CW00376242

Fate

Also by the same author

Fate

L. R. FREDERICKS

JOHN MURRAY

For
the music
and the musicians

First published in Great Britain in 2012 by John Murray (Publishers)
An Hachette UK Company

1

© L. R. Fredericks 2012

The right of L. R. Fredericks to be identified as the Author of the Work
has been asserted by her in accordance with the
Copyright, Designs and Patents Act 1988.

All rights reserved. Apart from any use permitted under UK copyright
law no part of this publication may be reproduced, stored in a retrieval
system, or transmitted, in any form or by any means without the prior
written permission of the publisher, nor be otherwise circulated in any
form of binding or cover other than that in which it is published and
without a similar condition being imposed on the subsequent
purchaser.

All characters in this publication – other than a few historical figures –
are fictitious and any resemblance to real persons, living or dead, is
purely coincidental.

A CIP catalogue record for this title is available from the British Library

Hardback ISBN 978-1-84854-331-7
Trade paperback ISBN 978-1-84854-332-4
Ebook ISBN 978-1-84854-442-0

Typeset in 11.5/15.75pt New Caledonia
by Servis Filmsetting Ltd, Stockport, Cheshire

Printed and bound by Clays Ltd, St Ives plc

John Murray policy is to use papers that are natural, renewable and
recyclable products and made from wood grown in sustainable forests.
The logging and manufacturing processes are expected to conform to
the environmental regulations of the country of origin.

John Murray (Publishers)
338 Euston Road
London NW1 3BH

www.johnmurray.co.uk

Hail, great physician of the world, all-hail;
Hail, mighty infant, who in years to come
Shalt heal the nations, and defraud the tomb;
Swift be thy growth! thy triumphs unconfin'd!
Make kingdoms thicker, and increase mankind.
Thy daring art shall animate the dead,
And draw the thunder on thy guilty head:
Then shalt thou dye, but from the dark abode
Rise up victorious, and be twice a God.
And thou, my sire, not destin'd by thy birth
To turn to dust, and mix with common earth,
How wilt thou toss, and rave, and long to dye,
And quit thy claim to immortality;
When thou shalt feel, enrag'd with inward pains,
The Hydra's venom rankling in thy veins?
The Gods, in pity, shall contract thy date,
And give thee over to the pow'r of Fate.

Ovid, Metamorphoses, Book II,
trans. John Dryden, 1717

Prologue

❦

An Artist of the Aether

'What are you?' Alice asked.

My great-great-great-great-granddaughter is full of questions.

'What I am,' I told her, 'is the story of my life. And it is too long a story for today.'

And yet the question remains. I return to my study, summon a pipe and my blue silk chaise longue, a fire and a brandy, paper and pen.

What am I? Not a ghost, though that is what most people believe. Not a Secret Chief, a Mahatma, an Illuminatus: also common assumptions. I'm not even enlightened, no matter how you define that. I am, and it looks like I shall forever be, Lord Francis Peter George St John Damory. I was born more than two hundred years ago and although I am not strictly speaking alive, I am obviously not dead. My appearance is as I choose, though usually I resemble my old self. I was a handsome man; I enjoyed it then and I enjoy it now. I am not beyond vanity, nor any other trick or trap of earthly existence. My body is a simulacrum, as is my study, my fire, brandy, pen, paper. I am an artist of the aether.

1

A Book that Cannot Be Written

❧

The 17th of November, my seventeenth birthday. I'm lying in a gutter in the stinking city of London. It's night, the fog is thick. Someone must have hit me, or I fell. I didn't even have time to draw my sword; the men in masks grabbed the girl and ran off. Sebastian vanished in pursuit; the link boy fled.

My brother Sebastian had arranged a pleasure-party in a private room at Lovejoy's Bagnio. The girl was meant for me. Her name was Rosie; she was from Shropshire. She was fourteen and a virgin, or so he had been assured. But I couldn't do it – the look of fear on her face was, I discovered, a compelling anti-aphrodisiac – so he'd decided to take her home for himself.

My head hurts; I close my eyes and slip away. It's my eleventh birthday; I'm sleepwalking through the rooms of Farundell. I've unpicked the knots in the cords that bound me, wrist and ankle, to the posts of my bed; I've opened the heavy door. Sure-footed, with glassy unfocused eyes, I descend the great stair and cross the stone-floored hall to the library, to stand before the portrait of my great-great-grandfather, Tobias.

His pale, serious face breaks into a smile and he leans forward, elbows on his gilded frame. 'May God be with you, Francis, on this anniversary of your birth. I have a gift for you, if you can find it.' He shows me a book bound in white vellum, yellowed with

2

age. There is no title, but on the cover a rose twines over a cross. As I watch, a new shoot unfurls, grows, buds. A flower appears, deep red and sweetly fragrant.

The cobbles are cold under my cheek; I smell piss, dead animal, rotten cabbage, dog shit. I taste blood where my lip has split. A rat runs over my hand.

I open my eyes and sit up. I'm still drunk, apparently; the world is swaying gently. The fog has congealed near the ground and as moonlight breaks through the clouds, I pull myself to my feet. I feel dizzy; I lean against the bowed front of a shop and press my forehead to the window.

There, right in front of me, within reach of my hand but for the glass, lies the book, red rose on pale vellum, one among a dozen dusty volumes on display. In the dark interior of the shop I think I see a light moving; I tap on the window, but no one comes.

Then Sebastian is shaking me, pulling me to my feet, dusting me off. 'Link!' he shouts, and the boy emerges from an alley. Sebastian aims a kick at his head but he dodges and grins.

'St James's Square, wasn't it, sir? This way, if you please.'

'That was Hetheringham and his gang, I'm sure of it.' Sebastian drags me along by my collar. 'If he wasn't a bloody earl I'd cut off his balls. I paid fifty guineas for that girl.'

I try to look back. 'Where are we? What street is this?'

'A foul, verminous, poxy one that we wish to leave as soon as possible.'

'Wait, stop . . . there was a shop, a bookshop . . .'

I awoke the next morning with an abominable pain in my head, sick and queasy in my bowels. I begged the servants to summon a doctor, who came promptly and was about to bleed me when Sebastian strolled in, took one look at me, fell over laughing and booted the doctor out.

'It is only,' he said, 'a temporary effect of excessive drink, in

3

particular the combining of wine with spirits. Their natures are incompatible, and make war in your body.' He sent for what he called his 'Morning Medicine' and made me drink a large cupful.

It was unspeakable. 'What in God's name is in this?' I asked.

'You don't want to know,' Sebastian said as he left. 'Give it a few minutes to work.'

Someone came to lay out a fresh shirt, another to dress my hair. A maid brought coffee; I felt almost myself again. I had not realised that something so pleasant, when taken in excess, could have such dire effects. I had paid no attention; I drank what was in my glass – which, I now recalled, was always being refilled by someone's generous hand.

I obtained directions from Sebastian's manservant Joseph, who gave me a complicit wink, and found my way back to the bagnio. I tried to retrace our steps. Things looked completely different by day, not that I had been in a fit state last night to make accurate observations. As soon as I left the main thoroughfares, with which I was somewhat familiar from my few previous visits to London, I was lost in a maze of tiny alleys, blind courtyards, narrow passages deep in filth. I told myself it was really just the same as farmyard manure, but a fastidiousness I had not known I possessed caused me to try to walk without setting down my feet, an awkward, mincing gait that I noticed immediately in others.

I wandered down Long Acre, turned left at the Dog and Bone, whose sign I vaguely remembered, then stopped, confused. Now which way? Down to the Strand? No. The link boy had cut through a court with a fountain – this was it. Yes, here was the spot where the masked men had waylaid us and here, rather to my surprise, for I half thought I'd dreamed it, was the shopfront I remembered. Above it hung a faded sign: *B. Lytton & Son, Antiquarian Booksellers*. I peered through the grimy window. The book was no longer there; the place it had occupied in the display was now taken by a treatise on gardening. I pushed open the door and stepped into a small room crowded with books from floor to low, sagging ceiling.

The smell was that blend of old leather and mould, tallow, crumbling paper and stale smoke peculiar to such establishments throughout the world. It never fails to trigger in me an acquisitive anticipation, a cunning hope that here, in some forgotten corner, in an utterly innocuous binding or perhaps misbound, will be the book, *the* book . . .

As my eyes adjusted to the dim light I made out an elderly man in an ancient periwig, evidently the proprietor, in conversation with a woman whose face I couldn't see. He glanced up, murmured, 'If you will allow, Contessa,' and turned to me. 'Good day, sir,' he said. 'In what way may I serve you?'

'Last night, as I was . . . passing, I noticed a book in your window, but it's no longer there. It had a rose on the cover, and a cross . . .'

'Oh, but that was not a *book*.' The woman turned to face me. It was impossible to guess her age; her features were striking rather than beautiful. She was tall, sumptuously if soberly dressed, with a cool and direct gaze. 'Why do you ask for a book that cannot be written?'

'That cannot be written? But I saw it . . . I thought I saw it. Tobias had it – my great-great-grandfather.'

'Tobias Damory?'

'Yes, my lady.'

'That is why you seem familiar. So he has led you here. Well, if we should chance to meet again, young Damory, it may be that I will be able to show you something of the . . . book you seek.'

5

2
This Is Beauty

❧

That night I walked in my sleep, for the first time in years. The London house felt strange to me, thin and lonely. It was a new house, only thirty years old, and we had scarcely made any imprint – unlike Farundell, so deeply imbued with the varied, subtle flavours of generations of my family that it simmers with life, even at night when its current denizens sleep.

I wandered from room to room, vaguely aware that I was looking for something, drawn down the chilly marble stairs and the steeper wooden ones at the back towards the warmth emanating from the subterranean kitchen. A single candle burned by the banked fire where a girl sat sewing, and silently weeping.

I must have made some noise that startled her; she looked up, saw me and shrieked. I awoke and realised I was barefoot, in my nightshirt, with a prominent erection. I tried to speak, but my teeth began chattering so hard I couldn't form any words, and my limbs shivered with such violence I feared I would fall down. She took pity on me, guided me to a chair by the hearth, found a blanket to put over my shoulders, poked at the fire until it blazed up, fetched a cup and poured me some wine.

Warmth slowly soaked into me; the girl returned to her sewing. She looked familiar. 'What's your name?'

'Matilda, sir.'

'You're Tildy Butterfield, aren't you?'

'Yes, sir. I came here four years ago.'

She was about my age, the daughter of one of our tenants; we'd played together as children. 'I remember your mother,' I said. 'She used to give me milk, straight from the cow. And your father let me ride his plough-horse.'

'They're both dead now.'

'Is that why you're sad?'

'Oh no, that was long ago.'

'So what troubles you? If I can help, I trust you will ask.' I was trying to act the kind master and put her at ease, but in truth I only wished for the shawl to slip a little further from her white shoulders.

'It's nothing you can do anything about,' she said. 'A silly little thing. The sort of thing that can happen to any girl.'

'My brother.' Behind Sebastian trailed a long line of pregnant serving girls. 'What will you do?' He was always generous – the girl could choose money for an abortion, or a return to the country to become a farmer's wife.

'I don't know.' She glanced up; our eyes met. 'Do you remember when we were children, sir, you and your brothers – we used to sneak up to the hayloft and take off our clothes.'

'I remember.'

'I always liked you best.'

The next day I took a horse from the stables and set out to explore, determined to see something of London besides bagnios and coffee houses. I rode along the Strand, lined with fabulous emporia and glossy equipages, and up Fleet Street to gawp at Wren's huge new cathedral of St Paul, which I supposed I ought to admire but which I found brutal. At its base the building is just large, with a ponderous and self-important air. If one did not know, one would think it the headquarters of some particularly recondite government department in a nation, such as France, that specialises in infuriating bureaucracy. I craned my neck to comprehend that dome. The stone and metal protuberance seemed to assault the softly varied greys of the sky; I found its immensity rather futile, and it made me sad. I thought of Tildy, and wondered what she would choose.

The streets were crowded; I was jostled from all sides and nearly run off the road by a scarlet coach with a liveried driver who looked neither right nor left but lashed out with a whip at everything in his path. A wide avenue leading north gave a glimpse of the open land beyond the city; I turned that way. Carts and carriages and drovers with cattle for the slaughter passed in great numbers, but the close-packed buildings gradually thinned. There were open fields to either side, and on my right glimpses of a slender river, which cheered me. Was I pining for Farundell already? Sebastian would be disgusted with me.

A shaft of sun broke through the clouds and shone on a wooded hill in the distance; I let the horse out for a canter. The road was muddy from recent rains and by the time we'd reached the foot of the hill the poor beast was heaving. I pulled him up at a trough outside a church, dismounted and let him drink, then tied him to a rail next to a pretty grey mare.

I looked back. Miles away, across the pattern of fields, woods and villages, London lay beneath a grey-brown pall of smoke. It crossed my mind that I didn't have to return; I had a horse and a full purse. I could go home to Farundell or ride on, wherever my fate might take me, like a knight errant in the romances of Mallory and Chrétien de Troyes that I had always loved.

Yes! I would do it! My heart suddenly fired with daring, I was turning towards the door of the church, intending to beg a scrap of paper to send a message to Sebastian so that he wouldn't be concerned about me or tell Father, when it opened and an old priest came out, accompanied by a woman. I recognised her at once.

'Contessa.' I bowed. And so this must be, I thought, La Belle Dame sans Merci.

She greeted me without surprise. 'Which way are you riding?'

'Wherever my fate might take me.'

'Then you may ride with me.' She mounted the grey mare and set off up the hill.

The road – if one could dignify the raw sluice of mud with that name – was so steep it had to be negotiated in a series of tacks. I forced my way past a line of overloaded oxcarts and caught up with her.

'Have you been to Farundell, Contessa?' I had reasoned that she must have visited our house; she could only have known what my great-great-grandfather looked like from his portrait, and as far as I knew, there were no portraits of him anywhere else.

'Why yes, I have,' she said. 'Many years ago.'

'I did not know that I resembled Tobias.'

'I am not certain that you do.'

'I know very little about him,' I said. 'My father will not have him spoken of.'

'Why is that?'

'He does not explain.' My one enquiry had led to such a rough and sudden cuff to my head that I did not broach the subject again.

Fields bordered the road, and a few new houses, bleak and neat. We entered a patch of woodland and turned off on a track to the right.

'Do you play music?' the Contessa asked.

'I am a most humble student of the harpsichord, my lady.'

'What music do you most love?'

I knew at once. 'The *Stabat Mater* created by Signor Vivaldi.'

'Why?'

'It makes my heart weep.'

'For sorrow?'

9

'No, lady. For beauty.' I looked up. Branches, nearly bare, met above our heads; a golden leaf drifted down. I gestured. 'Like that.'

She said nothing, but I felt as though I had passed some test. After a time we came to a gate; she told me to dismount and open it, and made no objection when I followed her in and closed it behind me.

1924

There is no more night in London; street lamps insinuate their unpleasant gloom into every lovely darkness, even here atop Highgate Hill. I'm standing on a grotesque iron bridge where the forest track once lay. A hundred years or so ago they failed to make a tunnel and made instead this chasm where traffic now flows unceasingly from morning till night. London spreads as far as the eye can see.

An old woman leans over the railing. She sees me. 'What are you?' she asks.

'Just a passing stranger.'

'Stranger,' she says. 'So you are.' She climbs up and stretches out her arms. 'I can fly.' She blows me a kiss, leaps into the air, rises and soars towards the moon as her body falls like a rag to the road far below.

I walk on.

The fields have been dug up for clay, the woods felled for timber: it is all still here, merely rearranged. I stand in the Contessa's garden, now a house, one of a hundred identical, with a narrow tiled hall lit by a stained-glass window of mediocre quality. A little girl pauses on the stairs, wide-eyed. She sees me.

'Are you sleepwalking, child?'

She nods.

'Shall I show you something wonderful?'

She nods again.

'Then look.' The walls of her house dissolve; the Contessa's garden spreads over the hillside. The avenue of yew trees, the pyramid pale in the moonlight. The divine Celestino is singing the *Stabat Mater*; of course he was not there that night, but whenever he sang it for me, this was the image that always came to my mind, and now I cannot separate them.

The child listens avidly; she's drinking in his voice as it swoops and slides, pure and passionate. 'This is beauty,' I tell her. 'Try to remember.'

3

A Jewel Beyond Price

🌱

Yes, it was a real place, or at least mostly real; though I came to doubt it. Set in the middle of woods, the Contessa's house was tall, half-timbered, with diamond-mullioned windows. A groom led our horses to the stables; the front door opened and a turbaned Oriental bowed us in. I was wide-eyed as a colt, but determined to appear a man of the world. A sweet-scented cherry-wood fire burned in a panelled drawing room; we had no sooner seated ourselves than another servant, also Oriental, also turbaned, appeared with wine and food. Before I knew it, I was talking with ease about Farundell and my family, about poetry, music, even about the part of me that questioned the existence of God. We talked all day as if we had known each other for ever, but I still did not know her name.

Did I fall in love with her? Yes, of course, but it was more than that. She saw into me and valued what she saw; she understood me. I had found my first true friend, or so it seemed. And there was her allure. Never by any overt sign – no provocative glances, no coquettish tilting of the head and fluttering of the fan – but I could sense, under it all, a pull that was purely erotic.

She showed me around the house, and although she said nothing about herself or her family, I had the impression that she had lived there her entire life. On the walls hung paintings of strange power, portraits and landscapes and dreamy still lifes, all her own work, as were the small carved figures, in niches and on shelves, of creatures part human, part animal or god, demon or angel. She had a library of beautifully bound books and a collection of Egyptian bronzes. She named them for me: Osiris, the sacrificed god; his sister-wife Isis, mistress of magic; Thoth, called Hermes, inventor of language; Horus, the child of dawn.

In the twilight we walked in the garden. A long arbour, entwined with the thorny bare stems of roses, bordered a pond where golden fish moved slowly in the cold green depths. There was a box-edged parterre, with santolina and senecio and fennel straggling in the cold. An avenue of clipped yew led to a strange structure: a pyramid of smooth-polished stone. I walked twice around it, but saw no entrance. When I asked the Contessa she shrugged and smiled as if to say: Eccentric ancestors; what can one do? I felt I understood; I had a few of my own.

When we turned back to the house it was dark. We went in and without another word she took me to her bed. I remember candles flickering in coloured sconces, wine-flavoured kisses, her soft sounds of pleasure, her scents of sandalwood and jasmine, her body, which was . . . a perfect expression of her spirit. I lost track of time; at seventeen one can go on for ever.

I slept for a while, our limbs entangled, and I dreamed that we rose up and went out into the night. It was summer, the garden was fragrant with lilies and roses, the grass tender under our feet.

She led me to the pyramid and pointed to a door in its side, then she turned and walked away.

I woke, and wondered to find myself weeping. She held me close and stroked my hair; in that moment she became everything to me. And that she should want me, too; well, it was a miracle. Is it any wonder I gave her all my heart and soul? Is it any wonder I flung my whole life at her feet?

In the morning I awakened alone. One of the turbaned Orientals appeared with a brass pot of coffee on a tray. When I enquired after my lady he moved his head in an inscrutable gesture midway between a nod and a shake, leaving me to ponder whether that meant she was not available; he could not speak English; he was mute; or he had nothing to say on the subject.

I left without seeing anyone else, though I found paper and pen and wrote a note saying that I would return in a few hours. My plan was to ride back to London as fast as I could, reassure Sebastian and beg his silence, induce him to give me a great deal of money, buy the biggest jewel I could find, hasten back and ask the Contessa to marry me.

Things went wrong. My horse found that damnable steep hill too slippery for his liking and refused to proceed; I had to dismount and walk beside him, cajoling. I slipped and fell, twisting my ankle rather badly, and I believe he laughed at me. He further obliged me by dropping a shoe at the bottom; we limped to a blacksmith, cursing each other. When I was finally able to remount, I found myself in the middle of a herd of a thousand bleating sheep and was forced to stop at a tavern to let them pass.

I returned, at last, to St James's Square, mud-spattered and dishevelled, only to learn that Sebastian was out – at a friend's house, a coffee house or perhaps a bagnio. I could not go in search of him without changing clothes, having my hair tidied, and – I realised I was ravenous – eating something. I did not find him until late in the day, deep in a game of faro. He was raking it in, and I had to wait until he felt the moment was right to pass on the bank.

Far from being concerned at my absence, he assumed I'd been out whoring and was pleased that I'd shown initiative. I did not disabuse him, and when he demanded details of the lady who had beguiled me, I smiled mysteriously and said that she was very expensive.

He gave me his purse, heavy with his winnings, but only after making me drink to Eros, to Priapus and of course to Aphrodite, then to Eros again. Between the third and fourth toasts I confided that I had found a jewel beyond price and therefore, by ineluctable logic, must buy one as well. We drank a final toast, to Bacchus, and set out gaily together; he knew just the shop and would ensure I was not cheated. We stopped for a coffee to counter the effects of the wine, and had a glass of ratafia to take the edge off the coffee. At the coffee house we collected a few of his friends, one of whom had to go back and pay while the rest of us waited on the corner. It was getting dark and beginning to rain.

We were within sight of the goldsmith's shop when we encountered Sebastian's nemesis Hetheringham with his friends and Sebastian started a fight. Fortunately the street was too narrow and too crowded with bystanders for swords to be drawn, but things got knocked over, an orange-seller had her dress torn and an old woman dropped her basket, spilling dozens of spools of lace into the mud. All this had to be paid for and Sebastian extracted from the mêlée. By the time we were once more under way, the shopkeeper was letting down his shutters and only grudgingly let us in, muttering about young gentlemen with no respect. Sebastian nearly struck the man and was all for walking out, but I had spotted a brooch that I knew at once was perfect – a ruby, cabochon-cut, set in rosy gold and encircled by three rows of pearls.

So old-fashioned, Sebastian said; he suggested something glittery, with sapphires, but I wanted the ruby. My brother was not the ruthless bargainer he had claimed, or perhaps he was not of a mind to bother. The Earl had kicked him in the balls. He wandered off and left me to negotiate, which I did very badly and undoubtedly paid far too much.

When I left the shop it was raining hard; the street had become a flowing sewer. Sebastian was climbing into a bright yellow carriage; he pulled me in and introduced his dear friends Lizzie and Lucy, twin sisters, who happened to be passing on their way to a party.

There were so many vehicles crowding the roads that we moved very slowly, but fortunately refreshments were on hand: the carriage was equipped with a cunning cabinet containing a selection of wines and spirits in crystal flasks, silver goblets and – I had to ask – dildos. Sebastian explained to the girls that it was my seventeenth birthday, give or take a day or two, I was new to town and in love for the first time.

'That is *so* sweet,' said Lucy, or Lizzie, and gave me a kiss.

We drank toasts, as before, and one thing led to another. I had not realised what went on in carriages, but Sebastian assured me it was *de rigueur*.

By the time we arrived at the party I was a little drunk, I had been unfaithful to my jewel already, and I decided it was best not to attempt that muddy hill – even if I could find it – at night in the rain.

4

The Place Had Charm

🌿

When I awoke at midday, mercifully in my own bed though I couldn't remember how I got there, I discovered to my chagrin that I had need of Sebastian's Morning Medicine again. Apparently it was not enough to intend to refrain from overindulgence.

In sober daylight the ruby brooch looked tawdry, risible; I saw that its inadequacy was very possibly a mirror of my own. Whatever had possessed me to think the Contessa would marry me? I must have been insane. I was not a great prize; I had no fortune, was the third son, unlikely ever to inherit the title – and of course I'd assumed she was herself unmarried. I had thought a married woman would not . . . but last night I had met a number of married ladies who obviously did, even within sight of, nay, positively encouraged by their husbands.

The afternoon was bright and cold. I made my way north out of London and through the countryside to the foot of the hill, where I paused to fortify myself at a tavern opposite the church. I had second thoughts. Perhaps I should write to her. I could be eloquent and erudite; I could present myself in the best possible light; I could enquire where I stood. I could wait for her to invite me, instead of charging in unannounced. What if she did not wish to see me? She would be embarrassed; she would not know what to do with me; it would be a disaster. But, if for no other reason than that I'd said I would, I had to go back, so despite a strong presentiment that it was not a good idea, I returned to her house.

I was surprised to find the courtyard bustling with activity. Men tramped to and fro, carrying crates and boxes and bundles, loading them on to waiting oxcarts. I watched, agape, as the Contessa's massive oak bed appeared in pieces and was loaded on to a cart of its own. As each cart filled, it trundled off and its place was taken by an empty one.

I went to the door and slipped in among the porters. When I stopped one and asked him where the Contessa was, he had no idea to whom I was referring. I walked from room to room, seeing no one but an army of men like ants. Furniture was carried away whole or taken apart if too large, paintings and sculptures were placed in padded crates, books packed into boxes, carpets and wall hangings folded into leather cases. No Contessa, not even any mute Orientals.

I went out to the garden; the fish, at least, were still in their pond, but as I started down the avenue of yew trees I saw four men dismantling the pyramid; I had to stand aside to let them pass as they carried the painted wooden sections up the path.

I sat on a stone bench and took the brooch from my pocket. In a strange way, it was all I had left of her; I had never learned her name. Nor, I remembered, had she told me about the book that was not a book. I had forgotten to ask; I had thought there was time for that. Everything I thought I'd known about her was merely an assumption; mistaken, as it turned out. I felt a desolation utterly new to my young heart; it was as though I had fallen off a cliff.

At the sound of footsteps I turned, my heart rising. A portly man in a bright blue coat approached, bowed, and gave me his card:

17

Edgar M. Bonnerby,
Property Agent, Letting Manager,
House Broker, Insurance, Surveying.

Nightingale Court by the Turk's Head, Fetter Lane.

From him I learned that the house had been leased and the lease expired today. He did not know any Contessa; the house had been taken by a Mr Pym. Was I perhaps interested in the property myself? Not many liked such a remote location, it was true, but the place had charm, did I not agree?

I did. I was better acquainted with its charm than he.

I left him locking up and returned to the courtyard. It was empty but for the great ruts scoured by the oxcarts and a few wisps of packing straw. In a sudden panic I saw that my one hope of finding the Contessa had disappeared with her furniture. I scrambled on to my horse and set off at a gallop. At the gate the churned track showed they had turned towards the main road; I followed as fast as my horse would allow, but by the time I got there they had vanished and I could not tell if they had turned north or south.

Of course I should have left it at that; if she'd wished me to find her she could have left word. And if she wished to find me, she knew where I lived. But I had become angry. I galloped back to the house; there was one last trail to follow.

I caught Bonnerby as he was leaving and asked for Mr Pym's address. He shook his head regretfully to indicate that the information had slipped his mind, inserted a finger delicately under his wig and scratched. I understood that his memory could be stimulated by a small emolument. I had never bribed anyone before; I hoped it didn't show. I took out a crown; he gazed off into the trees. I tried a half-guinea; he reached out and pocketed it in one smooth motion.

'Care of B. Lytton, by the Rose and Crown, Cecil Court off St Martin's Lane.'

18

'Lytton? The bookseller?'

'Wouldn't know; all I have is the address for correspondence.'

I made my way thoughtfully down the hill. As I passed the church where I'd met her, the old priest came out.

I greeted him. 'Good afternoon, Father. Do you perhaps remember a lady who stopped here two days ago?'

'Yes, indeed I do. A most generous lady.'

'Generous?'

'She gave us forty guineas.'

'Generous indeed. Who is she?'

'That's the strangest part. I had never seen her before; she asked to pray alone. When she came out she gave me a purse, which was rather heavy, though I assumed it was full of small coins. Then she rode off – with you, as I recall. When I opened the purse I found it was full of guineas. I had never seen so much money in my life; I sent a message straight away to the bishop and his man came to collect it.'

'And do you know her name?'

'I know her only as the most generous lady I ever met. Perhaps you would care to make a small donation yourself? For the poor of the parish?'

Was he, perhaps, soliciting a bribe as well? I gave him half-a-crown. 'You are sure you do not know her name?'

'I regret that I do not, for then I could name her in my prayers.'

It was dark by the time I returned to London; I went straight to Lovejoy's Bagnio, where Lucy and Lizzie were holding court. No sign of Sebastian, which was a relief. I drank, and laughed, and gambled; when Lucy chose me to accompany her to a private room, everyone toasted my good fortune.

5

The Man and the Image

🌺

I had intended to go to Lytton's first thing in the morning, but after a late breakfast Lucy wanted to take me shopping. I needed new clothes, she said, more colourful, fashionable clothes. I protested that I had little money; she explained about credit, and that a gentleman never pays tradesmen. I asked how I should pay her; she took me back to bed.

The acquisition of clothing had always been a chore. Once a year we children were herded together to be measured by Mr Abernathy, the tailor from Exley. A month later boxes of garments would appear, always of the same good serge and fustian, brown and grey and dark blue, with one court suit or gown each, in dull burgundy, a respectable year or two out of fashion. My sisters made the same protests every time, begged to be allowed to send to Paris for materials, willing to compromise on London, but never allowed. 'Where will it end?' Mother would ask, 'with you competing like strutting peacocks; what one had, the others would have to better.' They would clamour, and she, eventually, yield a little; the haberdasher was permitted to come with his lace and ribbons, beads, bows and feathers, and the plain gowns would sprout incongruous extrusions; these would be removed, rearranged, swapped, replaced until they became as drab as the gowns.

I had taken it upon myself to be Mother's champion in the

disdaining of vanities, but shopping with Lucy was a revelation. Under her tutelage I came to see that my disdain was neither true nor virtuous; my preference for black a mere affectation, and not even original. Lucy maintained that it was our duty as God's creatures to celebrate His handiwork, to enhance the beauty of the forms with which He endowed us. There was, as well, a science of colour; one did not wear just any colour one happened to fancy, oh no. Such lack of discrimination might have dangerous consequences. One had to choose colours to harmonise, augment or, if need be, counteract the forces of one's character.

At the tailor's she looked me up and down, exchanging critical glances with Monsieur Duplis, the maestro. My black worsted coat was whisked away by one assistant; I was measured by two others.

'You have,' said Lucy, 'a strongly Saturnine temperament, I believe; also somewhat Martial, which is quite nice in a man, to a degree. You should not wear black or scarlet, though grey might suit and pink would be sublime, don't you think, Monsieur?'

'Sublime,' M. Duplis agreed. 'This blush-pink organzine, this peony duchesse satin . . .'

'Not pink,' I said. 'Under any circumstances.'

'Green, then,' said Lucy. 'For Venus, and Nature. That will compensate for the heavy, intellectual qualities of Saturn, and balance Mars. Venus and Mars were lovers, you know.'

Bolts of shot silk, taffeta and velvet were unrolled and draped over my shoulders. 'This new Nile green bengal,' said M. Duplis. 'Or the verdigris moiré. Here is a marvellous leaf green velvet, with emeralds. We have this faille in forest green, moss green, lichen green. And paduasoy in lawn green, dawn green, sea green, pea green.'

I decided the man was mad, but harmless in his obsession.

Lucy looked on in delight. 'Or blue,' she said. 'For Jupiter: beneficence, prosperity, power.'

21

'The celestial blue bombazine, the mazarine and ivory damask,' said M. Duplis, snapping his fingers at an assistant. 'The cerulean sarcenet, the indigo barèges. This azure crêpe lisse, embroidered with silver thread . . .'

'Does it not tarnish?' I said.

M. Duplis sniffed. 'Send your manservant; we will teach him the correct method of cleaning it.' I dared not mention that I had no manservant of my own.

I was intoxicated by the dazzling colours, the voluptuous fabrics, the fawning attentions of M. Duplis and his assistants, Lucy's enraptured encouragement. I ordered six suits, to be delivered in a week; and although I repented almost at once and even more when I finally saw the bill, I cannot deny that I loved those suits and who they made me seem to be. There is nothing like the sense of assurance and ease that comes with exquisite tailoring and the best materials. And, of course, I have come to know only too well how the man and the image intertwine, how one imagines oneself into existence at every moment anew . . . though imagining myself out of existence has so far proved impossible.

Drunk with spending such ephemeral money, Lucy and I reeled on to the glove maker's (half a dozen each of grey, white and green; plus a dozen red for Lucy); the milliner's (a plumed tricorn in grey with a green feather, plus a little ditty for Lucy with a stuffed bird on a golden nest); the hosier's (two dozen white, one dozen black silk stockings for me, half a dozen grey, embroidered with roses and a dozen white, with tiny gold leaves, for Lucy), plus garters with gold clasps and obscene verses embroidered; the shoemaker's (two pairs of special city shoes for me, with elevated soles, two pairs of buckskin riding boots; for Lucy a pair of India brocade mules); the sword shop, where my sturdy *spada da lato*, passed down from Sebastian, was discreetly put aside and I tried out a wonderfully light rapier, an exotically bejewelled scimitar and a very modish *épée de cour*, before settling on a colichemarde with a rather plain leather scabbard and a niello hilt. Nothing there for Lucy, but next door was a goldsmith where she got a sapphire ring and I, an enamelled watch.

Lucy took me back to her tiny jewel box of an apartment in Hart Street, making sure I knew that it was a privilege she accorded few of her other lovers.

'Has Sebastian been here?' I asked later, as she served me oysters in bed.

'No,' she said, though the smallest of hesitations told me she was lying. I took it as a compliment that she bothered.

She unpacked the boxes and tried on her new hat, gloves, stockings and mules; I fastened her garters, then unfastened them again.

6

A Torn Stocking

🌿

The next day, and the next, I intended to go to Lytton's, but something always intervened: we went to Twickenham in the yellow carriage with Sebastian and Lizzie (and home in the dark, confusing but fun), there was an afternoon at the races, nights at the opera, a long house-party at Lord Kendrick's.

I acquired a manservant, a cousin of Sebastian's man Joseph. His name was Tunnie: a short, wiry fellow of indeterminate age who'd spent his youth in the Navy. I sent him to M. Duplis to learn how to care for my silver-embroidered coat.

I acquired a married mistress, Lady Kendrick, then another: her sister, Lady Rokesley.

One morning I realised that I had not seen Tildy for several days. I asked Tunnie to enquire among the other servants, hoping to hear that she'd returned to the country to marry a farmer. He reported, instead, that she had gone out one afternoon, no one knew where or why, and had not been seen again. Her place had already been filled. I did not believe that no one knew; I summoned the maidservants, one at a time, until I found one who would not meet my eyes. With the help of a few shillings, she was able to recall that Tildy had twice gone to visit a Mrs Pettiwood. She had failed to return from the last visit.

'Who, pray, is Mrs Pettiwood?'

She pointed to her belly.

'Ah. And where does Mrs Pettiwood reside?'

'I don't know, m'lord.'

I took out another coin. 'I'm certain you do.'

'Star Alley off Little Sheep Lane by Cary Street.'

'I wouldn't go there if I was you, sir,' said Tunnie, when I summoned him to accompany me. 'They'd knife you for the buckles on your shoes.'

'Then I shan't wear shoes. Fetch my oldest boots, and the brown coat. Bring a cudgel.'

Star Alley was dark at midday and squelched underfoot. It had escaped the Great Fire and the crooked, jettied upper storeys shut out the sky. The inhabitants scuttled away like rats as we approached.

'How do we know which house?' I asked Tunnie.

He pointed to a basket of bloody rags outside one door. 'That one. Don't you say nothing, sir. And keep your purse well hid until I tell you.' He led the way to the door, knocked once, then kicked it in. The boy who'd been lurking behind, eye to a knothole, fell over, was collared and lifted off his feet.

'We want Mrs Pettiwood.' Tunnie set him down with a thump but kept his hand tangled in the lad's hair.

'Dunno who you mean, sir . . . yow!'

I noticed a light at the end of the corridor where a door cracked open; I pointed it out to Tunnie, who dragged the boy along with us. We entered a dim parlour inhabited by a creature with gnarled hands, greasy grey hair and a single yellow tooth.

'Mrs Pettiwood, I presume,' said Tunnie. 'We're looking for a girl.'

Mrs Pettiwood cackled. 'Two doors down, good sirs, but I'll expect you back when you've caught the clap.' She laughed so hard I thought she was having a fit.

The boy squirmed out of Tunnie's grasp and fled.

With a combination of threats and bribery, we learned that Tildy had come for a medicine to bring on her courses; this having failed, she'd returned for more direct action. Pleased with the outcome – more cackles – she had left. Mrs Pettiwood prattled on and on, telling us what a nice, well-spoken girl Tildy had been, a good girl with a good job in a noble household, no harlot she, just unlucky; clean, too, quite remarkably clean.

Tunnie glanced around uneasily and gestured to me to leave, but as I turned, the doorway was filled by the shapes of three men, knives drawn. I began considering the alternatives, the most pleasant of which involved being beaten and robbed. I was reaching for my purse, hoping that by immediate compliance I could bargain for our lives when Tunnie exploded in a flurry of violence. One fellow took a cudgel blow to the side of his head that laid him out flat; a knife flew out of nowhere (Tunnie's boot, I later learned) and stuck in the next man's arm. I was too surprised to move. Tunnie head-butted the third man, grabbed me and bolted for the door. We didn't stop until we'd reached the end of the alley.

'Good God, Tunnie,' I said, when I'd recovered my breath. 'Where did you learn that knife trick?'

He tried to look abashed. 'It weren't the *regular* Navy I was in.'

I stared at him. 'You were a pirate. A pirate, Tunnie?'

'A liberator of foreign assets, sir.'

A one-armed beggar in a ragged cloak detached himself from a doorway and sidled in our direction. 'Beg pardon, sirs. I hear you're looking for a girl.'

'No, we're not,' said Tunnie, turning away.

'I seen the girl you're after.'

'What girl?' I said.

'Nice girl, pretty.' He described Tildy accurately. 'Came twice, last time four days ago.'

'And did she leave?'

'Maybe.'

I gave him a shilling.

'Yes, she left.'

'Where did she go?' I held out another.

'That way.' He pointed to the right.

'Not very useful.' I put the shilling away. 'Let's go,' I said to Tunnie.

'No, wait,' the beggar said. 'I might know something more.'

'Yes?'

'I was on my way to the brick kilns where I sleep when I stumbled over a girl in the middle of the road. I think it was the same one. She was dead.'

Although it was what I had prepared myself to hear, it felt like a kick in the stomach. I gave the man his shilling; Tunnie led me to a tavern and ordered us each a pint of ale. 'Maybe it wasn't her, sir. Maybe she got away safe.'

His tone told me he didn't believe that himself.

'What will have happened to her body, Tunnie?'

'If the watch found her, she'd have been taken to St Clement's. Or they might have sold her to the anatomists.'

I shuddered, drained my ale and stood. 'We'll ask at St Clement's.'

The church was chill and serene, but as the curate guided us through the graveyard the reek of rotting flesh made me gag. Even Tunnie looked a little green. The pauper's grave was at the far end: an open pit, half full of corpses. Three layers had been laid to rest, the curate explained; two more and then it would be covered over.

'Four nights ago, you say? The only body that night was an old man, but there was a girl brought in the next morning. We waited a day, to see if anyone claimed her. No one did. There, that's her.' He pointed to a small foot in a torn stocking near the middle of the pile. 'Or no, perhaps it's that one.' A dirty blue hand clawed the sky.

7

A Discovery of the Rosicrucian Fraternity

Weeks passed. I never told anyone about Tildy; there was no one to tell. Word would get back to her relations in the country; it probably already had. I tried to put it from my mind. I drank a bit more, bought Lucy new gowns, took up horse-racing in Hyde Park, made a woman cry for the first time, had fencing lessons and my first duel, with Lord Rokesley, an even greater idiot than I. We gave each other little nicks, ruined our shirts with blood, went home filled with *amour propre*.

As I was preparing to return to Farundell for Christmas I came upon the old ruby brooch in a drawer. I had done nothing about the Contessa; was I still hoping that she would write to me? I was turning the brooch in my fingers when Tunnie brought me a letter from Mr Lytton, the antiquarian bookseller, who begged leave to inform me that a book of possible interest to me had recently come into his hands.

The afternoon was already drawing in and fog was rolling up from the river as I walked to Cecil Court. Mr Lytton rose as I entered. His bow was so creaky that I feared he would fall over. 'I hope you will forgive my liberty in writing to you,' he said.

'I will,' I said. 'Out of curiosity, how did you know where to write?'

He gestured to the newspaper on his desk. It was open to the 'Out and About in London Town' page.

'You read that sort of tittle-tattle?' He did not look the type.

'I read everything,' he said mournfully. 'Business is slow; I have plenty of time. There is a very entertaining account of a party hosted by yourself and your brother at an address in St James's Square. I took note because I had received a book, in a lot amongst many, mostly uninteresting others, that I identified at once as coming from Tobias Damory's library.' He picked up a slender volume and showed me the inside front cover, where the initials TGHD were inscribed in a distinctive glyph that I recognised at once from the library at Farundell.

I took it from his hands and turned to the title: *Fama Fraternitatis, or, A Discovery of the Rosicrucian Fraternity: the most laudable Order of the Rosy Cross*. The mention of the Rosy Cross caused my breath to catch, which I covered with a cough.

'I come across books from your great-great-grandfather's library from time to time,' Lytton was saying, 'and I'd be more than happy to send them to you. Sometimes a true marvel comes my way. About six or seven years ago I had a beauty: Master Simon de Greer's famous *Alchymical Garden*, a great masterpiece.' A dreamy look came over him.

'But how have these books come to be bought and sold?' I

asked. 'I have never known any book to leave Farundell once it has entered.'

'A number of them came on the market some years ago, and are now widely dispersed. Occasionally they reappear. If you like, I can make enquiries among my colleagues in the antiquarian book trade. We have an arrangement of friendly co-operation, here in England and throughout Europe, helping each other to find what our clients require, with every discretion, of course.' He touched his finger to the side of his nose and gave me to understand that whatever heresies or erotics I fancied, he could obtain for me, at a price.

'Yes,' I said, 'please do. I will buy anything with his glyph.'

He wrapped the book in paper; I put it in my pocket and went to the door, then turned back as though a new thought had occurred to me. 'By the way, do you happen to know where the Contessa has gone?' I hoped that he might reveal her name without my having to ask.

'Ah, the lady who was here when you last visited? I do not; that was the first and only time I saw her. She merely called to leave a letter for someone else.'

I hazarded a guess. 'For Mr Pym?'

'Yes, for Mr Pym. Do you know him?'

I made an indeterminate noise.

'I have never met him myself,' Lytton said. 'I inherited him, you could say, from my father. Sometimes we act as his intermediary in small matters. We are his *Adresse de Correspondance*.'

8

I Am One of You!

❧

I sat up all night reading and rereading the *Fama Fraternitatis*. It told the story of a young man called Christian Rosenkreutz, who lived more than three hundred years ago. Although of noble birth, he had been, through poverty, placed in a monastery to be raised by monks. At the age of sixteen, having seen nothing of the world beyond its walls, he had begged to be allowed to travel and was sent to accompany an elderly monk on a pilgrimage to the Holy Land. When the elderly brother died en route, the young man seized his moment and decided to go to Jerusalem himself.

On the way, however, he encountered the wise men of Damcar, and beheld the wonders of magic that they wrought, and how the secrets of nature were revealed to them. This so fired his spirit that he immediately set out with a caravan of Arabs bound for that legendary city, deep in the desert. After many privations, he arrived at last and was received not as a stranger, but as a friend long expected.

He stayed for three years, perfecting his command of the Arab tongue and learning many things never imagined in his cloister: the science of nature and the rights and duties of Man as Microcosmos; the arts of Healing, Astronomy and Mathematics. He travelled across the Red Sea into Egypt, where he learned the ancient mysteries of Isis: Alchemy and Thaumaturgy, the secrets of the Philosopher's Stone and the Elixir of Immortality, knowledge lost to Europe but preserved among the ruined temples and tombs. From there he went to Fez, and although he felt that their Magia was not pure, their Cabala defiled by religion, he was able to make good use of all he learned. He compiled the *Book M*, which he brought with him when he returned to Europe. His intention was to initiate the Reformation of the entire world with his rediscovery of lost wisdom, his knowledge of the true heritage and destiny of Man and the glorious path of the Christian Reborn.

He went from nation to nation, seeking out the wise and learned, demonstrating the errors in their understanding and how they might be corrected. But they laughed at him, and called him an ignorant fool; no one wanted to admit that their whole science was founded on nonsense. So he returned to his homeland where he built himself a house by a lake with a tall tower where he watched the stars at night, a laboratory where he delved into the heart of matter and learned to unlock the pure spirit within. He had an immense library containing the whole of human knowledge and a collection of astounding automata, and although his mastery of the transmutation of metals could have brought him fame and riches, he instead dedicated himself to healing the sick and spreading God's love through kindness and charity.

But seeing the burden of suffering under which Man laboured, he still yearned for the Reformation of the world, and after some years he took on a number of students. These people learned all of his arts and dedicated themselves to healing and good works, to secrecy and to the passing on of their knowledge to the select few who, in every generation, would be revealed by chance or fate. They call themselves Rosicrucians, for the rose that blossomed from the Cross: the Christian Reborn, the perfected human. Adept in the arts of magic and alchemy, they travel the world incognito, taking on the clothing and customs of the lands through which they pass.

As I read, it seemed to me that I had always known about these

Rosicrucians, heirs to the wisdom of Egypt and Arabia. Or not known about them, how could I? But it was as though the space they now occupied in my mind had always been there, waiting. Of course, I thought, there must be some, in every age, who know the truths that are hidden from the masses of men. It would be too cruel, otherwise, to abandon us to ignorance and error.

The text concluded with an invitation to reply and a mysterious conundrum: that although the authors made no mention of their names or location, yet everyone's reply, in whatever language, would find its way to their hands; they would discern, somehow, whether your heart was true and respond accordingly.

I knew at once that the Contessa must be a Rosicrucian, as must the enigmatic Mr Pym. By chance our paths had crossed; now they awaited my response. I even knew where to write. Heart aflame and hand trembling, I took up paper and pen. At last I had found the quest for which my soul was destined. Yes, I declared, I am one of you! I waxed poetic: Let me sit at your feet, let me drink of the well of eternal wisdom, et cetera. I addressed the envelope with a flourish: *Mr Pym, care of B. Lytton, Bookseller, Cecil Court by the Rose and Crown*, and sealed it with an enormous dollop of scarlet wax to express my sincerity and my importance.

But with the light of dawn, doubts began to intrude. The book had been published more than a hundred years ago and referred to events earlier still; probably it was intended as a satire, or a provocative fiction. If Rosicrucians had ever existed, they had obviously failed in their grandiose mission – look at the state of the world. Mr Pym was an ordinary man of business who merely liked to maintain his privacy. At best he was a spy for some foreign power, and the bookshop a useful cover for a discreet correspondence with 'antiquarian booksellers' on the Continent. Perhaps Lytton was himself Pym, and maintained a double identity for any number of reasons. And the Contessa was an ordinary adventuress, who enjoyed playing with young hearts. She had used me and discarded me; she had already forgotten me. And the book, the rose and cross? That had been just a dream, a delirium. Lytton had heard me describe them; it was inevitable that he should then try to sell me a book about them. What had I paid? Three guineas, I recalled. Well, I'd made myself an easy mark; I had only myself to blame.

9

A Bargain with the Devil

🌿

The journey to Farundell promised to be unusually comfortable. Sebastian had won, at cards, a carriage from the Marquess of Blandford. It was very grand, with good springs, handsome upholstery and a drinks cabinet (no dildos). But to our dismay we were joined at the last minute by our brother Andrew, on leave from his regiment. It was a source of the most profound irritation to Andrew that Sebastian was the elder; in consequence, he took his role as the military second son with the utmost seriousness. Even as a child he had marched and saluted, stood ramrod straight and subjected himself to Spartan disciplines, such as naked swims in winter and long tramps inadequately attired. He was happiest when he could inveigle the rest of us into his war games, lead stealthy attacks in the middle of the night, defend the elaborate fortresses he built in the woods. Sebastian and I had mocked him, teased him and played tricks on him, but he never cracked.

He glittered with gold braid and clanking metal and took up three-quarters of the carriage. 'You look terrible, Francis,' he said.

'You are too kind.' I squeezed in next to Sebastian, who was trying to disentangle his legs from Andrew's very large sword.

'Can't you put that bloody thing on the roof?' Sebastian's temper finally snapped. 'Only a toy soldier wears his sword in a carriage. What you want, in case of highwaymen, is a brace of pistols.' He reached into his pocket, pulled one out, cocked it, opened the window and fired it into the air.

I screamed and clapped my hands over my ears; Andrew ascended directly into the roof of the carriage without changing expression, except for a tightening of his jaw. If the brakes hadn't been on, the horses would have bolted all the way to Farundell.

When the carriage stopped rocking, Sebastian poured a brandy for himself, and one for me. 'Your very good health,' he said.

'And yours,' I replied.

We arrived late. Torches illuminated the wide courtyard and the long, ivy-hung sprawl of the house; the windows shone with candlelight. Grooms came running for the horses, footmen unloaded our luggage. I managed to slip up to my room by the back stairs without going through my family's lengthy greeting rituals, waylaid only by the ecstatic salutations of my wolfhound, Japhet.

My youngest brother Clarence was curled up in the bed; I kicked him out over his drowsy protests. I was too old to share a bed; I felt, in fact, about sixty. Tunnie brought up my trunk and unpacked my clothes; the London suits looked extremely out of place here and I suspected I wouldn't have the courage to wear them. I sent him for wine and food and settled by the fire with my feet on Japhet, who made little snuffles of contentment. Tunnie returned sooner than I'd expected; it is remarkable how quickly servants are able to find their way in a new household.

The next morning I rode out early. The ruts in the road had iced over and patches of snow lingered in the shadows. The air was sharp and cold, with a whiff of burning as we passed the coppice wood. Japhet ran circles around me, wider and wider, then raced straight back in like an arrow, before spiralling out once more. My horse's breath steamed and he pranced to keep warm until I let him out for a canter past stubbly fields and close-cropped meadows dotted with sheep. We skirted a patch of woodland and climbed, trotting now, to the top of Belimor Hill. This, to me, was the centre of Farundell; our land stretched for miles in all directions. I could make out the town of Exley, the villages of Bridewell, Upper and Lower Belcombe, and our house far away in the valley, identified by the columns of smoke rising from its many chimneys, the glimmer of the lake and the River Isis, mist-wreathed and untouched, as yet, by the frigid sun.

The north wind bit my cheeks and seared my lungs. I breathed deeply, expelling the smoke and stench of London. For weeks I had rarely ventured out in daylight; I'd lived, it seemed, in a series of small, dark spaces – beds, carriages, coffee houses, bagnios. No wonder I'd felt old and tired.

A wave of sparrows fluttered over the field, pecking, twittering, moving on. Japhet scared up a hare, who led him in a mad zigzag before diving into the hedgerow. High above, a pair of red kites circled.

I rode back the long way and stopped at St Ælfhild's pool to call on Sally Bird. A woman with that name had lived in the little hut by the sacred spring for as long as anyone could remember, although I suspected that not one but a series of women had taken the name and residence. My Sally had a frizz of white curls, ageless, weathered skin, bright black eyes and nearly all of her teeth. As always, she seemed to have been expecting me. The door stood open; she turned from her cauldron and poured a fragrant, steaming stream into a cup. 'This will help clear your lungs and spirit of the foul vapours that lie upon them,' she said.

'Thank you, Sally.' I sipped cautiously, tasted honey and

elderflower, rosemary, mint and other flavours I couldn't identify. It was delicious.

Dried herbs hung in bunches from the rafters, the walls were lined with shelves of thick glass bottles and clay jars, the floor was beaten earth. I felt I'd travelled back in time; London seemed a thousand miles and years away. I settled on a stool by the fire as Sally resumed her work, shaking seeds from their papery pods, funnelling them into carefully labelled jars. As far as I knew, Sally couldn't read or write; her labels consisted of cryptic symbols derived from flowers, leaves and roots, legible only to herself.

'How is the Lady Anne your mother?' she asked after a while.

I shrugged. 'I didn't see her when I arrived last night. When I was in London I heard she was with child again. But you probably know that.' Sally always knew who was pregnant.

'She is not with child.'

'Oh? Well, I imagine she's relieved.' My mother had borne fifteen children; seven of us still lived. 'My sister Isabel is to marry next week,' I said. 'Will it be a happy marriage, do you think?'

Sally didn't answer.

Isabel's future husband, Reginald, was our third cousin twice removed, heir to the Harfield lands that adjoined ours to the east. He was very fat and, for reasons unknown, detested by his father, the present Earl, who was in his seventies and looked set to live for ever out of sheer spite. Harfield Hall was a decrepit pile, freezing in winter and full of noxious air and clouds of flies in the summer. I suppose my father considered the match a long-term investment.

'Do you know anything about my great-great-grandfather Tobias?' I asked.

'How old do you think I am?'

I laughed. 'I mean, do you recall any old stories about him?'

Sally eased into her chair, reached for her pipe, looked questioningly at me.

'I almost forgot,' I said, and took a pouch of tobacco from my pocket. 'Special from London, this is. The finest black Turkish.'

She opened the pouch, sniffed and smiled. 'You're a good lad.'

I waited while she cleaned her pipe and filled it, tamped it down and lit it. 'Tobias?' I said.

'He's not going anywhere.' She puffed slowly, leaned back and propped her feet on the hearth. 'Tobias the Alchemist,' she said, 'had two wives.' She always liked to start with something dramatic, to capture your attention. 'At the same time.'

'But in the graveyard there's only one – Clothilde, I think her name was.'

'There was another, and no one knows where she lies. They say he murdered her, or witched her away, or turned her into gold. Tobias had a secret store of alchemist's gold, magic gold, that could turn anything to gold just by touching it. It's hidden somewhere, guarded by a demon. I remember my gran told me that her gran knew a man who discovered the hiding place and tried to steal it; the demon sent him mad. He was found half drowned on the shore of the lake, gibbering nonsense. He never recovered his senses. They say Tobias made a bargain with the Devil and it all went wrong.'

The day had darkened; Japhet shuffled his paws in the doorway, watched by Sally's irascible tabby cat. As I left, Sally gave me a bottle of thick, dark liquid. 'Your mother may have need of this,' she said. 'Tell her, never more than one spoonful every eight hours. Repeat, please.'

'Never more than one spoonful every eight hours.'

'And tell her I will come if she sends for me, but not with a doctor in the room.'

'I'll tell her.'

'And tell her not to let them bleed her.'

'I'll tell her, Sally, but . . .'

'That is all.'

37

10

Someone's Fallen In

I rode back to the house perplexed, intending to seek out my mother at once, but Reginald and his entourage were arriving. Mother stood with Isabel and Father on the step to greet the guests; she seemed bright and gay enough.

At dinner I was able to approach her chair; I kissed her cheek and was surprised by the foulness of her breath. 'I apologise for not greeting you last night, Mother.'

She made a small gesture: it was forgiven. I had the impression she hadn't noticed my absence.

'And you are well, Mother?'

Another small gesture: as well as could be expected. Her hand moved to rest on her belly, where there was a distinct bulge.

'I hear we are to be blessed with a new member of the family,' I said.

She glanced at me and frowned. 'One does not discuss such matters at dinner.'

Dinner was followed by dancing; Sebastian and I, au fait with the latest gigues and bourrées from London, were much in demand.

Isabel, pale in ivory silk, looked about twelve next to Reginald, resplendent in puce. Gorgeous material, but ill fitting. Monsieur Duplis would have deplored the pinched armholes. Reginald retired after one dance, citing his gout. My mother did not dance;

but then, she rarely did. During a pause in the dancing, Isabel was asked to sing; I accompanied her on the harpsichord. While in London I had neglected my practice and it showed, but Isabel's sweet soprano slid over my mistakes.

That night the lake froze over; the next day was colder still. By Christmas Eve the ice was several inches thick and we had a skating party. I loved skating, and Isabel had always been the only one who could keep up with me. We strapped on our blades, I took her arm and we skated off.

'Reginald does not skate,' I said. He sat on the shore in a chair near the bonfire, swathed in fur, sipping chocolate.

'Which is a pity,' Isabel said. 'He might fall through.'

The ice near the shore was rough and pebbly; we went further out, where it was glassy smooth. I took her hand and swung her in a circle. She stretched one leg behind her, skirts billowing. I twirled her faster and faster until she was red-cheeked and laughing, then released her. She sailed away, inscribed a graceful arc and skated back to me.

The sky was iron-grey; a few flakes of snow drifted down. Arm-in-arm, we circled the lake. On the far side, out of sight of the house, some children were larking about with wooden skates, sticks and what looked like a frozen rat.

'Do you remember the night we swam over to the island?' Isabel said.

'Of course. In the morning you were afraid to swim back; I had to go on my own and fetch a boat.'

'Will you come and visit me at Harfield?'

I heard the catch in her voice. 'Of course. We all will. And you'll come here for visits as often as you like. During the Season you can live in London. Go to the opera and masquerade balls.' Take lovers, I thought, but didn't say.

'I think I hate him.'

'How can you hate him? You hardly know him.'

'He never looks at me.'

'So you hate him for that?'

'I am silly, I know.'

'He may die before long,' I said. 'I watched him last night; he drinks a great deal and that yellow tinge of his eyes is not a sign of good health.'

'Well, that is a comfort.'

We circled the lake again and again. 'How is Mother?' I asked.

'Glad to marry me off, fretful about all the entertaining she has had to organise.'

'You wrote that she was with child.'

'Her maid told my maid.'

'Sally Bird says it is not so.'

'Does she? I suppose she knows best.'

It was dusk; the line between land and sky blurred and skating felt almost like flying. Everyone else had gone back up to the house. As we rounded the island, we heard an ominous cracking sound, followed by shouts from the cluster of children on the far bank.

'Someone's fallen in,' said Isabel, skating closer.

'They'll be all right,' I said. 'Come away; the ice is too thin there.'

'We have to help, Francis, we can't just leave.'

I made her stay where she was and skated cautiously closer. 'Is all well?' I called.

In response came inchoate cries. In the shadows I could make out some children dragging a branch down to the shore and trying to push it out. Isabel appeared at my side. 'Look – the ice has broken, there.' She pointed to a darker patch.

I strained to see. 'There's no one,' I said. 'If someone fell in they've already been lost; the currents will have taken them.'

'No, no, we can't let her drown . . .'

'Her? How do you know – damn it, come here.' I caught hold of her cloak and pulled her back as a crack appeared and moved rapidly in our direction. We retreated, Isabel sobbing now; I held her firmly and skated away as fast as I could.

The bonfire had died to embers; the cries from across the lake had ceased. Snow fell in fat flakes and melted on Isabel's face, obscuring her tears. Above the long, dark slope of the meadow the windows of the house glowed with light.

11

There Shall Be Signs

Christmas morning was icy clear. Isabel and I walked around the old cloister to keep warm as we waited for the rest of the family; we had to enter the chapel in the correct order.

'I think I might have liked being a nun,' Isabel said. 'Can you imagine? Twenty or thirty women living here – an infirmary, a herbarium, a school. A library and a scriptorium.'

'Poverty, chastity, obedience,' I said. 'You might have had some difficulty with the last.'

'True. But I'm glad they left some of it standing, so I can pretend.'

The cloister, or what remained of it, linked the old part of the house, built in 1540 by Roger Damory, Tobias's father, with the twelfth-century chapel. Cool and pleasant in summer, it was a draughty place in winter, open to the courtyard on one side and the kitchen gardens on the other.

'Francis, what is it . . . what is it like . . .' Isabel stopped, face crimson.

'What is what like?'

'Oh, you know. What married people do in bed.'

'Surely that is a question for Mother?'

'She said, "Do your duty. Produce an heir." As though it was a cabbage, or a conjuring trick.'

'What makes you think I'd know? I'm not married.'

She gave me a look. 'I know what men get up to in London. Are you a rake yet, or a libertine like Sebastian?'

'How do you even know those words?'

'Novels.'

'And you assume these fictions are real?'

'Aren't they?'

'I have not read your novels.'

'You are merely being evasive.'

'Yes.'

'Francis, please. Please give me some idea what to expect. Surely if it's as awful as Mother implies, mankind would not be so numerous.'

'It can be heaven,' I said.

'Aside from probably being blasphemous, that doesn't answer my question at all.'

'Look, here's everyone. We have to go in.'

We filed into the chapel, Mother and Father first, then Reginald, then the rest of us in order: Sebastian and Andrew, Isabel and I, Gertrude, Catherine and Clarence.

The chapel was punishingly cold, cold rising from the floor and emanating from the walls, cold light from the bare windows, cold shadows across the nave. It made one feel like a sinner. The old priest – a distant cousin – who had always conducted our services had died and his replacement was unknown to me. An old man as well, though quite spry, with white hair and spectacles. I didn't catch his name.

His voice, when he began the first lesson, was unusually reso-nant. 'The people that walked in darkness have seen a great light:

42

they that dwelt in the land of the shadow of death, upon them hath the light shined.'

I studied the walls, where traces of painted saints bled through the whitewash: the corner of a blue robe, a halo, the outline of a cross, with a patch of mould blooming like a rose.

'And there shall be signs,' said the priest.

I thought of the Rosy Cross, and, unwillingly, of the Contessa. When I'd spoken of heaven, it was her I'd meant.

'He came unto his own,' said the priest, 'and his own received him not. But as many as received him, to them gave he power to become the sons of God.' I thought of Christian Rosenkreutz, disregarded by the world, imparting his secrets to a chosen few.

'Who rose to the life immortal,' said the priest. According to the *Fama Fraternitatis*, immortality was the destiny of all true Christians.

We knelt to receive communion. 'Most precious body and blood,' said the priest.

The wine tasted strangely of roses; the cloth covering the table was embroidered with roses. As I watched, they twined and blossomed, releasing a sweet fragrance. I heard a sound like bells ringing, though the bell tower was long fallen. Isabel reached out and took my hand. Her gloves were embroidered with roses, alive and growing. I shook my head; the ringing faded and the roses stilled.

After the service, as the others hurried inside, I walked up the wooded hill behind the house. The communion wine had had an odd effect – for a moment I wondered whether I was sleepwalking. There was a peculiar tingling beneath my skin, not unpleasant, and a sensation of floating a few inches above the ground. I'd ceased to notice the cold.

Tobias's oratory chapel looked forlorn; no one ever came here except for burials – its graveyard deemed more appropriate, if less convenient, than the nuns'. It was a small building, with narrow windows and an unusual pyramidal roof. I pushed aside a briar rose that had sprawled across the path and opened the door, rusty hinges creaking. The single, square room was completely plain with the exception of – I noticed for the first time – a large, elaborate stone rose at the apex of the ceiling. Had the world always been so full of roses?

In the graveyard Tobias lay beneath a simple slab. I brushed away the dead leaves and read the inscription:

Tobias Geoffrey Herbert Damory
1538–1620
God made Eternity, Eternity the World,
the World Time, and Time Generation.

There was, of course, a rose. It must have been here all along; I'd never really looked. A cross was carved the entire length of the slab; at its centre, over Tobias's heart, bloomed the rose.

12
The Child

I returned to the house. One feast in the hall for a hundred or so tenants, villagers, minor burghers, with music from the gallery, trumpets and violins – unbelievably noisy; another upstairs for local gentry, a slightly lesser din. I went to my room, took up the *Fama Fraternitatis* and looked for the letter I'd written to Mr Pym. Unable to find it, I summoned Tunnie, who said he'd posted it before we left London.

'In future, Tunnie,' I said, 'don't post anything unless I specifically ask you to. I need to allow for second thoughts.'

I couldn't remember exactly what I'd written, but it had been a not altogether clear-headed, middle-of-the-night sort of thing. No doubt Mr Pym, whoever he was, foreign spy or ordinary man of business, would find it utterly incomprehensible and take me for a lunatic. Unless – the thought niggled at the back of my mind – he was a real Rosicrucian, he'd understood my letter, and all those roses were his reply.

Isabel was married two days later, in murrey damask embroidered with roses and pearls. I had no chance to speak with her, just kissed her and wished her luck along with everyone else as she and Reginald set off in his carriage. She waved and smiled bravely from the window.

My mother collapsed the moment the carriage was out of sight, and was helped to her room. A footman was dispatched to Exley to fetch the doctor. I remembered what Sally Bird had said, and when the doctor arrived, waylaid him in the hall.

'Do not bleed her,' I said.

'Ah, you are a medical man, my good young sir; I had not realised.' He swept off his hat and made a deep bow. 'Such a pleasure to meet a new colleague. I gather you have made a thorough examination of the patient; of her urine and her stools, of the odours of her breath, the markings on her tongue, the condition of her finger- and toenails, the texture of her skin. And of course, since she has been your patient for many years, you will know her medical history. I am most eager to learn your diagnosis.'

Before I could reply, my father appeared, frowned at me and ushered the doctor upstairs. I followed, but was barred at the bedchamber door by Nancy, Mother's dour-faced maid. 'Tell Lady Anne that Sally Bird will come if she asks,' I said. Nancy gave me a horrified look, crossed herself and closed the door.

45

The thaw began the next night, the darkness broken by great cracks and groans as the lake ice shifted. Rain fell, hard and heavy. In the morning the Isis flooded the water meadows; when I rode out at midday the lake had spread among the willows and hazel that lined the shore. Two men were at the weir, struggling to raise the sluice gate and poking beneath the water with a long stick.

'Jammed by a log,' one said.

'Or a bag of gold,' laughed another.

One man stood to the side, watching anxiously. He stepped forward, hesitated.

'You have another idea?' I said to him.

'My daughter, m'lord . . .'

'Stop poking about with that stick,' I said, dismounting. 'Can you not climb in and reach down with your hands?'

'Too deep, m'lord.'

'Too bloody cold.'

'Can't swim, or I would,' said the father.

I stripped down to my breeches and jumped in.

The shock nearly killed me. It was unimaginably cold; I went numb immediately. An immense tiredness filled my mind, blackness spread like ink. Faces floated past: the Contessa, Lucy, Isabel, Sebastian . . . But wasn't it just too stupid to die like this? I really shouldn't. Had I not come here for a reason? Oh yes, the child. I forced my eyes open, groped downwards, grasped what might have been a limb, pulled. It was trapped, wedged in by a log. My lungs were on fire, but if I went up for another breath I knew I would never dive again. I kicked at the log, too numb to tell if I was having any effect until at last the body slid free and I clawed for the surface.

I must have lost consciousness for a moment – the next thing I remember I was lying on the bank, looking into the blue eyes of the child. Her eyelids had been eaten by the fishes.

Two of the men slung me across my horse and made for the

house. The last I saw of the father, he was sitting in the mud holding his daughter's white and fingerless hand.

13

The Missing Books

❦

I recovered quickly. My sisters and Clarence thought I was a hero, coddled me in furs with warming pans at my feet and spent the afternoon running back and forth bringing me hot drinks and titbits of food. Sebastian wept with laughter when he learned that I'd nearly killed myself for the corpse of a peasant child; Andrew was aggrieved that I had not summoned him to do it.

It rained all week. My mother remained in her room, seeing no one but the doctor, who called every day. I learned from Tunnie, who at my suggestion cultivated a friendship with Mother's maid Nancy, that he was not bleeding her, but dosing her with mercury concoctions of his own devising, with which he claimed to have had much success in similar cases.

'Cases of what?' I asked; Tunnie said Nancy did not know. There was no more talk of pregnancy.

I spent most of my time in the library, looking for anything with the TGHD glyph. Tobias had had one of the largest collections of books and manuscripts in England; scholars had come from afar to consult it. I'd always thought we had kept them all. We are a family of bibliophiles, with some notable exceptions, and the library had expanded considerably in the last hundred years. Most of Tobias's books resided in glass-fronted cases, though some had escaped to mingle with the common fellows on the open shelves.

There had always been a librarian to maintain order. One of my earliest memories was of Mr Trevelyan, with his tufts of mousy hair and his musty odour, who held me on his bony knee and let me turn the pages of the magnificent *Crèvecoeur Book of Hours*, the pride of the collection. But when Trevelyan left, my father had not filled the post and disorder was creeping in.

The library was dim and quiet, the tall windows streaming with rain. I passed many blissful hours flicking through some of the books, lingering over others: an introduction to the Chaldean and Armenian languages; a translation of Plato by Marsilio Ficino. I got lost in Jean de Léry's fascinating *Historia Navigationis in Brasiliam, quae et America Dicitur*. Many books had copious marginalia in Tobias's hand – berating, correcting and very occasionally commending the author.

After a time, I noticed that I'd found no books whatsoever on alchemy or any related field; a bit odd, considering Tobias's renown as an alchemist. Could these be the ones to which Lytton had referred?

After a fortnight on the doctor's remedy, my mother was deemed well enough to dine with the rest of the family. She looked feverish to me and, despite the padded robe, extremely thin. She was sweating and swallowing convulsively and only pretending to eat.

Sebastian, who had gone up to London for a few days, arrived late and drew disapproving glances. He rolled his eyes, slipped into his seat across from me and applied himself to the roast venison. As the plates were being cleared he leaned back in his chair and reached into his pocket. My first thought was that he was about to bring forth a pistol and fire it at the ceiling; I prepared to cover my ears. Instead he took out a parcel and tossed it to me. 'This arrived at the house for you.'

I unwrapped it. There was a book and a letter, which I looked at only long enough to see that it was from Lytton and put in my pocket. As I turned to the book, my mother gasped. She seemed so stricken I thought she was having a seizure of some sort; Andrew leapt up and rushed to her side.

She pointed at the book. 'You told me Trevelyan destroyed those books.'

'I beg your pardon?' I said, then realised she was addressing my father.

I glanced at the book. It was beautiful – blue leather binding with silver corners and hasps set with opals, a rose and cross outlined in gilt on the cover. Vellum pages, not paper: a bound manuscript. A very valuable book indeed.

My father stood. 'Come with me, Francis,' he said, and led the way to the drawing room. He paced for a while, then sat in an armchair by the fire and gestured me to the chair opposite. I could not recall another occasion, aside from meals or in chapel, when I had been seated in my father's presence.

He was silent for a long time. I heard a stealthy rustling as people gathered to listen at the keyhole, which he didn't seem to notice. It occurred to me that he might be growing deaf. His mouth worked as though he was chewing words and swallowing them. He was badly shaved; his valet was an ancient dim-sighted fellow with a tremor. It was a wonder my father survived his daily ministrations.

He crossed his legs; I did the same. He glared at me – was I mocking him? I uncrossed my legs.

'I must ask you to give me that book,' he said.

I only just stopped myself from obeying instantly. 'But I have not read it yet.'

His eyes widened; he too had expected immediate obedience. He stood, and perforce so did I. 'Not a request. Give me the book, Francis.'

We realised at about the same time that I was now taller than he was. He restrained himself from taking a step backwards, but he pulled in his chin. I restrained myself from hiding the book behind my back.

He moved faster than I'd imagined possible, striking me across the face with one hand while snatching the book with the other. As I staggered back he flung the book on the fire, seized the poker and rammed it into the heart of the flames.

I lunged at him; we fell in an ungainly tangle. His wig slipped over his eyes and he flailed blindly at me. I tried to get my hands around his neck. I was bleeding like a pig where his ring had opened a cut over my left eye and the blood spattered over his contorted face and white cravat. He made horrible grunts and wheezes; I fought in silence, determined to kill him.

Sebastian and Andrew burst in and separated us, accompanied by a crowd of servants. Father got to his feet, straightened his wig and walked unsteadily from the room. The crowd parted to let him pass. I turned to the fireplace and poked at the embers, but all that remained of the book were a few bits of twisted silver. Tunnie handed me a cup of wine; I sank into a chair and let him press a cloth to the cut on my brow.

It was not until later, when I was preparing for bed, that I came upon Lytton's letter. After the usual salutations and courtesies, which took up half the page, and further declarations of the very great pleasure, et cetera, it gave him to deliver into my hands this quite special, et cetera, item from Tobias's library, came the words: '. . . *which your friend the Contessa has brought in and asked me to send to you*'.

I read and reread the words. The Contessa, the Contessa, the Contessa. I had persuaded myself that she was a shallow adventuress; I had almost managed to forget her. How I had misjudged her!

I headed straight for my father's room with the intention of throttling him in his bed. What a fool I'd been, what a stupid, trusting child. I'd done everything but put the book on the flames myself. Why hadn't I put it in my pocket? I'd stood there holding it out for him. Had I expected a civilised conversation, an attempt to persuade me with reason? Had I thought he would take no for an answer? Had I thought he would ask more than once?

He was not in his room; he, and everyone else, was across the passage outside my mother's room, where she had collapsed again. His face was so full of distress that it stopped me in my tracks. He glanced at me but I don't think he really saw me.

I returned to my room, sat by the fire and drank a large brandy. What had Mother said? You told me Trevelyan destroyed that book – no, *those* books. But I couldn't imagine Trevelyan destroying any books; they were his life, his children. And Tobias's books, the foundation of the library? Never. He would sooner have died, I was sure. I knew, then, what had happened to the missing books, the ones about alchemy, magic, cabala. Trevelyan had been ordered to destroy them but had sold them instead, and lied to my father.

14
Her Last Words

🌿

My mother's condition deteriorated from that night. She kept to her bed and started moaning with pain, a low, continuous sound that penetrated doors and walls. The doctor came and went, prescribing new medicines and finally attempting to bleed her, though I heard from Tunnie that the blood would not flow. The moans grew louder; she never slept.

With Tunnie's help, I obtained one of the doctor's empty bottles and filled it with Sally Bird's medicine. I made rather a good forgery of the doctor's label, with instructions: *Not more than one spoonful every eight hours*. For verisimilitude, I sent Tunnie into Exley, where he was to hire a lad to deliver it to the house as though from the doctor himself. The moans ceased that night; my mother, we learned, slept peacefully. The doctor was credited with a miraculous cure.

Sally's medicine eased the pain but there was no cure. Mother weakened steadily; she never ate or drank and soon could not even raise her head. The priest came, and we were summoned to her bedside to say goodbye. I scarcely recognised her; she looked like a tiny bird, sunk among cushions and furs, her skin shrunken over her face so that the skull showed through. I thought we had come too late, but then her eyes opened and moved from face to face. When she came to me a spark appeared and she beckoned me close.

I leaned over, but could not make out her whisper. I lowered my ear to her mouth, then jerked back as she shouted, 'You are an idiot.' Everyone gasped; my father bundled me out of the room.

Those were, apparently, her last words.

Isabel came back for the funeral. It was a mild day, with wood doves calling and snowdrops pushing through the dead leaves in the graveyard. After the burial we rode out together.

'Well,' I said, 'how is married life?'

'Not what I expected,' she said. 'Reginald went off to stay with friends. He never, we never, that is . . . well, we never even shared a bed. Nothing happened at all.'

'So that is a relief?'

'Yes, I suppose it is. Though of course the dread event may only have been postponed. But he's left me at Harfield with his ghastly father. If you can believe it,' she lowered her voice, as though the horses could hear, 'he wanted to inspect me.'

'Inspect?'

'He came to my rooms and ordered the maids to undress me. So he could see if I was likely to produce an heir. I am glad to see you looking shocked; if you had told me this was the usual thing I would never have forgiven you for not warning me.'

'I'm speechless,' I said. 'What did you do?'

'I took up my sewing scissors and prepared to defend my honour.'

'What did he do?'

'Blustered a bit and left.'

'First round to you, then.'

'Yes. I've scarcely seen him since. But you have been busy as well – I heard that you tried to kill Father, but no one knows why.'

'Do I need a reason?' I touched my brow. Half an inch lower and I'd have lost the eye. The cut had not healed well; I would have a scar, which secretly I thought gave me a dashing air. People would assume I'd acquired it in a duel rather than from being cuffed by my father like a disobedient child.

'And I also heard about the drowned girl. Thank you.'

'I was an idiot.'

'Were those really Mother's last words?'

I laughed. 'Apparently so. I'd no idea she cared.'

15

Snares for the Unwary

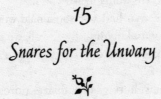

Father fell ill with a fever and we thought he was soon to join Mother, but as winter turned to spring, he began slowly to recover. Isabel went back to Harfield; Andrew was sent to Norfolk to train with his regiment. Sebastian and I slunk off to London, only to be called back to Farundell a month later when Father took a turn for the worse. Again he recovered and we fled; again he weakened and we returned.

One day he summoned Sebastian with particular urgency; we thought for a final blessing, but my brother emerged in a state of repressed mirth.

'What did he want?' I asked.

'To give marriage advice. I believe he has given me up as a lost cause and is pinning his hopes on my future wife, whose responsibility it will be to save the Damorys. His only regret is that he has not yet secured this paragon for me, but he gave me two lists.' He held them up. 'Qualities, Persons. Desirable qualities are: moral fortitude, robust constitution, intelligence but not too much, devotion to duty, ability to manage servants. Undesirable qualities are: attractive appearance, frivolous manner, excessively revealing attire. Is that a quality? And the Persons, well, see for yourself.'

I perused the list. It was headed, of course, by the daughters of our nearest neighbours. With Isabel's marriage we had achieved the Harfields, to the east; Father now cast his eye on the Shereham-Waverly lands to the north and the Plachards to the west. 'Does he know what Lavinia Plachard gets up to in London?'

'Apparently not. He wants to see you now.'

'Me? What for?' We had not spoken or even looked at each other since I'd tried to kill him.

'How should I know? Go on.' He gave me a shove towards the door.

The room was sweltering, fire ablaze, dozens of candles. My father sat propped up in his bed, arms covered with scabs where he'd been bled. He coughed constantly and spat thick greenish phlegm into a basin at his side. 'D'you want to strangle me now, boy, eh?'

54

The thought of touching him was revolting. 'No, sir.'

'Sorry, are you? Now's your chance to beg forgiveness, secure your inheritance.'

'I'm not sorry,' I said.

He wheezed with laughter. 'Sit.' He pointed to the bed.

I sat down gingerly next to the phlegm.

He hawked and spat. 'Serious matter,' he said.

There was a long pause. Had he been referring to the phlegm? 'Yes, sir,' I said.

'I mean your mother.' Tears welled in his eyes.

I was astonished and appalled. I tried to edge away, but he seized my wrist with a surprisingly strong grip.

'She saved me.'

Was I, too, to get a lecture on marriage? There was another long pause.

'It killed her.'

'What killed her?'

'Seeing you with that book.'

He was obviously losing his mind; best to humour him. 'I am very sorry, sir.'

'Trevelyan betrayed me.'

That made sense, though I pretended not to understand.

His hand tightened on my wrist. 'You. Must. Be. Ware.'

'Beware of what, sir?'

He fixed his red-rimmed eyes on me. 'There is a streak of madness in our family.'

'Really, sir? How fascinating.' I had heard of certain cases of extreme eccentricity, but not actual madness.

He sat up suddenly. 'Never touch those books!' he shouted, then subsided, weeping uncontrollably. 'Promise me,' he said. 'For your mother's sake. Never touch those books.'

I tried to think how I could phrase a promise in such a way as to avoid taking on any significant limitations. 'Which books?' I stalled.

'Snares for the unwary,' he muttered, and his eyes slid away. His hand loosened on my arm; I withdrew slowly and tiptoed out of the room.

His ravings had aroused my curiosity. Why had he ordered Trevelyan to destroy Tobias's books, and from what had my mother saved him? I wondered what had happened to Trevelyan, and sought out our housekeeper, Mrs Garson. She had been in the post for more than twenty years and might recall him.

'Mr Trevelyan,' she said. 'Of course I remember him.' She did not even have to consult her record books. 'He retired ten, or was it eleven years ago? An unexpected inheritance, apparently. A cottage in Witney.'

I rode over to Witney the next morning, enquired after Mr Trevelyan at the inn and was directed to a small stone cottage on the outskirts of the village. A garden ran down to the River Windrush, and that is where I found him, sitting on a bench beneath a flowering cherry tree in the mild April sun.

I recognised him easily, though the tufty hair had gone grey. He also recognised me – or if not me, exactly, then he certainly recognised a Damory and an expression of concern passed over his face. Nevertheless, he greeted me warmly and invited me to dine with him. We went into the house and sat by the open window as an elderly maid served us a simple dinner of cold meats and cheeses, pork pies and small beer.

He asked about Farundell, about my family and, in particular, about the library. It was clear that he missed it a great deal; it was clear, also, that he longed to talk about what had happened and why he had left.

When the meal was finished he poured brandy and we lit our pipes. 'But you have not come just to visit me in my old age,' he said.

'No.'

'You want to know about the books.'

'I know you were ordered to destroy them,' I said, 'and I know you disobeyed.' I showed him the *Fama Fraternitatis*.

He took the book, opened it and smiled as if at an old friend. 'I could not have destroyed them, and I have always hoped they would find their way back to Farundell some day when it was safe for them . . . when your father and mother . . . oh, please forgive me. I do not mean to imply . . .'

'I understand,' I said. 'And I promise you, I will try to find them and bring them back where they belong. But why? Why did my father wish them destroyed?'

Children can never imagine their parents as other than they are, and it seemed all but impossible that the man Trevelyan described was the father I knew. He, like me, had been a third son. Before he unexpectedly inherited the title he'd lived a wild life, having fallen in with a group of like-minded hell-dogs whose favourite activity was breaking into churches to perform sundry blasphemies. Locked into his room by his father, he had nearly burned the house down by starting a fire intended to invoke Beelzebub.

With the title came debts; my mother's dowry was soon exhausted. Convinced that Tobias the Alchemist's treasure was buried somewhere at Farundell, my father had developed an obsession with him that culminated in a midnight ritual to raise him from his grave and compel him to reveal the location. He had commanded Trevelyan to assist him, but despite lengthy recitations of the barbarous names of evocation and the most exact tracings of the appropriate sigils, nothing happened except that they got soaked in a downpour and chilled by an unseasonal north wind. My father had fallen gravely ill and nearly died. When he recovered he was a changed man, exhausted and meek. It was my mother, Trevelyan saw, who ruled now, and it was she who ordered that the books be destroyed. Trevelyan had burned a pile of worthless books instead and sold Tobias's discreetly over a period of several years before he dared to announce his 'sudden inheritance'.

Thanking him profoundly – for the revelations and for saving the books – I rode back to Farundell in the dusk, feeling as though I had stumbled upon an unexpected vista in a landscape I thought I knew well. My father was not who I had assumed him to be and although I cannot say I liked him any better, I felt a curious kinship with him that I had never felt before.

16

The Most Frivolous and Degenerate of Occupations

It would have been so tidy if Father had obliged us by dying promptly, but it seemed he had found a way of life that suited him. He ailed; we attended. He improved; we hied to London. He ailed; we returned. He enjoyed giving the appearance of a witless old man – he even drooled – then springing an acute and malicious comment like a trap. When his children were not available, he tormented the servants; Tunnie reported that Mrs Garson was deluged with requests to be sent to the London house. Doctors came and went, the latest specialists called in, subjected to an increasingly well-informed questioning as to theories and practices, their remedies tried and always found ineffective, or effective in unwelcome ways.

A year and a half crawled by in this way, and Sebastian had

begun to evade our father's summons. He was not in; he could not be found. I, too, tried to be 'not in', but even when I succeeded, my mind was troubled, and I went the next day, tardy, knowing I would be excoriated for my tardiness, but I had to go. The sight of that man, my progenitor, in his bed, so repulsive, was yet compelling. Of course I hated him, for no reason and for good reasons, but his long dance with dying fascinated me. For dying he undoubtedly was, beneath the pretence. I saw it; he saw that I saw it, but we pretended he was only pretending.

I had agonised over what I should do about the Contessa. She had become, in my mind, a potent and painful presence, reminding me always of what I had lost. I caught myself wishing I'd been used by a callous adventuress rather than touched so deeply by a real Rosicrucian.

But I could not let her gift go unacknowledged. I wrote to Lytton and enclosed a sealed letter for the Contessa, care of Mr Pym. To her I could only be truthful. I confessed that I had lost her gift, that I regretted it more bitterly than I could say, that I was obviously unworthy of it in the first place, and that if my life had any meaning it would only be to find her and beg another chance. No. I crossed that out and started again. One must not be sentimental. Powerful as were my feelings for her, some part of me recognised that this was not love in the ordinary sense. Perhaps she had already given me, by her brief passage through my life, everything I could hope to obtain. With the letter I enclosed the ruby brooch, an honest if insignificant gift. I had it inscribed on the back with the words *Gemma Ultra Pretium*: the jewel beyond price.

At the end of the summer of 1719, Andrew's regiment returned to the county, he took up his rightful role as dutiful son and I finally escaped. It was with strangely mixed feelings that I set out for university on a mild early-October morning. I felt I was cutting the traces even though I was not really going far. Oxford was less

59

than a day's easy ride away if you went cross-country; longer by road. Tunnie had set out the day before with my trunks.

I left Farundell at dawn on my favourite horse, a bay gelding called Lancelot, with Japhet trotting alongside. We paused where the drive curved and I looked back at the house, the lake, the hills in the distance touched here and there with the golden flame of a birch. The sky was clear and colourless above, pink-tinged in the east.

It was an uneventful journey; it was a perfect day. Fields, woodland, streams, hills and gentle valleys familiar as my own hands, yet imbued on that day with the poetic light of adventure. Rosehips, red berries of white bryony, blue-bloomed sloes, ragged stalks of hemlock, beech trees with muscular lace of roots gripping the bank – all seemed to mean something, to be speaking to me as I passed.

We took the horse ferry across the Isis at Bablock Hithe and made our way over the flat fields of Berkshire to approach Oxford at twilight. We crossed the Isis again by Folly Bridge and came into St Asher's College as the bells were ringing. Tunnie was waiting for me at the porter's lodge, and after seeing Lancelot stabled, fed and watered I inspected my three modest rooms on the first floor.

The largest room, facing the quad, would be for eating and entertaining. The harpsichord that I had arranged to hire stood in the corner and a fire blazed in the hearth. Tunnie had stocked the sideboard with my wines and set out a plate of food; Japhet had a bowl of water and a dish of meat. A small bedchamber overlooked the college meadows, which ran down to the Isis near its confluence with the infant Thames. The adjoining study held my books; paper and pens, ink and penknife were neatly laid out. It pleased me more than a palace.

'And you, Tunnie, you are well housed?'

''Tis a garret, sir, but I have it to meself, and that's a rare thing.'

I knew what he meant. When he left, I was alone – except for Japhet, asleep on the hearthrug. I took a cup of wine and walked from room to room. Mine, mine, mine. Farundell was far more than a day away – it was my old life, and it was finished; this was my new life, and I was free.

The next day my tutor, Mr Davies, invited me to supper. He assured me that as the son of a peer I was exempt from attendance at chapel or dinner in Hall, the Proctors' authority did not pertain, nor did curfews. I need undertake no studies, would sit no examinations, could receive a degree if I chose. He kept an excellent cellar, and was kind enough to advise me that Gibbon & Whelk, wine merchants in the Cornmarket, would give me a good price if I mentioned his name. He reminded me that once term began, I would have to wear appropriate robes, tassels and so forth, and mentioned that Pelliston & Carell, in Magdalen Street, were the best tailors. They, too, would give me a special price if I mentioned, et cetera. I obtained, in this manner, a comprehensive list of establishments to cater for my every material need; he obtained, no doubt, many little luxuries to ease the difficult life of a scholar. He stopped short of recommending the best brothel, not from delicacy, as I assumed at the time, but because he had as yet no idea of my taste in such matters.

I settled into an agreeable routine. Tunnie brought my breakfast at ten – hot rolls with butter – and I made my own coffee on a little Turkish stove. My study got the morning sun, and I sat at my desk to count and admire the night's children: the pages I'd written. I was writing a novel about a young man who travels the world: his amorous adventures, his quest for the secret of immortality, his encounters with spies, assassins, alchemists and Rosicrucian adepts with strange powers. I intended it as a trifle for the amusement of Isabel but became quite caught up in the story myself, all the more so when I realised that I had no idea how it was going to end. It gave me the keenest satisfaction to know that my father would abhor novel-writing as the most frivolous and degenerate of occupations.

17

On the Matter of the Philosopher's Stone

🌿

During my first week at Oxford I found, with a thrill of acquisitive pleasure, one of Tobias's books in an upstairs room of Enderby's, the oldest and largest of Oxford's many bookshops. I was reaching for another book when it all but fell into my hands. I opened it, and there was the familiar TGHD glyph. It was a Greek text by someone called Hermes Chrysotum – the Golden Hermes.

I took it to the front desk where a young woman with pale skin and dark brows sat with her nose in a book. 'How much for this?' I asked.

She took it from me and examined it. 'I'm afraid this book is not for sale.'

'But I found it on the open shelf.'

'I regret, sir, that it is already spoken for, as it were.'

'Already spoken for? That is most unfair. If you have a book on display for a customer to see, surely it is your duty to sell it to him.'

'If I had known we had this book it would not have been on display for you to see but sent off to the person who requested it before you. Well, not this book in particular, but any book with this mark, see?' She pointed to Tobias's initials on the inside cover.

'Ah. Would this request have come through Mr Lytton in London?'

'Yes . . .'

'Then it was on my behalf. I'm the one who's looking for books from Tobias Damory's library. He was an ancestor of mine.'

'I see.' She looked doubtfully at me as though I might be trying to deceive her for some unfathomable reason.

'I am not trying to deceive you. My name is Francis Damory, I'm at St Asher's. Shall I send for someone from the college to vouch for me? Swear an affidavit? Or, I know, let me send a messenger to London to ask Mr Lytton to write a description of the person he knows as Francis Damory, seal it and send it to you.'

'Is that an attempt at humour?'

'No, of course not. This is no laughing matter. I am deadly serious.' I put my fists on the desk and leaned over her. 'If I am not permitted to purchase this book at once I may have to resort to murder and theft.'

She frowned but also, perhaps, repressed a smile, turned to the title page and rattled off the Greek with astonishing fluency, which I later learned was her favourite defence. '"*On the Matter of the Philosopher's Stone, the Elixir of the Wise, and Diverse Other Formulae, Sacred and Mundane,*"' she translated. 'Oh, alchemy.'

'You are interested in alchemy?'

'My great-uncle is. He was a student of Robert Boyle. You've heard of him, I'm sure.'

'The famous chemist – Invisible College, Royal Society and all that?'

'That's the one. My great-uncle was his assistant for many years. Boyle's long dead, but Uncle Erasmus carries on the work.'

'Agnes, where is last year's inventory?' A weedy, balding man came down the stairs and peered at me through thick spectacles. 'Good afternoon, sir. I trust my daughter is helping you?'

'Are you helping me, Agnes?' I asked.

'Of course, sir. Of course, Father, and here is the inventory.

This book is four shillings and sixpence, sir. I am delighted you have found what you were looking for. Would you like to start an account with us?' She opened a ledger, dipped a pen and wrote: *Francis Damory, St Asher's. Four and six.* 'Thank you, sir, good day.'

The book was a compendium of recipes for a variety of potions and substances, including several for the Stone or Elixir of Immortality. I was immediately irritated by the imprecise use of terms. Were the Stone and the Elixir the same thing? A liquid or a solid? Or was one made from the other? Perhaps both were a metaphor for something else. I understood why alchemy had such a dubious reputation; surely if there really was anything to it, they would just say what they meant instead of wrapping everything in so much mysterious verbiage that any reasonable person was bound to suspect some flimflam. Nevertheless, it drew me in, with its potable gold and philosophic mercury, red lions and green dragons, trees, eggs and crowns. I spent weeks making a translation. If my Greek had been better, it would not have taken so long.

The material was arranged geographically: from Persia, India, China and Japan, Greece, Egypt and Arabia. The object sought was referred to by many names ('Stone' and 'Elixir' just two of dozens) and seemed to have many properties, from the sacred (immortality, godhood) to the mundane (health, longevity, wealth). The premise seemed reasonable enough: God made man and nature, nature within man and man within nature, and by manipulating natural substances in accordance with the laws of correspondence, hidden potencies could be released. The texts were extremely devout, and construed the operations as part of God's plan for the perfection of His creation.

The recipes ranged from simple essences and distillations to extraordinarily complex concoctions with dozens of ingredients and mythical properties. Mithridate, for example, is a substance which, if taken regularly, purports to keep the body safe from all poisons. It was named after an evidently very unpopular ancient king, Mithridates, who with its help survived more than a hundred attempts on his life. It contains: costmary, 66 grams; saffron, ginger, cinnamon, 29 grams each; rhubarb root 28 grams; shepherd's purse 26 grams; nard and opobalsam, 25 grams each; castoreum, frankincense, hypocistis juice, myrrh, opopanax, malabathrum leaves, flower of round rush, turpentine resin, galbanum, Cretan carrot seeds, 24 grams each; storax 21 grams; casia, saxifrage, darnel, long pepper, sweet flag, 20 grams each; poppy tears and parsley, 17 grams each; Gallic nard, gentian root and dried rose leaves, 16 grams each; anise, 12 grams; hypericum, sagapenum, acacia juice, Illyrian iris, cardamom, 8 grams each. This was to be ground together with dried scorpion and mashed viper, distilled, recombined, fermented and left to mature in a dung heap for a year, then re-distilled, et cetera. It might well have been worth the trouble; many years later I saw some for sale in Paris at a hundred times the price of gold.

My classical Greek dictionary was entirely flummoxed by the late Greek colloquialisms, and many of the terms for ingredients and processes were simply incomprehensible. I tucked the book in my pocket and returned to Enderby's.

Agnes was at the desk with an older woman she introduced as her mother. I showed her some of the passages with which I'd struggled, and once again she read them off with great fluency, translating as she went, ignoring her mother's increasingly urgent *tsks*.

'Yes, Mother,' she said at last, 'what is it?'

'You know what it is.'

'I do not.'

'You certainly do.'

'I certainly do not.'

I gazed from one to the other, intrigued.

'If you will accompany me to the office for a moment, I would like a word with you,' said Mrs Enderby.

'But there is a customer,' Agnes said.

I nodded vigorously, to show I was on her side, whatever it was.

Mrs Enderby closed her eyes for a long moment, compressed her lips, gave Agnes a final glare and left the shop.

Agnes sighed. 'I apologise for Mother's strange behaviour. She has an unfortunate affliction.'

'An affliction?'

'She despairs of my matrimony.'

'Surely not.'

'I reveal what should be concealed, and conceal what should be revealed.'

When I looked perplexed, she sighed again. 'Too much learning, not enough bosom.'

'I find your learning beguiling, and as to your bosom, well, what I can see of it looks beguiling as well.'

I thought she was going to slap my face, but another customer walked in and she recovered her composure with admirable speed. 'Greek dictionaries are in the front room on the second floor, sir, but you might find an alchemical lexicon helpful as well; that would be in the back room on the first floor, third shelf from the top on the right.'

I bought a dictionary, and a lexicon, but I knew already that they would prove inadequate and I would have to return, quite soon, for more of Agnes's learning.

18

A Web of Hidden Connections

And indeed, the books were no match for the arcane vocabulary. A few days later I returned to Enderby's, bearing a list of questions about alchemical terminology with which I hoped to confound the learned Agnes. It was a dull day and she sat by the window holding a book so close to her candle that she was in danger of singeing the pages.

'Perhaps you should consider spectacles,' I said.

'I have spectacles, but my mother hides them. Is there anything we can do for you, sir, or have you come merely for idle chit-chat?'

'I have come for your guidance, O gracious Sophia, infinitely perspicacious goddess of Wisdom.'

'I have no wisdom. If I had wisdom I would not be spending my life in this . . . I beg your pardon. You can have no possible interest in how I spend my life.'

'On the contrary.'

'In any case I have no interest in discussing it with you, so if you would like to look around, please do.'

'I need your advice on these terms,' I said, taking the list from my pocket. 'What is Narbasaphar, for instance? And is Spodion the same as Pomphilix?'

She took the list and studied it. 'Glisomarga, Hartwerch, Idraogiris. You made these up.'

'Certainly not.'

'Well, I'm afraid I have no idea what they mean.'

'Dictionaries fail me, my Sophia spurns me; I despair. Whatever shall I do?'

She folded her arms, considered me and shook her head. 'All right, I don't know why I'm doing this.' She went to the stairs and called up, 'I'm going out, Father,' took her cloak and hat from a peg and beckoned me to follow. 'I'll take you to Uncle Erasmus,' she said. 'If he doesn't know what your words mean, no one does.'

She led me along Church Street, past St Æbbe's and down an alley by the old wall of Grey Friars. A path led through a derelict apple orchard towards a long, low building that looked out across the Thames towards the remains of Osney Abbey. As we approached, a cloud of black smoke billowed from the chimney, followed by a loud wail.

'Oh dear God, what have you done, please no, you idiot, you scum, you worthless . . . Oh sweet Lord Jesus, I will kill you, oh God it is ruined.'

The door flew open, a boy ran out and fled past us up the path.

'Oh dear,' said Agnes. 'It's happened again.'

'What's happened again?'

'Some mishap always occurs at the last minute. Poor Uncle. At least this time it seems he has someone else to blame. Let us wait a moment before we enter.'

She turned and walked among the gnarled old trees. The apples were small, bird-pecked and worm-holed, but I found a few that were whole and offered one to her.

She hesitated.

'It's just an apple,' I said.

'That, no doubt, is what the serpent said.'

'This apple's manifest imperfection should be proof that we are not in Eden.'

'Oh, but we are. Did you not know? This place is called Paradise. The monks named it. It's the old orchard of Grey Friars.'

'In that case, we really must partake.'

'No, thank you,' she said. 'They may not be as good as you hope.'

She was right. Two were rotten at the core, one was bitter. Only one was sweet, and that only on one side.

As we turned back to the path an old man came out of the building, eased himself on to the bench by the door and put his head in his hands.

'Good morning, Uncle,' Agnes said. 'I've brought a visitor.'

He looked up with bleary eyes and struggled to his feet to make a bow, then sat heavily. 'I am defeated, my dear,' he said. 'I will never be able to begin again.'

Agnes sat beside him and patted his hand. 'That is what you always say.'

'And something always goes wrong. The stupid boy. Too much heat, after all these months. Well, it cannot be entirely his fault. No doubt my instructions were insufficiently precise. He is a good lad. I hope he comes back.'

'Show Uncle Erasmus your words,' she said to me. 'I'm sure it will cheer him.'

I handed him my list.

'Oh yes,' he said. 'Narbasaphar is the Chaldean word for brass. Spodion is a type of Pomphilix, as is Antispodion. Glisomarga is chalk, a corruption of the Arabic, I believe. Hartwerch is calcinated copper and an Idraogiris – an Armenian term – is a dunghill used as a furnace. Perhaps that is what I should have used, instead of trying to hurry. Too much hurry, too much heat. When will I learn? It always seems the right thing to do at the time; I am always sure. There are signs; I follow the signs. So how can I go wrong? Tell me, how?'

'I do not know, sir,' I said.

'Oh, you *sir* me, do you, a young lordling like you in your lace and silk?' He referred to my college gown, which I wore twisted into a scarf and tied around my neck. 'Ah, you're after the gold, all of you. Can't you see I haven't got any?'

'There is other gold, isn't there? The Stone of the Wise, the Elixir of Immortality?'

He looked sharply at me. 'And what do you know of that?'

'Not as much as I'd like. I have a book that belonged to my great-great-grandfather Tobias Damory, and I think he knew about it.'

'You are Tobias Damory's . . . well, that is something. Do you know where he is?'

'Where he is? He's in his grave at Farundell, as far as I know.'

'Well then you don't know much, do you? Last I heard, he was living in Paris. Boyle was corresponding with him until he died. Boyle, I mean, of course.'

'You are saying Tobias Damory was alive thirty years ago?'

'Oh, indeed.'

'But then who's buried in his grave?'

'How do you know anyone is buried there? Have you dug it up?'

'No.'

'Perhaps he faked his death. Wouldn't you? If they,' he waved his hand at the world, 'if they knew what you'd done, what you'd achieved, you'd never have a moment's peace. They would imprison you, torture you and the ones you love, all for your secret. It's happened many times.'

'I take your point. But anyone could say they were Tobias Damory. What happened to this correspondence? I would recognise Tobias Damory's handwriting if I could see it.'

'You have a very suspicious mind,' said Agnes. I detected a note of admiration.

'They destroyed the correspondence,' Enderby said. 'The great man's reputation, don't you know? But it was all science to him, you see. All knowledge was good, was only to the benefit of mankind. He said that what we saw, what we were able to understand of the cosmos was only the tiniest piece of it. We discovered many things, Boyle and I, witnessed many mysteries right here in this workshop that only future generations will comprehend. You separate, you combine, changes happen, why? How? The more I see, the less I understand. Obviously, obviously there must be a web of hidden connections beneath the world as it appears to our senses. We get flashes of insight, an occasional faint glimmer in the gloom of our ignorance, and it's enough to go on, somehow, somehow.' He sighed. 'Come again another time, young man.'

'Thank you, sir, I will.' I bowed to him, and to Agnes, and made my way back through the orchard, not picking any apples.

19

By the Grace of Isis

🌿

I was awakened in the middle of the night by a sonorous voice. 'All hail Osiris!' I sat upright and a bag was dropped over my head. I called out, and a cold blade was pressed to my chest.

'Silence,' the voice intoned, 'is the word of night.'

'Oh, nice,' murmured another voice.

Japhet barked; not, I regret to say, with any aggression. I could tell from his tone that he felt left out and wanted to play.

'Give it the bone,' said the first voice.

Japhet made happy, gnawing noises.

My wrists were tied behind me, my feet lashed together. I

reckoned there were at least four of them, and resistance utterly pointless. My mind, frozen between deep sleep and blind panic, struggled to assess the alternatives. It was either a bad dream, a genuine and hostile abduction, a Rosicrucian initiation (though that was really too much to hope for), or a joke. I decided on the last when I heard suppressed laughter from my bearers as they picked me up and carried me down the stairs.

We passed under the archway, then the changing odours told me we were crossing the meadow. Beneath my nightshirt I was naked, and the night not warm. I made myself as heavy as possible, and was glad to hear them breathing hard. Soon I heard the soft burble of the flowing Isis; were they going to toss me in? Through the coarse fabric of the bag I saw a glimmer of torches, and smelled the pitch. I began working urgently at the rope that bound my hands.

They laid me out ungently in a wooden box and nailed down the lid; the box was dragged to the riverbank and pushed over the edge. As it slid towards the water it occurred to me that even if this was a joke, I might not survive it.

My fear abated when I realised that I was being loaded on to a boat, then rekindled when the boat tipped alarmingly. There were muffled curses and I was dropped on someone's foot. 'Hurrah!' I shouted, but I don't think they heard me.

Clunks and splashes indicated that oars were being deployed; we pushed off and headed upriver. The slight flow of air and the clarity of the sounds reassured me that my box had holes in it. Suffocation, at least, was not imminent. I continued working at the rope binding my wrists.

The men rowed in silence for what felt like hours, then we bumped against a shore where others were waiting. My box was hauled up a bank with much slipping and cursing. The bearers paused, and I thought I would finally be let out and everything explained. But they were only catching their breath. They lifted my box – I was reluctant to call it a coffin – and lowered it into a shallow hole. 'Hallo-ooo,' I called.

'Harken to the voice of the dying god,' said someone from near my head.

'All hail Osiris,' intoned several voices in approximate unison.

'Who journeys through the dark halls of the Underworld,' said the first voice.

'All hail Osiris!'

'Who dies and is reborn by the grace of Isis.'

'All hail Osiris!'

A few spadefuls of earth thudded on to my – I had to admit it – coffin. I called out again; no one answered. I heard footsteps withdrawing, then noises from the shore as the boat departed. I surmised that they planned to leave me overnight.

It took some time and cost some skin, but I managed to free my hands. I pressed my arms against the lid of my coffin and pushed as hard as I could. It shifted half an inch. A few more pushes, and I had raised it enough to permit me to roll over and use the strength of my back to heave it aside.

I pulled the bag from my head, untied my feet, sat on the edge of my grave and tried to get my bearings. The moon was full, high in a sky of scudding clouds. I was on a small treeless island in the river, halfway to Binsey.

It was rather chilly, and I considered climbing back into my cosy coffin, pulling the lid over me and waiting for morning. No, damn it. Too easy. I gathered mud from the riverbank and carried it to the coffin, where I sculpted the shape of a man. I crowned him with ivy, gave him a laughing face and a large, erect phallus, replaced the lid and pushed the earth back over.

My labours had warmed me up; I waded into the river and swam for the Oxford bank. It was steep, overhung with roots and tangled branches, and I had to work my way along for some distance before I found a place to scramble ashore.

The night was silent but for the soft murmur of the river and the sound of a child crying. A glimmer of light appeared in a lone cottage at the edge of a field; the crying stopped. Shivering in my wet nightshirt, I picked my way through the muddy stubble and bent to look in at the window. A young woman sat in a chair, a child in her arms. For a moment I thought she was Tildy, alive after all. But no, this was a different girl.

I tapped lightly at the window; she looked up in alarm.

'Don't be afraid,' I called out. 'I have need of dry garments and will pay very generously. I am a gentleman,' I added.

A combination of persistent pleading and mentions of a half-crown overcame her fears; she unbarred the door, seated me in her chair, gave me ale and cold turnip stew. She ladled a second helping into my bowl even when it became apparent that I did not have the half-crown on my person at that moment. The child sat on a sheepskin by the hearth, watching me with grave grey eyes beneath golden curls.

The woman's name was Johanna Brown; her daughter was Grace. Johanna's parents, brothers and sisters had died in the plague when she was an infant. She'd been raised by the curate of St Thomas's and had married a farmer, who had died just before Grace was born: an accident with a scythe. She earned a few pence cleaning the church and doing fancy embroidery, at which she was very skilled.

Johanna offered me her husband's best breeches and shirt and would have given me his shoes, but they were far too small. She turned away modestly as I dressed, then laughed when she saw how my arms stuck out of the sleeves and the breeches failed to cover my knees. I assured her that they suited me perfectly and were certainly worth a crown at least.

The setting moon paled to white as I left her cottage and made my way across the misty fields. Mr Corwin, St Asher's long-suffering porter, roused from his bed by my knocks, let me in without any indication of surprise at the hour or my attire. 'Sixpence,' I said.

'Thank you, sir,' said he.

I went back to bed.

Tunnie came in as usual at ten and I enjoyed his puzzlement at the strange clothes on the chair, the abrasions on my wrists, the muddy footprints on the floor.

At midday a letter arrived:

> All hail Osiris, the crowned and RISEN god!
> Wykeham's Coffee House in South Street.
> Eleven o'clock tonight.

20

The Cup of Freedom

W ykeham's. The word evokes an atmosphere: smoke-hung ceiling, din of laughter, conversation and argument; the sudden hush as the poet of the moment climbs on to a table and recites his latest satire or panegyric; somnolent waiters dispensing coffee, ale, wines and spirits at their whim; light ladies of the better sort, who could appreciate a witty turn of phrase.

It was my first visit to that hallowed Oxford institution. As I paused in the doorway to shake the rain from my cloak, two men rose and beckoned me to a table at the back. I had seen them around St Asher's.

Mr Edward Alexander Meryll and Lord Marcus Victor Annesley de Montague Purefoy were cousins, yet utterly unlike. Meryll was dark-haired, with that white skin that flares red when feelings are roused. He was tall and easy in his movements, with expressive hands and a lively temperament. Purefoy was slightly built, reticent and decorous in manner, with pale hair and lashes. Their mothers, sisters, had married respectively a fabulously wealthy Bristol shipping magnate (Meryll) and an impoverished ex-Catholic duke (Purefoy).

I recognised their voices: Meryll had been the first speaker, the one I took to be the leader. Purefoy I'd heard only once; his had been the wry murmur, 'Oh, nice,' as he commended Meryll's turn of phrase.

We were joined by four others: Sherbourne and Winstanley, Gordon and Everleigh, all St Asher's men. This was the Isis Society, an ancient association revived after many dormant years by Meryll, who had found the Society's original Book of Records beneath a floorboard in his bedroom. Or so he said. Poetic licence, I came to understand, was a way of life for him; his Welsh ancestry, he claimed, gave him the right, if not the duty.

'And why,' I asked, 'have I been chosen for the singular honour of joining you?'

'Because you are a Damory,' Meryll said. 'The Society was founded by a Damory at St Asher's in 1556 and there are Damorys in the membership lists for every decade from then until the Civil War, when the records cease.'

'Fifteen fifty-six,' I said. 'Would that be Tobias Damory?'

'Yes, Tobias.'

From the Book of Records, Meryll had gleaned the information that the Society's initiation ritual involved spending a night in a sarcophagus in an underground chamber, somewhere upriver. It didn't say where, so he had improvised. I told him it had been very effective and that I'd had moments of genuine terror. He looked pleased.

As for the rest, the aims of the Society and so on, Meryll was making it up as he went along. He was a passionately religious man, but his religion was Paganism, or at any rate his interpretation of it. He loved the Roman gods, the Greek even more, but was convinced that the religion of the ancient Egyptians was the greatest of all. There had been a Golden Age, he said, when divine harmony had pervaded creation. Since then, the world had passed through a dark time of ignorance, fear and misery. But that was ending; a new Golden Age was at hand when men would throw off the shackles of superstition and step into their true destiny, free as gods.

We went back to Meryll's rooms and he showed me the Society's Book of Records. I recognised Tobias's handwriting at once. In 1556 he had been just my own age. The book began with an essay about St Asher, the patron saint of our college, that put a new slant on the familiar story.

St Asher, like the earlier St Ælfhild, came from very near Farundell; the area has spawned more than its share of saints over the centuries. As a child, he wandered the woods in communion with birds and animals and carried a pet snake coiled around his arm. He was assumed to be mute until one day he began to speak in what turned out to be Greek. They thought he was possessed by the Devil, so they tried to drown him by tying stones to his feet and tossing him into the River Isis. He sank from sight, but emerged, impossibly, on a tiny island a mile upstream, naked and free of stones. He remained on that island for the rest of his life, living at the top of its single tree during floods.

At first it was only the common people who came to him, but word of miraculous cures and prophecies that came true eventually brought lords and princes. When he died, there was a great debate about what should be done with his bones. The Franciscans prevailed, and in 1186 built for him a chapel which grew into a priory; in 1418, this became St Asher's College. His gilded, bejewelled casket was a popular attraction, credited with many wonders.

When it was smashed by Cromwell's mob, his scattered bones sprouted tall stalks of wheat which were surreptitiously harvested and baked into a hundred loaves with miraculous healing powers – the origin of the famous St Asher's Bread.

All this was well-known, but Tobias closed with an astonishing claim. He had discovered (he did not say how) that St Asher had never been a Christian; rather he was a priest of Isis, whose ancient temple had not vanished with the Romans but survived, hidden somewhere near the source of the river to which it had given its name. Asher, he said, was a priest name rather than a personal one, Asher being the Anglo-Saxon form of the Egyptian god Asar, known more commonly by his Greek name, Osiris. Hence the initiation ritual of the Isis Society involved the aspirant taking on the role of Osiris: being entombed, rising reborn.

Since the Book of Records gave no details of the activities of the Society, Meryll was at liberty to invent: moonlight swims in the Isis to commune with that goddess in her riverine form; the evocation, through poetry and music, of every deity in the combined pantheons of the ancient world, in alphabetical order, one a fortnight during term-time; the decipherment of the Egyptian hieroglyphic language in weekly study-group meetings, following the work of the Jesuit Athanasius Kircher.

And, of course, intoxication. Dionysus rated very high: he was Eleutherios, the Liberator. Meryll had created a beverage that he called the Cup of Freedom. He warmed wine and added honey, cinnamon, cloves and saffron. Taking an object folded in waxed silk from a rosewood box, he unwrapped a black slab, cut off a piece the size of a half-crown and dissolved it in the wine.

'*Lachryma papaveris*,' he said to my questioning look. 'The tears of the poppy. Far richer in the natural form,' he tapped the slab, 'than as laudanum.'

The effects of Freedom lasted until midday, when I awoke on Meryll's couch with an atrocious headache. I stepped over the slumbering bodies of my companions and crept back to my rooms. Tunnie prepared some Morning Medicine, but it had no effect. Only coffee and brandy, I eventually learned, in a ratio of five-to-one, followed by a pipe of hashish, would do for opium what Morning Medicine did for wine.

21

The Great Work

When my head finally cleared I rode out on Lancelot, with Japhet running alongside. It was one of those autumn afternoons when, if you did not see the bare trees or scent the sweet tang of dead leaves crushed by your horse's hooves, you would think it summer still. We came to Johanna's cottage just as she was setting out, with Grace toddling alongside and an empty basket over her arm. At the sight of Japhet – bounding and slaver-ing in his eagerness to make friends – she shrieked and lifted Grace high above her head. I don't think she recognised me at first, towering over her in hat and sword and boots. I dismounted hastily, took off my hat and made her a bow.

'You look so grand,' she said.

'I could only improve. Japhet, sit!'

Japhet, to my astonishment, sat. His nose reached Johanna's shoulder.

'Dog,' said Grace, trying to pat his head with her fat little hand. Johanna stepped back hastily.

'Don't be afraid,' I said. 'He is completely harmless.' Grace was squirming out of Johanna's arms in an attempt to reach him.

'Would she like to ride him? My sisters used to, when they were little.'

I tied Lancelot to a tree and we sat Grace on Japhet's back. She clutched his fur and he set off at a gentle amble with Johanna's hand on the child's shoulder to steady her, though she didn't need it. The expression on her face was one of ecstatic concentration. She rode all the way to our destination – a grove of chestnut trees about half a mile away. When we arrived, Johanna set her on a blanket; Japhet stood guard, nosing her back whenever she tried to wander off.

We strolled among the trees and I helped Johanna to fill her basket with chestnuts. I was touched by her readiness to trust Japhet, who could have killed the child with one bite. Grace was too sleepy to ride back, so Johanna carried her. I carried the basket, which seemed to surprise her. At the cottage I took her husband's shirt and breeches from my saddlebag and gave them to her, with two crowns. She refused to accept the money. I had returned the clothes; there was no debt. I insisted that I owed a debt to her kindness and her turnip stew. She said they were worth nothing. I said they were priceless. It was an impasse, so I kissed her.

She won the argument; I kept my money. She gave me to understand that she had let me kiss her because she liked me; she was not the sort of woman who sold her kisses for coins.

I rode back to Oxford along the river, past the shell of Osney Abbey. The path took me towards Grey Friars, and Enderby's workshop at the edge of Paradise. The smoke rising from the chimney seemed a peaceful shade of grey, so I left Lancelot and Japhet in the orchard and knocked at the door. It was opened by the boy I'd last seen in flight, evidently restored to grace.

'Is Master Enderby available?' I asked, stepping into a dusty, empty room. 'Tell him Francis Damory would like to see him, if it is convenient. I will wait here.'

The boy went off and I looked around. Other empty rooms flanked the one I'd entered, each with a pair of squat furnaces and a row of windows looking out over the orchard.

The boy returned. 'My master will see you, sir,' he said, and led the way to the furthest room, larger than the others. One wall held shelves of jars and bottles like an apothecary's shop; glass and earthenware vessels ranged down a long workbench. Some I recognised from illustrations in books – crucibles, beakers, alembics, retorts – and that extraordinary thing with glass globes one atop the other, linked by double arms of glass tube, had to be a pelican. The impression was one of order and cleanliness: floor well swept, glassware gleaming, apparatus tidy, and but for a strange burnt odour and a fresh black soot-stain on the ceiling, there was no evidence of catastrophe.

Enderby sat at a table by the window. 'I am writing up the report of the experiment.' He prodded at a small lump of black matter. 'It is a result, even if not the one I'd hoped for. The importance of accurate records cannot be overstated. Who knows? It might make sense to someone, some time. Boy! Fetch some wine for my guest.' He waved to a chair; the boy brought a cup.

I took the wine; it was thin and sour, and I put it discreetly aside. 'I hope I did not seem discourteous when I doubted whether Boyle had corresponded with the real Tobias Damory.'

'I regret that I spoke of him; I was perhaps not in the best frame of mind. And whatever else I may be, I am not naive. It has not escaped my notice that scoundrels, thieves, impostors and all manner of avaricious scum crawl over this world. I've met some, Boyle met many more. They flock to the famous like flies to sugar.'

'But what made Boyle certain that it was Tobias?'

He gazed at me steadily for a long time before speaking, then he lowered his voice. 'A man came. We were working late, but afterwards I realised that Boyle had been expecting him. I worked alongside him and Boyle through the night. He knew his chemistry, that was without doubt. But to this day I do not understand what he did that turned a lump of lead into the purest gold ever seen by any assayer in Oxford or London. He left before dawn. Boyle told me, many years later – the last time I saw him, in fact, before he died – that the man had been Tobias Damory. All I can say is, that is what he believed. There is no way to prove it, none whatsoever. You have to decide, first, if you think it's possible that a man can live so long, perhaps even be immortal.'

'I don't know. I've seen plenty of evidence of death; none of immortality.'

'Would you know it if you saw it?'

I had no answer to that. 'I will try to keep an open mind,' I said. 'In the meantime, I'd be grateful for anything you can tell me about Tobias Damory. You say he was living in Paris – you don't happen to recall the address, do you?'

'No. The correspondence went through an intermediary. We never referred to Tobias Damory by name; we called him Thank God He's Dead.'

'Why?'

'TGHD.'

'Oh, I see.'

The light was fading; the boy came in and lit the candles. I stood. 'May I come again, sir? And perhaps you could show me what you've been working on.'

He nodded. 'You may come. And bring some decent wine.'

I went back the following day, and the day after; he took me on as a student of sorts, though we never called it that. He began his work again, the Magnum Opus, as it was known – the Great Work. Over the months I learned about distillations, calcinations, sublimations, fulminations, triturations and projections. I shared with him the sleepless watching through the night and the awe as matter changed before our eyes. It was his twenty-seventh attempt at the Great Work, and I came to wonder if it was defined at least in part by its futility. Among the thousand things that could go wrong it was hard to know, when failure had again been achieved, which ones were to blame.

22

The World Is Full of Suffering

The day before I returned to Farundell for Christmas, I visited Johanna again. I brought her some thick worsted, a lovely deep blue, that I thought she might like for a winter cloak, and a few yards in a soft creamy white for Grace. I couldn't resist adding a handful of silk ribbons and a big bag of candied ginger.

Grace greeted Japhet with cries of delight and immediately tried to climb on to his back. He obliged her by lying down, then, looking over his shoulder to make sure she was ready, levered himself upright and walked gently round and round the yard.

It was a mild day. Johanna brought me a cup of ale and we sat on the bench outside her door as Grace tried, in vain, to get Japhet to trot. I presented my gifts; Johanna refused, relented, wept a little, and finally smiled. I kissed her again. I stayed for supper, and afterwards, when Grace was asleep in her crib and Japhet was asleep by the hearth, we climbed together into her bed.

Farundell was dismal. We were still in mourning for Mother, and a year in unrelieved black, with another year to come, had sapped my sisters of their will to live. Father continued to enjoy his flirtation with death and his hold on the puppet strings of familial duty but I, who had not seen him for more than two months, was shocked at his decline. Tired veins stood out on his arms, the flesh of his neck hung scrawny as a rooster's. There was no more phlegm, but his breathing was a laboured wheeze.

I had thought at length on what Enderby had told me about Tobias. In the graveyard behind the chapel I stood once again over the slab that marked his final resting place – or so I had always assumed. I wondered how difficult it would be to dig it up, whether it would be a sacrilege, whether I could get away with it. But there was no point. If I found bones, it proved nothing; they could be anyone's. If no bones, it would most likely be that they had rotted away. I went back to the house and, after some searching, unearthed the old ledgers that listed Damory births, marriages and deaths. What I found confirmed my uncertainty. A brief note appended to the entry for Tobias's burial stated that he had died abroad and only his bones, in an urn, had come back to Farundell.

Sebastian appeared for a few days, then left with no word of his destination. Andrew strutted unbearably. Isabel, from Harfield, wrote entreating me to visit, so a week after I'd arrived I departed, taking Tunnie, Japhet and Lancelot. At the last minute, Clarence begged to be allowed to come too. I was reluctant, but then Andrew forbade it, so of course he came.

After a frosty night, the sky was clear, our spirits high. Clarence, at twelve small for his age, sat his horse well. His face lit up when I commended him, and he demonstrated how he had trained the horse to prance and pirouette on command.

It was a pleasant ride; we reached Harfield by midday. The house sits at the head of a little valley and looks quite imposing until you realise that only the east wing is habitable. Isabel received us – even Japhet – with joy. She had done wonders with the place: new hangings hid the mouldering walls, bright carpets covered the floors. The dark, woodwormed furniture had vanished, replaced with softly cushioned chairs and sofas; gilded mirrors and mirrored sconces dispelled the gloom. The scent of beeswax and the cherry-wood fires blazing in every room nearly overcame the venerable dank. She had spent a fortune, and I wondered how she had persuaded the old Earl to loosen his notoriously tight purse-strings.

Dinner was lavish, if moribund. Here, too, everything was new: plates, serving dishes, silver. My memory may have exaggerated, but I seemed to recall that the last time I'd dined at Harfield, we ate off wooden trenchers, stabbing at overcooked, gristly stews with the points of our own daggers.

Reginald said nothing; the Earl, at the head of the table, was barely visible. Also present, also silent, were Reginald's brother and his wife; his sister and her husband. Out of a sense of my responsibility as a guest to provide my hosts with amusing conversation, or perhaps from other motives, I tried to engage Reginald on every topic I could think of, from agrarian reform to zoophilism. Would we join the declaration of war against Spain? Would Voltaire's sensational Oedipus get him thrown back into the Bastille? Had he misunderstood Sophocles? Isabel kicked me under the table, but I pretended not to notice. Dinner was followed by a walk in the park and card games, then a dreary supper and early to bed. Harfield, I decided, would be a good place to catch up on my sleep.

I was awakened by a pair of hands sliding over my chest. I reached out; it was a woman, that was all I could tell. The brother's wife or the sister? Whoever she was, she knew exactly what she wanted. Having achieved her goal, twice, she left and I went back to sleep. I was awakened – it seemed only a minute later – by another pair of hands. A different woman, but similarly single-minded. The following nights the two women arrived together.

The day before we were to return to Farundell, Clarence took me aside after dinner and, with a mischievous smile, beckoned me to accompany him. He led me through the first-floor salons, up the private stairs, along a passage and into a windowless closet linking two bedchambers.

'What are we doing here?' I whispered.

'Hush, just wait.'

We heard footsteps in the room on our right; a few minutes later a second person entered and the unmistakable sounds of erotic activity ensued. Clarence bent to the keyhole, then stepped back and gestured to me. I saw a young man whom I recognised as Reginald's valet; of his companion I could see only a pair of fat white buttocks, but it was enough to identify Reginald. Well, that explained a great deal.

We withdrew silently. Clarence seemed to be waiting for me to comment. 'Some men like other men,' I said, as we walked back downstairs. 'But how did you find out about this?'

He explained that he'd made friends with the son of the steward, a lad his own age, who'd grown up at Harfield and knew every nook and cranny and, no doubt, every secret.

'You mustn't tell anyone,' I said. 'Even if you think they already know. Great harm would come to everyone, not only Reginald, but our sister, too, and the rest of our family. It is something one never speaks of – do you understand?' Clarence nodded.

I went to Isabel later, in her sitting room. 'Reginald's valet,' I said, 'is a man of many talents.'

'Indeed he is.' Isabel gave me a speculative look as she poured chocolate into exquisite cups. 'And such a dedicated servant of the family.'

I returned the look. 'I gather that he has a . . . unique position in the household.'

'Reginald and I,' Isabel smiled demurely, 'are both very appreciative of his services.'

I was not quite sure how to interpret that. 'He seems to have special . . . skills.'

She sipped her chocolate. 'Yes, he does. His . . . skills help to make Harfield an altogether more agreeable place than I had at first thought it to be. All this,' she waved her hand at the new furniture, 'was just the beginning. I have plans, Francis. The Earl will refuse me nothing so long as I keep the little family secret. When I was in London I saw hundreds of children begging on the streets. Many are the children of prostitutes, and through no fault of their own they fall into a life of sin, for no other choice is offered them. I have seen them with my own eyes, dying in the gutter, not fifty yards from our house. No one pays any heed; people will step over a dead child as though it was a dead dog. Surely you have seen this.'

'Yes.'

'But you accept it. That is so typical of a man. Do you think they deserve their fate?'

I shrugged. 'The world is full of suffering.'

'Oh, could you not possibly be a little more pompous if you try?'

'I doubt it.'

She whacked me with her fan. 'It is not immutable fate that condemns people to a life of suffering and disease. People think that the sin of the parents lives in the child, that a child born out of wedlock is worthless, unredeemable. But of course, if you had a bastard, and chose to acknowledge him, this wouldn't apply; he'd have a place in society. Only the poor are tainted, apparently. I want to prove that if a child is properly looked after and educated he can be the equal of anyone. I will start a school, Francis. I will take children from the streets, the lowest, poorest ones I can find, and make for them an environment of health and beauty. You wait and see – they will be as clever and good as any.' Her eyes were bright with excitement. 'Who knows what genius there might be in such people, who are thrown away like rubbish?'

87

Most unwillingly, I remembered the pauper's grave at St Clement's. 'I will help you in any way I can,' I said.

'I knew you would.'

23

A Hanging

🌿

I went back to Oxford a week before term began. I thought it was simply to get away from Farundell, where my father's rasping breath drifted through the corridors day and night like a peevish ghost. But when I found myself turning away from the gates of St Asher's and riding up the river path, I realised it was Johanna I'd come to see.

It was a dark afternoon and her cottage looked very lonely at the edge of the field, though the tiny window glowed with light. I peered in. She sat by the fire working on some embroidery. I knocked softly; she looked up, smiled and came to the door. Grace and Japhet had a joyous reunion.

'I was just thinking about you,' Johanna said as she helped me to stable Lancelot in the byre next to her cow. She was warm and sweet-smelling as hay beneath her new blue cloak.

There was turnip stew for dinner, with a slice of the smoked ham I'd brought from Farundell. Grace and Japhet fell asleep together by the hearth.

In the morning a foot of snow had fallen. I went out to the byre, broke the ice on the trough and tossed down some hay for Lancelot and the cow. After breakfast, Johanna and I climbed back into her bed. In the afternoon I chopped wood and carved a little toy

Japhet for Grace. When I left some days later, the woodshed was stacked to the rafters, Grace had a small menagerie and my shirt was beautifully embroidered with roses.

Meryll and I fell into an easy friendship, but after my introduction to the Isis Society, I'd seen little of Purefoy. He rarely attended the meetings – I had the impression he had come along on the night of my initiation merely to make up the numbers – but one morning in February he came to my rooms and shyly invited me to a hanging. Shadrach Smith, a Gypsy, was to be executed for murder.

The entire population of Oxford, town and university, had turned out to witness the event; Smith's victim had been a popular tavern-keeper's pretty daughter. The castle's vast courtyard was already crowded when we arrived, but Purefoy led me to a door in the tower, where he exchanged brief words with a guard and handed him a purse. I followed, mystified, as Purefoy walked rapidly down a narrow stone stair and along a passage. Another purse changed hands, a door was unlocked with a great clanking of keys and we were in the presence of Shadrach Smith himself.

'Did you bring it?' he said.

'Of course,' said Purefoy, and set a bottle of gin on the table.

Smith drank a long draught. 'Thank you, m'lord. You are a kind and Christian gentleman.'

'It has preservative properties,' Purefoy said to me. 'Drink up, Smith.'

'Quite right, m'lord,' said Smith. 'No point saving any for later, is there?' He crowed at his marvellous wit and drank a toast to his own good health, and that was so amusing he toasted himself once more.

As he was about to slip into a stupor, Purefoy prodded him with his walking stick. 'Wake up, Smith,' he said. 'You are about to die and I want to know: do you believe you have an eternal soul?'

Smith began to sob.

'Oh, don't snivel, man. I merely want to know your opinion. As a man about to die, you have a certain perspective. Do you have a soul, and if so, where do you believe it is located?'

Smith blinked slowly and gave every appearance of considering the question. Then he slid, snoring, to the floor.

Purefoy poked at him again, to no effect. 'Damn. Gypsies cannot hold their drink. Irishmen are best. They can absorb astonishing quantities and still give interesting answers.'

As we left, we passed the hangman coming to collect the prisoner and another purse changed hands. Then, instead of going to the castle yard, we joined a group of a dozen or so university men waiting by the tumbrel.

Smith was led out, or I should say dragged, and we followed the cart to the gallows. Last prayers said, the noose was tightened, the horses were whipped, the cart pulled away, the body dropped. At first I thought the people rushing to pull at Smith's legs were his relations, seeking to shorten his suffering, but it was our lot. Some held the body as it flailed; others, directed by Purefoy, fended off the family.

Women screamed, men shouted and cursed. Smith's family threw stones at us and waved cudgels and knives; the university lads unsheathed their swords. The hangman and the guards inspected their fingernails as Purefoy cut the body down. The family had brought a coffin, and they now seized Smith by the legs and tried to pull him towards it. The university team pulled on his arms, and for a horrified moment I thought they would tear him limb from limb.

Purefoy paced cautiously around the edges of the mêlée, calling occasional instructions. The family retreated, then surged forward en masse with their women in the front rank. The gentlemen fell back in disarray; the family swarmed around the corpse and bundled it into the coffin, but as soon as they had set it upon their shoulders our lads regrouped and attacked. The coffin was dropped and shattered, the body trampled. Purefoy shrieked in dismay, flung himself into the fray and with a strength that surprised me, dragged the corpse from beneath the scuffling feet.

He whistled and four men detached themselves from the fight, seized Smith, ran for the west gate and vanished in the crowd. Purefoy tossed a handful of coins into the air; in the chaos that ensued he stepped back, straightened his clothes and led me back to St Asher's.

24
God's Most Perfect Creation

🌿

Smith had been stripped and laid out on a marble slab in the anatomy theatre when Purefoy and I slipped in. The steep tiers of seats were packed with students and buzzing with anticipation. Mounted on the back wall and suspended from the high ceiling were life-sized anatomical models made, I assumed, of coloured wax – flayed men, women and children, displayed as though posing, with limbs extended in graceful gestures. One man lifted aside the muscles of his own abdomen with delicate fingertips to reveal the organs; a pregnant woman peeled back her belly like an orange to show the perfectly formed babe within.

The college's celebrated Dr Grimani would perform the dissection; he had earned his degree at the University of Padua and it was said that he could dissect a man blindfolded, skull to feet, sternum to spine, in one hour. He beckoned to Purefoy, who gave me his coat and stick to hold, pushed up his sleeves and joined the doctor behind the body. It was the first time I had seen him smile.

After a strange moment, when I seemed to feel the doctor's blade slicing open my own chest, I found I was able to watch with interest. Two students stood by with sketchbooks and pens to make a record as the doctor, assisted by Purefoy, folded back the skin. Blood flowed along channels in the marble and dripped into buckets at their feet. Starting with the hands and arms, then the feet and legs, the cords of muscle meat, given dignity by their Latin names, were cut away to reveal the bones. The skull was sawn in half, the brain removed with eye-stalks and eyeballs attached.

The grotesque mass of organs that spilled from the cave of the abdomen looked like slimy subterranean reptiles, coiled inside God's most perfect creation. Each one was named and described, dissected in turn, its workings explained. Cut from the body and pinned out on boards, the heart and liver, lungs, spleen, pancreas, stomach and kidneys were passed around the hall for closer examination.

When Shadrach Smith had been so analysed and anatomised and sorted into his constituent parts that he had all but ceased to exist, Dr Grimani and Purefoy stepped back, wiped their hands on a towel and bowed to each other. The spectators applauded. Purefoy caught my eye and worked his way through the crowd of students to where I waited. His clothes were spattered with blood, and blood caked beneath the nails of his slim white hands, which were trembling with fatigue as he took his coat and stick.

It was dark when we emerged and Purefoy seemed not to know where he was; I guided him towards Wykeham's, but he recoiled from the lights and noise. He was shivering now, his teeth chattering, so I took him to my rooms, sat him by the fire and tossed a blanket over his knees. Japhet nosed at him, whether from kindness or for the smell of fresh blood I don't know, though his antics kindled some light in Purefoy's tired eyes. 'Good dog,' he murmured, and I realised those were the first words he'd spoken since the dissection had begun.

I sent Tunnie to fetch some supper and he came back with roasted woodcock, cold mutton and venison pasties. I piled a plate for Purefoy, set it at his elbow, poured him a glass of wine, which he took without seeing it, sipped, then drained. He looked around the room and seemed to take in where he was for the first time, then he looked at his hand holding the glass and set it hastily down.

'I apologise; I beg you to forgive me.' His mouth twisted in distress as he stared at his bloodstained hands.

'It is quite all right,' I said, 'but Tunnie will bring some hot water and you can wash in my closet.'

When he came back, his hands were pink with scrubbing and some colour had returned to his face. 'I have intruded enough on your hospitality,' he said, and made as if to leave.

'Don't be absurd,' I said. 'You must eat. I cannot possibly eat all this myself and it is far too rich for Japhet.'

'You are very kind,' he said. 'You are sure I do not disgust you with my stench of dead flesh?'

It was true; he carried the smell of the anatomy theatre wherever he went, but I insisted I had not noticed it. He saw that I lied, but said nothing, betrayed by the look of gratitude in his eyes.

25

A Hidden Beauty and Logic

✼

The following week Purefoy sent me an invitation to supper in his rooms; I replied, accepting. That afternoon at Wykeham's, I mentioned it to Meryll.

'He has invited you to his rooms? Well!'

'Well what?'

'Well, you shall see for yourself.'

'See what?'

'His rooms.'

At the appointed hour I crossed the quad to Purefoy's rooms with a bottle of my best claret under my arm. The first thing I noticed was the smell of burning pine resin. Clouds of smoke hung in the air, almost obscuring the gentle, pervasive reek of putrefaction. Tall folding screens hid all of the room save a small area between the window and the fireplace, where there was a narrow bed, two wooden chairs and a table set for two.

The candles were tallow, the goblets pewter, the food standard fare from the college kitchen. Purefoy was a gracious host, but with a stiff formality that suggested he did not often entertain. I tried to put him at ease by asking about his home. Not a good topic.

'Cold and remote.' He shrugged, or perhaps shuddered, and I didn't know whether he meant the house or the people. Gradually I managed to extract some details. 'I was the fifth son,' he explained, 'born far too early – before, they said, my soul had the chance to take root in my body. It killed my mother and was a great inconvenience to everyone. I was so sickly I wasn't expected to survive, and required a great deal of expensive care on which I am unlikely to produce any return. They leave me alone and I leave them alone, so we are in perfect accord.' He had come to St Asher's two years ago, at fifteen, and had never gone back. When he asked about Farundell, I tried not to paint too glowing a picture, dwelling instead on the ghastly dying father and the insufferable older brother.

A scout brought in the next course and I realised Purefoy had no servant of his own. The meal resumed in silence, the screens edging closer the longer they went unmentioned.

At last Purefoy tossed down his napkin. 'It's no good, is it? I never should have, of course you want to leave, you were so kind to me, I thought I ought, we should have gone to Wykeham's, it's the smell, isn't it? I am such a fool, this must be awful for you.' He said all this in a rush, staring down at his plate.

'Not at all.'

'Let's go out,' he said, and stood so abruptly that he knocked over his chair. When he turned to right it, his foot caught the frayed corner of the tablecloth. It jerked and slid, the goblets overturned, the plates crashed to the floor, the wine bottle lurched, tipped and rolled towards the edge. I lunged forward to grab it in midair and collided with Purefoy; he stumbled and fell. The bottle landed and shattered.

He sat in a pile of spilled food and a spreading puddle of wine. 'This is a disaster,' he said.

'Not at all.' I gave him my hand and helped him up.

'Ha,' he said, tentatively. 'Ha, ha.'

He was laughing, but didn't quite know how. I laughed too; soon he caught on and we were howling together, doubled over, wiping tears from our eyes, whooping and with grand gestures imitating the inexorable slide of the tablecloth, the flight of the wine bottle, the fateful collision, the fall.

The scout appeared at the door, astonished; no doubt he'd never heard such laughter from Purefoy's rooms. When he'd tidied the mess and withdrawn, I asked Purefoy to show me what was behind the screens.

With an air of resignation he folded them aside and stood back. In the dim light I could make out at first only rows of glass jars lining the walls. I took a candle and approached. Suspended in clear fluid were organs and body parts, human and animal and – I flinched when the light first revealed it – an entire infant with yellow-grey skin, oddly wrinkled at the joints and marred by a few torn patches.

'It's terribly hard to get a human foetus,' Purefoy said. 'Sometimes a midwife will sell me a miscarriage, but they want a lot of money and seem to feel it's unchristian. This one was still-born, to a woman sentenced to hang. That hardly ever happens. I could do it much better now.'

'You made these yourself?'

'Oh yes, I could not possibly afford to buy them. I sell the best ones – to Dr Grimani, and to other colleges. You saw some on display in the anatomy theatre.'

'I thought they were wax models.'

'No, real flesh.'

'But how is it preserved?'

'Are you truly interested? Meryll says it's a hideous business.'

'I'm fascinated,' I said, and I think he was so pleased he almost wept.

The tools of his art were laid out on a long table. Purefoy showed me how a specimen was first washed to remove the blood and other fluids, then soaked for several hours in a warm bath called a bain-marie. The veins and arteries were then injected with a mixture of white wax and oil of lavender, with ground talc and cinnabar for colour. It had to be done quickly, while the tissue was warm enough for the wax to remain liquid as it penetrated the finest capillaries, yet with extreme care, for the flesh was weakened by the bath and easily distorted. For this delicate task Purefoy had devised a set of hollowed, sharpened quills of different sizes to which he attached bladders containing the molten mixture.

Prepared in this way, a body could be allowed to harden in the air, in which case it would last for several years, or, in the case of smaller items, be placed in a jar with the *liquor balsamico*, a mixture of clarified wine, spirit of amber and oils of rue, rosemary and black pepper, where it would be preserved for ever.

In the second room, Purefoy worked on anatomical drawings from fresh specimens. He showed me a book of his plates that had been published in London to accompany a text by Dr Grimani, depicting in minute detail the stages of dissection of the hand and arm. For another series he had carved a man's brain into thin slices, front to back, revealing hidden structures of organs and ducts that astonished me.

My lack of revulsion was a tonic to him, and from then on he regarded me, I believe, as his greatest friend. He would show me each new specimen as he acquired it – human body parts when he could get them, any sort of animal when he could not. His skill was extraordinary. His knives, probes, clamps and forceps revealed a hidden beauty and logic in the body's inner workings, and while at first my interest had been partially feigned and revulsion overcome with an effort, very soon I was genuinely intrigued.

26

The Wrong Tree

❧

Early on a drizzly morning in March Purefoy appeared at my door. I had never seen him so distressed. 'Damory, please, you must come quickly, I cannot, I don't know what, they are taking, they will break, you must make them stop.' He pulled me down the stairs to the quad.

A team of scouts, cleaners and porters was carrying his specimens out of the building and stacking them on the lawn. He dashed across just in time to steady the baby as they stumbled with its glass jar.

Mr Corwin watched from the door of his lodge. I summoned him over. 'What's going on here?'

'Orders from the Vice-Chancellor. Lord Purefoy has been conducting a business on college property. Not to mention the evil smells and foul emanations. As you know, sir, no one will share a stair with him.'

'But he is a member of the college, you can't evict him.'

'It is not he who is being evicted, sir, merely his business. He is of course free to live here as long as he likes.'

'But without warning, what is he meant to do at such short notice?'

'Without warning? Short notice? He has received many notices, requests, warnings. He has ignored them.'

'Yes, there may have been a letter,' Purefoy said, when I joined him in the midst of the growing pile of specimens. 'Was it last year? I thought it said . . . I don't remember what it said.'

We watched as the final items emerged, the dog brain, the pregnant cat, the skinned lizard. Inevitably, someone dropped something; the gouty human foot, a particular favourite, lay in a puddle of shattered glass and *liquor balsamico*.

Passing students stopped to stare, pointed and whispered. There had been many rumours about what Purefoy did in his rooms. Since Meryll and I were the only ones he invited within, the stories had grown to encompass not merely strange smells, but mysterious cries, demon visitors, animal familiars.

Purefoy was beyond words. He paced around his collection wringing his hands, stopped, moaned, pressed them to his head, then resumed pacing.

'No plan, then?' I said.

He bit his lip. 'No plan.'

'Wait here.'

I found Tunnie and sent him to hire a cart while I went to see Erasmus Enderby. I was renting, for my own experiments, one of the spare rooms in his workshop. It had once accommodated four chemists; but, as Enderby lamented nearly every day, no one was interested in *real* science any more. I caught him as he was cohobating a distillate and, taking his distracted 'What?' for assent, I committed Purefoy to a rent of five shillings a month and returned to St Asher's where Tunnie was already loading a cart.

What Enderby would think of his new tenant's occupation I had no idea. I had never heard of chemists and anatomists having much to say to each other. As to the smell, chemists are well acquainted with foul-smelling substances. A rotting corpse is sweet as lilac compared with the boiled urine required to make icy noctiluca.

Enderby visited Purefoy's room soon after he'd moved in, blinked at the rows of specimens in their glass jars and perused the equipment. 'Nice bain-marie,' he said, 'but you will get a more even heat by mixing the ash with sawdust.'

'Thank you,' said Purefoy. 'I will try that.'

'Microscope from Holland, I see.'

'Yes, a new one. Four-hundred-times magnification.'

'Is it so? I must send for one. Very nice indeed. It is too bad, altogether too bad, that you are barking up entirely the wrong tree.' He returned to his end of the building.

Agnes Enderby avoided me, but since it was obvious that was what she was doing, I took it as incitement to pursue. She had many opportunities to practise her avoidance as not only did I frequent her bookshop, but Uncle Erasmus, who had no children of his own, often invited me to dine with the family. My pursuit took the form of mock-worship and blatant provocation, but I soon found that I genuinely liked her, and could only stand in awe of her learning. Solely from books, and a few lessons from passing scholars, she had acquired Latin, Greek (classical and late) and several modern languages. She devoured books as other girls devour sweet-cakes. She read all day and, I suspected, half the night, and seemed to remember all that she read. It turned out that she had the remarkable facility of being able to picture, in her mind, anything she had seen, including every page of every book she had read, in such perfect detail that she could simply read the page again any time she liked. She had been astonished to learn that not everyone could do this; no wonder we all seemed so stupid to her. As a corollary to this – and extremely useful in the shop – she remembered exactly where every book was shelved and where, in any book that she had read, a particular passage was located. She would walk straight up to it, pluck it from the shelf and turn immediately to the page. 'Here,' she would say, stabbing the spot. 'Read it for yourself. I am right; you are wrong.' She wore her learning as an armour.

Her mother tried to make up for it by flirting with me herself, which was rather amusing but also excruciating. Her father, I think, was secretly proud of her. Also, she was their only child; if she married and went away, who could ever run the shop so well?

She abhorred Purefoy from the beginning, and while it would have been beyond her to be so discourteous as to fail to include him when she brought, as she sometimes did, her mother's gorgeous rum and raisin cake to the workshop for her uncle and me, I could see how she steeled herself to politeness. Purefoy saw it too, and made little excuses: he had urgent work to finish, was about to go out, had just had dinner. The trouble was that once one knew where his fingers had been it was difficult to watch him eat.

27

The Prima Materia

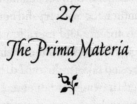

I tended not to take Japhet to the workshop – long, exuberant tails and fragile glassware do not go well together – but one day Purefoy asked me to bring him the next morning. 'Now, Purefoy,' I said, mindful of his penchant for dead animals – any number of mice, rats, stray cats and dogs had, with his help, donated their lives to science – 'you're not thinking of pickling him, are you?'

'Oh my, of course not, I know how fond you are of him, I would never, not to anything you cared for. I just want to borrow him for, well, less than a minute, probably.'

Japhet knew what it was about before I did. As we crossed the orchard he bounded ahead and scrabbled at the door of the workshop with that eager whine that signalled uncontrollable lust. Purefoy opened the door; Japhet surged in and mounted the bitch, who was tied to a table leg; it was over in seconds. Japhet lay down and panted happily.

'The pups might be a little big for her,' I said – the bitch was a collie cross, less than a third of Japhet's size.

'It doesn't matter,' said Purefoy, turning an hourglass. 'The pregnancy won't get that far along.'

I stayed to watch, fascination triumphing over revulsion. After three hours, Purefoy prepared the *spongia somnifera* and held it to the bitch's nose; her struggles ceased as she inhaled the laudanum. He lifted her on to a table, tying her legs apart. As he made the incision and opened her abdomen Japhet whined and I put him outside.

'The question is,' said Purefoy, reaching into the still pulsing mass of organs, 'whether the new life-form exists already, infinitesimally small but complete and unique, in either the ovum or the sperm – or whether each life stems from a common, undifferentiated substance and takes individual form only as it develops. Hartsoeker published drawings of homunculi he claimed to have seen in human sperm. I have more powerful optics than he did but I have never seen any such thing.'

He pushed aside the intestines, delved deeper and lifted out a handful of organs and ducts. He seemed to know his way around this bloody mass; making a slit with his scalpel he scooped some substance on to a glass dish which slid beneath the microscope. He positioned the lamp so that the flame was magnified by a polished glass sphere, adjusted the eyepiece and stared intently. 'Damn, nothing.' He removed the dish with its disappointing contents and prepared another. 'Ah yes. Here, Damory, look. Your Japhet's sperm.'

I saw tiny creatures like tadpoles, tails twitching, swimming urgently. 'Where are they going?'

Purefoy looked again, probing with his pincers. 'They are going towards . . . that. Look: an ovum.'

I had no chance to gaze for long; Purefoy nudged me aside. He watched intently for over an hour, making a series of quick sketches. At last he looked up, sighed and tipped the bloody mass carefully into a glass phial, added some of the bitch's blood and set it gently in the bain-marie. 'I have no great hopes for its survival, but who knows?' He untied the body of the bitch, took it to the back door and tossed it out.

Over the following weeks Purefoy borrowed Japhet regularly, allowing each pregnancy to proceed a bit further along. His plan was to observe and record the development of the dog embryo from conception to birth. Being evicted from the college had liberated him; no one noticed what he did, so no one complained. He moved his bed into the workshop, though he rarely slept. No matter how late I worked, he was still working when I left. One morning I found him asleep with his head on his arm and his knife in his hand, a dried-up specimen of God knows what pinned out on a board.

Enderby was growing vague; he started to call me Roderick, the name of an assistant he'd had twenty years ago. When I reminded him that my name was Francis he did not always believe me.

I came in one morning to find the laboratory in disarray. He had taken the bottles from the shelves and put them on the table; the instruments from the table were on the floor. He was on a ladder, searching the top shelf.

'Where have you hidden it, Roderick?'

'I'm not Roderick, sir, I'm Francis.'

He climbed down and approached me, tears in his eyes, and touched my shoulder gently. 'You are not!' he shouted, leaping back.

'I beg your pardon . . .'

'If you are,' his look grew canny, 'you will be able to tell me where it is.'

'Where what is?'

He folded his arms and studied me sceptically. 'You are a ghost, are you not?'

'I'm Francis . . .'

'Or a spirit; do you prefer that term?'

'No . . .'

'In either case you must know.'

'Know what?'

His voice dropped to a whisper. 'Where it is.'

'What . . .'

'Ah, very clever. I see. You are testing me. What? you ask. Indeed, what is it? Is it the beginning or the end? You think I will fall into the trap of time. I will not. It is both and neither. It is red and white, dark and light, matter and spirit, the first and the last. Hah! I have it and I have it not. The *prima materia* is everything and nothing.' He sat down, sighed, rubbed his face with his hands, looked up and frowned. 'Roderick, what on earth is all this mess? Why have you put everything on the floor?'

'We were looking for something, sir.'

'Looking for what?'

'The *prima materia*, I believe.'

He laughed, harder and harder, then he gasped and fell over. One side of his body had frozen, his face pulled askew. I'd seen cases of apoplexy before, and knew there was nothing I could do. I made a pillow with my coat, waited as the seizure ran its course, then summoned Purefoy.

'I wish I could see inside his brain,' Purefoy said as we struggled to lift him on to a plank. 'I could remove the top of the skull, but of course the damage may be deep within. Do you think they might let me have his brain when he dies?'

'I think he may be able to hear you,' I said.

'If that is so, it would mean that portions of the brain are able to act independently of each other, and the part to do with speaking is separate from that to do with hearing. What I'd really like is to get at a brain while the person is alive, probe it in different places and find out what they feel. I have tried, of course, on cats and dogs, but they are unable to tell me anything.'

We carried Enderby home; Agnes came running from the shop and helped prepare a bed for him on the ground floor. 'Something like this happened two years ago,' she said, 'but they bled him and he recovered.'

'I'm sure he'll recover again,' I said.

'Possibly not,' said Purefoy. 'The second stroke is usually fatal; if it isn't, a third and final one will soon follow. Do you suppose I could have . . .'

'Not now, Purefoy.' I led him away.

He was right; Enderby suffered another seizure the next day and died. They did not allow Purefoy to remove his brain.

28

The Red Lion and the White Rose

❧

I stayed on in Oxford through the long vacation, except for a brief sojourn at the Plachards' for Sebastian's wedding. From his perpetual deathbed my father had arranged the purchase of Lavinia's fourteen-year-old sister Cornelia. She was a plain girl but I don't think Sebastian really noticed; he was occupied with her very pretty maid.

Enderby had left behind some confusion; it turned out that he was embroiled in more than a dozen lawsuits. Far from being the impoverished scholar I'd imagined, he was a considerable landlord, owning, besides the workshop, twenty or so buildings in Oxford bringing in an annual income of over four hundred pounds. His will divided his estate between Agnes and, to my shock, me. I immediately tried to give my half to her, but she refused. She nevertheless gave me all of the lawsuits to manage.

It was a hot summer. Mornings were spent in sweltering lawyers' chambers, being informed of the content of torts, codicils, disclosures. Early on, I asked what it would cost to settle all the lawsuits at once. It was as though I had suggested we sprout wings and fly to the moon. It was not that such a thing was undesirable, though clearly it was, as it would put them out of work. No, it was actually impossible. The web of legal entanglements was so intricately woven that no thread could be unpicked. As Enderby's heir, I was obliged to pursue his lawsuits unto eternity, if need be. Even death would not bring release, as the duty would fall upon my own heirs.

The workshop was a cauldron of heat, and with the added heat of the furnaces was only tolerable at night. Purefoy's specimens began to decay almost as soon as he got them; he tried to compensate by working harder. I called in one noontide to check on the progress of a calcination of pitchblende, and looked into his room as I passed. He was slumped over the table and his face was so red that I thought he'd bathed in blood. But it was the heat. I dragged him outside to the shade by the well, hauled up bucket after bucket of water and doused him until he revived. He confessed that he couldn't remember the last time he'd eaten or drunk anything.

Most afternoons I went to Johanna's. We'd walk by the Isis, Grace riding Japhet. Grace had begun to call me Da; we laughed and corrected her, but secretly we liked it. There was a place where the bank was hollowed into a shallow pool; we splashed about in bare feet and tossed sticks into the river for Japhet. One day I bought a little skiff and, rowing upriver, tied it by our paddling place. When we came upon it later I pretended to steal it for a lark. Johanna was so shocked that I had to laugh, and gave the joke away too soon.

In the evenings I went to the workshop, where, with the windows open to the cool night air, it was just about bearable. I was working on a recipe from the Hermes Chrysotum text, the most complex and the one most heavily annotated by Tobias. It required the simultaneous preparation of the substances known as the Red Lion and the White Rose. These must be several times separated and recombined, then introduced, somehow, to a fulmination of mercury, a substance I found not excessively difficult to make but extremely hard to keep, as it explodes upon the slightest provocation. I knew the recipe was well beyond my abilities, but I was learning all the time and relished the many disasters for what they taught me.

I told myself that I conducted these experiments purely out of curiosity, to see if the results were as predicted, avoiding the question of whether I believed in the ultimate goal of immortality. I tried, as I'd told Enderby, to keep an open mind. But when things went wrong, as they frequently did, the disappointment fed a growing determination to succeed. I was becoming addicted.

I had seen little of Agnes, but one night she came to the workshop with some cherries and wine. It was a still night, with barely a breath of wind. We sat talking, mainly about Uncle Erasmus. I hadn't known that he'd had a son, also named Francis, who'd died as a child after accidentally swallowing some potion in the laboratory. Enderby had made the rest of the family promise not to tell me.

'What he never knew,' Agnes said, 'was that I was here with Francis when it happened. We were pretending it was our wedding feast. He drank a toast to me, because that was what we'd seen people do.'

A small breeze arose, the candles flickered, a moth flew in and immolated itself. Agnes removed her kerchief, replaced it over her shoulders, removed it again, lifted her arms and pushed back her hair. She ate a cherry, adding the stone to the neat pyramid we'd been constructing. Her lips and fingertips were stained red. She ate another, and suddenly the companionable silence seemed strained.

I was wearing a loose shirt, open to the waist, cotton breeches and not much else, and I wondered how women could bear to wear so many garments. I pictured Agnes in just her shift, loose and cool and free, and experienced such a strong urge to undress her that I had to sit back and try to think of something to talk about.

She reached for the wine at the same moment as I reached for a cherry; our hands met and fell together to the table. She turned hers palm upwards under mine; of their own volition, my fingers moved to stroke her wrist.

'Francis,' she said, then said nothing else for a long time as I undressed her. 'Should we blow out the candles?' she whispered when I reached her shift. I blew out all but one.

I had relit most of the candles and Agnes was mostly dressed when we heard Purefoy returning. 'Halloo, Damory!' He appeared at the door holding aloft a bloody bag. 'Look what I've got, it's a human . . . I beg your pardon, I thought you were alone.' He withdrew hastily.

Agnes looked as if she would have liked to disappear. 'I must go at once,' she said.

'I'll walk you home.'

'Nonsense, I can find the way quite well, thank you.'

'I'll walk you home.'

The walk was silent; when I tried to take her arm she drew away.

'Agnes,' I said at her door.

'I don't want to talk.' She went inside and closed the door in my face.

It was the same every time we were together. She would come to the workshop, not often, perhaps two or three times a week, always very late. In the days her manner was as cool and patronising as it had ever been, but on those nights her body told another story.

29

Our True Natures

❧

Towards the end of August I forsook my lawsuits and my alembics to help Isabel find a property for her educational project. I enlisted the help of Mr Bonnerby, the house broker I'd met in Highgate. He had taken on a partner, Henry Pinchon of Gray's Inn, to handle the legal niceties of deeds, leases, conveyancing and so forth, and was proving very helpful.

Isabel was now the Countess of Harfield, the old Earl having finally died; it was clear that the power and the money of the Harfields were in her hands. She had acquired a very polished veneer and it was no longer so easy for me to read her.

Meryll had left Oxford that year and was living in town; I introduced them over dinner and was pleased to see a mutual attraction flare at once. Neither was adept at the arts of dalliance; Meryll was too sincere and Isabel too inexperienced. I contrived to leave them alone whenever possible, but it was weeks before they progressed beyond ardent glances and shy hand-holding.

Isabel's vision had expanded over the months and she had secured donations from nearly all of society, even the King. There was to be a hospital and a school for boys and girls of all ages, with gardens for recreation and the cultivation of vegetables to provide a healthy diet. At first she had wanted to convert an existing property in the City or Westminster but it proved impossible to find one with enough land for a garden so she had decided to try further afield. Having looked in Islington, Stepney and Camberwell, today we were in her carriage on our way to view a property west of the city, outside the little village of Chiswick on the Thames.

Meryll had architectural ambitions and threw himself into the planning, producing wonderfully detailed drawings of buildings with courtyards, wings and pavilions, Corinthian columns and ornamented pediments.

'This looks like Versailles,' I said, as Meryll unrolled his latest plans. 'Is that a boating lake?'

'Do not mock, Francis,' Isabel said, and I began to wonder if she had lost her sense of humour. 'It will be revolutionary. We will wrest the children from the wasted lives to which they were destined and they will remake the world.'

'They will be the golden children,' Meryll said, 'making a new Golden Age . . .'

'From the discarded rubbish of the old,' said Isabel, as we passed a night-soil cart drawn by a scrawny, filthy boy.

Just then a blind musician on the corner took up his fiddle and began to play. The instrument was scratchy, the playing inept, but the unmistakable strains of Vivaldi wove their way through the clangour and stench of the street. The night-soil boy lifted his head and an odd look – part pain, part longing – passed across his face.

As I watched him disappear into the crowd a strange sensation came over me, as though a piece of my soul went with him. It had

110

never occurred to me that such people could feel as I felt, could respond as I did to the call of beauty. How would it be for me, I wondered, to have such sensibilities yet be trapped in such a life? A wild panic spread through me, a sense of dread, horror, hopelessness.

For the first time I understood Isabel's passion. I'd caught a glimpse of the golden child that survived, somehow, locked away even in the lowest-born, the poorest, the most ignorant and debased. And music, I suddenly realised, was the key to unlock that gold.

'Listen, you two,' I said. 'I have had a revelation. The children must learn music. It won't be enough just to rescue their bodies and teach them letters and numbers, we must nurture their souls as well. We must teach them about beauty, and poetry, and art. They must all learn to play instruments; I'm sure everyone has a natural talent for one or another. And all must sing; we shall have a choir, a famous choir, and an orchestra.'

'Oh, is it *we*, now?' Isabel was smiling.

Mr Bonnerby's carriage was drawn up at a pair of rusty gates; he was striding about, whacking at nettles with his stick. We pulled up alongside and he came to open the door and hand Isabel down.

'Would you care to walk?' he said, after kissing Isabel's hand and bowing to Meryll and me. 'So you can view the acreage. Fourteen and three-quarters, to be precise, with four hundred feet of river frontage.'

Insects buzzed in the humid air and the drive was so overgrown we had to go one by one between the encroaching brambles, stopping at intervals to free Isabel's skirts from the thorns. The house was close-pressed by trees all around and the soft pink brick had almost vanished under a living green wall of ivy. On closer inspection one saw that the ivy was holding up the house, not the other way around. The building listed to one side, as though seeking support from the giant elm whose roots had undoubtedly caused its subsidence. And indeed, the tree was doing the best it could; several branches had penetrated the upper windows and emerged through the roof.

'You'll want to tear it down and rebuild, of course,' Bonnerby said.

'But it's charming,' Isabel said, swatting at gnats with her fan.

Bonnerby knocked at the door, which was so riddled with woodworm that it almost fell off its hinges. I think we were expecting an owner to match the house and were shocked to be greeted by a young woman with blooming cheeks and merry eyes, introduced by Bonnerby as Miss Miranda Hathaway. She invited us in with a graceful flourish, the irony of which immediately became apparent: the entrance hall had no roof; the staircase ascended to nowhere. A few of the ground-floor rooms were intact and she showed these with gestures that invited us to imagine things as they once had been. A salon looked out over a sheep meadow which revealed traces of a vanished garden running down to the river – bowers, parterres, the remains of a box maze.

Meryll and Isabel wandered out to the tilted terrace and I drew Bonnerby and Miss Hathaway on to the next room, where a harpsichord lay broken beneath a great chunk of the ceiling. Satyrs and nymphs frolicked by an Olympian river in faded murals.

'The music room,' said Miss Hathaway.

'But how has this come to such a state?' I asked.

'Deaths and debts, more deaths and more debts. A fire. Subsidence. Rot. If we get the asking price we will just about clear the debts, so please don't try to drive me down. We cannot accept any less.'

'Quite,' I said.

A shriek from Isabel drew us running towards the river.

Isabel had turned modestly away and Meryll blushed scarlet. Behind them on the riverbank a man and three women scrambled for their clothes amid unmistakable signs that we had interrupted one of those erotic pastoral interludes depicted on the music room walls.

'Do not disturb yourselves, good people,' I called. 'It is we who intrude upon your idyll. Or are you, perhaps, not mere men and women but gods and nymphs, disporting here in mortal guise?'

The man stopped trying to hop into his breeches. 'You have a canny eye, sir, and have discerned our true natures. Would you care to join us? Even I, a god, sometimes find all three of my nymphs a trifle tiring.'

'Don't you dare, Francis,' said Isabel.

'Another time, perhaps,' I said.

'I hope this doesn't put you off buying the place,' Miss Hathaway said. 'I promise you that my brother and I will leave the instant it's sold.'

'And the nymphs?'

'Oh, they might stay, if you ask them.'

'We will withdraw and leave you to your . . . your amusements,' Isabel called over her shoulder as she set off for the house. Meryll and Bonnerby hastened after her.

Miss Hathaway and I walked slowly up the meadow and I learned a little about the family. She and her brother Jack had grown up here and now lived in the gardener's cottage. The house had been built by the Duke of Warminster for his mistress. She'd borne him three children, the youngest of whom, and the only one surviving past childhood, was Miranda and Jack's grandmother. When the Duke died the property passed to her, but with no provision for maintenance, it soon fell into disrepair. A fire took out the central core of the building, dry and wet rot set in. It turned out to have been built without foundations, of inferior bricks inadequately mortared.

'The price is for the land,' she said. 'We do not pretend the house is worth anything. We know you'll tear it down.' Her voice caught and I saw that her blithe air was entirely contrived.

'What will you do?'

'There are relations in the North who will . . . who might agree to take us in. Sheep farmers, charmingly rustic, I believe.'

Isabel and Meryll stood on the terrace with the drawings rolled out on the one remaining upright section of balustrade.

'How is the drainage?' Isabel asked Bonnerby. 'And is the subsoil clay or gravel?'

'I will enquire,' he said, making a note in his pocket-book.

'Pleasure gardens,' Meryll said. 'A pavilion on the riverbank – no, many small pavilions.'

'An opera house,' I said. 'Half a dozen little palaces for visiting royalty. Will fourteen and three-quarter acres be enough?'

Isabel gave me barely a glance. 'So far from London, we will need housing for the staff as well as the children.'

'So you'll buy it?' Miranda said.

'Yes,' Isabel said. 'I'll buy it.'

'Oh, that's wonderful.' Miranda looked as if she was about to cry.

'Isabel,' I said, 'we are going to need a great deal of help – people to do all sorts of things, planning, building, organising. And then, of course, teachers, administrators and so on. Miss Hathaway was just telling me that she and her brother, whom you met just now, are very good at many things. Aren't you, Miss Hathaway?'

'Oh, not really . . .'

'Many things. And they have the advantage of knowing the terrain, the local people and so on. They will prove indispensable.'

'I suppose you would like me to hire the nymphs as well?'

'Indeed, why not?'

30

The Organ of the Soul

❧

I called at Enderby's bookshop the first morning I was back in Oxford for Michaelmas term, uncertain how Agnes would receive me. Perhaps she regretted our indiscretions and would wish me to pretend they had never occurred.

She greeted me unsmiling as ever. 'We have received a first edition of the *Hypnerotomachia Polyphili* that might be of interest to you,' she said. 'Father, would you please mind the shop while I take Mr Damory upstairs?'

Enderby's rare book room was on the top floor. Agnes unlocked the door and relocked it after us. She took the book from its shelf and opened it on a padded stand. 'It has exquisite woodcuts,' she said, unpinning her bodice.

'Agnes,' I said, afterwards.

'I don't want to talk.' She ordered her clothes, closed the book and held it up with a questioning look.

'Oh yes, certainly,' I said. 'It's beautiful. Irresistibly seductive.'

She led me downstairs, entered the purchase (six guineas) on my account and walked me to the door. 'Francis,' she said, as we stepped outside.

'Agnes,' I said. I leaned against the shop window and waited for her to speak. It was market day and the Broad was crowded with stalls and tables, thronged with shoppers. Purefoy emerged from the apothecary next door. 'Ah, Damory, look,' he said. 'They've

115

received some saffron from Madagascar, very pure, see?' He unfolded the packet and showed me the yellow filaments, more precious than gold dust. 'I will try mixing it with cinnabar to give a more realistic colour. I've got a new foetus to try it on, a nice early one – four months . . .'

Agnes turned away.

'Oh I do beg your pardon, Miss Enderby. I know Francis shares my enthusiasm; I had forgotten you do not.'

'That is quite all right,' Agnes said. 'I do not mind in the least.' A brisk wind tugged at her shawl and she pulled it closer.

'I was just about to buy you some flowers,' I said, beckoning to a girl with a tray of nosegays.

'Well, hello, Francis,' the girl said. 'You keeping well?'

'Oh, er, very well, thank you. Molly, isn't it? Taken up a respectable profession, I see.'

'Oh, not really. Day work and night work, you might say. A girl has to make a living.'

'Quite. Here is a shilling.'

'Thank you, sir. Hope to see you again soon.'

I gave the flowers to Agnes with a little bow. Her expression was unreadable. 'Friend of yours?' she said.

'An acquaintance of my early days in town.' I gazed off into the distance, pretending to be fascinated by the activity on the other side of the Broad. The crowds parted and I caught a glimpse of Johanna and Grace, their backs to me. Johanna was bending over a display of vegetables. When she straightened and turned, the wind blew her skirt against her body, revealing a roundness to her belly that had not been there when I'd last seen her. As she chatted with the vegetable seller she pressed her hand to the small of her back and I knew she was with child. I was transfixed by a completely unexpected joy.

'Francis?' said Agnes, and I tore my eyes away. 'Another acquaintance of yours?'

'Certainly not.' Not my doxy, I wanted to say, she is a respectable
. . . But that would only dig me deeper.

'Are you coming to the workshop, Damory?' Purefoy said.

I glanced at Agnes; she looked away.

'Yes, I am,' I said.

Purefoy took my arm and we walked up the Broad. 'As I was
saying, saffron in the white wax, slightly less cinnabar. I think the
saffron itself may have preservative properties. I intend to try it on
the brain. I am not certain whether to slice it, to examine the
development of the glands, or preserve it whole. Only four
months, you must see it, so perfect! It seems a shame to dissect;
one might almost think it could yet live, if somehow I could feed
it what it needs. No, I think I must delve further. I am sure it contains the organ of the soul. The question is, is it there from
conception – in which case it must be visible from the earliest
stages, though perhaps beyond our optics at present – or does it
only develop later? And then it must be something not found in
animals, and so far, every structure I have found in the human
brain is present also in dogs', cats', even rats' brains. Who knows,
if I could see within a spider's brain, or a fly's, or a gnat's . . . my
God, Damory, do you suppose it goes on for ever, smaller and
smaller?' He gazed at me wide-eyed.

I had stopped listening; I was thinking only of Johanna. 'I beg
your pardon, Purefoy,' I said. 'I forgot something. I'll be along later.'
I returned to the Broad but Johanna was nowhere to be seen, so I
made my way to the cottage and sat on the bench outside the door.

I saw her coming along the path by the Isis, Grace running
ahead, stopping to examine something, being overtaken, running
ahead again. Jo was singing; a melody drifted on the wind. 'Green
Grow the Rushes, O'. I wanted to run across the fields and kneel
at her feet. I sat still and waited as she came up, smiling.

'You're back,' she said.

'You're pregnant,' I said. 'I love you.'

'Oh, don't be daft.' She laughed and went into the cottage.

'Where's Jafa?' said Grace.

'I'm sorry, sweetheart, I didn't bring him. I'll bring him tomorrow. He said to say Woof, and give you a big lick.' I grabbed her and tried to lick her all over; she shrieked, squirmed out of my grasp and ran inside.

Johanna came back out, gave me a cup of ale and sat beside me. 'Yes,' she said. 'I am.'

'Let's get married.'

'You really are daft.'

'I mean it.'

'Oh la, and me the lady of your manor.'

'I'm not lord of any manor.'

'That you'll look after us, that's all I want, and when you go away . . .'

'I'm not going away. I'll stay in Oxford; I'll be a chemist. We could build another room on the cottage.'

'You are daft. That will never happen. Don't speak of it any more; it'll bring bad luck. Are you staying for dinner?'

'Yes.'

'Then I'd best start cooking it, hadn't I?'

31
An Unfinished Piece of Embroidery

🌿

In early November I was summoned to Farundell; it seemed this time my father really was dying. Clarence came to fetch me; he'd galloped all the way, and we galloped all the way back.

Death's arrival, so long awaited, was something of an anticli-
max. Father had no last words, just one final wheeze and it was
over. Everyone was there: the sisters managed some tears;
Clarence looked like he was trying not to run out of the room.
Sebastian, I think, was both shocked and exhilarated to find
himself Lord Damory at last, though he was doing his best to look
bored. Andrew surprised me, taking it harder than I'd imagined.
I knew how deep was his distress by the fact that he stood exceptionally straight and refused to meet my eyes. Isabel took charge
of the household and saw to it that the funeral and corollary
entertainments went off with military precision.

It was nearly dark when we waved the last guests away from
the last dinner; a full moon was rising in a clear, cold sky. The
others went inside but I stood in the courtyard and turned slowly
around. The stone of the house glowed pale, bare branches
rattled as a gust of wind passed through the wood. Everything
looked different now. It was Farundell; it was home; it was
family; and though I was still tied to it by a thousand gossamer
strands, the heavy chain that was my father had dropped from
my neck.

I'd left Japhet at St Asher's with Tunnie; there was no one to
look after and no one to whom I need give any account of myself.
I had a groom saddle Lancelot and set out for Oxford. The night
was almost as bright as day and I made very good time, arriving at
Johanna's cottage with the glimmer of dawn. I stabled Lancelot in
the byre, patted the sleepy cow, pulled down some hay for both of
them, added water to the trough.

The cottage was silent; she'd left the door unbarred. Had she
known I was coming? Sometimes she did, and would be waiting in
bed. I felt my way across the room, just able to make out her
rounded form under the covers. Grace was sitting up in her crib.
'Da,' she said, and began to cry.

'Hush, hush, sweetheart, let's not wake Mama with crying.' I picked her up and swung her around as she liked, but she wailed more loudly.

'Jo, what's the matter with Grace?' I was certain the noise would have awakened her, but she didn't answer. I set Grace down and went to the bed. Johanna hadn't moved. I touched her shoulder; it was cold and stiff. 'Ma,' said Grace, trying to climb on to the bed.

'Mama's sleeping, we'll let her sleep, shall we?' I carried Grace to the chair by the hearth and held her on my lap. She stopped crying and fell asleep, sucking her thumb. My mind had gone blank.

At last I got up, bundled Grace into her coat and shoes and took her to the byre where she sat on a bale of straw while I saddled Lancelot. I went back and put my cloak over Johanna so she wouldn't get cold.

'Sir, children are not allowed,' said Corwin, when he came to let me in at St Asher's gate.

'Half-a-crown,' I said.

'No sir, I mean truly not allowed . . .' but I was already in the quad and up the stairs. Japhet greeted Grace with licks and yips; she wrapped her arms around his neck and cried a bit, then fell asleep. I summoned Tunnie, who raised his eyebrows but went for porridge and milk without a word.

'Make sure she eats a whole bowl,' I said when he returned.

'How?'

'Spoon, bowl, mouth, Tunnie. Nothing could be simpler. And show her the chamber pot; she knows how to use it.'

I went back to Johanna's cottage on foot, more convinced with every step that she would be fine when I got there, warm and cosy with a fire blazing and breakfast cooking, laughing at me for having abducted Grace in the middle of the night. But how would she know it had been me? She might be, she must be terribly distraught. I hastened my steps until I was running, and arrived at her door panting. 'Jo,' I called, 'it's me, I took Grace to see Japhet . . .'

The cottage was cold; she was cold, still and grey.

Daylight revealed the red stain that soaked the bedclothes. She must have suffered a miscarriage, her life bleeding away in the night with no one to staunch the flow. 'I'm so sorry, love,' I whispered. It can't have been a painful death; she looked very peaceful.

I smoothed her hair and kissed her pale lips. I knew I should go to the church where she'd worked, make arrangements for her burial, decide what to do about Grace. Later. I sat on the floor at the side of the bed and stroked her hand, which lay outside the covers. Something niggled at my mind, a smell, familiar, but not right in this place. I leaned close to Johanna's face and sniffed. Laudanum. Why would she have dosed herself with laudanum? I wondered, even as another part of my mind knew that she had not.

'No,' I said aloud, stood up, crossed the room, stared back at the bed. 'No,' I said again, but I had already returned to the bed and flung back the covers. In the midst of the blood, the curling purple edges of a long, neat incision.

I was outside, on my knees, retching great empty gasps. There was a ringing in my ears as from the aftermath of an explosion and the wind was howling, though the branches of the trees were still. The sky was an abyss; I knew that if I did not cling with all my strength to the two dry tufts of grass I clutched in my fists I would fall into utter darkness.

Time moved in staggered jumps. I was crossing the fields; I was at the door of the workshop. Purefoy looked up as I came in. The room seemed to be filled with blood; I moved as though swimming. The specimen was in the bain-marie. 'Was it a boy or a girl?'

'What?' said Purefoy. 'Oh, a male. Well-developed testes – see, I've removed them to examine later.'

The point of my sword was at his chest. Comprehension dawned in his eyes. 'Oh God, Damory, if I'd known, you know I would never, I was there, Agnes asked, you said you didn't know her . . .'

The blade slid smoothly between his ribs. His eyes filled with sorrow and then, curiously, relief. He leaned gently forward; the blade slid in up to the hilt and he rested his head on my shoulder. A thin river of blood flowed from his mouth as I lowered him to the floor. I went around the workshop smashing every jar, then tossed down a lighted candle. As the flames spread, I walked away and did not look back.

Grace was sleeping on my bed with Japhet. I lay down beside them, closed my eyes and drowsed. Rain was falling; it pattered on the thatch, trickled over the eaves, dripped on to the rose-bush outside the window. Johanna murmured in her sleep; I slid my hand over her firm round belly and rubbed my nose in her hair, which smelled like roses. I dreamed we were walking by the Isis, Grace riding Japhet, and Johanna with our new son in her arms. A wind came up and blew all the leaves off the trees.

Tunnie was shaking my shoulder. It was still morning. 'Mr Corwin is at the door, sir, but I wouldn't let him in. He insists that I tell you that children are not allowed; also that Miss Enderby is waiting to see you.'

Grace woke, started to cry, climbed on to me and wrapped her arms around my neck very tightly. I stood and tried to detach her, but she tightened her grip.

'You should change your clothes,' said Tunnie, 'before you go out.'

I looked down. I was still wearing the clothes in which I'd ridden from Farundell, mud-splattered and bloodstained. I lifted Grace out of the way – she would not relinquish her hold – as Tunnie stripped off my coat, shirt and breeches, washed me and dressed me in fresh garments. 'I cleaned your sword, sir,' he said as he buckled it around my waist.

At the door I discovered that he planned to accompany us; so did Japhet. Agnes was waiting by the porter's lodge. She looked from me to Grace and back to me. 'Is she yours?'

'Yes, she is,' I said, 'in every sense that matters. Grace, this is Miss Enderby. Miss Enderby, Miss Brown.' Grace hid her face in my coat.

'I came to tell you that there was a fire in the workshop,' Agnes said. 'It's all been destroyed. I don't know what happened to Lord Purefoy. I asked your porter, but he said he's not seen him for weeks.'

I shifted Grace to my other arm. She made a small whimper and pressed closer.

'Well,' said Agnes. 'So you're all right, then.'

'Yes.'

'I also, although this is undoubtedly not the best time, nor does it in any way resemble the scene as I had imagined it, or certainly ever wished . . . indeed, I would very much have preferred not to be in this situation in the first place but, nevertheless, I must conclude that it is best if I tell you sooner rather than later that . . .'

'Agnes, what are you talking about?'

'I am pregnant.' She turned on her heel and walked briskly away.

The cow was lowing in the byre when we arrived at Johanna's cottage. I put Grace in the manger; Japhet sat down to watch her. 'Do you know how to milk a cow, Tunnie?'

'Yes, sir.' He took the bucket from its peg, pulled up the stool and set to work.

The cottage door stood open as I'd left it. I straightened the bedclothes and replaced my cloak neatly, covering Johanna's face. I tidied the room, putting the scraps out for the hens. An unfinished piece of embroidery lay by the chair; I folded it and tucked it into the work basket. A few of the spools of coloured thread were unwound; I rewound them and arranged them in order. I gathered Grace's clothes, her rag doll, the carved animals, and tied them in a bundle.

Tunnie was at the door. 'She drank some milk and now she's asleep, sir.' I gave him Grace's things to hold while I finished sweeping the hearth.

'I always wondered where you went,' he said softly.

I stepped outside, closed the door behind me and sat on the bench.

'Should we report this, sir?'

'Yes, of course.'

'Did you see this?' He pointed to a curl of wood on the step. 'It came from here.' A pale strip showed on the doorframe. 'Someone used a blade to lift the bar.'

'Yes.'

'Should I fetch the constable?'

I nodded.

'What parish is this?'

I pointed across the fields to St Thomas's.

'I'll go and get him.'

I nodded again. It was too much of an effort to speak; a great stone sat on my chest.

The constable came at a trot, looked and left, then returned with an assistant and the priest from St Thomas's. They took Johanna away on a cart; also the cow, the chickens, my sword and my dagger. They wanted to take Grace but we didn't allow that.

32

A Wonderful Automaton

❧

The next afternoon I received a request to call on Sir Sidney Cranston, Justice of the Peace. I was unable to persuade Grace to stay behind, so we dressed her in her best, combed her hair and tied it up with ribbons. She wanted to take Japhet, but graciously agreed to settle for toy Japhet and her rag doll.

Sir Sidney was exceedingly polite and apologised for the inconvenience, but his gaze was sharp. He gestured me to a comfortable chair on the other side of his desk. 'You understand that this is a criminal investigation?' He placed his hands on a neat stack of documents.

'Yes.'

'It is clear that Mrs Johanna Brown was murdered on the night of the eighth of November, and it is my duty to determine the facts of the case. Is this Mrs Brown's daughter?'

'Yes.'

'And is she also your daughter?'

'Her father was Johanna's husband; she is no one's bastard, but I intend to make her my ward.'

'For how long were you acquainted with Mrs Brown?'

'About a year.'

'She was a friend?'

'Yes. A close friend.'

'It is known that she was with child. Was the child yours?'

I nodded.

'Had you quarrelled recently?'

'No.'

'On the night of the eighth you called on Mrs Brown.'

'It was just before dawn.'

'Was it usual for you to call at that hour?'

'I was returning to Oxford after an absence; I had ridden all night.'

'Was Mrs Brown expecting you?'

'I don't know.'

'Was the door open when you arrived?'

'No. It was closed, but not barred.'

'Would Mrs Brown have unbarred the door to you?'

'Of course.'

'So you would have no need to lift the bar from without by means of a blade?'

'No.'

'And indeed, we have found that neither your sword nor your dagger are thin enough to have penetrated the gap between door and frame.' He glanced down at his papers. 'Are you acquainted with Miss Betsy Jerrold?'

'No.'

'With Fionella Hawkin, a Gypsy?'

'No.'

'With Mrs Dorothy Slebb?'

'No.'

'With Miss Ellen Baker?'

'No.'

'With Lord Marcus Victor Annesley de Montague Purefoy?'

'Yes.'

'Are you aware that the workshop which you shared with him was destroyed by fire on the morning of the ninth of November?'

'Yes.'

'Is it true that the premises contained many highly combustible materials?'

'Yes.'

'I regret to have to tell you it is now certain that Lord Purefoy perished in the fire. He was a friend of yours?'

I made no answer.

Sir Sidney steepled his hands, pressed his fingertips to his lips and studied me for a long moment, then stood and showed me to the door. 'Thank you for your assistance, Mr Damory. You may collect your sword and dagger as you leave.'

On the way back to St Asher's I stopped at the hostelry and ordered a carriage to take us to Farundell the next day. I thought I was doing very well – looking after Grace, managing the details – until I saw Agnes waiting at the porter's lodge. I'd forgotten all about her and the shock must have showed on my face. She turned, saw me, took a step towards me and a step back.

'Agnes,' I said.

'Francis,' she said at the same time. 'I . . .'

'We . . .'

'Don't want to . . .'

'Have to . . .'

'Talk.'

'Talk, but not now.' Grace was asleep in my arms, growing heavier by the minute. 'May I call on you later?'

She nodded briefly and walked away.

Corwin reminded me that children were not allowed. 'We are leaving tomorrow,' I told him, and gave him half-a-crown.

'I will miss you, sir,' he said.

Tunnie had some dinner set out; he cut Grace's portion into small pieces, warmed wine for me and milk for her. I fell asleep in my chair.

When I awoke I was alone. I didn't know where I was; I didn't know who I was. There was only cold darkness, with cold hands that pulled at me from all directions. Tunnie caught me as the current was about to carry me away. I had walked in my sleep, down to the Isis and deep into the icy water. Had I thought I'd find her there?

Tunnie led me back inside. I remembered who I was; it came with such a weight of pain that I staggered on the stairs.

With daylight came habit and routine. I dressed, ate, drank. Grace woke; we dressed and fed her. I made lists in my mind of what had to be done and set Tunnie to packing.

Having persuaded Grace to stay with Japhet in my rooms, I called at Enderby's as soon as they opened. Agnes led me to the rare book room. 'I know you do not love me,' she said. 'And I do not blame you for anything; I made a choice and this is the consequence.'

I started to speak, but she held up her hand.

'I'll go away for a while. I thought maybe France. I'll tell everyone that I have taken employment as a lady's companion. My chance to see the world. Perhaps that is what I will actually do, at least at first, and then retire to some lying-in place. I will find a decent family to raise the child, and then I'll return to my old life as if none of this had ever happened. I don't want any money, I have more than enough. I just need to forget about this, you . . . us. That's all I wanted to say, so you see, there's nothing to talk about.'

'You are right; there is nothing to talk about. You will marry me. Let us go and ask your parents to publish the banns.'

'What? No, Francis, wait. Please don't . . .'

Agnes's mother was so thrilled she felt faint and had to lie down. Her father's regret was obvious, although he tried to conceal it. Agnes said almost nothing and if her face gave anything away, I was neither able nor willing to notice.

Many years later I came across a wonderful automaton – a man, life-size, who walked, bowed and even played the harpsichord. That is what I was. Although I did everything that I had to do, I was only acting; my soul was with my ghosts in the land of the shades. I never spoke about it, but Agnes certainly realised that something awful had befallen me and I suppose eventually she must have worked it out. She was tolerant, even kind, though I know it was not easy for her.

We were married in early December at St Æbbe's church in Oxford. Isabel was the only member of my family in attendance, though the presence of a countess caused such a stir that she left before dinner. Meryll stood by me, though he was deeply baffled.

After our wedding I took Agnes and Grace home to Farundell; it didn't occur to me to live anywhere else. Sebastian never came out to the country; he was in London, or abroad. Andrew was with his regiment, Clarence with his horses. Sebastian's new young wife Cornelia spent her days gossiping with my sisters and being rude about Agnes and Grace. Agnes did not tell me until much later about the malicious pranks they regularly played on her. She took refuge in the library, organised it and updated the catalogue. At her request we had separate bedrooms, which was just as well, as Grace had to sleep with me and Japhet had to sleep with Grace.

Grace, Japhet and I walked or rode out together every day; as the days lengthened we went further and further afield. Soon Grace was too big to ride Japhet and I got her a fat, placid little pony whom she named, confusingly, Jafa. She liked to visit Sally Bird, who always gave her a candy or a sweet, chewy piece of dried fruit.

On the first warm day of spring we rode over Belimor Hill and down to the Isis at Carey's Ford. After dinner at the Fox and Duck I hired a little skiff and we rowed about on the river. Johanna was so strongly with us that I felt her weight in the boat. We rode back to Farundell in the long twilight, Grace asleep in my arms, Japhet and Jafa following.

We arrived to find the house swarming with doctors. Agnes had fallen from a ladder in the library; it had brought on her labour, too soon. I had not imagined that she could scream so loudly. She screamed herself hoarse and cursed me in several languages. When a night and a day passed with no issue, I dismissed the doctors and sent for Sally Bird. I have no idea what she did, but an hour later my son Christopher Sebastian Erasmus was born, small, tired but alive.

The next month Cornelia was delivered of a daughter but the child died within a few hours. It had been born, the doctor reported discreetly, with symptoms of the pox already well advanced.

'It didn't work, anyway,' Sebastian said when he arrived. 'Do you suppose she really was a virgin? So ugly, I thought no one else would have had her, but I do recall she wasn't as tight as I'd thought she'd be.'

'What are you talking about?'

'Why d'you think I married her?'

'Land?'

'Bugger land. She was meant to cure me. A virgin fuck cures the pox, don't you know that? Useful information, baby brother, make a note of it. But you can't trust the virgins they sell in London. They have a little trick, the whores, that they do with alum. So I had to marry one.'

'But it didn't work.'

'Therefore she was not a virgin. I should send her back to those whoremongering Plachards.'

We saw no more of him. Cornelia recovered her health, more or less, though she was subdued and no longer insisted on being addressed as Lady Damory. Christopher thrived with his wet-nurse, a niece of Sally Bird's. Agnes returned to the library as soon as she was able; Grace and I continued our rambles. It was Clarence who told me, months later, about the string he'd found tied to the leg of the ladder and running under the carpet to the door. He had heard Agnes's cries for help; he had seen our sisters run away.

We left the next day: Agnes, Grace, Christopher and his wet-nurse, Tunnie, Japhet and Jafa. Isabel took us in and installed us in the old dower house at Harfield. To my surprise, she and Agnes became friends. Agnes I rarely saw; she'd discovered Harfield's mouldy, derelict library.

Grace and I went everywhere together; if I tried to leave her with anyone, she cried until I returned. In the rush to get away from Farundell, Johanna's ghost had been left behind and I missed her terribly. We rode down to the Isis, a couple of miles from Harfield, to see if she was there – linked, somehow, to that river – but I never found her again.

Isabel had purchased the Chiswick property and we drew up the charter of New Eden, as the school was to be called. It was an optimistic name. More than optimistic, it was hubris, pure and simple. One never, of course, recognises hubris while one is in the midst of it.

Meryll, having designed everything down to the doorknobs, was supervising the construction of a school, dormitories, infirmary, dining hall, kitchens, staff cottages, gardens, pavilions, terraces, greenhouses and – his *pièce de résistance* – a small amphitheatre built into a natural declivity with a view of the river framed by picturesque Doric columns. For himself (and Isabel) he was building a villa on the riverbank, with an orangery and a private garden; he made room for another, next door, for me.

I threw myself into the creation of a curriculum. Music, of course, but also history, literature, philosophy, mathematics. I looked back on my own childhood, recalling the efforts of my various tutors to stir and beguile my mind. Some were better than others; one, I remembered, had been too drunk to do anything more than recite Chapman's Homer at the top of his lungs – but somehow they had made me love learning, thinking and wondering. That, I believed, was what the children needed, at least as much as they needed food and shelter.

The building work went on for three years, partly due to the larceny and incompetence of the workers, but also because Isabel and Meryll were continuously changing and expanding the plans. In the spring of 1724 we finally moved in and New Eden was opened with a grand dinner in the vast dining hall attended by our donors, patrons and the new Board of Governors. The first children, looking rather terrified but tidy in their grey worsted uniforms, marched in to cheers and applause. Our great project had begun.

33

New Eden

1730

I awoke, as one must in New Eden, at dawn. Meryll was leading the children in the Hymn to the Sun. Not all had beautiful voices, but his vibrant tenor covered their mistakes. 'We hail,' they sang, 'the glorious Light, the golden One. We are the golden children of the radiant Sun.' The song ended and Jack Hathaway took up the melody on his panpipes.

I had only just fallen asleep, having been on night duty in the infirmary. We were in the midst of another outbreak of smallpox; three children had died, but the rest would probably pull through. Better than last year, when we'd lost almost a quarter of the schoolchildren, several staff and Miranda's and my own new daughter.

Agnes appeared at the door, shepherding Grace with coffee on a tray and Christopher with bread-and-butter on a plate. Grace climbed on to the bed and, commanding Christopher to hold up the plate, dipped pieces of bread into the coffee and fed them to me. I did not like bread dipped in coffee, but it was years too late to tell her that.

Agnes sat on a chair across the room. 'I want to leave,' she said.

'Leave what?'

'New Eden.'

'But you can't leave,' I said. 'Who could possibly run this place if you left?'

'You?'

I snorted. 'Not half so well as you. And anyway, where do you want to go?'

'I want to travel. Jack and I want to travel together.'

'Travel? Where?'

'I don't care really. One starts with France, does one not? Then Italy . . .'

'Have you told Isabel?'

'Not yet. I was hoping you . . .'

'Well, not today. She'll be too busy. And tomorrow is the Governors' meeting, surely you can't expect her to . . .'

'Oh Francis, I don't expect anything. Not. Anything. At. All.' She kept her voice low but I saw Grace frown.

'*Pas devant les enfants*,' I said.

'*Comme tu, mon cher*,' she said as she left.

'You always have to have the last word, don't you?' I called as her footsteps receded.

'Unlike you,' she called back. A door slammed, bounced open, slammed shut again.

'Oh-oh,' said Grace. 'You're in trouble.'

'You're right,' I said.

'You should marry me and we'll go away together.'

'With me,' said Christopher.

'If there's room in the carriage,' said Grace. 'We're taking Japhet.'

'Japhet's dead, sweetheart.'

'No, he's not. I saw him last night.'

'Maybe that was his ghost, coming back to make sure you're happy. The real Japhet got tired, don't you remember? He was just so tired he lay down and went to sleep for ever and we buried him in the garden.' I pointed out of the window. 'Under the cherry tree, remember? You cried so much I had to read out the poem you'd written.'

'That wasn't the real Japhet, silly. That was only dog-Japhet.'

'Oh, I see.'

Tunnie came in with a bundle of clothes. 'What will you wear tonight, sir? I thought the blue-and-rose damask for dinner, then a quick change into the emerald moiré for the concert and the ball, with the peacock mask.' He held the feathered mask against the green coat.

'What do you think?' I asked Grace.

'Very handsome,' she said, with such a serious air that Tunnie smiled. 'And I'll wear my green dress so everyone knows I belong to you.'

'Oh, you're coming, are you?'

'Of course I am.'

'Who's given you permission to stay up so late?'

'My aunt, of course.'

'Which aunt?'

'You could give me permission.'

'You may come with us to the concert, and if you're still awake when it ends, which I will bet you a pinch and a tickle you're not, you may come to the ball.'

'Me, too,' said Christopher.

Miranda put her head round the door. 'Isabel's here, my love, and wants to talk to you.'

Grace ran to her and tugged at her skirt. 'I can come to the ball! Help me to dress.'

'That's not exactly what I said. And it's not for hours yet. And take Christopher.'

Miranda gave me a quick kiss, scooped Christopher up in a flurry of breadcrumbs and disappeared.

Isabel was pacing the terrace. 'Sebastian's coming.'

'Yes, I know. He wrote.'

'Have you seen him lately?'

'Not since Christmas.'

'He's in a very bad state, Francis. He looks quite ghastly, all crusty under the powder. He's half blind and his twitch is worse.'

'You don't want him to come.'

'Of course I don't. He really shouldn't be out in public.'

'You'd rather we didn't know him.'

'Frankly, yes. He can't be trusted to behave properly. The last time I saw him he was not entirely coherent. I think perhaps reason was never his strong point, and now . . .' she made a vague wave with her fan.

'Do you remember the time Andrew tied you to a tree and Sebastian rescued . . .'

She snapped her fan shut. 'Childhood's long over. No use remembering.'

'He will stay at my house; you can pretend you don't know him.'

'Thank you.'

'Talk to Agnes.'

'Why should I talk to Agnes?'

'She wants to talk to you, but hesitates.'

'Well, there won't be time today or tomorrow, and then I have to go to Harfield for a few days, and after that London. But when I come back next month I'll talk to her.'

'She will be so grateful, I'm sure.'

'What is the matter with you, Francis?'

'Matter? How could anything be the matter in New Eden?'

Isabel sighed. 'I only hope it doesn't rain.'

'Do you not believe Meryll's solar invocations are effective?'

'Edward loves playing the druid.' She gazed up at the cloudless sky. 'And it does seem to be working.'

I sought out Jack and found him organising the choir's procession. At a signal from his panpipes the children, dressed in their white robes, followed him down the colonnade, past the statue of Apollo and into the amphitheatre, where our music master waited with the student orchestra to rehearse their songs.

They would provide an introduction to a recital of works by Maestro Handel, one of New Eden's most enthusiastic supporters, who was bringing a new castrato. Celestino was only nineteen but they called him, already, *Il Divino*. His voice spanned nearly three octaves; I'd heard that he had caused men to weep uncontrollably and women to swoon in ecstasy.

The children's voices drifted sweetly on the breeze; these were the ones who could sing, some of them very well indeed. I had been right about that, in any case: if introduced to music at an early age, a surprising number of children manifested a real talent.

Jack joined me on a bench beneath Apollo. 'That'll do, I think,' he said. 'If they remember what order they're in. Meryll wants me to wear a white robe but I damn well won't. You're not, are you?'

'Certainly not.'

The lawns were bustling with activity. Supervised by Miranda, teams of children swept the paths and set out tables and chairs. Others, on ladders, draped swags of greenery along the colonnade and hung coloured lanterns in the trees.

'Agnes talked to me,' I said.

'Oh, I told her to wait.'

'You're planning a trip to Europe.'

'Is that what she said? Well, we haven't really decided yet.'

'She sounded decisive to me.'

'Oh, I don't know, Damory. Is this the right time?'

'I think it is the right time for Agnes to get what she wants.' I turned to face him. 'Make her happy, my friend. If you don't, I'll kill you.'

He started to laugh, then saw that I was serious. 'All right, I'll take her to France. Tomorrow, if you like.'

'If she likes, you mean.'

'But I haven't any money and it's hell having her pay for everything.'

'Put up with it.'

I found Agnes in the office. 'Go whenever you want,' I said. 'I'll handle Isabel.'

'Oh Francis, I don't think I can. Look at this.' She pointed to the stack of bills on her desk. 'And I don't know what the Governors will decide about . . .'

'We will manage. Somehow.'

She burst into tears.

'Agnes, what's the matter? Isn't this what you want?'

'Yes. No. I want . . . I don't want . . . oh God.'

I held her for a while until her tears subsided. 'I have to say something, Francis, before I go.' She wiped her eyes. 'When I started with Jack it was to get back at you for Miranda.'

'I know.'

'Although now I'm rather fond of him.'

'That's good.'

'But that's not what I wanted to say.'

'No?'

She hid her face in my shoulder. 'You know I didn't want to marry you.'

'Yes.'

'Well, it wasn't because I didn't . . . it was because I was so in love with you.'

'Oh, sweetheart.'

'I'm not, any more. I've got over it.'

'You'd better start packing. Take plenty of warm clothes.'

'Look after Christopher.'

'Of course.'

'He loves Miranda more than me, anyway.'

'I don't think so.'

'Maybe I should stay . . .'

'Nonsense. You'll have a wonderful time. I'll envy you, larking about Europe, seeing those wonderful places, meeting fascinating people. Don't forget to write and tell us about it. And Agnes, get Jack to carry the purse. It will be so much nicer for you not to have to deal with money.'

34

A Distillate of Roses

In the infirmary, Dr Bayliss was completing his rounds. He had discharged all but the last few children, who were sitting up in their beds, eating heartily. 'Well done, Francis,' he said. 'I think we've beaten it.' He was a diminutive, round-faced man somewhat past middle age, whose habitually mild expression hid an iron core.

We went into the laboratory. It was very like Enderby's – ovens, alembics, retorts – but where Enderby had worked with minerals and metals, Bayliss worked with plants. He was obsessed with finding the perfect substance, the quintessence of matter that would provide the link with spirit. Death and disease, he was sure, were caused by the gradual separation of spirit from matter; without spirit, matter inevitably decays and dies. This process, so easily observed in nature and man, began, he believed, at birth, but he refused to concede that suffering, disease and death were our inevitable fate.

'There is nature, yes,' he would say, 'and in nature life engenders death as death engenders life. But man is both within nature and outside of it, for he is the only creature who can imagine himself and nature, and speculate about their relation.'

Bayliss's radical views had got him expelled from Cambridge; he'd travelled to Europe and studied with the Paracelsians in the Low Countries for a decade before returning to England. Meryll and I had met him in a coffee house in London, where he had attracted a circle of admirers with his indignant, erudite diatribes aimed at the medical profession.

For him, light was the key. His *prima materia* was not material at all: it was light itself, and his efforts were directed towards making a medicine of light. He wanted to heal not only the material body but the spiritual body, which was made, as Aristotle said, entirely of light. In his view, there was no point in treating merely the flesh; it was this invisible body that governed health because it was the link with God.

For a long time after Oxford, I'd wanted nothing to do with chemistry. The fire that had destroyed Purefoy's workshop had destroyed mine as well, and I'd felt no regret. I'd put away the books on alchemy and even wondered if my father had perhaps been right about their dangers, and my own susceptibility to madness. When Bayliss first came to New Eden and set up his laboratory I'd been unable even to enter the room, which was dominated by a huge bain-marie. The glimpses I'd caught as I hurried past the open door had filled me with horror, and more than once I'd had to convince myself that the bloody baby I saw in it was not really there.

I'd learned that the nightmares which plagued me could be thwarted by a dose of laudanum at bedtime. My sleep was thick and dark; if I dreamed, I remembered nothing. And then early one morning I awoke in Bayliss's laboratory.

'What am I doing here?' I said.

'You seem to be cohobating a distillate of roses.' He was watching me with an expression of wonder.

I looked at the phial in my hand, at the cucurbit into which I'd been pouring it.

'Several times in the last few months,' he said, 'I've noticed that someone had been here during the night. Sometimes my own work was furthered by this helpful visitor; on other occasions new work had been commenced, then abandoned. I admit I considered a supernatural explanation – angelic intervention would have been so gratifying. But I could tell that my unseen helper, while certainly a skilled chemist, was not a perfect one. I started sleeping here,' he gestured to a couch in the corner, 'last week. You came three hours ago.'

The laboratory was full of the fragrance of roses; the rising sun flooded the windows. The sight of the bain-marie had ceased to terrify me. Eventually I discovered that I no longer needed the laudanum; my nightmares dwindled to a manageable few. I returned to chemistry with renewed dedication, sure that Bayliss's gentle, spagyric methods were the way to a true understanding of nature. I became convinced that flowers, roses in particular, could by their beauty and their scent operate directly on the soul.

In the gardens of New Eden I planted roses of every variety: damasks, albas, gallicas. In the laboratory, Bayliss and I worked together, experimenting with the essences of many flowers, combining, distilling, making and perfecting our salves and elixirs, which we administered liberally to ourselves, the staff and the children. As far as I know we did no harm, and everyone smelled wonderful.

35
Ravished

🌿

Sebastian arrived during dinner. It was a very grand occasion, hosted by Lord Langton, our patron, and attended by the Governors and our most valued donors. Isabel saw him at the door and with urgent glances alerted me. I caught him halfway to the table; he was a bit unsteady and reeked of brandy. I steered him gently aside and took him to my house.

He had a bottle of medicine in his pocket at which he swigged continuously, alternating with brandy from a silver flask. His man-servant Joseph appeared with his luggage; the quantity indicated that a stay of some length was planned.

'Isabel doesn't want to see me,' Sebastian said.

'Oh, I don't . . .'

'I can tell. She exudes that haughty Harfield superiority. Wouldn't want to soil her skirts, so I'll keep out of the way. Just wanted to see you, baby brother. I was thinking about, oh, what was it? Something to do with family. Mother. Is she dead? Yes, she is, isn't she? Had too many babies. Father misses her so much. You wouldn't have thought so. He talks about her constantly, how she saved him from a great . . . a great something. He doesn't think I know about it, but I do. Andrew is her favourite, can you believe it? D'you remember the time we crept up on Andrew when he was asleep, pretending to be ghosts?'

'I was pretending to be a ghost. You were the Grim Reaper himself. Remember that enormous scythe we borrowed from old Butterfield?'

'Remember Tildy Butterfield in the hayloft? Oh God, what a sweet arse. I wonder what ever happened to her?'

'Have a bit of a rest, Sebastian. Shall I have someone bring you some food?'

After dinner the guests retired to their pavilions to change and don their masks; it was dusk as we made our way to the amphitheatre. The seats had been spread with rugs and cushions; children, dressed as shepherds and shepherdesses, moved about serving wine and sweetmeats. The riverbank was crowded with pleasure-boats disembarking more guests. At last all were seated; Lord Langton made a little speech and the music master stepped forward to lead the choir.

Miranda and Grace had saved me a seat; Agnes, next to Jack, was holding Christopher, already asleep. 'We're leaving tomorrow,' she whispered.

The children performed well and were politely applauded; the professional musicians filed in and tuned their instruments. Grace tried to conceal her yawns.

Maestro Handel entered, bowed and took his place at the harpsichord. Celestino was nowhere to be seen. 'Where is he?' A whispering ran around the seats. 'Celestino!' someone called, echoed by others. It became a chant, accompanied by clapping and stamping, so loud that no one heard the first note. As it swelled, a sudden hush descended. Celestino was still invisible; the unearthly voice seemed to come from everywhere and nowhere. For more than a minute without pause for breath it swooped and soared until at last Celestino stepped from behind a column and finished on a long, liquid trill. Miranda leaned against my shoulder with a sigh; all around me, people were gasping, weeping, throwing flowers.

My limbs were frozen, my eyes were burning. Somewhere inside me I felt a great shifting, as though the cogs of an ancient machine had begun to turn. As Celestino continued the aria I staggered to my feet and left.

The voice pursued me. He was singing about his lost beloved: '*Cara sposa, dove sei, dove sei?*' Where are you, where are you? There was such a pain in my chest that I wondered if I was dying. I found my way down to the river, leaned against a tree and wept. *Ritorna*, come back, oh, come back to me.

'It's about her, isn't it?' Miranda's voice was gentle. 'The one you never talk about. Grace's mother.'

'You should stay away from me, Miranda. I don't think knowing me is beneficial to health. It might even get you killed.'

'I'll take my chances.'

'You don't know what you're talking about.'

'Not unless you tell me.'

'Tell you? What shall I tell you? That I'm a murderer? That people are dead because of me, including my own son? And I don't even know how many other deaths I might have prevented if I'd been paying attention. None of this can be undone.'

'And you wouldn't want to, if you could.'

'What?'

'Because it's your special treasure, your secret pain that keeps you locked away where no one can touch you.'

'Damn you.' I turned away. When I turned back she was gone.

I sat on a bench by the river as the music flowed on and on. It no longer seemed to me that I was listening to a man singing notes written by another man; it was pure beauty: incorporeal, transcendent. I wished I could dissolve.

At last I returned to the amphitheatre and watched from the side of the stage as Celestino sang a final encore. He was a slender, handsome man, splendidly dressed in a white coat embroidered with gold, an elaborate white wig and high golden shoes. It seemed impossible that any human could produce a sound of such inhuman perfection, though I was close enough, now, to see the effort – the sweat that ran down his face, soaking his cravat, the powerful expansion and contraction of his chest and abdomen as he breathed, the fluttering muscles of his throat, the vibration of his mouth and lips as he shaped the sound.

He finished, bowed right and left. There was silence, then ovations that went on and on. The floor was strewn with flowers; he picked one up, kissed it and tossed it back. His people were waiting to take him to his pavilion; they closed around him, clearing a way through the gathering crowd. Hands reached for him, offering gifts or just trying to touch him.

I looked for Miranda; Agnes told me she'd left before the concert ended with a very sleepy Grace. 'We're going quite early in the morning,' she said, 'so if I don't see you . . .'

'Have a wonderful time. Write. Come back safe.'

'I will.'

The guests were making their way to the dining hall, now cleared for dancing and blazing with hundreds of candles. Our best student musicians played a lively chaconne; light and laughter spilled out of the open doors. I donned my mask, danced with everyone and drank a great deal of wine.

It was long past midnight when I looked out of a window and caught a glimpse of the bright disc of the moon. During a pause between dances I excused myself and stepped outside. The night was mild; couples strolled the lantern-lit paths and from shadowed bowers came an occasional sigh or giggle. As I walked along the river the sounds of music and revelry faded. A nightingale was singing from the top of a tree and a masked woman sat alone on a bench in the moonlight.

'May I join you?' I asked.

'Please do.' She made a graceful gesture and pulled her skirts aside.

Her gown was iridescent silk, blue-green and gold, and her mask, like mine, was of peacock feathers. 'Birds of a feather,' I said.

'Perhaps we are.'

'You are tired of dancing?'

'A little. And the noise. After a time one's ears must rest.'

Her English was clear and precise, but there was a slight accent that I couldn't place. 'Have you been in England long?'

'Not so long.'

'You speak English very well.'

'Thank you. I studied before I came.'

Her voice was light and demure; I pictured a château, private tutors, a careful upbringing. But then what was a carefully brought-up girl doing with such an intoxicating décolletage? There was a tiny heart-shaped black patch on the gentle curve of her left breast, an unmistakable signal that her heart was not spoken for.

'Have you enjoyed your evening?' I said.

'Yes, very much. I think it is wonderful work that you do here.'

'Ah, so you know who I am?'

'I asked a friend.'

I removed my mask and with a gesture invited her to do the same.

She shook her head.

'And who is your friend?'

'Lord Langton.'

That put a new perspective on things. Was she a new mistress of his? A bastard daughter? I was more and more intrigued. 'Langton has been a great help to us. It was he who persuaded Maestro Handel to stage these benefit concerts.'

'Maestro Handel is the greatest genius who has ever lived. Do you not agree?'

'Well, yes . . .'

'But you walked out of the recital.'

'Oh, you saw me?'

She nodded.

'That was not because I disliked the music.'

'No?'

'It was because . . .'

'Tell me.'

'That voice . . . Celestino ravished me. I couldn't . . . I can't put it into words. May I kiss you?'

Her mouth smiled below her mask; I kissed her. 'Who are you?' I whispered.

She leaned close to my ear and began to sing, so softly that only I could hear. It was the opening phrase of 'Cara Sposa', repeated exactly as Celestino had sung it. Once again, it ravished me. I lifted aside his mask.

'Do you still want me?' he asked.

I kissed him again; it was impossible not to.

36

Celestino il Divino

For you who have not heard Celestino sing, I have only pity. Your life will always be incomplete. For you who think perfection is impossible, I know that you are wrong. If I could have bestowed immortality upon anyone, it would have been him, which is not to say that there were not times when I wanted to kill him out of sheer exasperation.

Sandro – Alessandro Zanetti, as he was born – was a fanatic. As effortless as he made it seem, that voice was the result of a lifetime of discipline. No matter that the night's revels often went on until dawn, he would begin his morning exercises at exactly six o'clock: three hours of vocal drills, accompanying himself on a harpsichord which he'd had specially built with a double keyboard and long legs so that he could stand. In the late mornings he prepared new material; in the afternoons he ran through the role he was currently performing. In the evenings he sang before ever more ecstatic audiences. When he missed one performance due to a cold, there were riots.

Deploring the tendency towards fat to which many of his rivals succumbed, he ate only vegetables and fish, fruit in great quantities and no bread, cheese or meat. Wine he drank sparingly, always well-watered. He never touched spirits, coffee, tea or chocolate. He had rented a sumptuously furnished house in Jermyn Street, convenient for the Queen's Theatre in the Haymarket and Maestro Handel's house in Brook Street, and large enough for his entire staff, which included a German secretary, a Swiss valet, a French hairdresser, an Italian cook, a Hungarian harpsichord tuner, a blackamoor driver and footmen, all very well paid and extremely loyal. I was astonished to learn that he was paying rent of £20 a month; to him it was an inconsequential sum. His fee for the London Season was two thousand pounds but he received thousands more in gifts – jewellery, swords, golden watches and enamelled snuff-boxes, diamond-encrusted shoe buckles, a carriage and pair of matching greys. When he donated an enormous diamond-and-ruby ring (a gift of Lady Melbury, a very fond patroness) to New Eden, it made the front pages of the newspapers; the gossip pages were full of speculation about which lady had replaced her in his affections.

It was early June; for nearly a fortnight I'd been slipping in and out of his house at all hours to accommodate his schedule. The building had a back door reached through an alley off Portugal Street; necessary, because there were always journalists lurking outside the front door.

It was past midnight; the room was bright with candles and a fire blazed in the hearth. Sandro stood at the window shivering in his dressing gown. 'Is there a word for this rain that is mixed with little balls of ice?'

'We call it hail, or sleet if it's a bit wetter. Come to bed.'

'I was told that June was a summer month in England.' He took an orange from a bowl and reclined on the pillows next to me.

'This is typical English summer weather.'

He stared at me in disbelief; I enjoyed it when he didn't know whether or not I was joking. 'Does it not rain in Italy?' I asked.

'Hardly at all, in the south.' He peeled the orange and fed me a piece. 'I would like to take you to my village, Francesco. It is dry and hot; there are vines and olive trees and goats.'

'We have goats.'

'English goats are too well-mannered to count.'

'I beg your pardon; do go on.'

'There are vines, olives, goats and the church. My brother Giovanni and I sang in the mountains with the goats and we sang in church. We were so poor we sang instead of eating.' He rolled on to his back and sang, 'Giovanni', stretching the word into a song. 'All we wanted was to become great *musici* like Bernacchi and Senesino. When Giovanni was eight and I was seven the bishop came to hear us; it was the most exciting day of our lives. We sang and the great man was pleased; some money changed hands and we went to live in his palace. Well, it seemed a palace to us; it's really just a large house. We were given splendid clothes, wonderful food, a soft bed and music lessons all day. The Signore was a kind man, and if he sometimes had certain needs, well, he never hurt us. He was rather sweet.'

'Are you saying he . . .'

'Oh, you are so full of dis – pro . . . what is the word, Francesco?'

'Which word?'

'The word for how you are being.'

'How am I being?'

'Well, you are not being so any more, but you made a face like a prune.'

'Disapproval?'

'That is the word. *Grazie*. Disapproval. You disapprove?'

'Yes, I disapprove of an old man doing – what did he do, anyway?'

'Why, do you want to do it too?'

I laughed. 'Maybe.'

'And anyway he was not so old. Not much older than you.'

'So he was your first?'

'No, that was his maiden sister; she pounced on us the night we arrived. Hah, you don't know whether to believe that, do you?' He smiled triumphantly. 'You will never know.'

When I asked him about Giovanni, he looked away and his voice was sad. 'He died from the operation. I was lucky and he was not. But he's still with me; I feel him inside me when I sing. He helps me to get through the difficult parts. Sometimes I think I have no more air and he gives me some.' He took my hand and pressed it to his chest. 'Can you feel him?'

I felt his heart beating strongly in his strange and beautiful body.

'I have to go home for a while,' I said in the morning. 'I seem to recall that I had a rather full life before I met you and I suspect it is still there.'

'*Non lascia me, caro, carissimo,*' he sang.

'Stop it.' I'd told everyone that I had family business in town; Sebastian's condition made it plausible. When that was no longer tenable, I pretended to go to Oxford to deal with Erasmus Enderby's lawsuits, whose endlessness finally proved useful.

149

'I will visit *you*,' he said. 'Next week, when the Season ends, I will have more time. I want to meet your Miranda, your Grazia and your Cristoforo.'

'Oh, how wonderful . . .'

'And I will give a singing lesson to your students.'

'Now that really is wonderful. They will be so excited.'

'I will have my secretary arrange everything so it is all, *come se dice*? *Comme il faut*. And then I will come, and we will meet for the first time. It will be *delizioso*.' He made an elaborate bow. 'Meester Damory, what a pleasure to meet you! Meester Zanetti, the pleasure is all mine! Will we be friends, do you think? Or perhaps rivals: shall I seduce your Miranda?' He let loose a cascade of trills and arpeggios that followed me down the back stairs.

37

Just with His Voice

🌿

New Eden prepared for Sandro's visit as if for royalty. His secretary, Herr Meintz, came the day before to view the arrangements. 'If I may suggest,' he said.

'Please do.'

'An area should be roped off for the journalists.' He consulted his papers. 'There will be about a dozen, plus a few artists to make sketches. If you do not separate them, they will mingle and make nuisances of themselves.'

'We certainly can't have that.'

'And the children who will meet him – they are clean and healthy?'

'Of course.'

'I would like to inspect them, please.'

'Now?'

'If that is convenient.'

We inspected the children.

'They are not as clean as they could be,' Herr Meintz said.

'They will bath in the morning and put on new clothes.'

'That is acceptable. And the private dinner afterwards . . . if I may ask, will Lord Damory attend?'

'No, I do not believe so. He is ill.' I made a mental note to lock Sebastian in his room.

'Indeed. So those present will be the Countess of Harfield, Mr Edward Meryll, Miss Miranda Hathaway and yourself.'

'Also Miss Grace Brown and Mr Christopher Damory.'

'Oh? I did not have those names on my list. Who are they, please?'

'They are children. Clean children.'

He made a note. 'And you are aware of Signore Zanetti's dietary requirements?'

'Yes, we are.'

'So the menu will be . . .?'

'Er, it will be . . . I don't know precisely. Miss Hathaway instructed the cook.'

'Shall we speak with her now?'

'By all means.' We found Miranda at home, supervising the most thorough cleaning the house had ever known. At Herr Meintz's suggestion she summoned the cook, and although he clearly felt that a meal without meat was not really a meal, he read out his menu: clear fish soup with crab and saffron; artichoke hearts *en croute*; baked lobster with butter and parsley sauce; sautéed sole with spinach and peas; pike in corbullion; asparagus ravioles with almond sauce; prawns with fennel and rice; strawberries in Madeira wine; vanilla ice cream; peach fritters and syllabub.

'Next time, let's have the King to dinner,' Miranda said when Herr Meintz left at last. 'It will be far less trouble. And expense. Do you know what it costs to get lobster, packed in ice, by overnight coach? But Cook would have nothing less. And the maids had to have new bodices and aprons to wait upon His Marvellous Wonderfulness.'

'And you have a new gown as well – I saw the dressmaker leaving.'

'Yes, well, frankly I have never been so excited in my life. What do you suppose he's like? Does he even speak English? I've learned a few words of Italian, but I'm not sure I'm pronouncing them correctly and I don't want to make a fool of myself. Listen, does this sound right? Bon joorno, Seenori Zanetti. Ben-ven-ooto ah New Eden.'

'That sounds good. But I believe he does speak some English.'

'Oh, that's a relief. We can converse. What might he like to converse about? Music, obviously. And perhaps travel? He's travelled widely, I understand. Did you know, it said in the paper that when he was only sixteen he was the lover of the Queen of Bohemia?'

'Don't believe everything you read,' I said, although that one was true.

'Of course not. But I heard that he caused her to . . . experience the highest ecstasy . . . just with his voice. Is that possible?'

It certainly was. 'You could ask him for a demonstration.'

'Oh Francis! No, you're joking, aren't you? Oh my, I could never. Do you suppose he would?'

Knowing him, I thought, anything is possible. 'I don't know,' I said.

'Would you mind if he did?'

'Not at all. I would not want to deny you such a unique experience.'

'That is good of you. I am trying to remain angry with you but you make it difficult.'

'Why are you trying to remain angry?'

'Well, why do you think? I ask a civil question, you damn me and disappear for two weeks.'

It took me a while to work out that she was referring to the night of the concert; I'd forgotten our conversation. 'I didn't disappear; I told you where I was going – London, Oxford.'

'Yes, you said. London and Oxford.'

'You don't believe me.'

'I don't know where you went, or with whom. All I know is that I intruded on your . . . your pain, your past, so you found another woman to console you. It's what men do.'

'I have not found another woman.'

She looked carefully at me.

'That is the truth, I swear it,' I said. 'I will swear on the Bible, if you like. You are the only woman in my life.'

'All right, I believe you. No need for oaths. And anyway, as I said, I just can't stay angry, I'm too excited. Bonjoorno, Seenori Zanetti, ben-ven-oto, ben-ven-ooto . . .'

We had two really exceptional singers at the school, a boy named Stephen, now about thirteen, and his eight-year-old sister Abigail. Isabel had found them three years ago on one of her trawls through the streets of London. When they arrived, filthy, lice-ridden, half-starved, barefoot and covered with infected sores, we couldn't even tell what sex they were. It was a huge battle to undress and wash them; they were so full of fear and mistrust that they didn't speak for days. They ran away as soon as they could and, after searching all night, I found them begging by the side of the London road. I had to carry them back kicking, one under each arm.

When at last they realised that no harm was intended, they flung themselves enthusiastically into school life. They learned to read and write in just a few months and though it took them longer to join in the singing lessons, when they did it was a revelation. The purity of their voices brought tears to my eyes, and I immediately summoned everyone to listen. Lord Langton came, and the Governors. Stephen and Abigail were our great success, the proof of our methods, the justification for all the expense. Donations flowed in; we expanded, took in more children, hired more teachers, built a new wing.

Like many of the children, they had not known their surname; it was our practice to give them names in keeping with their qualities, as these came to be known. Stephen and Abigail were given the name Silver, in recognition of their voices and, in a perhaps unintentional double entendre, their value. The Silvers were famous, and if Stephen sometimes lorded it over the other children, well, I couldn't blame him.

He had blossomed into a child of great intelligence and charm, very quick and perceptive, with a passionate determination to make something of himself. Aside from music, which seemed to flow from his very soul, he excelled in my weekly philosophy seminars, where I introduced the brightest of the children to the realm of thought. I had the notion that certain pure ideas – such as reason, beauty, truth – could act on the mind as medicine acted on the body. I imagined myself pouring good ideas like molten gold into their young, receptive minds, gradually washing away the fear, greed, envy and hatred that had polluted them.

More than once, as I watched Stephen devouring books and soaking up knowledge like a sponge, I caught myself imagining that he was my own son. My Christopher was a sweet lad, but Stephen's thirst for understanding moved me deeply. In a few years, I thought, I'd send him to Oxford; I might even make him my ward.

I was touched to see how much care Sandro took with the children. He had a kind word and a bit of advice for each, though I wasn't surprised to see that Stephen and Abigail were singled out for special instruction. Before he set to work with them, he insisted that the whole school, including the teachers and other staff who'd crowded into the hall, practise breathing together.

'You think you know how to breathe,' he told us, 'but you do not. What you call breathing is like the little gasps of a dying fish.' He wheezed melodically to demonstrate. 'Most of you breathe only with your noses,' he sniffed and snuffled; 'some with your stomachs.' He puffed his abdomen in and out comically. 'But it is the ribs that must breathe as well.' He held up his hand, fingers pressed together, splayed them open, closed them again. 'Like this. You think there is no space between your ribs? You are mistaken; the ribs can be taught to move freely, although for most of you, it is too late to learn. I have been stretching my ribs since I was a child. Without this, you cannot control the breath; if you cannot control the breath, you cannot control the sound. Now, everyone breathe in slowly, then out, in and out. Try to fill your lungs more each time. Now all together: aaaaahhhhh . . .'

We sang together. Some collapsed into coughs, some gave up after a few seconds. Sandro sang on and on. At last his voice faded; we thought he'd run out of air. He turned away, shaking his head sadly, then let the sound swell again and we saw he'd only been teasing. He added ripples and trills, stronger and stronger, smiling and bowing all the while, and finished in laughter. 'Ribs,' he said, rolling the *r*. 'It is all in the ribs.'

I had steeled myself for an awkward dinner, but Sandro was a consummate actor, perfectly controlled yet apparently bubbling with spontaneous bonhomie. He was the gracious prince, taking pains to put us at ease with his naturalness, his simplicity, his humility. He was delighted with the house, the gardens, the setting. With Meryll, he discussed architecture, apparently just sufficiently knowledgeable to appreciate Meryll's superior scholarship. He flirted outrageously with Miranda, and she glowed. With Isabel he discussed the school, which he said was indeed an

Eden compared to the conservatory in Naples where he'd spent most of his life. I don't believe anyone noticed that he rarely spoke to me, or caught the few glances. His foot pressed mine from time to time under the table but no doubt pressed others' as well.

Grace and Christopher were presented before we sat down to eat. They had insisted on singing something for him, and had chosen the Hymn to the Sun. They weren't too awful, although I thought I saw Sandro's shoulders twitch in the smallest of involuntary cringes. He praised them effusively and insisted that they sing it again. Having heard it once he had, of course, learned it and sang along with them, correcting the missed notes, adding small embellishments.

We were halfway through dinner when the banging began. At first we tried to ignore it, which clearly puzzled Sandro. 'What is that noise?' he said.

'I suspect that is my brother,' I said, 'who has discovered that he is locked in his room.'

'Ah, the ill Lord Damory. He sounds very, *come se dice, robusto*.'

'Unfortunately, although quite ill, he retains a vile temper,' said Isabel.

It sounded as if Sebastian was kicking his door down. 'If you will excuse me,' I said, 'I will just go and see what he wants.'

Joseph was outside the room. He made a helpless gesture. 'I did make sure he took his laudanum, sir, but . . .'

'Seb,' I called out, 'will you please stop that.' The kicks doubled in ferocity. 'If you do not stop I cannot open the door.'

'I do not need you to open the damned door, baby brother. I can open it perfectly well by myself.' The kicks stopped and I moved forwards, then started back as a heavy object thudded against the door, cracking a panel.

'Where does he get the strength?' I said.

'I do not know, sir,' said Joseph.

'Stop it, you stupid shit,' I shouted.

Another crash, another panel cracked.

Miranda appeared. 'Anything I can do?'

'Fetch my pistol.'

'Are you going to kill him?'

'No, but I feel the need to make a very loud noise.'

Isabel brushed past her, followed by Meryll and Sandro. 'Seb, dear,' she said, 'please stop. We want you to join us for dinner.'

'You lying cunt.' Another crash. He was evidently ramming the door with a large piece of furniture.

'If you will allow,' said Sandro. He approached the door, rested his hand lightly on it, and began to sing. There were no words, just a single pure note that moved into a melody, but in that melody was all pain and sorrow, lamentation, loss and regret.

The crashes stopped, replaced by the sound of sobs that rose to an eerie howl. I unlocked the door, pushing aside the remains of a mahogany desk. Sebastian was huddled in a corner; he turned his face away.

Joseph knelt at his side, hiding him from view. 'I'll take care of him now,' he said.

38

Doomed to Rot

We returned to our dinner and tried to talk of other things. Only Sandro seemed at ease, but then dramatic scenes were his speciality. After he left, with kisses all round and promises to return, I asked Bayliss to come. Sebastian had refused to see him before, but now we found him unusually compliant. I wondered if Joseph had increased his laudanum dose, but he said not.

Sebastian apologised for the desk and the door, his sudden courtesy more shocking than his rage. I left Bayliss alone with him; when he came downstairs an hour later he found me in the garden. 'Let us walk by the river,' he said. 'I need to think.'

The sun, declining towards the west, was still strong; the air was full of the shouts of the children. Every day they had two hours of vigorous games devised by Meryll, in which there were no winners or losers and a spirit of comradeship was – supposedly – engendered. Shouting was encouraged, as it helped to loosen the hold of anger and war-like thinking. I had noticed, though, that some of the children remained quite competitive, and a great deal of covert pushing and pinching went on behind the teachers' backs.

'Lord Damory,' Bayliss said at last, 'has many diseases; the French pox, more properly called syphilis, which he exhibits in all of its stages simultaneously. Virulent gonorrhoea, gout, an unspecific chronic fever. He has been greatly harmed by repeated dosings with mercury, over-vigorous purgings, and, of course, excessive bleeding. You know, Francis, I used to think it was mere foolishness that was taught in the medical schools; now I am certain they teach chicanery as well. They must know that their remedies are worse than useless, but they continue to prescribe them. I have heard that in China, you pay your doctor to keep you in health; if you fall ill you stop paying. That is how it should be. But forgive me, I digress. I digress because I am reluctant to tell you that your brother is dying. It is not the diseases that are killing him; it is not even the treatments. No, he is dying because his soul is rotted. I do not know how else to put it.'

'Because he has sinned, is that what you mean?'

'I find that discussions about sin usually degenerate into trivial word-quibbles. But, essentially, yes. His actions, even his thoughts and feelings, are the cause of this rot, which is the cause of death. If we can affect our health through the right use of nature it would be illogical to think that our acts have no effects. We eat food that agrees with us: we are strong and happy. We eat food that disagrees: we weaken and suffer. Somehow the nature within the food affects our nature. Perhaps this is so obvious that the miracle of it is overlooked. The miracle, and the lesson. There are poisons in thoughts and actions just as in food; this is what most people call sin.'

'So sinners are doomed to rot.' I laughed, to make a joke of it, but I felt my sins crawling like worms inside me.

Bayliss glanced at me. 'I do not know what sins you believe you have committed, Francis, but I know that you are a good man. Your brother . . . is not.'

'Does he know he's dying?'

'No, he has hope, which we must help him to preserve. He believes he has turned a corner, that here in New Eden he will find the cure he's been seeking. All we can do is make his end as comfortable as possible. We will give him the elixir of roses; he will believe it is helping. He must have sunshine, fresh air, light food. I think that being around the children may bring him a little peace. Has he any of his own?'

'None acknowledged. His wife died in childbed four years ago.'

'Well, we have plenty of children. And music; music will benefit him. Let him listen to children singing as often as possible.'

And so Sebastian spent his days sitting in the sun, with a blanket over his knees like an old man. He had grown feeble; that last burst of violence had exhausted him. He was so benign that it was hard to remember what he'd been like. I arranged for Stephen and Abigail to come and sing for him every day; Grace insisted on joining them. To make up for not singing nearly as well as the other two, she was sweetly solicitous of her Uncle Sebastian's health, making sure he was warm enough, that the sun was not in his eyes, that he had enough to eat and drink. He seemed genuinely touched by the care, and the singing.

39

It Would Make a Wonderful Opera

When the London Season ended, Sandro was deluged with invitations to visit his many patrons and admirers in the country. Isabel had him for a week in July and invited me as well as Lord and Lady Langton. She had restored the long-disused central section of Harfield Hall with its vast ballroom, Jacobean dining hall and long first-floor gallery lined with ancestors. Everywhere were bright brocades, exuberant gilding, gay carpets from Persia. I had begun to suspect that her extravagant redecorating was a form of revenge on the Harfields.

Four years ago she had borne a son. The child was, of course, Meryll's, but the Harfields pounced upon any semblance of an heir with all the force of the law behind them. Isabel was not allowed to raise him; he lived at Harfield in the care of Reginald's aunts. Reginald himself had all but ceased to exist; when he was at Harfield, which was not often, he occupied a suite of rooms in the east wing and was never seen.

Sandro arrived with his harpsichord and his entire staff. His routine was much the same as in London, except that instead of huge crowds at the theatre he sang before intimate gatherings in the salon. He knew that, rich as he was, supreme in his art, his position was in certain ways similar to that of Lady Langton's trained capuchin monkey, Melchizedek. He stretched the bounds with the size of his entourage, the particularity of his culinary demands, his insistence on his six-o'clock practice sessions, but he knew that if he did not oblige with gracious entertainment, the invitations would soon dry up.

He had found a copy of my novel in the library. 'You did not tell me you were an author.'

'My misspent youth,' I said. 'There were just a hundred copies printed. It was meant for Isabel and a few friends.'

'Tell me the story; it is too hard for me to read so much English.'

I told him about the young traveller, his quest for the Elixir of Immortality, his encounters with alchemists, Rosicrucians, foreign spies and mysterious ladies.

'It would make a wonderful opera,' he said. 'With me, of course, as the young seeker. Maestro Handel is looking for a new idea. May I show it to him?'

'Do you really think . . .? Well, of course, if you want to, but I can't imagine he'd be interested.'

He shrugged. 'I think it is the sort of thing he likes – a quest, love, magic. We are so tired, you know, of the same old stories about ancient foreign kings.'

One night he appeared at my bedside. 'Francesco, can you come, please, I need your help.' He led me on tiptoe to his room and pointed to the settee where Lord Langton sprawled in his dressing gown, eyes wide and staring at the ceiling.

I felt for his pulse; there was none. 'What happened?'

'It must have been his heart; he cried out and clutched at his chest. It is not what you think. He liked to talk to me, that is all. But he mustn't be found here. We have to move him to his own room.'

With Sandro's valet as look-out, we half-carried, half-dragged Langton's not inconsiderable bulk through the corridors. We were nearly there when Melchizedek sprang from behind a potted palm. Sandro gave a muffled shriek and dropped his end; the creature leapt on to Lord Langton's chest, pawed at his face and began chattering.

'Shhh,' I hissed at it.

It spat at me and chattered louder.

'I know what he wants.' Sandro fumbled in Langton's pockets. He came up with a handful of nuts; the monkey snatched them and scuttled off.

We deposited Lord Langton in his own bed and tiptoed away. At breakfast it was announced that he had died peacefully in his sleep.

During dinner the next day a messenger appeared bearing a letter from Miranda. *Come at once*, it said, and on the gallop back to New Eden, through nine changes of mount, my mind fretted over the possibilities. Had something happened to the school – a fire? Or to the children – a new outbreak of smallpox, some other disease? Could Sebastian have run wild, or had Miranda herself fallen ill, or suffered some hurt? Or, God forbid, my children. Not Christopher, and oh, please not Grace, I prayed, though I knew it meant that if I had to, I would choose her over my own son. I offered God many promises if only He would spare Grace.

By the time I arrived, all other feelings had given way to rage at Miranda. I wanted to throttle her; nothing could have been worse than not knowing.

Had God heard me? Had he accepted my bargain and if so, which of the many mutually contradictory promises I'd made was I to keep? Grace was well; Christopher was drowned. He and Grace had been playing by the river with Stephen and Abigail.

'You left them on their own,' I said, though I knew perfectly well that they were always going off on their own.

'I don't know how it happened.' Miranda was red-eyed, twisting her hands in her skirt. 'Grace came running for me, said he'd disappeared. We looked for him everywhere. It was Stephen who found him downriver, in the rushes.'

Sebastian was distraught not to have been of any use and Miranda was so abject that to have shown my anger would have been like kicking a dog. And . . . I had never found the time to teach Christopher to swim, as I had Grace.

The only mercy was that I could defer telling Agnes that I had failed to look after our son, though I did write to the Enderbys in Oxford. I received a long letter back, expressing huge sorrow; they had doted on their only grandson far more than I'd realised. They recounted every detail of his visits to them, his pranks, his cleverness, the great career at Oxford that they had envisioned for him as a scholar and bibliophile. It seemed they knew him better than I did.

I took his body in its small coffin home to Farundell to be buried. I didn't bring Miranda. It was unreasonable, but I blamed her. I could not be angry, so I was cold.

It was the first time I'd been back to Farundell since I'd fled to Harfield. Andrew, now a major-general, had married two years ago; I had not been invited to the wedding. I recall nothing about his wife except that she had an extremely small mouth, through which she spoke rarely and without moving her lips.

If Andrew had been insufferable before, I do not know the word for what he was now. He had become as tight and tense as a fist. He'd always condemned Sebastian's and my – in his view – excessive drinking, but I caught him surreptitiously downing a large brandy before breakfast. When he saw me he turned red and marched stiffly from the room. I had the feeling he wanted to hit me.

My youngest brother Clarence was somewhere in the West Indies, seeking his fortune as a sugar planter, but I was expecting, if not precisely hoping, to greet my sisters. They were nowhere to be seen. When I asked about them, supposing that they'd been married off and relieved that I'd not had to attend their weddings, Andrew told me they had both died of the smallpox the previous year. He had not even bothered to write to me or to Isabel with the news. I wanted to hit him.

40

An Impossible Ideal

In Agnes's absence the administration of New Eden had slipped somewhat. Meryll's gifts were more in the fields of invention and inspiration, so it fell to me to wade through the pile of unanswered correspondence. It took the better part of a week, but I resolved most of the issues.

There remained one mystery: several children had vanished. It was our practice to place the children in work when they were ready to leave New Eden, at the age of fourteen or fifteen. Because they could read and write, were clean and well-mannered, they were much in demand and we always had a waiting list. The boys went into the better trades, some into clerking; a dozen or so had been sponsored by one or another of our patrons to attend university. The girls were much prized as upper servants, seamstresses, ladies' maids and so on, and went only to the best households. A few were training to be midwives, one had been taken on by an apothecary, and several had joined our staff.

In the last few months, four girls had not taken up their positions as arranged. The most recent case involved a girl named Jane who had been expected to begin work in the London household of a duke, where we had placed several other girls over the years. The letter from the duke's housekeeper said that she had never arrived, though our own records showed that she had left New Eden.

I summoned Mrs. Goode, the matron, who said that Jane had been issued with a new dress, cloak and shoes as was usual, and had been collected by one of the duke's servants. She could not recall any details about the other missing children.

I wrote to the duke's housekeeper, who replied irately that no servant of theirs had collected Jane; they were expecting her to be delivered, and if she was not available, could I please send someone else at once?

Had Mrs Goode been deceived, or was she deceiving me? I sent for her again. She repeated exactly what she'd said before; it sounded a trifle rehearsed. I sympathised; she had an ailing mother, had she not? Whose care was no doubt expensive. I pressed her, made veiled threats. She wouldn't give an inch, but she forgot to feign concern for the missing children.

I pretended to be taken in, shrugged, suggested that they had probably run off; ungrateful children, good riddance. With obvious relief, she agreed.

I was mulling this over when Meryll came in. 'How long has Mrs Goode been with us?' I asked.

'About four months, I think. Before that we had Mrs Yates. Who left to look after her father.'

I told him about the missing children. 'Of course it's possible that some of them have run away, but Mrs Goode is definitely lying about Jane.'

'But why?'

'I think she's been selling them. Jane is especially attractive, isn't she? And these others,' I read out their names, 'all good looking, as I recall. Don't look so incredulous. There is a market for pretty virgins. My brother once paid fifty guineas for one. What do we pay Mrs Goode? Two pounds a month.'

Meryll shook his head. 'But how could she? We trusted her. We thought she believed in New Eden.'

'Perhaps she can't afford to.'

'Am I a fool, Damory? To trust people?'

'I don't know.'

'You don't trust people, do you? You're always suspicious.'

'Obviously I haven't been suspicious enough.'

'We have to try to find the children, get them back.'

'Go and talk to Mrs Goode, see if you can get anything out of her. Tell her we won't prosecute her if she tells us everything.'

He went to find her, but returned almost immediately. 'She's run off. Packed a bag and left.'

I sought out Sebastian and found him in his room. The subject I wished to discuss seemed very out of place here, with warm sunshine flooding in the open window and the sounds of happy children floating up from the riverbank.

'If you wanted to purchase a virgin, where would you go?'

'I didn't think virgins were your sort of thing.'

'They're not.' I told him about Jane. 'I have to try to get her back.'

He laughed. 'You realise that this is like diving into the lake after that dead child?'

'Jane's not dead. At least I hope she's not. So where should I look?'

'Practically anywhere.' He picked up a newspaper and turned to the back page, which was filled with advertisements.

"'*Mrs Grimsby, the Lady Abbess of Marlborough Court, has laid in a new stock of virgins for the Season and has refurbished her rooms to accommodate gentlemen of all ages, sizes, tastes and caprices as, it is judged, will surpass every seminary of the kind yet known in Europe.*"

Here is another:

"Mrs Cleland of Berwick Street wishes to announce that several novices have recently entered the nunnery and, having been schooled in every nice manner and the most advanced techniques of pleasure, desire to present themselves to gentlemen of discernment. Doctor-certified."'

'Doctor-certified?'

'Some old quack sticks his finger up and says they're intact. You get a piece of paper with seal and signature. But it's nonsense, of course. Those girls are no more virginal than I am. You could trawl every brothel in London and never find a real one.'

'I can't give up before I start. Surely someone will have noticed Jane – a genuine virgin, pretty and well-mannered – she'd stand out from the crowd.'

'Try the auction at Mrs Quill's in King's Square. Top floor, first Thursday of every month, starting at midnight. The password for the door is . . . is . . . oh damn my memory. Something to do with tongue. Ah, that's it. Cunnilingus. Eliza Quill specialises in rarities, and if she says a girl is a virgin, it may possibly be true. Her clientele is of the highest rank. It's where the Prince of Wales goes for his special treats. I warn you, though, it's expensive.'

Over the next two weeks, while I waited for the first Thursday of August, I visited dozens of brothels from Soho to St James's. The merchandise on offer was, as Sebastian had predicted, of dubious quality, and nowhere did I find anyone like Jane. It was difficult to hold on to my memory of her, and after seeing hundreds of drab, derelict girls, all of whom were happy to be called Jane if it pleased me, the image of the real Jane had become a glowing, impossible ideal of youth, beauty and purity.

41

A Fortunate Girl

❧

Meryll had been relieved when I told him there was no point in accompanying me on these grim expeditions, but by the time the date of the auction came around, he'd worked himself up to it.

'Can't let you do it by yourself,' he said. 'And we may need this.' He showed me his purse – a hundred guineas of his own money to fund the purchase, if it turned out we had to buy her back.

'We probably won't find her,' I said, 'so don't get your hopes up.'

'We'll find her. I'm sure we will. If we were to abandon her I'd never forgive myself.'

Mrs Quill's establishment occupied a wide, bow-fronted house. A number of fine carriages were drawn up outside; I recognised many of the liveries. We arrived a little after eleven and, after paying a door fee of two guineas each, joined a glittering throng. The rooms on the ground floor were for dancing; light from extravagant crystal chandeliers shone on silk and lace, diamonds and gold. A grand marble stair led to the first floor, with gambling rooms and a restaurant. On the second floor an Italian pastiche was being performed by scantily-clad nymphs.

Meryll had not expected to see so many people he knew; everyone was astonished to see him. Not quite as astonished to see me, though a few mistook me for Sebastian and were surprised to find me still alive.

The activities on the lower floors discomfited Meryll for their frivolity and excess, but when we returned to the second floor, the pastiche had been replaced by a series of tableaux. Though based on the classical myths that he adored, the interpretations were so obscene they rocked him back on his heels. Men and women, some naked, some costumed as animals, frolicked with each other and with real animals – a goat, a swan, a pig, several snakes, a small horse, a large dog – in every permutation of the sexual act it was possible to imagine, and a few that were impossible to imagine and had to be seen to be believed.

Meryll covered his eyes, then lowered his hands, straightened his shoulders and willed himself to look. His expression flickered between horror and unwilling fascination. I tried to remember how I'd felt when Sebastian had first taken me to a place like this; perhaps just as shocked as Meryll, but far better at concealing it. My main concern had been not to embarrass my brother by appearing unsophisticated.

'Sebastian, is it you?'

I turned. 'No, it's Francis – Lucy?'

'No, it's Lizzie, but I'm called Eliza now. Mrs Eliza Quill.'

'Ah, so you're the famous Mrs Quill.' I bowed. 'Sebastian sent me, but he didn't say who you were. You're doing well, I see.' She was richly dressed and bejewelled, elaborately coiffed and powdered.

'Yes, I am.' She smiled, and I saw that beneath the lead-white paint, her face was badly scarred with smallpox.

'And how is Lucy?'

'Not so well. In the Fleet since last summer. Ten thousand pounds, she owes. She always was the stupid one. I send her money for rent and food, but . . .' She shrugged, took my arm and we strolled among the tableaux. 'Francis, my dear, do you recall that party where Lucy and I posed in a fountain of champagne?'

'Yes, who could forget it?'

'Well, what I cannot remember is where it was held. I'm writing my memoirs, you see, and I want to be sure I do not inadvertently suggest the correct house.'

'I don't know – it was during my first few weeks in London and I had no idea where I was most of the time.'

'You were delectable.'

'I was seventeen.'

'And now you are so ancient.'

'Sometimes it feels that way.'

'Are you married? Have you children?'

'Yes, and . . . yes.'

'That ages a man, though not always disagreeably. And how is Sebastian? I'm afraid I had to ban him last year. The last time I saw him he was being thrown out of Mrs Perry's establishment across the road.'

'He's dying, but seems to be doing it peacefully.'

'Peacefully? Sebastian? Don't you believe it.' She stopped to give instructions to a footman, then consulted her watch. 'So what brings you here, my dear? Anything special in mind?'

'I'm looking for a girl named Jane.'

When I described her, Eliza nodded. 'Oh yes – we call her Janine, more refined. She's from that school of yours.'

'And we want her back!' Meryll pushed between us.

'Be quiet, Meryll.' I took Eliza's arm and drew her away. 'Could we speak with her?'

'She will be preparing herself; she is the top item in tonight's auction, you know. New Eden girls always are.'

'Always are?' Meryll had followed, bouncing on his toes in agitation. 'How many have you stolen?'

Eliza narrowed her eyes. 'Francis, would you please inform this gentleman, though I am not certain that is the correct word, that I will not be spoken to that way in my own house.'

'Meryll, may I introduce Mrs Quill, an old and dear friend. Eliza, may I present Mr Edward Meryll, also a dear friend.'

They stared at each other with loathing.

'A gentleman would bow at this point,' I said.

'To a lady,' said Meryll, between clenched teeth.

I kicked him lightly behind his left knee; he bowed.

Eliza inclined her head fractionally.

'Meryll, would you be so kind as to wait here?' I led Eliza aside.

'Francis, you are so . . . commanding. You are ageing well, if I may say.' She squeezed my arm. 'If Janine proves to be beyond your means I may, perhaps, be free later.'

I kissed her hand. 'I will remember that. But first, could we not see Janine, just for a moment? It would set Meryll's mind at ease.'

'His mind, is it? Very well, but only as a favour to you. One word from him and I'll have him thrown out.'

She led us away from the public rooms and up the back stairs to a room full of laughter, chatter and the scents of many perfumes. A group of women clustered around a dressing table where a girl was having her hair done. A pile of silk gowns covered the bed, the floor was strewn with shoes and stockings.

'Not too much powder,' Eliza said. 'And keep it simple. Just the wreath of flowers.'

'Oh, Mrs Quill, you said I could wear feathers.'

'I did not. Janine, some old friends of yours have come to see you.'

The girl turned, saw us and gasped. 'Oh Lord, am I in trouble? You can't take me back, don't let them take me back, Mrs Quill. I know I didn't go where you put me, sirs, but you never asked what I wanted to do. And I don't want to be a lady's maid, truly I don't. I want to be a lady, a fine lady like Mrs Quill, who has a dozen maids of her own.'

'Oh Jane, you don't know . . .' Meryll began, but I stamped on his foot.

'We can't make you come back, Jane,' I said.

'My name is Janine now.'

'Janine. I know that this,' I gestured to the rich furnishings, the gowns, 'is very attractive. But have you considered the cost?'

'Every penny that Janine earns tonight will be her own,' Eliza said. 'Her nest egg.'

Meryll could not contain himself. 'Oh, so you get nothing in return for these gaudy clothes, these baubles and trinkets . . .'

Eliza turned on him. 'And good food, better than what your wonderful school provides, and excellent accommodation, a room of her own, with feather pillows and silk curtains, not a draughty dormitory with mice. She has dancing lessons and French lessons, and protection, and friendship, and a promising future, if she follows my advice and invests her money wisely. As long as she is happy here, she will pay me ten per cent of her future earnings. No one could possibly consider that unfair. She is a fortunate girl to have come to me. And now get out.'

'Wait for me downstairs, Meryll.' I pushed him none too gently out of the door. 'I apologise for my friend, Eliza.'

'What I despise,' she said, 'aside from the rudeness, is the assumption that he is good and I am bad. That his motives are pure, mine not. If I wanted only money, I need not take so much trouble.' She turned to the girls who'd listened, smiling. 'Carry on with your work, girls. It's our little Janine's birthday tonight.'

She led me out and closed the door behind us. 'I had a daughter, Francis. I think she was Sebastian's. I tried to raise her well, and keep her out of this, but . . . life was difficult then. I don't know why I'm telling you this. Maybe because Janine reminds me a bit of her. When she was six, a man I trusted sold her to a friend of his, who shared her with his friends. They had extreme tastes. They dumped her body in the river and I do not know if I am glad that it was, eventually, found.' She turned and strode away.

I found Meryll pacing up and down in front of a door which was guarded by two burly footmen. 'They won't let us upstairs without a password,' he said.

'We should go home, my friend. I don't think Jane can be rescued, if that's the word. You heard her; this is her choice.'

'Damn it, I'm not letting her go. We'll buy her back, and teach her to make a better choice. Any honest life is better than this degradation. You let that unspeakable woman wrap you around her little finger, Damory. Now what's the password?'

'Cunnilingus.'

'What?'

'Need I explain? You know Latin.'

He turned bright red. 'I can't say that.'

'Then you'll have to leave, won't you?'

'Please, Damory. Don't abandon her. She doesn't know what she's saying; she's just swept along by the excitement. It may start with pleasure and gratification, but this world will suck her down and drown her.'

His chosen metaphor could not have been more effective. 'All right, we'll go to the auction and we'll bid for her. If we win, we'll drag her kicking and screaming back to New Eden and lock her in, with a hard bed and draughts and mice and drab food and a grey worsted gown. She will be eternally grateful.'

42

A Dark and Bottomless Sea

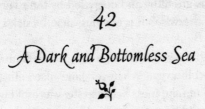

I gave the password; we ascended to the top floor and were shown into a large room filled with tables and chairs. At one end, below a curtained dais, a string quartet played. Pretty girls, fetchingly dressed in silk ribbons, flowers, feathers and nothing else, moved about offering beverages and informal sexual services. I ordered wine, Meryll a bottle of brandy. When it came, he drank two glasses off at once and poured another.

Across the room I noticed the duke into whose household Jane was to have gone as a lady's maid. I pointed him out to Meryll. 'She would have earned a few pounds a year in his house,' I said. 'He would have seduced her and, when she got pregnant, very likely thrown her on to the street. If not killed at once by a botched abortion, she would have had no choice but to become a street whore of the lowest sort. In all likelihood, drink and disease would have finished her off in a couple of years at best.'

'Is that the world we send them into? It is Hell. This is Hell. What have we been doing all this time?' He drained his glass.

'A great deal of good, but . . .'

'But the world is a vile and filthy cesspit. I look at these people, these rich people in their rich clothes, do you realise that we could support a dozen children for a year on what that man's coat cost, or that woman's hat, my God, Damory, that hat, and beneath it I see a skull, with maggots crawling out of her eyes, everyone, my God, everyone is full of maggots, they're all rotten, corrupt as all flesh is corrupt. There's no hope, we have been deluding ourselves, humans are filthy and degraded by their very nature, who can suppose otherwise? It is obvious, sick . . . sick . . . sickeningly obvious.'

He was beginning to slur his words; when he reached for the bottle I moved it away. 'Whatever Jane's fate,' I said, 'she has a better chance of happiness because she was at New Eden. If she hadn't come to us she would probably have died years ago.'

He stretched across the table, seized the brandy and refilled his glass.

'You really should not drink any more,' I said.

He stared blearily at me. 'Who are you . . . you . . . to tell me . . . tell me anything? I can see for myself, this, all this. Cesspit. And you're on her side, aren't you? That vile woman, that unspeakable whore.'

Eliza strolled among the tables greeting the patrons, pausing to sit for a few moments with one or two. When she came to us I rose and bowed. She sat down next to Meryll, who glowered at her.

She smiled graciously at him. 'Mr Meryll, I wonder if you will do me the honour of accepting a small gift as a peace offering?' She beckoned and a girl approached, wearing nothing but a flower in her hair and a pink ribbon around her waist. 'This is Angélique. She is a little like your sweet Jane, is she not?'

The girl knelt between Meryll's legs and began to unfasten his breeches. He leapt up with a cry and pushed her away. Eliza snapped her fingers and two footmen appeared behind his chair, seized his arms and held him down.

I felt I should protest, but she raised a warning finger. 'This is nothing to do with you, my dear. But if you truly think it is not a fitting gift, I will desist.' I could not say that he did not deserve it.

Eliza stayed to see the act completed. 'Thank you, Angélique,' she said. 'That was beautifully done.' She offered Meryll her handkerchief and stood. 'Enjoy the auction, Mr Meryll, and I do hope you come again.'

I stifled a laugh and turned away to allow Meryll to compose himself.

'Pass me the brandy,' he said after a time. 'I've disgraced myself.'

'Not at all. You have merely done what any man could not help but do. You are not above nature.'

'That poor girl.'

'It looked to me as if she enjoyed it; you obviously did – where is the harm?'

'To my pride, damn it.'

'We can go home now, if you like.'

'No. I will not admit defeat.'

The auction began. As Sebastian had said, Eliza specialised in rarities. First was a handsome black-skinned girl, shiny and polished as ebony, with startling white teeth and intricately plaited hair. A pair of fair-haired twins were next; they performed some remarkable contortions. There was a golden-brown girl from India with strangely orange hair down to her knees and a pale, doll-like girl from China, with slanted eyes and feet so tiny that she could not walk, but had to be carried out on a cushion.

Meryll had long since slumped in his chair. I'd decided the best policy was to encourage him to drink, in the hope that he would lose consciousness before Jane appeared. By the time she was announced he was snoring and, with a footman's help, I carried him out. He flailed about as we were dragging him into the carriage, muttered something about lost paradise, then collapsed into weeping and fell asleep. I took him home.

He woke as I was putting him to bed. 'It's all over,' he said.

'What's over?'

'No. . . noble exper. . . experiment. My life. Oh God, I think I'm going to be sick.'

I passed him the chamber pot.

'Better?' I said.

'Worse, far worse. Been so . . . so wrong, such . . . such a fool.' He reached for the chamber pot, retched again, then fell back on the pillow. 'You will see now, how it will fall apart, because I am . . . what am I, Damory?'

'You are very drunk.'

'No, I am nothing.'

'Oh, what nonsense.'

'I am worse than nothing, because I thought I was something.'

'You are becoming maudlin. Go to sleep.'

I made my way through the gardens to my house. It usually gave me pleasure to walk by the river, but tonight I felt a hollow sadness. Meryll had infected me with his despair. He'd lost some innocence I hadn't realised he'd possessed, perhaps because my own, if I'd ever had any, had been lost so long ago that I'd forgotten it existed.

I had not given much thought to the fate of our children after they left; many had no doubt deviated from the course on which we'd set them and I would never know. I stopped and listened to the water lapping at the bank. New Eden seemed an ineluctably eroding island in the midst of an ocean of corruption. I pictured the children falling, one by one, into a dark and bottomless sea.

That night I couldn't sleep. I stood in the doorway of Grace's room, watching her. I thought of Eliza and her lost daughter – my niece perhaps. I thought of Jane; had her transformation into Janine been a flight to freedom or a plunge to destruction? I thought of Lucy.

43

An Angel Taking Flight

🌺

The next morning I called on Meryll bearing a large cup of Morning Medicine. He was green and queasy and, mercifully, remembered almost nothing of the previous night, though a dark cloud still hung over him. 'We failed,' he said. 'We should have saved her.'

I envied his blotted memory. I, unfortunately, recalled every detail, and could find no excuses to put off a visit to Lucy. As I rode into town I pictured her as she had been when we met: luscious and light-hearted, with silky skin and laughing eyes. She must have been about twenty then, near the height of her fame.

I'd heard that she'd gone on to become the mistress of an earl, or a duke or, some said, a royal personage.

Nothing could have prepared me for the Fleet. The prison was stuffed with more than three hundred debtors, many sharing cramped cells with their families. Those who could afford the fee – about six shillings a week – rented rooms on the first or second floors, many of which had a chimney and a window, while others made do with a few feet of floor space in one of the larger rooms on the top floor. Those still less well off were accommodated in the cellar, where I was, for a shilling, directed. These rooms had no windows, though the better ones had tiny square openings high in the walls.

'Looking for anyone in particular, sir?' asked the guard.

'Yes, a woman named Lucy, a pretty woman, here since last summer.'

'Can't say I recall anyone by that name.'

I gave him a shilling.

'Ah, you must mean Lucy Loosecunt. Oh yes, she was quite the tasty morsel when she arrived.'

'Was? She's not dead, is she?'

'No, but she's not pretty any more.' He guffawed. 'She's a proper bitch, that one. Got into fights with everyone, had her eyes gouged out. That detracts somewhat from her appeal.'

'Where is she?'

'She clawed me last week.' He indicated a red weal on his cheek. 'So I had to put her in the back room to cool her temper. And she's behind in her rent.'

'I want to see her.'

'She's not allowed visitors until her rent is paid, plus the fines for fighting and for wounding a warder. That would be, let me see, one pound, nine shillings and tuppence.'

I paid, and he let me into a room so low-ceilinged that I had to stoop. The walls were running with water, the unpaved floor was deep in sewage. The stench was unbelievable. Rats blinked incuriously in the dim light and at first I thought they were the only inhabitants; then I discerned two piles of rags from which protruded what might have been human limbs, manacled to the wall. I bent over the nearest, but I could tell from the smell that the rags covered a corpse. I was gagging now, and the desire to flee was almost overwhelming, but I made myself approach the other. I recognised Lucy by the weeping sores that had been her eyes.

I staggered to the door and summoned the guard. 'Get her out of there.'

'Can't do that, sir. Warden's orders. Assaulting a guard means a month in the back room.'

'Or a fine, I'm sure.'

'Five pounds.'

'That is highway robbery.'

'If you say so, sir.'

'I don't carry that much money.'

He shrugged.

I fought the urge to run him through with my sword and reached for my purse instead. 'All I have with me is two pounds. I will bring the rest later.'

'What do you take me for? No money, no release.'

I seized him by the throat and rammed him against the wall, squeezing his windpipe until he gasped. 'I will go and get your money, you piece of shit. But you will take her out of that dungeon at once or I will kill you. Is that clear?'

He wheezed and his eyes began to roll back in his head. I gave him a final shake and propelled him towards the door. He unlocked Lucy's shackles, led her out and, at my order, took her upstairs where I secured a room for her on the first floor. I left her there, went to my bank for the money and, on the way back, bought a bed and blankets, a cup, bowl and spoon, a dress, shift, stockings and shoes from the shops outside the prison walls. I chose the least insalubrious of the food stalls and made arrangements for her to be sent two meals a day. Back in the Fleet, I paid her fines and three months' rent in advance, and ordered some water brought to her room with a basin for washing.

Lucy had remained huddled in the corner where I'd left her. I could barely bring myself to touch her; she was crawling with lice and covered with ulcerated sores which stank of pus. She seemed not to be aware of me but when I tried to peel off the rags which were glued to her body by blood and excrement, she roused from her stupor and in a graceful gesture I remembered well, took out her mottled, flaccid breasts and offered them to me with a toothless parody of her old smile and wink.

'Not just now, Lucy,' I said. 'Look, I've bought you a new gown. From Monsieur Duplis. The scarlet paduasoy, embroidered with golden thread. And this shift, the finest lawn, with Alençon lace and satin ribbons. Touch it, it's very soft.' I took her filthy hand and stroked the coarse fabric. 'Let's have a little wash, shall we? And then you can try them on for me.'

When I returned the next day, she'd sold the clothes and furniture for gin. I chided her and replaced them, but in a couple of days they were gone again. She said she was starving, and I should give her money for food. I checked that the meals I'd ordered were being delivered; they were, but she was selling them on immediately. The following week she had rented out her room and was back in the cellar. A few days later she was dead.

I could not bear to imagine her in a pauper's grave, so I bought her a resting place at St Bride's and a marble headstone with an angel taking flight. I invited Eliza and Sebastian to her funeral; neither came, but Meryll did, and Tunnie, who remembered her.

44

A Paroxysm of the Heart

❧

We had received a few letters from Agnes, and I discovered that she was one of those people whom one comes to know better in writing than one did in person. The letters showed both wit and exuberance, neither qualities that she'd had much opportunity to display at New Eden, or, indeed, in Oxford. The first, posted from Calais, described a six-hour crossing from Dover. Jack, she related with thinly disguised relish, had been sick from the moment he set foot on board. He'd spent the entire voyage curled in a miserable ball below deck while she stood in the bow, whipped by wind and rain, earning the admiration of old sailors and fancying herself Odysseus, strapped to the mast and listening for the sirens' song.

The next letter recounted the journey by diligence to Paris. She was shocked by the prices of food, transport, accommodation. Assuming that Jack's easy-going nature was making him a ready dupe, she'd taken back the purse only to find that, as a woman, she was routinely charged double. The countryside was uninteresting, though she was thrilled to realise that she was travelling on what must be a Roman road: absolutely straight, and planted with evenly spaced poplars receding across the flat plain before and behind. Having been accustomed to English roads and carriages, she was surprised to discover that standards were not universal. Despite her wide reading, she acknowledged, she'd had little idea of the world. Twice the carriage had run off the road due to the carelessness of the postilion; the second time had resulted in a broken axle. They had to pass the night in Amiens, where they were unable to find space at a decent inn and had to sleep in a very dirty room shared with two others.

With Paris itself, she was disappointed. There were English and Germans in all the parks and cafés; the costs were astronomical. She did not speak the perfect French she thought she had and was everywhere misunderstood. Then came a short letter posted from Lyons, saying that they had resolved to head for the Alps and cross into Italy, visiting Paris on the way back if time allowed.

After a long gap came an exultant letter from Rome, which was everything she had dreamed, and more. She was in rhapsodies about the Coliseum and the Pantheon; she walked among fallen columns and obelisks reciting Cicero while Jack fended off importunate beggars. They had rented rooms – the cost seemed reasonable to her – and she had signed up for a month-long course in antiquities taught by a Cambridge don. Being Agnes, she could not help but complain about the neglect and decay brought about by the ignorance and laziness of the populace, and had joined the Society for the Preservation of Ancient Monuments.

I discovered that I missed her rather a lot. Frequently I found myself wanting to tell her about some little thing that had happened, or some amusing thought I'd had, then realising with a jolt of disappointment that I could not. I saved them up for her return and wondered if, perhaps, I had always loved her after all.

One rainy afternoon in November I was standing at the window when a carriage pulled up and Jack descended. I rushed outside, my heart rising. Had Agnes returned already? I pictured her aglow with the satisfaction of her travels, burnished with sophistication, brimming with stories to tell. I brushed past Jack with a careless greeting and reached into the carriage to hand her out. It was empty.

'Where is she?'

He shook his head and wouldn't meet my eyes.

'Where the hell is she?'

'She's buried in the English cemetery at Leghorn.'

I hit him so hard that it lifted him off his feet and laid him flat on the ground. Miranda came running, looking wildly from him to me and back again. 'Oh my God, Francis, you've killed him!' She knelt at his side; he moaned. Servants came; he was carried indoors. I stood for a long time in the courtyard, then had a horse saddled and rode into town where I spent the night with Eliza Quill and two of her charming girls.

The next day I returned to New Eden and apologised to Jack. I had broken his nose, which made it difficult to understand him, but he managed to tell me what had happened. Agnes had wanted to spend the autumn in Florence, where her Cambridge don would be teaching. Rather than endure the terrible roads, they had booked passage on a coastal felucca to Leghorn, from where it was but a short distance inland to Florence. The journey had taken several days and Jack had drunk so much brandy to combat the seasickness that he'd paid no attention when Agnes complained that she'd been bitten in the night, by what she didn't know – a rat or a scorpion or a spider. She wanted to be set ashore, but the sailors had refused to stop as long as the wind was favourable. It was not until they reached the port and Jack emerged from his stupor that he realised her entire leg was swollen and she was delirious with fever. She died two days later without regaining consciousness. I still wanted to hit him, so I left.

All the time Agnes had been away, her presence had remained in the house; only now did it seem that she was gone. I went into her room and lay on her bed. It had neither memories nor comfort for me; I had not shared it for years. I stared at her dressing table, bare except for a small figurine of a dancer that I had given her. She had been a surprisingly good dancer, although it had taken much effort to persuade her to participate in such frivolity. When I first met her she'd thought of herself as someone who did not dance.

At least I was spared having to tell her about Christopher; she must already know. Were they together in Heaven? Surely Christopher had gone straight to Heaven; it would be too cruel to keep a mother from her child, so Agnes must be there too. If there was such a place. I wanted to believe in Heaven; but would I then have to believe in Hell? If I did, I would have to imagine that I might end up there, suffering for eternity. What would it be like? To bodily suffering one might become accustomed, but if it was truly Hell, the anguish would be of the mind and soul as well – loss and despair, remorse twisting like a knife in one's heart. Like life, but without the hope of an ending. Or was Hell in fact where I now was, and the hope a cruel illusion? For a moment I glimpsed a world of Heaven and Hell mixed together, that both was and was not the same as the daily life of man on Earth. I felt a twinge of vertigo and sat up abruptly. The room seemed to tilt, then righted itself. I realised I'd eaten nothing since the previous morning.

I sat for a while on the edge of the bed, unable to summon the will to go in search of food. I imagined that I might remain sitting there for ever, dust accumulating around me, rising finally to bury me.

There was the sound of footsteps in the passage and Isabel appeared at the door. 'Miranda sent a message and I came as soon as I could.' She sat beside me. 'You mustn't blame Jack.'

'I don't see why not.'

She took my hand. 'She was having a wonderful time, wasn't she?'

I stared at the dancing figurine. 'I think she was happy for the first time in her life. It's what she'd wanted to do when I made her marry me instead.' I pictured a different course that Agnes might have taken, a happier one.

'You gave her a good life, Francis.'

'Do you think so? By what reckoning? I got her pregnant, forced her to marry me, took her to Farundell where our sisters mocked her and nearly killed her, put her through a ghastly childbirth, abandoned her while I went riding out every day with another woman's child, then hauled her off here and all but chained her to a desk in the office as though she was nothing more than a clerk while I took up with Miranda . . . and others. She'd have been better off if she'd never met me.'

'You can't know that.'

'But I feel it.' I stood. 'I have to write to her parents.'

I knew that I should bring the news to them in person but, coward that I was, I couldn't. What I really wanted was to punish Jack by making him go. Unfortunately, as far as the Enderbys were concerned, he did not exist. Agnes had concocted an elaborate fiction for them in which her travelling companion was Lady Jacqueline Hathaway, a wealthy and respectable widow. I had been impressed by the fluency with which she had constructed this alternative scenario, embellished with details such as Lady Hathaway's penchant for extremely large hats and her fondness for her pugs, Paulino and Sylvestra, who accompanied her everywhere in a specially designed case with little windows and cushions embroidered with their names.

In my letter to the Enderbys I had to invent a fate for Lady Hathaway: after having written to me with the sad news, she fell from her chair while crossing an Alpine pass and was lost in a bottomless ravine. It was what I wished had happened to Jack. While I was at it, I invented a more pleasant death for Agnes: a paroxysm of the heart while strolling blissfully in the moonlit Forum in the company of scholars and poets.

After Jack's nose healed, he took himself off to his and Miranda's relations in the North. I had let it be known that I couldn't bear the sight of him. Miranda attempted feebly to plead his cause, but I was still angry with her about Christopher's death and now, in my remorse, could not stop myself from implicating her in the guilt I felt about Agnes.

45

Whom Can We Trust?

🌿

As much as possible the school's administrative dilemmas, though quietly multiplying, had been put off until Agnes's return; 'Leave it for Agnes' had become a refrain. But that was far from our only problem. With the death of Lord Langton we had lost our most powerful advocate and protector; in his absence, the Board of Governors was revealed to have very mixed feelings indeed about our ideas and methods.

Meryll had hoped to improve matters by hiring a stern Scottish lady named Mrs McMurkle to replace Mrs Goode. Her chief qualification seemed to have been the vehemence of her loathing for moral turpitude in all its forms. She had her own ideas about the efficient management of children and reorganised our procedures so thoroughly that half the staff left and the remaining half worked at odds with each other. New Eden was in a state of barely controlled chaos which I did my best to ignore, but one morning I was summoned to the office to confront a gang of irate creditors. I assured them that the delay could only be due to a misunderstanding, collected their invoices and, after asking them to form an orderly queue, slipped out of the back door.

Meryll was sitting under a tree transcribing its thoughts. He'd been spending more time with the trees than with people since our visit to Eliza Quill. 'Does your friend here have any money?' I asked. 'Or perhaps advice on how to obtain some?'

'If only,' he said. A golden leaf fluttered down. 'Thank you,' he called up.

'I have a feeling it won't be enough to go round. We seem to owe,' I flicked through the bills, 'nearly three hundred pounds. Why, by the way, did we need two dozen silver candlesticks?'

'What?'

'At four pounds nine shillings each.'

'That's mad.'

'You signed for them, look.'

'That's not my signature.'

I looked more closely; he was right. We perused the rest of the invoices and found that Meryll's signature had been forged twice, mine once. We spent the afternoon searching every shed, office, storeroom, barn, cellar and attic for the silver candlesticks, three cases of fine claret and eighteen damask rose-bushes. We found none of them. We did find, under a pile of sacks at the back of a coal shed, a box containing eight silver coffee pots; in a cellar, a case of French brandy; in a stable, five ormolu clocks; in a disused storeroom, a hundred yards of Mechlin lace and in an attic, four bolts of crimson velvet: items for which the bills had not yet arrived.

Meryll would have hauled it all out and returned it to the merchants immediately, but I persuaded him that it would be more satisfying to let it remain, pretend ignorance and then catch the thief when he came for the spoils.

We went back to my house and drank a large glass of brandy apiece. 'I have begun to suspect everyone,' said Meryll. 'Except you, of course.'

'Likewise.'

'Could it be Wimberly?' Meryll named the head gardener. 'Or that weasel fellow who works in the office – what's his name?'

'Edwards?'

'That's him. He'd know our signatures. Maybe he and Wimberly together.'

'I remember Agnes said that things were always going missing.'

'This isn't petty theft,' Meryll said. 'It's too well planned. I wonder if the merchants are in collusion.'

'They must be – surely they would know we hadn't ordered all that.'

'Whoever it is must have accomplices outside.'

'Could you ask the trees if they've seen anything?'

'They do not notice such tiny flitters,' Meryll said. 'Our movements are much too fast for their perception.'

'I was joking.'

'Oh.'

'We must set a watch on all five hiding places. And there may be more we haven't found.'

'We need help, but whom can we trust?'

I summoned Tunnie, who pointed out that although things might be hidden in many places, they could only leave by three means – the main gate on to the road, the side gate, or the river.

'So we need two people at each location,' Meryll said. 'One to watch and one to fetch the others at the first sign of any activity. Are there three other people we can trust?'

'Joseph,' said Tunnie.

'And me.' Sebastian came in with Miranda. 'I am not as useless as you seem to think.'

'Nor am I,' said Miranda. 'We have been listening at the keyhole and insist that we be allowed to help.'

Sebastian was full of high spirits and exchanged conspiratorial glances with me; I could tell that he was remembering the games we'd played as children. We agreed that I would watch by the river with Miranda, Meryll and Tunnie at the side gate, Sebastian and Joseph at the main gate.

'Will they try it tonight, do you think?' Meryll had been so morose, it was good to see him taking an interest.

'I would imagine that the less time the things have to remain hidden, the better for them,' I said. 'But we'll keep watch every night if we have to.'

We pretended to retire as usual, then slipped out and took up our posts, armed with pistols. At Tunnie's suggestion we'd dressed in dark clothes and blacked our faces and hands with soot. Miranda and I, bundled in coats and blankets, concealed ourselves in a clump of trees on a slight rise, with a view of the riverbank in both directions.

'Thank you for letting me help,' she whispered.

The sky was overcast but the unseen moon shed a dim grey light. We waited. After a while Miranda moved closer and tentatively slipped her hand into mine. We waited some more; she fell asleep with her head on my shoulder. Nothing happened.

The next day we made surreptitious checks on the hiding places; they were undisturbed except one, to which two unmarked crates had been added. Meryll rather got into the act, playing the oblivious dupe. When the creditors returned, he made a great show of telling them that their bills would certainly be paid, even though he'd had no time to look at them as yet.

At night, equipped with flasks of coffee, we returned to our vantage points. The sky was clear, and when the moon set it was very dark indeed, the trees only discernible as murky blots. The river glimmered faintly with reflected stars.

Miranda curled up with her head in my lap. After a while I thought she was asleep and kissed her softly on the forehead.

'Oh, Francis,' she whispered.

'Shhh.'

I heard the splash of oars in muffled oarlocks; a shielded lantern in the bow of a wherry revealed two men. As they pulled in to the shore I sent Miranda off to alert the others.

The men climbed out with the lantern. A shadow detached itself from a clump of bushes, words were exchanged and all three men moved off. Sebastian came up silently behind me and, a moment later, Meryll.

'They've gone off to fetch things,' I said. 'We'll wait till they come back. Are the torches ready?'

'Yes, sir,' said Tunnie.

'What should I do?' whispered Miranda.

'Stay right here.'

We heard grunts and curses as the thieves returned, heavily burdened. I indicated with gestures that we should spread out in a line: Meryll, Sebastian and I in the centre, flanked by Tunnie and Joseph with torches ready to light. We got to within twenty yards before they saw us.

'Stop where you are,' I called out, 'or we will shoot.'

'You are outnumbered, villains!' cried Sebastian. 'Surrender or die!'

Tunnie and Joseph lit the torches, momentarily blinding me. I caught a glimpse of a pistol raised to fire and flung myself sideways, pulling Sebastian to the ground. The bullet whizzed over our heads. Meryll returned fire, discharging both of his pistols. There was a cry and a splash. I fired in the general direction of the boat and we rushed forward. One man was desperately rowing away; Sebastian fired at him but missed. A second man was lying in the shallow water; we hauled him up the bank. He'd been hit in the abdomen and was bleeding badly. The third man had vanished.

The shots brought people running and I looked to see if anyone was conspicuous by their absence. Wimberly was first on the scene, but that could be simply because the gardener's cottage was closest. In the throngs that followed I saw Edwards, looking convincingly sleep-addled. The wounded man was carried to the infirmary; I followed, hoping to question him, but he died. I sent someone to fetch the constable and we all made statements. No one, unfortunately, was able to say whose bullet had felled the man, and I pointed out that it might well have been the other thief, firing wildly in the dark as he had. The constable seemed inclined to favour this explanation.

When he left, we went to my house for brandy, moderately pleased with ourselves. 'It would have been better to have caught at least one of them alive,' I said. 'Now we may never know who their accomplice was.'

'Surely he will have run away by now,' Meryll said.

'That would advertise his identity,' Sebastian said. 'Maybe he'll try to carry on as normal.'

'And start the thieving all over again as soon as we let down our guard,' I said.

Meryll groaned. 'I don't think I could bear to live indefinitely with this level of distrust.'

'Shaken your faith in human nature?' Sebastian asked.

'Oh, that was quite thoroughly shaken a while ago,' said Meryll, yawning on his way to the door. 'I'm going to bed.'

'And I,' said Sebastian. He looked pale, with bright spots of colour on each cheek.

'You're all right?' I said. 'Not hurt when I knocked you down?'

'Not at all. Haven't had so much fun in years. I . . . I . . . my God, this is hard, baby brother. I owe you my life.'

'Nonsense. It would have missed you by a mile.'

'I don't think so.'

I followed him upstairs. Miranda must have fallen asleep waiting for me – we'd been two hours with the constable. For the first time since Christopher died, I wanted her. I undressed without lighting a candle, slipped into bed and reached for her.

She wasn't there. Nor was she in her sitting room, her closet,

Grace's room, the drawing room, music room or library. I even went downstairs and roused the maids; they had not seen her. I found her at first light exactly where I'd left her, in the clump of trees where we'd waited. She must have been standing in the shadows; the bullet meant for Sebastian had torn through her chest.

46

The Accumulation of Choices

🌱

The day of Miranda's funeral was cloudy and still, with a thin cold drizzle. After the service and the burial in the parish churchyard everyone returned to Meryll's house for dinner. I slipped out and walked along the river, then sat on a bench, transfixed by the minute drops of water that beaded on the fabric of my cloak. Each drop, I saw, fell along its own path and landed where only it could land, its fate determined from the moment it left the heavens and began its descent to earth. In time, several drops would coalesce, grow heavy and slip, catching others and pulling them down.

After a time I became aware that Meryll was sitting at my side. 'Come into the house,' he said.

I shook my head. 'I'm not fit company.'

He lit his pipe and stretched out his legs, indicating that he had no plans to leave me in peace. 'Go away, Meryll,' I said. 'Proximity to me is hazardous to health.'

'What are you talking about?'

'Not so long ago I warned Miranda to stay away from me. She didn't listen and now she's dead.'

'Miranda was shot by a thief. It wasn't your fault.'

'No? But it was. She was there because she was desperate to please me. I'd been unkind to her, unreasonably angry, blaming her for things that were my own fault. I was there because in my arrogance I persuaded you that we should try to catch the thief ourselves. The thief fired his pistol because I threatened to shoot him. The bullet found her because I leapt out of the way. She was standing in its path because I told her to stay there.'

'She was there because she wanted to help,' Meryll said. 'We were there because it was the only way to find out what was going on. We were armed because it would have been mad not to be. You warned them because it was the fair thing to do. The thief fired because he was a violent criminal. You leapt to save your brother's life. Anybody might find themselves in the path of a bullet at any time. She could have stood a few inches to the right or left and it would have missed her. In the end it was just fate.'

'That is meaningless. What is fate, then, if not the accumulation of choices?'

'If that is what it is, all the more reason why you cannot blame yourself for what happens to another – their choices, in fact the choices of dozens of people play their part. And it is illogical to suppose that keeping a distance from you will affect anyone's fate, or affect it in the way you hope.' He leaned forward, enjoying the disputation. 'It may even have the opposite effect, might help to bring about the very thing you hope to avoid.'

'You always come up with a convenient twist, don't you? I should have remembered that it is impossible to win an argument with you.'

'You always say that when you know that I am right and won't admit it.'

Later that day Jack appeared. Meryll had written to him, summoning him from the North, but he hadn't made it in time for the funeral. I walked with him to Miranda's grave. Wet leaves lay thick on the ground; the mound was covered with a golden blanket. I would not have blamed him for anger, but he said nothing, his face unutterably sad. He put his hand on my shoulder; we leaned against each other.

47

The Perfect Substance

🌿

I resumed the routines of my old life and tried to keep busy, but I was always falling into holes where Miranda had been, or Agnes or Christopher. I would find myself paralysed by memories, unable to recall where I was going, what I was doing. As much as possible, I retreated to Bayliss's laboratory. In that place of careful processes, precise measurements and scrupulous observation of cause and effect, I kept pain and disorder at a distance.

I admired Bayliss; he seemed to be well on the way to transcending the mess of human miseries that had entangled me. He was relentless in his struggle with the sufferings of material existence but possessed of an inner serenity that made him certain, despite all setbacks, that the goal – the perfected man – could and would be reached. I found myself telling him things I had never told anyone. He would listen closely, sometimes nodding, sometimes putting a gentle query. I told him about Johanna and Purefoy. He did not judge; he made no attempt to comfort or excuse but somehow just being with him eased my soul.

The weather turned frosty. Sebastian weakened, but was beset by strange excitements. He had grown very thin; his hands were like claws, blue-veined, and his rings became so loose that he stopped wearing them. He rambled on about salvation, how near it was, how soon it would come. Stephen and Abigail sang for him every day, often staying to play a game of cards or backgammon. Grace had stopped trying to sing with them; instead she assisted the cook in the preparation of nourishing possets. I asked Sebastian if he regretted not having children of his own but he only laughed, a great raucous cackle that went on and on until it frightened me.

My sleep was again plagued by awful dreams, but laudanum failed to bring oblivion; it merely made them more real. The details varied, but all were the same in essence: Grace was dying and I could not stop it. In some she wasted away, in others she burned or drowned. In one she shrank and shrivelled into a tiny, hideous doll before she dwindled into nothing and vanished. She was eaten by rats or shot; she bled to death or was crushed; she turned to water and slipped through my fingers; she turned to ice and shattered; she crumbled to dust in my arms.

When I was with her I was filled with fear, torn between a desire to hold her close and terror that if I did, she would die as she did every night in my dreams. Whenever Isabel came, Grace would run to her for comfort, and when, near Christmas-time, Isabel suggested that Grace should stay with her at Harfield for a week or two, I agreed to let her go. Grace immediately shed the air of caution and restraint that had come over her and was soon chattering about a new pony and the promise of puppies. I realised that it must have been very black for her, alone with only me, sad and silent, and Sebastian, mad and dying.

At night, to fend off sleep and dreams, I paced the gardens. One night, as I was passing the laboratory, I heard voices within. One I recognised as Bayliss's, though he spoke softly. His companion only whispered and I was unable to make out any words or guess who it was. I stayed to listen because they obviously did not wish to be overheard, and I could not imagine what Bayliss was being so secretive about. Then I heard him say, quite clearly, 'But

I love you.' The other person immediately hushed him; Bayliss continued in a whisper. I could only distinguish a few words, but it was clear that he desired a sexual act which was being withheld. 'I cannot get any more money for you so soon,' Bayliss said, his voice breaking. 'I was almost killed.'

They moved away from the window then, and only small groans suggested that Bayliss had prevailed. I heard him cry out, a few words which sounded like 'perfect substance'. There followed some minutes of silence, then footsteps approached the door around the corner from where I stood. 'Come back tomorrow night,' Bayliss said. 'I will have the elixir for you, and you will see what will happen this time – it will make you . . .'

'To the devil with your elixir,' whispered his companion. 'If you don't have the money I will tell them about you.'

Soft footsteps receded; I heard Bayliss weeping quietly and almost made my presence known, but thought better of it. If he wanted to confide in me he had plenty of opportunities.

The next morning I told Meryll what I'd heard. At once he suggested that Bayliss had been behind the thefts, the man who'd got away.

'Bayliss a thief? I cannot believe it.'

'Obviously not by choice; he's being threatened.'

'But if anyone believes in New Eden, it's Bayliss,' I said. 'And if there's anyone I trust . . .'

Meryll shook his finger at me. 'Ah, Damory, I never thought to find you the credulous one.'

'Nor I to find you so ready to believe evil of a friend.'

He shrugged. 'Give me another explanation, then.'

I could think of none.

'And his companion,' Meryll said. 'You are sure you have no idea who she was?'

'I heard only whispers. All whispers sound alike.'

'They plan to meet again tonight?'

I nodded.

'Then we must place ourselves where we can hear, and if Bayliss is innocent, we will leave him to sort out his difficulties as best he can.'

It was so like a plan I might have suggested that I had to agree.

48

One Step Away from Eternal Life

That night, while Bayliss was at supper, we slipped into a storeroom adjoining the laboratory. It had a slatted opening above its door through which we would be able to hear, and a lock which I fastened from within, wedging a nail into the keyhole so it would seem jammed if anyone tried to enter.

After about an hour had passed we heard Bayliss come in. He lit a candle; there was the clink of glass, the grate of coal being shovelled into the furnace.

'It must work,' he muttered. 'This time it will surely work.'

Whatever was afoot, it was clearly not just an assignation; his medicine was involved somehow. I thought I'd known every detail of his work; it perplexed and saddened me to realise that he had hidden things, evidently very important things, from me.

I'd heard no one enter and almost jumped when Bayliss said, 'Ah, thank God you've come.' He was immediately hushed, and continued in a whisper. 'Soon there will be no need for secrecy. You will be revealed as the perfect . . .'

'Do you have the money?' whispered the other.

'I have the elixir. All you need do is drink this and money will be nothing to you. You will see everything that is hidden to human eyes . . .'

'I see you, old man. I know what you really are.'

'Just drink this, please.'

'Are you mad? You think to get rid of me with poison.'

'As God is my witness, I love you and would never harm you. This is life that I offer you, not death.'

'You drink it, then.'

'You know I cannot. It is made with your substance, and will work only for you.'

'I will not drink any more of your filthy potions, old man. Give me the money.'

'I told you. There is no money. I cannot do it again, they are watching too closely.'

Meryll nudged me; he'd been right but I hadn't wanted to believe it. What hurt me most was to hear Bayliss refer to me as one of 'them'. In our shared love of chemistry, it had always been he and I united against 'them': the uncomprehending masses.

'Just be patient,' Bayliss was saying, his voice breaking above a whisper. 'Maybe in a month or two.'

'Too late, old man. Tomorrow I will land the big one and then we're away. I will leave a letter telling about you and the children you've poisoned.'

Abandoning all attempt at whispering, Bayliss cried, 'You are a devil not an angel! You are Satan disguised as a child!'

Footsteps receded, a door opened and closed. There was only the sound of Bayliss weeping.

Meryll began fumbling at the door; when he finally got it open Bayliss was staring, agape.

'We heard everything,' Meryll said. 'Who was that you were with?'

'It's all over.' Bayliss sank into a chair. 'I think I will go to China. I have always wanted to study the medical practices of China.'

'I'll be damned if you go anywhere before you tell me what's been going on.' Meryll was angrier than I'd ever seen him.

'Oh, it is nothing you could understand. Now Francis here, he might understand, but he would object nonetheless, wouldn't he?'

I shook my head, at a loss for words.

'You're no better than a common thief,' Meryll said. 'And a murderer, apparently. What children have you poisoned?'

'They were one step away from eternal life, you idiot. Is that not worth a small risk?'

Meryll seized him by the collar, lifted him from his chair and shook him. 'That was a child you were with, wasn't it?'

'A child? He's no child. He has never been a child. He is Satan incarnate.'

'Put him down, Meryll,' I said. I had already grasped what Bayliss had been doing; after all, it was no different in principle from what he and I had done, making medicines, testing them on ourselves and others. It had just gone further than I'd realised, and several mysterious deaths among the children were now explained. A deep chill crept over my soul. 'What did he mean, your friend, about the big one?'

'I have no idea,' Bayliss said. 'He always has some scheme in hand.'

'You will tell us who he is,' Meryll said, 'or we will see you hanged for theft and murder.'

'There is no proof and I will tell you nothing.'

'Why should you protect him,' I asked, 'if he is Satan incarnate?'

'I love him.'

We locked Bayliss in the storeroom and made our way back to my house. Meryll's anger had turned to despair. 'It really is over,' he said, so quietly I almost didn't hear.

I could make no argument. With Bayliss's betrayal some final blow had been struck to the edifice that had been my life. I sat heavily in a chair and stared at the empty grate.

'We have to find the child,' Meryll said at last. 'And he must testify against Bayliss, who must hang.'

I had no enthusiasm, nor any ideas about how the child could be identified.

'Whoever he is, he has a bag of money. We must search the boys' dormitory, question all of the children.' He leapt up, fired once again. 'It is our only chance. And we must do it right away, too fast for anyone to slip away or hide.' He was halfway out of the door. 'Aren't you coming?'

I shook my head. 'You don't need my help. I think I'd rather just sit here for a while.'

'I do need you. We must act fast. Come along, damn it.' He seized my sleeve and pulled me outside.

The night air was bracing; a sharp north wind brought a light, stinging rain as we made our way among the staff cottages, rousing the teachers and nurses. We positioned some at the doors and windows of the boys' dormitory, then sent the others in with instructions to take the place apart.

49

The Painless One

We waited in the office and received the results before dawn. Hidden under floorboards or in the mattresses of thirty-eight of our fifty-two boys the searchers had found knives, slingshots, truncheons, gin, tobacco, opium and small amounts of money. But one find stood out – three purses stuffed with coins from the mattress of Stephen Silver.

I was shocked speechless, convinced that the searchers had made an error, but they insisted they had not. Nor had Stephen tried to deny that the money was his, kicking and scratching like a fiend and cursing them for thieves and puggards.

I emptied the purses on to the desk. A pile of golden guineas spilled out and, almost buried, a jewelled ring – no, three massive jewelled rings that I recognised as Sebastian's.

'"The big one",' I said. 'I should have known.'

'What do you mean?' said Meryll.

'My brother. All along he's been after one thing. Send for Abigail.'

Abigail proved not yet to have been violated. When questioned, she revealed that under Stephen's guidance special games had been played, in which Sebastian had been allowed progressively greater liberties. She knew that something important was to happen very soon, for which she would be rewarded with extra sweets.

A sudden look of terror crossed her face. 'Please don't tell Stephen, sir. He'll punish me for sure. It was supposed to be a secret.' She began to cry.

'You've done nothing wrong, Abigail, and no one will punish you if you tell me everything.' Awash with a nightmarish sense of foreboding, I tried to speak softly. 'Did Grace play these special games, too?'

She nodded. 'Grace was good at them, but then Stephen did something to make her go away, and after that Lord Damory said I was the best one.'

She left the office in the care of a nurse. I think Meryll tried to speak to me, but I couldn't hear him. Red rage blotted my vision and roared in my ears. I went to my house and climbed the stairs to Sebastian's room. He was asleep in his bed and if Meryll had not stopped me I would have run him through with my sword where he lay. He woke, smiled at us and sat up.

'Is it morning already?' he said. 'No, no thank you, no breakfast today. I must rise and dress. Where's Joseph?'

'Here, sir.' Joseph appeared at the door, wigless, hastily stuffing his shirt into his breeches.

'My silver suit, Joseph, and the waistcoat embroidered with silver and pearls. Silver, ha! And a pearl, indeed! Today I will be saved. Maybe some champagne is in order, what do you say, baby brother? Champagne for breakfast, like the old days. You have been so good to me. I am so glad that I came here.' He tried to take my hand.

I leapt back in revulsion and turned on Joseph. 'Did you know, you bastard? Did you know what was going on?' I pushed him out of the room and would have strangled him on the spot if Meryll had not again prevented me. The passage was full of staring servants.

The look on Joseph's face told me he had known. 'He is my master, sir, and I . . .'

'Get out of my house. Now, at once. Go!' I shoved him towards the stairs; he tripped, fell, tumbled to the bottom and limped away. I locked Sebastian's door. 'No one, absolutely no one, is to enter this room or let Lord Damory out. Is that clear?' The gaping faces nodded in unison. 'Now be gone, all of you.'

Only Meryll remained. He took my arm, led me gently to the library and poured me a brandy. My fury had evaporated, leaving me deflated and so exhausted I could barely lift the glass.

The sun rose, golden rays pouring in at the windows and glowing on the rich colours of the carpet. From the riverbank came the sweet strains of the Hymn to the Sun. It seemed impossible that light and beauty should continue to exist. With all my heart I wished the sun extinguished and the world cast into eternal blackness.

'I will not allow you to murder your own brother,' Meryll said. 'For your sake, not his.'

He was right. I could not kill him, but neither did I have to sustain his life. I sent for the carpenter and had the windows of Sebastian's room boarded over from the outside, his door reinforced and extra locks installed.

Morning classes began and the school returned to normality, as much as was possible with so many of the boys undergoing punishments, mild or severe in proportion to their transgressions. Stephen Silver was locked in a room apart. I could not bear to remember the bright and beautiful child I had imagined him to be.

Meryll insisted that Bayliss should be prosecuted, at least for his part in the thefts, so we sent for the constable and returned to the laboratory. When Meryll opened the storeroom door a very bad smell emerged; Bayliss had hung himself from a hook on the wall, soiling his breeches. I made myself look at the round face, now black and contorted, the bulging eyes and protruding tongue. You were like a father to me, I thought.

The constable and his assistant took the body away. Meryll paced the room, furious and frustrated. I set to work, and after a while he stopped pacing and came to watch me.

'What are you doing?' he asked.

I said nothing. I knew exactly what I wanted, and it took only a few minutes to prepare the two vials. Meryll followed, silent and perplexed, as I went back to my house and entered Sebastian's room.

'You have some choices, Sebastian, but not many. You can starve to death or you can take poison.' I put the two vials on the table. 'Death by starvation is long and painful, I'm told, so I would recommend the poison. As you see, there are two vials, two choices. One will provide a painless death, the other an extremely painful one. They look alike, they smell alike. Even I cannot now tell which is which. Let fate decide.'

I wanted him to say something, but he only nodded, a terrible understanding in his eyes.

I went to the door.

'I will take your poison, baby brother,' Sebastian said, very quietly. 'My soul is already damned.'

'And may it rot in Hell for ever.' I went out with Meryll and locked the door behind us. We were halfway down the stairs when the screaming began.

Meryll shuddered. 'I was praying for him to choose the painless one.'

'There was no painless one.'

'But you said . . .'

'I lied.'

50
You Cannot Go On Like This

🌿

As Meryll had predicted, his life – indeed all of our lives – unravelled. Everything that we had believed in and worked for was revealed as idiocy and delusion. We were dismissed from our posts at New Eden and evicted from our houses. The school was taken over by well-meaning improvers who replaced the Hymn to the Sun with catechism classes and music lessons with Bible study. In a final blow, they changed the school's name to Our Saviour's School for the Redemption of Fallen Children.

Stephen had escaped from the room in which he'd been held, broken into the office, picked the lock on the strongbox, taken not only his bags of gold but the school's money as well and disappeared with his sister Abigail.

I left New Eden in January with Grace and Tunnie. We lived for a while at the London house in St James's Square, then at Farundell, but Andrew made it plain we were not welcome in either place. He had swelled almost instantly to fill the role of Lord Damory; he took Sebastian's death as a personal vindication. In his view, trivial obstacles had been swatted away and now, as a reward for his extreme virtue, he had come to his rightful place. His satisfaction was alloyed by the fact that, although he inevitably had to inherit Farundell and the title, Sebastian's will left a great deal of the money to me.

I had known, of course, that Andrew resented Sebastian merely for being the elder; it had rankled him deeply that Seb had not taken his role seriously. I'd known, too, that he disliked me, considered me frivolous and dissolute. But I had not known how profoundly he had always, always loathed us both. Now he did not try to conceal it; hatred oozed from him like poison.

I, who had only come to hate Sebastian in the last minutes of his life, was torn. For a long time I remained irrationally convinced that there were two Sebastians: the evil one, already rotten, whose end I had helped to hasten, and the other one, my brother, my friend – still alive somewhere, still selfish, unpredictable, exasperating yet powerfully attractive.

I had brought his body home to Farundell to be buried next to our parents, not sure whether the torment of his soul would be greater if he lay in consecrated ground under false pretences or whether he would suffer more outside, as a suicide; nor did I know whether, indeed, I wished to heighten or lessen his suffering.

I rented a house in London and set about trying to make a life for Grace. I hired a governess, a French maid, tutors, a dancing master. I took her shopping and spent a fortune on clothes.

Monsieur Duplis, who seemed not to have aged a day, doted on her and decked her in sky blue and pale peach, grey to match her eyes, gold embroidery to complement her fair hair. She was becoming a beauty, which worried me.

I watched her closely for signs that Sebastian had harmed her. She developed a slight rash that I feared was the pox, but I treated it with a salve of marigold, rose and orris root, my own recipe, and it vanished. Other than that, she seemed well, though prone to occasional bouts of lethargy and melancholy when she would not tell me what she was thinking.

I went to parties, balls, theatres and brothels, but whatever I did, I experienced only a slow slide into darkness. I caught a glimpse of myself in a mirror and had a jolt of terror when I thought it was Sebastian's ghost. There were grey hairs at my temples, more, it seemed, every day.

The house developed a pervasive odour of putrefaction, but the most painstaking searches revealed not so much as a dead mouse. Furred patches of mould resembling faces, hands, staring eyes and open mouths bloomed on certain walls, disappeared overnight, reappeared elsewhere.

I got into fights. I took offence easily, demanded satisfaction, refused to accept apologies. After three duels in which I wounded my opponents with moderate severity while receiving not a scratch, I'd acquired such a reputation as a swordsman that no one would take me on.

A year and a half passed in this way until one morning I came home after a night at Eliza Quill's to find the house bustling with activity, servants running to and fro, packing cases in the hall. I found Isabel sitting in my chair by the drawing-room fire.

'What the hell is going on?'

She stood up and seemed to brace herself. 'You cannot go on like this, Francis. We are taking you to Paris with us. It will be best for Grace.'

A number of angry retorts came to mind, but none emerged from my mouth.

Grace appeared in a flurry and flung herself into my arms. 'Oh thank you, thank you! Paris! How did you know?'

51
A Very Well-Brought-Up Girl

❧

1733

We had been in Paris for a year, renting a house on the western outskirts of the city. It was called Les Pommiers and had been built in the fourteenth century, when this was wild countryside, as a hunting lodge. Extended a few years ago, it now had a dozen or so comfortable bedrooms and spacious salons whose tall windows opened on to pretty gardens with espaliered apple trees.

Isabel and Meryll lived together openly here, as they had not dared to do in England. She had begun to make a reputation for herself in society as a woman of taste and wit. Meryll became enthralled with the architecture of Lemercier and Le Vau and spent his time making the most exact drawings of the Palais du Louvre.

I stayed more or less out of trouble; knowing few people, I had few occasions to pick fights. I jousted instead at the gaming tables where I found that I had, if not luck, then a ruthless instinct that showed me exactly where my opponent's weaknesses lay.

I set up a small chemical laboratory in an outbuilding where I conducted simple experiments, combining mineral and plant extracts with no particular end in mind, just to see what would happen. Some led to disasters, most to nothing useful, but a few had interesting results. I made a salve that was quite effective on minor burns, a potion that alleviated the gripe, a powder with salix, astragalus and mould that seemed to hasten the healing of cuts.

Paris was full of alchemists. Every few weeks a new Wizard would appear, claiming to have lived for thousands of years, witnessed the Flood and the Crucifixion, conversed with angels who whispered a secret cabala in his ear. Miracles of healing and divination were attested by the most reliable witnesses until his methods were exposed as fraudulent, his transmutations revealed as sleight of hand. He would vanish and another would take his place.

Grace, now fifteen, had acquired considerable polish. Her French was excellent, though she had abandoned Latin. She had vulgar taste in novels, which Isabel said was natural in a girl her age. She was a good dancer, adequate on the harpsichord, a passable singer. Her passion was the lute, which she played with real skill. Her music master said that he might one day get her an invitation to play at court. I don't know if he meant it but he succeeded in persuading her to practise for hours every day. I liked to watch her when she thought I wasn't looking: her slim fingers on the strings, the way she bit her lip as she struggled with difficult chords. She played Lully and de Visée, Purcell and Dowland: slow, plangent melodies that lingered in the mind.

She was still subject to episodes of fatigue, rashes and occasional fevers that seemed to have no cause, and disappeared as suddenly as they appeared. Isabel said I spoiled her; it was true I refused her nothing. She loved clothes and always had to have the latest fashion. Her possessions would have filled the cottage in which she'd been born several times over.

One day, taking me unawares, she asked me about her mother. 'What was she like?'

'She was beautiful and kind.'

'Did you love her?'

'Yes, very much.'

'But you didn't marry her.'

'There wasn't time before she died.'

'How did she die?'

'She died peacefully in her sleep.' I lied smoothly, pleased to have come up with a decent answer at such short notice.

'And what about my father?'

'He died before I met your mother, but he was known to be a good man, very well-respected.' More lies; he'd been a lazy drunkard, according to Johanna. I added further lies, to make the whole thing more convincing. 'He played the organ in the church. Perhaps that is where you get your musical talent. I know he would be proud of you.'

'Do you wish I was really yours?'

'You are really mine.'

'But not your own daughter.'

'As dear as.'

She gave me a kiss on the cheek, her way of introducing a subject, such as an expensive purchase, that she thought might provoke some slight resistance on my part.

'What do you want?' I said.

'I think I am too old to call you Uncle Papa any more.' That had been her name for me since she outgrew Da. 'I have agreed with Isabel that I will call her Isabel and not Aunt. Will you be terribly hurt if I call you Francis?'

'But how thoughtful you are to show such tender solicitude for my feelings, sweetheart. I can see that you are a very well-brought-up girl. You may call me what you like.'

209

52

Enragés

❦

One mild and sunny day in early summer I was teaching Grace to drive in the quiet country lanes near our house. We were in my curricle, a light, two-wheeled chariot pulled by a pair of greys. We practised walking and stopping, turning right and left, negotiating herds of sheep, single indecisive sheep, cows, pigs, flocks of geese, barking dogs and peasants with barrows. The horses were frisky; so was Grace. I consented to a trot.

She held the reins tightly in her gloved hands, clucked to the horses and broke into a grin when they stepped out smartly at her command. Her cheeks were flushed with excitement and I remembered how she had ridden Japhet with the same expression of concentration and delight. We went twice round the lanes; when, for the third time, we came to a straight stretch of road that ran alongside the high wall of some great estate, she pleaded to try a canter and I relented. She touched the horses lightly with the whip and almost lost her seat when they surged forward. I braced her with my arm.

'Ease off on the reins just a little, that's it. Hold them steady, good girl. You can breathe now.'

She laughed; the wind tore at our clothes and whipped our hair. The other chariot came up so fast it was right behind us before we heard it, alongside before we could react. There were two men in a racing curricle, pulled by a pair of fierce bays that I recognised as *enragés*, the specially bred horses from the King's stables. The driver was standing, wielding his whip; the other was hanging on for dear life, but laughing.

'Pull up,' I said to Grace, 'let them overtake,' but our horses wanted to race; they stretched out their necks and increased their speed. I grabbed the reins and hauled hard; they began to slow, but not in time. A stand of trees narrowed the road; the *enragés* passed us and cut across our path. Our horses swerved, the left wheel dropped into the ditch and we were flung to the ground.

I was dazed, the wind knocked out of me. I crawled to where Grace lay, very still. Time froze, then she opened her eyes and sat up.

I held her close, reassured myself that she was not hurt and helped her to her feet. She seemed most concerned about a small tear in her skirt. Our horses had stopped nearby and were grazing at the side of the road as if nothing of note had occurred. One wheel-spoke was broken; otherwise the chariot was muddy but undamaged.

The sound of hoofbeats approached; the other curricle was returning. I went and stood in the middle of the road. The driver made no move to pull up; I'm certain he would have enjoyed seeing me jump, but his companion shouted at him to stop and he slewed to a halt a few yards away.

My anger was, no doubt, only too apparent; when I approached an expression of alarm appeared on his face and he raised his whip.

My sword was out in an instant and with a flick of my wrist I severed the whip just above his hand. He leapt from the chariot, drawing his own sword. He was a handsome man of about my own age, richly dressed. For a moment, as we faced each other, swords poised and vibrating with the desire to touch, I had the odd sensation that I was seeing a reflection of myself.

The other man jumped down and grasped his arm. 'Jean, stop, please.' And to me, 'I do most humbly beg your pardon for my cousin's terrible driving and worse manners. Please tell me that you and the young lady have taken no hurt.'

'Of course we have taken hurt. It is only a wonder we are not dead. Does your cousin here have sufficient wit to arrange a time and place that we may get to know each other better before I kill him?' Even I was a trifle taken aback by the strength of my feelings. I wanted to fight this man more than anything in the world; it seemed like ages since I'd felt so alive. I allowed the tip of my sword to brush lightly against his with a sweet metallic whisper.

'Please, Francis.' Grace's voice penetrated my fury. She was at my side, her hand on my sword arm. 'I am not hurt; well, only my pride. And some bruises no doubt.'

'Mademoiselle, please accept our most sincere apologies, and allow me to introduce myself. I am Etienne du Bellay and this is my cousin, Jean de Grenville, Visconte d'Armillac.'

Du Bellay was slighter and younger than his cousin, with soft brown eyes and a winning smile. I had no choice but to lower my sword and introduce myself and Grace. He bowed and kissed her hand.

'Now please,' he said. 'You must let me take you home for a little rest and refreshment. This is my house, just here.' He gestured to the gates that stood open in the high wall. 'I will send someone to collect your horses and your curricle, which I will have repaired immediately.' He turned to his cousin. 'Jean, thank you so much for showing me your new horses. They are truly magnificent, and well-deserved, I have no doubt.' He offered Grace his arm, which she took with a smile.

D'Armillac and I were left staring at each other with undisguised enmity. We sheathed our swords with equal reluctance; he climbed into his chariot and galloped off in a cloud of dust.

53

Connected by Fate

🌿

I followed Grace and du Bellay up the gravelled drive towards an imposing château, white-walled, with slender ornamental turrets under slated, conical roofs. The house, called La Ronce, was set in a manicured parkland of clipped hedges, fountains, neat parterres and immaculate lawns.

After giving orders for my horses and curricle to be brought in from the road, du Bellay led us to a small salon overlooking a garden. The room had flowered wallpaper, a Chinese carpet, silk drapes, upholstery, cushions, all profusely flowered as well. Flowers stood in vases on small tables and marble pedestals, paintings of flowers hung on the walls in gilded frames.

'Maman, look what I have found,' du Bellay said. 'You told me we would have a visitor, and as always, you were right. Monsieur Damory, Mademoiselle Brown, may I present my mother, Marie-Louise de la Rochefoucauld Derain, Marquise du Bellay.'

It took me a moment to discern the woman in the flowered dress who sat on a flowered settee. She was in her forties, rather thin, with angular features and pale amber eyes beneath high, powdered hair.

'I said there would be *two* visitors,' she corrected, putting aside her embroidery (of flowers). 'You are most welcome,' she said to us. 'And your chariot? It is not too badly damaged?'

It was impossible that she could have heard about the

incident so quickly. I opened my mouth to reply, but she forestalled me.

'Do please sit down. I have been expecting you.' She rang a little silver bell and a footman entered almost immediately, bearing a tray with chocolate in a flowered pot, four flowered cups of delicate porcelain and a pile of cakes decorated with sugar flowers.

After we were served I again turned to the Marquise with a question on my lips, and was again forestalled. 'Naturally you are wondering how I knew you were coming,' she said.

'Naturally,' I said. We studied each other.

'You have a very suspicious mind,' she said, with a scolding wag of her finger.

'So I have been told.'

'And you will no doubt demand proof when I tell you that the cards foretold your coming.'

'I would not presume to demand anything, Madame, certainly not something impossible.'

'And if it was possible?'

I shrugged.

She rang the bell and the footman reappeared. 'Bring the ivory box from my sitting room.'

We sat in silence as we awaited his return, Grace perplexed, du Bellay with a small smile, the Marquise with no expression whatsoever. We sipped our chocolate.

In a few minutes the footman returned, bearing an ivory box a foot or so square, with a rounded lid. He placed the box on the table in front of the Marquise and withdrew. She unlocked it with a key from her pocket, took out a small leather-bound notebook and, opening it where a green ribbon marked the place, handed it to me.

'Read the entry for today,' she said.

The book was laid out like a journal, with a few lines for each date. I read out the most recent: "'*A chariot overturned, a fight averted. Visitors: a man and a girl. Connected by fate.*'"

'I suppose there are a great many road accidents outside your gates,' I said, without much conviction.

'Perhaps there are; the cards do not see fit to inform me.'

'Why should they bother to inform you about us?'

'Why indeed? We are connected by fate; in what manner has yet to be revealed. Shall we ask them about you?'

'What cards are these, that concern themselves with my doings?'

She delved further into the box and brought out a silk pouch, opened it and took out a deck of old playing cards. They were long and narrow, with gilded borders, very worn and scuffed. She shuffled them and turned the deck face down before I could see any details. Her white, bony hands, webbed with fine veins, stroked the cards with a delicate, questing touch.

'Please cut them into three piles,' she said, and I obliged, reluctantly.

'Now choose one of the piles.'

I chose the one furthest from me.

'And now shuffle those, please, without looking, and cut once.'

I did so.

She touched the top card. 'This card represents you.' She turned it over. It showed a knight on a horse, sword held high in the air.

'The Knight of Swords,' she said. 'A fine mind, but a quarrelsome temperament.'

Grace smothered a laugh.

The Marquise turned the next card, which showed a man at a table on which were three golden pyramids. Behind him was a running horse and a pair of tall poles with waving flags. 'Ah, the Magus. Let us merely say, for the moment, that you will journey to distant lands and learn many secrets.'

It was my turn to smother a laugh.

The Marquise was undeterred. 'And this,' she said, 'represents your purpose in life.' She turned the next card. It showed a golden-haired child in a garden beneath a bright, many-rayed sun. 'Horus, the Child of Dawn,' she said with some surprise. 'Perfection, the highest transmutation, rebirth, redemption, immortality.'

I said nothing.

'Your past,' she said, turning the next card: a corpse-strewn battlefield under a wan, sickle moon. 'Loss, remorse, the unforeseen consequences of one's actions.'

This was becoming uncomfortable and I would have stopped her there but she had already turned the next card. It showed a strangely twisted skeleton wielding a scythe. At his feet lay the severed parts of a man's body; the head, in the foreground, had open eyes and a smiling mouth. 'Death,' the Marquise said. 'Your enemy. Though it was reversed, so perhaps he is your friend as well.'

'I think that's enough,' I said.

'Not quite,' she said. 'We must learn what power directs you.' She turned another card: a woman enthroned, with a crescent moon above her head and a babe in her arms. 'The Priestess.' Her tone was again astonished. 'This card comes up very rarely; I can think of only one or two others who have had it, in any position. Here, the meaning is unmistakable. You are an initiate of Isis.' She turned to stare at me. 'Perhaps this frivolous appearance of yours is a disguise. Have you undergone initiation?'

'I have no idea what you're talking about,' I said, remembering Meryll's Society of Isis, and my mock burial. But surely that had been a joke.

'The near future,' said the Marquise, before I could stop her. The card showed two naked, crowned figures, a man and a woman, embracing in a fountain. 'Ah,' she said, with a small smile.

'Thank you, I do believe we've seen enough.' I was suddenly overcome by the strongest possible desire not to see the next card.

I reached out and, with a sensation of breaking through some barrier, moved my hand abruptly over the table, disturbing the order of the cards.

The Marquise tightened her lips but said nothing.

'These are interesting cards. A form of tarot?' I picked up a few at random. 'Hand painted, I see. How charming.'

The colours were faded, the gilding rubbed away in places. Before I could examine them more closely, the Marquise took them from my hands, gathered the deck together, cut it once and turned up a single card. It was entirely black within its gilded border, and quite blank. At the centre was a small egg-shaped hole.

She stared at it for a long time. 'The Stone of the Wise,' she said. 'So that is what you are about.'

It was time to go; I rose, thanked Madame du Bellay and her son and extricated a clearly rather smitten Grace. The curricle was waiting at the door, broken spoke repaired. I drove home as Grace chattered about du Bellay; Etienne, she called him already.

'Is Etienne married?' I asked.

'Oh no. It's so sad. He was telling me. He was twice betrothed – one girl died, the other ran away with an Irish pirate.'

'That is tragic.'

'Why don't you like him, Uncle Papa, I mean Francis? He's very handsome, and so polite.'

'I don't dislike him.' Of course I disliked him, if only because he flirted with Grace, who was far too young to flirt.

I mentioned the incident to Isabel that evening, and was not surprised that she knew both du Bellay and d'Armillac from court. 'Etienne du Bellay is the fourth or fifth son. His mother the Marquise is said to be somewhat odd.'

'No, truly?'

'Yes, quite eccentric. But she is related by blood or marriage to absolutely everyone. Her mother was the famous Duchesse de

Cossé-Brissac, who had children by both Richelieu and the Duc d'Orléans. It's not quite clear who Mme du Bellay's father was; some say the King, some say the Comte de St Germain. Her eldest son, Charles, is the fourteenth Marquis; one of the others is somebody important in the Church. I have seen young Etienne occasionally at court, though only on the fringes. He has an air of someone who hopes to make a good impression but has no real expectation of being noticed.'

'He was quite attentive to Grace,' I said.

'Well, it is not an unreasonable match, depending on the dowry you give her and the income you settle upon her. He has no title but neither have you. If you like, I can let it be known that Grace has, if not a fortune, certainly a substantial . . .'

'You will do no such thing.'

'No? You are sure?'

'Grace is far too young to think of marriage.'

'She is not. I was betrothed at fourteen and married at sixteen, and just look at how marvellously well it has turned out.'

I laughed. 'What about the other fellow, d'Armillac?'

'Visconte d'Armillac is a very good friend of the King. Did you say he had a pair of *enragés*? Hardly anyone gets those horses. It's rumoured that he is the King's, well, how can I put it? He provides the King with amusing companions.'

'He's a pimp, you mean?'

'One does not say that, even in France. But the King has the most refined tastes and is apparently quite difficult to please. He will only go where he can be certain that no one has, as it were, preceded him.'

'He requires virgins.'

'Only the finest. And d'Armillac seems to have a most exact understanding of the King's taste.'

I shuddered. 'I shall keep Grace well away from him. Perhaps I should have killed him there by the road.'

'My dear, duelling is ubiquitous, deaths not uncommon and for the most part easily covered up. But killing the King's friend in a public place with witnesses would perhaps attract some unwelcome attention.'

'It would have been self-defence.'

'Too late now, *tant pis.*'

Late that night, when I couldn't sleep, I thought about the Marquise and her cards, her obscure pronouncements, her mystic airs, in which I could not quite believe. When I tried to recall her face, my memory swam with images of flowers instead, yet she in no way reminded me of a flower; more like a spider hidden among flowers. But everything she had said – everything the cards had showed – was right. What had she written in her little book? *Connected by fate.*

The next day I received an invitation to return to La Ronce the following week for 'a special evening'.

54

An Unspoken Question

Dressed well, although not in my best, I arrived at La Ronce at around dusk, uncertain what to expect. There were several other carriages in the drive; evidently this was not to be a private meeting. I was simultaneously disappointed and relieved.

A footman showed me through the house to the gardens at the back, where a dozen or so men and women strolled among the softly splashing fountains. I took a glass of champagne from a passing footman and studied my fellow guests for a clue as to the nature of the occasion. At first I thought there was no one I knew, then I glimpsed a familiar, slender figure. It was Sandro; I had heard that he was in Paris, performing a series of recitals at court. After kisses and embraces he took my arm and we walked slowly up and down.

'I was so sad to hear about Miranda,' he said, and I think he might have gone on to ask about her death, but something in my face stopped him. He moved on quickly. 'And the school? I heard that you left. Will you start a new school in Paris? The need is just as great.'

'You must speak with Isabel and Meryll about that,' I said. 'I have ceased to believe in education, but perhaps they still do.'

'*Da vero*? But everywhere I go, I tell people about the wonders you worked. That sweet child, Stephen was his name, *n'est-çe pas*? An angelic voice, I remember him so well. I predicted he would have a great career.'

'I'm certain he will, though perhaps not in the profession we anticipated.'

'How do you know Madame du Bellay?' Sandro asked, and I explained about the encounter with her son and the uncanny card-reading.

'Yes, she is well-known for her card-readings. I was introduced to her at court; she said we had been great lovers . . .' he lowered his voice to a whisper, '. . . in a previous life.' He lifted his hand in an eloquent, bemused shrug. 'This nation must be more tolerant than I thought if such ideas are so casually spoken. Where I come from she would be burned for even thinking such a thing, but here she moves in the best circles. An invitation to one of these mystical soirées is *très recherché*.'

'Mystical soirée? Is that what this is?'

'*Certo*, did you not know?'

'I had no idea. I thought it was purely a social occasion – then when I saw you, I thought we were come to hear you sing.'

'I am not singing, *caro*. My contract specifies that I shall only sing at court, in the King's presence. Madame du Bellay – how did she put it? She "discerns my spiritual essence". She wants me for myself, can you imagine? Or if not my self exactly, my colour. According to her, I have a unique colour between violet and green. My presence completes her spectrum.'

'You are making this up, Sandro.'

'I am not. Has she not told you what colour you are?'

'No.'

At this point we were summoned within and shown into a dimly lit salon. A semicircle of chairs with our names on cards faced a single chair at a table, on which stood a candle and a large sphere of translucent stone. I was seated between Sandro and a dark-haired beauty he introduced as Madame Caroline Harper, from Virginia in the colonies.

'Have you attended many of these mystical soirées?' I asked her.

'One or two,' she said. 'And you?'

'My first. Are we arranged by colour, do you think? Monsieur Zanetti tells me he is green-violet, or was it violet-green? but I have no idea what I am.'

'I am orange-blue,' she said. 'Can you not tell?'

'I'm afraid my senses are too dull for such refined perceptions.'

'Perhaps you are mud-brown,' she said, and peered at me with mock intensity. 'Yes, I do believe you are. That is unfortunate; there is no hope for mud-brown people.' She closed her fan and opened it again, stroked it lightly against her bosom. It meant both approach and desist; evidently she liked to keep one off balance.

Madame du Bellay entered and, after greeting us, introduced an elderly man named Monsieur Gribois, lean-cheeked and crook-backed. With him was a small, pale boy of perhaps ten or

221

eleven who sat at the table. M. Gribois said a brief prayer, calling on Jesu Christus and all the saints to bless and guide us, then he leaned over and began speaking into the boy's ear in a soft, continuous mutter. The boy gazed into the stone, which seemed to hold and magnify the flickering candlelight.

I sat back and prepared to watch an amusing charade, but then something changed. A chill seemed to pass through the room; people murmured and shifted in their chairs. I felt a brief twist of nausea, accompanied by the sudden dreadful certainty that the ghosts of my dead were about to appear. Images of Johanna, Purefoy, Miranda, Christopher, Agnes, Sebastian, Tildy, Lucy and others hovered at the edges of my vision, then came my father, my mother . . . No! I pushed them back with all the strength of my will. They retreated, but still I felt them pressing in, and others behind them, hundreds, thousands. My God, was this how things really were, countless hordes of grey dead surrounding a few bright pools of the living? Lord Jesu bless and protect us. I understood now why M. Gribois was repeating that phrase regularly. Gradually the waves of dead receded beyond the walls of the room and I told myself firmly that I had experienced a delusion brought on by the extreme ridiculousness of the occasion.

The boy gave a soft moan and lowered his head so that his eyes were just a few inches from the surface of the stone.

'What do you see?' asked M. Gribois. 'Lord Jesu bless and protect us.'

'An angel,' said the boy in a light, curiously uninflected voice.

'Ask him his name.'

'His name is . . . Arazael.'

'Yes, that is a good angel. Lord Jesu bless and protect us. Ask him his number.'

'He says his number is two hundred and forty-nine.'

M. Gribois looked up and addressed us. 'That is correct. He is who he claims to be.' He turned to Mme du Bellay. 'Have you a question for the angel, Madame?'

Mme du Bellay stepped forward, handed a folded piece of paper to M. Gribois and returned to her seat. He held it in the candle flame, then dropped the burning wisp into a dish.

'It is possible that he is the one,' said the boy. 'If you are true of heart. But you must give before you receive.'

'Yes, I see. Thank you,' Mme du Bellay said.

'Anyone else?' said M. Gribois.

Mme Harper rose and handed over a piece of paper; again it was burned and the boy spoke. 'Investments made on a waning moon will fail. Sell the Stratford shares immediately. Buy copper.' The mundane advice sounded very odd in the child's high, thin tones and I almost laughed aloud.

Several others submitted questions and received answers, then the boy fell silent for a time. 'Are there any unspoken questions?' asked M. Gribois, followed by another pause, then the boy twitched in his chair and moaned.

'Others are coming in now,' he said. 'The angel has stepped aside. There are some messages. For Pauline from Henri. You betrayed me but I forgive you. Beware of Montrachet, he only wants your money.' There was a long pause, then, 'For Madame Perpillon, from Charles. He is holding out a pot of salve for you. It is made of angelica, hyssop . . . Do not be concerned about Régine. She will marry, but not soon. For Gérard, from Géneviève. I curse you, I curse you, I curse you.'

A man at the end of the row got up and left the room.

'For Sandro,' the boy said, and Sandro gasped. 'From Giovanni. I am so proud of you but I must leave you now. You do not need me.'

'No,' Sandro whispered. '*Non lascia me . . .*'

The boy was silent for a time. 'Is that all?' M. Gribois asked.

'Yes . . . no. Wait a moment. There is more. Here is someone coming. I do not know him.'

'What does he want?'

'He has a message for . . . Francis.'

I twitched involuntarily.

'What is his appearance? Is he man or angel, ghost or some other spirit?'

'I cannot see him. There is something – a book . . . no, a stone . . . no, a rose. *Dieu merci . . . Dieu merci il est mort.*' The boy sighed and slumped in his chair. He was ashen and trembling with fatigue.

'That is all for tonight,' said M. Gribois. He picked up the boy and carried him away.

Footmen moved about the room lighting candles; the vaguely sinister atmosphere lifted. Mme Harper turned to me and fluttered her fan. 'How delightfully enigmatic. What could it mean?'

'I have absolutely no idea,' I said, but I had. *Dieu merci il est mort*. In French the phrase had no special meaning, but in English it did, though only for me. Thank God he's dead. TGHD. Tobias.

Sandro left almost immediately; I walked him to his carriage. 'I cannot believe that Giovanni has gone,' he said. 'And yet it's true. I no longer feel him. There is such a strange, empty space here.' He was pressing his hand to his chest. 'I suppose I must go on alone.' He gave me a small, sad smile. 'But you are my friend, Francesco. I am so glad. When will I see you?'

I invited him to Les Pommiers; we made an arrangement for the following week. After he had left I strolled through the torch-lit gardens, trying to assemble my thoughts.

Perhaps the whole thing was an elaborate hoax, the Marquise either complicit or a dupe herself, M. Gribois a charlatan, the boy good at memorising and reciting. Opportunities to be relieved of funds would come later. The 'messages' could easily be based on facts or rumours known to Mme du Bellay or M. Gribois. But try as I might, I was unable to imagine how they could have known about TGHD. My confused feelings settled into annoyance. If someone wanted to tell me something, why be so cryptic?

'Damn you,' I said aloud.

From the other side of a tall hedge came a low laugh.

'I beg your pardon,' I said, but there was no reply.

I made my way back inside, where supper was being served. I had no appetite and sought out Mme du Bellay to take my leave.

'You are leaving so soon?' she said. 'You are displeased with the answer to your question?'

'I asked no question.'

'Are you sure? Sometimes there is an unspoken question in one's heart.'

'I harbour no unspoken questions,' I said, but even to my ears such a swift and complete denial suggested its opposite.

There was a pause as we weighed each other's resolve not to be the first to yield. Finally she smiled. 'I have been told I must give in order to receive. If you would call on me tomorrow afternoon at four, there is much I would like to show you.'

I could not sleep that night. I sat up reading until my eyes grew tired and the letters swam about, then I closed the book. I went up to Grace's room and stood in the doorway; it always soothed me to watch her sleeping. The moonlight fell across her pillow and what I'd thought was a shadow seemed to glisten as though wet. I rubbed my eyes. Was I becoming prone to hallucinations? But no – I crept closer. There was a dark red stain on the pillow.

I cried out. She woke and sat up. Blood covered half of her face.

'Uncle Papa, what is the matter?' she said.

I lit a candle with shaking hands; she saw the blood on her pillow, touched her face and looked at her fingers.

'It is only a nosebleed,' she said.

'Only? What? You have had this before?'

'Once or twice.'

'When?'

'A few weeks ago.'

'Why was I not informed?'

'Because it is nothing. See, it has already stopped.'

I sent for a doctor; he came within the hour, diagnosed a bleeding from the nose, announced that it had stopped, collected his fee and left.

55

The Cabinet of Curiosities

The next day I prepared for my visit to Mme du Bellay. I was unusually indecisive about what to wear, which provoked a wry comment from Tunnie to the effect that the lady upon whom I was calling must possess exceptional appeal.

'Quite the reverse, Tunnie,' I said. 'She is old, scrawny, deceitful and not in the least appealing.'

'Indeed, sir,' he said. 'In that case, the turquoise velvet?'

'Don't be absurd. Something dark. Sober. Serious. Something to keep her at a distance.'

'A suit of armour, sir?'

'That might be best. Have I one?'

'I did see one in an attic, though it was a trifle rusty. Shall I fetch it down, give it a bit of a polish?'

We settled on a dark brown twill coat with a great many shield-shaped brass buttons over a black damask waistcoat in a subdued pattern of roses with prominent thorns. I took the caroche with four horses and put a footman on the box with the driver and two more on the footboard. Did I feel the need for an army at my back?

I arrived precisely twenty minutes late. This time there were no other carriages in the drive. I was escorted to a small salon on the first floor, informed that Madame would come soon and served strong, sweet coffee from a silver pot.

The chairs were shaped like butterflies, with tufted wings and gilded antennae for feet and arms. There were pictures of butterflies on the walls and, in glass cases, specimens showing the stages of larva, chrysalis and imago. A mild breeze stirred sheer curtains, on which embroidered butterflies seemed to flutter.

'They know the secret of transmutation,' said a woman's voice.

I turned, expecting to see Mme du Bellay, but a younger, far prettier woman stood before me.

I bowed, and only when I met her eyes on the way up did I realise that this was indeed Mme du Bellay. 'Marquise,' I said, almost bowing again in my confusion.

'Please call me Marie-Louise.' She gestured, smiling, and we seated ourselves on butterfly chairs at a low table whose shimmering surface was made of hundreds of overlapping butterfly wings under glass.

I studied her between sips of coffee as we made small talk. Ground pearls might explain the luminosity of her complexion; a well-designed bodice shaped her waist and lifted her breasts, but this was not enough to account for the transformation. Even her hands, which had reminded me of spiders, were now smooth and graceful. I looked at my cup; did the coffee contain some drug that had altered my perceptions? I felt perfectly lucid, though there was no denying that Marie-Louise was attractive in a way she had not been before. After all, she was not so old, perhaps forty? Maybe only in her late thirties. And I was past thirty myself, not so great a difference. Her voice, too, had a lilt and subtle melodiousness I'd not noticed before, though I was forgetting from one minute to the next just what it was we were talking about.

'Would you like to see my little cabinet of curiosities?' she asked.

'*Certainement,*' I said, giving myself an inner shake and resolving to keep my wits about me.

She led me through a short gallery and up a flight of stairs. The room we entered was octagonal, about twenty feet across, lit from above by a glass cupola. The only furniture was a pair of elegant chaises longues upholstered in violet silk and a table set with wine and small delicacies. The floor was inlaid with various woods in a complex geometric pattern; on the domed, star-strewn ceiling painted cherubs held a banner that said *Rosa Æterna Clavis*. Wall panels carved in low relief depicting Greek gods and goddesses alternated with tall, mirror-backed display cabinets.

Treasures from every land crowded the shelves: narwhal tusks, ostrich eggs, crystals and shells, Greek bronzes and Egyptian faience figures, clocks, orreries, music boxes, obelisks, stuffed birds with outlandish plumage, skeletons of fish, reptiles and snakes, insects in amber, carved gemstones, murrhine vases, shark's teeth set in gold, mythical beasts cast in silver, nesting ivory lattice spheres of astonishing delicacy, a mechanical boat with jade sailors and bronze sails, a clockwork gilded coach-and-six with horses covered in horsehair, a porcelain driver and footmen.

Marie-Louise took my arm and led me around, explaining the meaning and history of the objects. Her pride and pleasure were evident and unfeigned; I allowed myself to be charmed.

56

Rosa Æterna Clavis

🌹

When my curiosity was slaked we sat and drank chilled wine, a delicious Muscadet from her own vineyards in the Loire Valley. She looked at her watch. 'I wonder,' she said, 'if you have noticed that there is more to this room than meets the eye?'

As I gazed about, perplexed, a harp began to play, though I could not discern the source. I traced it to the carved panel depicting Apollo, but then it ceased and a new melody appeared from elsewhere, a trumpet, muffled but distinctive. As soon as I had traced it to Ares, it too ceased, and now the sound of a viol floated through the air, emerging from the panel showing Hermes. Looking closely, I noticed a hairline gap at the edge. I traced it with my fingers; this was not a wall, but a door.

Marie-Louise smiled mysteriously and made a gesture inviting me to open it if I could. As the music moved around the room I studied the panels; each one must be a door with a secret catch. If so, it was well hidden, and after ten minutes of fruitless search, during which Marie-Louise continued to smile, I flung myself down in frustration. My glance fell upon the cherubs and their banner. *Rosa Æterna Clavis*: the Rose is the Key to Eternity. There had been roses in several of the panels; I leapt up and looked again. Every panel had at least one carved rose. I started with Aphrodite, whose rose, half-open, concealed her private parts. I pushed it and pulled it; it moved but nothing happened. I

229

tried various manipulations until I found the right combination: pull, twist right, push, twist left. There was a tiny click; Marie-Louise applauded.

I opened the door expecting to see a musician, but there was no one. The room was about fifteen feet across, with walls at oblique angles and a single high round window. It contained a curtained bed, two tall porphyry columns, a few tables and chairs, paintings and sculptures of Aphrodite in various poses, a mirror and copper sconces. The floor was richly carpeted and the walls were painted a deep shade of green. I sniffed; there was a strong scent of sandalwood and rose whose source I couldn't identify.

'The scent is in the paint,' Marie-Louise said. She pulled a silk cord that hung by the door. There was a brief pause, then music appeared from, it seemed, nowhere: a lute, joined in a moment by a flute and a viola da gamba. I stepped back into the main room – the sound was fainter. I returned to Aphrodite's room – it increased. But there was nowhere for a musician to hide. 'I am at a loss, Madame. Whence this music? Have you unseen spirits at your command?'

She showed me a grate set into the back of the columns, which were not stone but painted wood, hollow, and open at their bases to a chamber below.

'Beneath each of these rooms is a chamber lined in copper for resonance, with its ceiling shaped to channel the sound into these two apertures. I have three musicians; between them, they play ten instruments. They wait in the central chamber until I give the signal to play.'

'But they began before you pulled the bell.'

'I instructed them to begin at six o'clock.' As I was to learn, precise timing was her forte.

I made my way from one secret room to another. Each one opened by means of a carved rose; in each, a bell-pull commanded the musicians below. The music, the furnishings, the colours and the scent of the paint were particular to each room's presiding god or goddess. The intention was to create conditions conducive to the presence of the deity, to draw its qualities into manifestation.

The rooms – indeed, the whole tower that housed them – had been created for Marie-Louise's mother, the Duchesse de Cossé-Brissac, by an architect skilled in the magical arts: the designer, as well, of the tarot cards I'd seen on my first visit. It was from her that Marie-Louise had inherited both the château and her mystical inclinations.

We ended up, of course, in Aphrodite's bed, and it was not until I returned home the next day and Tunnie was undressing me that I remembered the wariness with which I'd set out.

'Polish up that suit of armour, Tunnie,' I said. 'I'm invited to return tonight.'

That night's encounter had an altogether different flavour. It took place under the auspices of Ares, in a red chamber, with iron ornaments and the scent of tobacco; accompanied, until I pulled the bell to make it stop, by martial music. It was not a room in which sleep was possible, so we adjourned after a time to Jupiter: blue, calm and cedar-scented.

Marie-Louise woke me before dawn and we repaired to Artemis, where the setting moon traversed the silver-hung bed, a flute played below and jasmine filled the air. After that, we crossed the *cabinet* to enjoy the golden, olibanum-scented chamber of Apollo. A brief pause for sustenance, then a sojourn in Saturn's black chamber, with myrrh, oboes and soft, insistent drumbeat. During the following day and night we made the circuit of the seven rooms a number of times.

When we were not erotically engaged, she showed me around her domain. In the cellar was the most sophisticated alchemical laboratory I have ever seen. She employed a dozen chemists who laboured around the clock. She was obsessed with finding an

Elixir of Immortality, though for her the quest was entirely personal, unlike for Enderby or even Bayliss, who were driven by a desire to penetrate the secrets of nature, to know for knowledge's sake, for the benefit of the human race, for the fulfilment of God's design. Marie-Louise simply believed that she should live for ever.

She had lately, however, begun to doubt whether it was advisable to seek to prolong the life of her present earthly accommodation. Her consultations with higher realms, through the mediation of Gribois and his boy, had led her to a new theory and a new plan. She would conceive a magical child, a perfect hermaphrodite, who would contain within him-herself all possible qualities; into this ultimate human she would transfer her soul, fully conscious and in possession of her memories, knowledge and intentions. The cards and Gribois had led her to conclude that I was the one whose sperm was required for this operation. Our passage through the realms of the gods and goddesses had been timed according to abstruse and exact astrological calculations to collect their influences and funnel them into her womb.

When she told me this, at the end (though I did not know it was the end) of our liaison, I was so tangled in her ambience that I was neither surprised, incredulous nor amused. At the time it seemed to make sense. Looking back on it, I cannot account for the attraction that I must have felt, which gives support to my suspicion that she had, if not drugged me, certainly cast some sort of glamour over me. Even now, my recollections have the feel of a dream remembered, not an incident of waking life.

She sent me home when she was done with me; I called the next day and was told she had left for her country estate in the Loire. When I saw her the following night at the theatre, she greeted me as an acquaintance of little importance and made no mention of our encounters nor of the extraordinary speed with which she had travelled to and from the Loire. I noted that I felt no attraction; she had shed her magic and looked once again old and rather stringy. As far as I know she failed to conceive a child, perfect or otherwise. She never told me what colour I was.

57

An Exhibition of Monstrosities

🌾

Grace received a letter from Etienne du Bellay. It was full of compliments, expressed his wish to call on her and asked which day was her *jour chez elle* – the day she received visitors at home. I forbade her to reply; she was far too young to have any sort of *jour* of her own, and although Isabel offered to play chaperone on her *jour* I did not wish to set a precedent. I attempted to make up for my strictness by taking Grace and Isabel shopping the following afternoon. We had a tiring but gratifyingly acquisitive trawl through the Palais Marchand and settled into a café opposite to recover our strength. It had striped umbrellas to shade the ladies' complexions and the most comfortable chairs, of woven reed with cushions in printed cotton. I ordered coffee with milk, Isabel tea *à l'anglaise* and Grace a *bavaroise*, a rich, sweet beverage that she loved, made with strong tea, hot milk, egg yolk, cane sugar and kirsch.

Street peddlers offered fruit, nosegays, candied rosebuds; Gypsies read fortunes and picked pockets; musicians, acrobats and rope-dancers performed in the middle of the boulevard, stopping carriages, then slid ingratiatingly among the tables collecting coins. A woman with a trained monkey gave way to a boy with a dancing dog, a tiny creature whose fur was dyed in blue dots on a pink ground, with yellow feet and ears. Yipping and prancing on its hind legs it approached Grace, who reached out her hand to pet it.

'Don't touch it,' said Isabel, pulling back her skirts. 'Give the boy something, Francis, make him go away.'

I gave the boy a few sous. He had a thin, hunted look about him; I called him back and gave him a few more.

A black-clad flock of nuns went by, walking quickly with their heads down, escorted by two scarlet-robed priests.

'We visited another nunnery yesterday,' Isabel said. She and Grace were touring the religious houses near Paris. 'Notre-Dame de Sion; they have a number of English nuns there.'

'Miss Bambridge and Miss Wootton,' Grace said. 'I thought Miss Bambridge too pretty to be a nun.'

'Miss Bambridge wore rouge,' said Isabel. 'I didn't think nuns were allowed to do that, but she leads quite an independent life. She plays the harpsichord, knows Latin and has many books.'

'What do they do all day, the nuns, when they are not at prayer?' I asked.

'Chess and backgammon,' said Grace. 'For money.'

'And they bet on anything,' said Isabel. 'Who will fall asleep in church. Whether the priest will have cut himself shaving. How many kittens the cat will have.'

'You used to want to be a nun,' I said to Isabel.

'Did I really? I don't remember that.'

'Oh look,' said Grace. 'It's Etienne.'

Unfortunately, it was. He was one of half a dozen overdressed foplings circling Mme Harper, the beautiful Virginian whom I'd met at Mme du Bellay's mystical soirée. In her retinue, besides the usual *demoiselle de compagnie* and footman, was a blacka-moor page in a citrine satin coat and breeches, leading an ocelot with a jewelled collar.

They stopped at our table. 'Ah, the unfortunate mud-brown Monsieur Damory,' said Mme Harper.

'Glorious orange-blue one,' I rose, bowed and introduced Isabel and Grace.

The group was on its way to an exhibition of monstrosities; Mme Harper invited us to accompany them. Isabel and Grace agreed at once, which left me no option but to go along.

Etienne offered Grace his arm and when I would have interfered, Isabel deftly stepped between. 'Let her have her little flirtation,' she said, and changed the subject before I could respond. 'So that is the famous Mme Harper. You didn't say you'd met her.'

'I didn't know she was famous. What is she famous for?'

'Money. Vast quantities of it. She's the only child of Edgar Allport Peabody, who owned half of America. And the widow – so young, so tragic – of Hiram Harper, who owned the other half. Now it's all hers and she's shopping for a title.'

I recognised several counts and a duke in the flotilla surrounding Mme Harper. 'Why tragic?'

'I thought you disdained tittle-tattle.'

'I'm only interested in the facts.'

'Well, the facts are that Hiram Harper was ugly and old; she, as you can see, is young and beautiful. The tragedy is that he died on their wedding night; her father died on the same night, in the next room. She's only just come out of mourning.'

'Very well, what's the story?'

'I knew you'd want to know.' She lowered her voice. 'They say that there was an arrangement whereby the father would watch the consummation. She turned the tables on father and husband by providing such intense erotic stimulation that both expired on the spot. She dragged her father's corpse to his room with the help of her devoted slave.' She indicated the blackamoor with the ocelot. 'And,' she lowered her voice still further, 'there is the suggestion that she planned it all and laced their wine with cantharides. Her revenge for being married against her wishes.'

I gazed at Mme Harper with new admiration. She must have felt my eyes upon her. Her glance flickered from me to Isabel and back; she guessed we'd been talking about her, smiled and inclined her head fractionally. I sketched a bow.

Monsieur Hercule Babinette's *Exhibition of Monstrosities: A Complete History of the Oddities of Nature* occupied three rooms on the ground floor of a building on the Quay de l'Ecole. The sign proclaimed that this was no mere display of curiosities to shock, titillate and amuse; scientific knowledge was the objective.

In the first two rooms were drawings and preserved specimens from across the globe; the final chamber promised living exhibits. Upon entering, one was greeted by a large engraving of the famous Monster of Ravenna: one-legged, bat-winged, with a single horn in the centre of his forehead and a phallus like an enormous claw. He had two serpents emerging from his waist and an eye embedded in his knee. The accompanying card analysed the creature in the context of the fall and sack of the city of Ravenna, which had occurred a few days after he was born. Other instances were cited of disasters heralded by the birth of monsters. In all cases, the characteristics of the creatures represented the moral failings of the populace, which brought about their downfall. The deformed genitalia represented their sodomitical practices, the wings their frivolity, the horn their pride, and so on.

Isabel shuddered. 'How can something like that exist? Surely God should prevent it.'

'Here, look.' I pointed to the next card. 'It says the cause may be the evil thoughts of the mother, or a fright, or the sight of some wicked thing. Alternatively, it is a product of carnal relations between a woman and an animal, or a friar and a nun.'

'It can't be that. We'd be tripping over them.'

I was twisting around, trying to see what Grace and Etienne were doing.

'Stop it, Francis.'

'They have been tête à tête too long,' I said. 'You go and join them. If I do I will only become annoyed. Please.'

Isabel rolled her eyes at me but obliged. I strolled about the exhibit, surreptitiously watching them.

A lamb with two heads and seven legs, badly stuffed; engravings of a pig-faced child from Basel; a dog-faced child from Russia; a child with no face at all. In a glass jar, wrinkled and yellow, a baby whose head was three times the size of its body, lumpy as a cauliflower. A skeleton of an infant with flippers instead of arms, said to have been born to a woman who consorted with a dolphin.

A curtained archway led to the third room. Here an additional door fee was demanded by a dwarf in a filthy orange coat who introduced himself as Hercule Babinette, the proprietor of the exhibition. He offered, for a further sum, a pamphlet written by himself and available in French, English, German, Italian and Latin, entitled *The Fallacy of Ultimate Causation*. I declined.

The room was divided into three alcoves separated by curtains and screens. In the first, a group of very diminutive, very black persons dressed in colourful scarves and imitation palm fronds rose from a table at which they had been playing cards and bowed. One took up a fiddle and began a desultory screeching; the rest began to dance a clumsy chaconne. The sign proclaimed them to be Hodmandods, a people living on the bottom of the world. They were apparently not born black, but made themselves so by the regular application of soot.

'And the chaconne is their ancient tribal dance,' said Mme Harper, appearing at my side. 'How remarkable.'

Her retinue crowded in behind her; one of the gallants, reading the sign, called for soap and water and demanded that the exhibit be scrubbed. Mme Harper made a small, exasperated noise, took my arm and turned away.

The next alcove contained a girl – one supposed her to be female for she was attired in a stylish mantua – completely covered in fur, with the exception of her lips, which were rouged and smiling. She rose from a chair, put aside the book she had been reading, curtseyed gracefully and began to recite an ode of Horace in excellent Latin. When she had finished she curtseyed again and returned to her chair.

The final alcove was dimly lit and at first I thought it was empty; then I discerned the sound of harsh breathing emanating from a pile of rags. The accompanying card said only '*Le Polypus*' – the many-footed one.

'What could it be?' Mme Harper peered into the darkness.

Monsieur Babinette appeared, took up a long stick that had been leaning against the wall and prodded the pile of rags, which emitted a feeble squeal and slowly unfolded itself to reveal a twisted, gangly creature.

'*Réveille-toi*, Polly,' he said, not unkindly.

The creature shuffled forward into the light and lifted two heads to gaze at us with four bleary blue eyes. It moved in a crab-wise fashion on six limbs, while two other limbs waved erratically about.

'*Lève-toi*, Polly,' said M. Babinette, poking it again. It batted irritably at his stick but, groaning softly, raised itself upright.

'*Montre-nous*, Polly.'

Hissing through its two sets of teeth, the creature pawed at its breast, parting the rags to reveal a single smooth torso dividing into two necks above and four legs beneath. It pulled the rags back over itself quickly, allowing only the briefest glimpse of what appeared to be two sets of male genitals.

'Oh, the poor thing,' Mme Harper said. 'Is it human? Do you think it has a soul?'

'As much as you, Madame,' it answered in thickly accented English.

58
The Best Day of My Life

❦

Sandro sent a message postponing his visit to us; then another, regretting that he would not be able to come at all. Our disappointment was allayed by an invitation to attend his final recital at Versailles; it included Isabel, Meryll and Grace. We immediately ordered new clothes, summoned *perruqiers* and perfumiers, had the caroche's paint touched up.

This was to be Grace's first grown-up occasion outside of our own house. When, on the day, she finally came downstairs after four hours of preparation I almost didn't recognise her.

'You are not going out in that dress,' I said when I had recovered the power of speech.

'Why not, Francis?' Her voice had acquired a new, cooler tone. 'Isn't it a pretty dress?'

It was a gorgeous dress, ivory stripes alternating with pale blue, a leaf motif embroidered around the bodice in silver thread with seed pearls. 'You are showing . . . it reveals . . . far too much.'

'It is the fashion.' She turned to Isabel, whose bodice barely covered her nipples. 'Isn't it?'

'Isabel is a married woman nearly twice your age,' I said. 'While it may be appropriate for her to flaunt her. . . her attributes, it is not the same for you. You are still . . . that is, I certainly hope you are still . . . In any case, I forbid it.'

Grace sniffled and looked as if she was about to cry. I softened

239

at the sight, because it made her seem a child again, until I caught her swift sideways glance at Isabel.

'Can she not at least put a kerchief over her . . . over that part of her . . . chest?' I asked Isabel.

'A kerchief!' Grace forgot to sniffle. 'Do you want them to think I'm a goose-girl?'

Meryll came in, saw Grace, made an elaborate bow and utterly undermined me. 'Mademoiselle! *Enchanté!* Do I know you? Have we met? Francis, you must introduce me at once to this beautiful young lady.'

Grace simpered and gave him her hand; he kissed it and winked at her. I had lost.

The recital was held in the Hall of Mirrors, which made it seem as if there were thousands rather than mere hundreds in attendance. The place is justly famous; some call it beautiful, but it gave me a headache. Also, my new shoes pinched. Only the King and his family sat; the rest of us stood about looking ornamental.

Grace tugged at my arm. 'Do you know who that is?' she whispered.

'Yes, that's the King . . .'

'No, not him. It's Monsieur de Visée, there, with the lute.'

I looked at the group of musicians assembled to accompany Sandro. 'The old man?'

'Yes. Robert de Visée. He has written the most beautiful music. You've heard me play his *Sarabande* over and over.'

'Oh yes, of course. That's the slow, plaintive one, isn't it? How marvellous that he is still able to perform. But hush now, Sandro is about to sing.'

Out of respect for his hosts, Sandro mixed French songs by Rameau and Lully with a selection of his most popular Italian arias. For an encore he performed extempore with each of the accompanying instruments. He accorded M. de Visée the honour of being last; I could see that this pleased the audience and the King.

After the performance Sandro came to find us. 'Thank God that is over,' he said, leaning on my shoulder in mock exhaustion. 'I hate French music.'

'You were superb,' said Isabel.

'Astonishing,' said Meryll.

'Not so bad,' I said.

'Monsieur Zanetti,' said Grace, 'do you think you could introduce me to Monsieur de Visée? I so long to meet him.'

'My fame is, apparently, second to some,' said Sandro, laughing. He offered Grace his arm and escorted her to the old man. All three sat down together, talking animatedly. M. de Visée played a few bars on his lute, then offered it to Grace. She shook her head, he insisted; she smiled shyly, took it and began to play. Through the din of chatter that filled the room I couldn't hear what she played, but Sandro and M. de Visée were gazing fondly at her. I had one of those moments of almost unbearable sweetness, with pleasure and pain in exquisite balance.

'She is lovely,' said a voice at my side.

It was Etienne du Bellay. I stifled the urge to smack his mild, pleasing face.

'I wonder if I might speak with you.' He took my arm and guided me out to the gardens. 'About her.'

So this is it, I thought. Her first marriage proposal. Of course I would refuse. I imagined a long line of young men seeking her hand. I would refuse them all.

We walked about for a while, du Bellay dropping names quite shamelessly though I pretended not to notice. I strolled, stopped, ignored him, interrupted him every time he seemed about to hit his stride.

'I wonder if I might perhaps speak more directly,' he said. 'You English are so fond of directness.'

At last, I thought. At last I will be able to tell you to go away. 'Please do,' I said.

'Mademoiselle Brown . . .'

'Yes . . .'

'I believe that you introduced her as your ward.'

'Yes.'

'I am not certain that I fully understand the term.'

'She is like my daughter.'

'Ah yes, I see. So she is not . . . you do not . . .' He intertwined his hands in a delicate gesture.

'What?' Surely I had misunderstood.

'I beg not to offend. I only wished to ascertain whether she was . . .'

I turned to face him. 'She is a daughter to me. I do not know what the custom is here, but in England we do not lie with our daughters.'

'Of course, of course. But this is good, this is what I had hoped to hear.' His manner was soothing; he took my arm and led me on. 'So you have given thought to her future, I am sure. A girl with her beauty and that fresh, natural charm . . . a special girl, and so many possibilities.'

It occurred to me that his incoherence was the result of his being so in love with Grace that he was unable to think straight. Although naturally I was pleased that my Grace inspired such raptures, I wished he would get to the point so that I could skewer his hopes as viciously as possible. 'Get to the point, du Bellay.'

'Indeed. Well. Here it is. Now of course there is no immediate financial benefit to you, or, for that matter, to me. No, but the possibilities for influence, which after all is both a more subtle and a more lasting currency, are nearly infinite.'

I gathered he meant that although he himself had no fortune, neither would he expect a great dowry. He seemed, as well, to have an inflated idea of his family's importance. Presumptuous pup.

'Especially if she were to have a child,' he was saying. 'And if the child was a boy . . .'

I had waited long enough. 'Even with a long betrothal, surely we cannot yet speak of children.'

'Betrothal?'

'I'm afraid she is too young for me to consider it, du Bellay. And even if she were of marriageable age, well, let me be direct as well. You are not good enough for her.' Now plead, I thought. Reiterate your attributes so that I can shoot them down one by one.

'Ah, my excellent Monsieur Damory, you misunderstand. But yes, you are right. I am not good enough for her, but I know someone who is . . . the very highest someone of all.'

I had not known it was possible to be icy-cold and burning at the same time. I was for a moment unable to move or speak, though I am surprised my look alone did not kill him. He stumbled backwards as though struck.

'Name your second, du Bellay.'

'Monsieur Damory, I apologise most sincerely. I meant no offence; indeed, I meant it as an honour to you and your family . . .'

'Name him or I will kill you right here.'

He opened his mouth and closed it again. 'D'Armillac.'

'Mr Meryll will call on him by midnight.' I stalked away, shaking with rage, and almost ran over Meryll before I saw him.

'Ah, there you are,' he said. 'I've been looking everywhere for you.'

'And I for you. You know Visconte d'Armillac? Yes? Go and see him, arrange a time and place for me to meet du Bellay. The sooner the better.'

'Oh Lord, Francis, not again. Never mind that now. We're going home. Grace . . .'

243

'Grace? My God, what has happened to Grace?'

'Nothing, that is, just the nose-bleeding again, but it won't stop. Anyway she's with Isabel in the caroche. Come along. I'll find d'Armillac later.'

Grace sat in the corner of the carriage, bleeding, weeping and furious. 'I've ruined my dress,' she said between sobs. 'I'm going to die of shame. I'll never leave the house again. I was so happy. Monsieur de Visée was so kind, and then the King came to speak to him, and he looked at me, and I curtseyed, and he smiled. He's so handsome, and not very old. It was the best day of my life and I've ruined it.'

59

I Laid Out this Path, I Planted that Rose

We arrived in the Bois de Boulogne at first light: Meryll, Tunnie, an extra footman, a surgeon. Du Bellay and d'Armillac were waiting. The exact terms of the offence and the challenge were read, swords were measured, the ground paced out, then du Bellay and I took off our coats and opened our shirts. D'Armillac insisted on looking under my shirt for concealed mail; he did it to insult me, of course. Meryll immediately did the same to du Bellay. The bystanders withdrew to the edge of the clearing. The two surgeons were laughing together about something and Meryll had to ask them to be quiet.

'*Prenez vos places,*' said d'Armillac.

We moved to the centre of the ground and touched the tips of our swords.

'*En garde,*' said Meryll.

Something moved in the woods; an old man stepped from behind a tree. No, it was just a shadow. Or was it? I looked again. It *was* a man, white-haired, bespectacled, thin, a bit stooped. He seemed familiar; I knew I'd seen him before, though I couldn't remember where.

'Who is that?' I called.

Everyone turned to look. I blinked; the stranger had vanished.

'Does your man wish to withdraw?' d'Armillac asked Meryll.

'No,' I said. 'Let us begin.' I lifted my sword.

Meryll looked concerned and was about to approach me; I shook my head. He stepped back to his place.

'*Commencez,*' said d'Armillac.

Duels, for the participants, happen too fast to remember; also, one is using an aspect of one's intelligence very far removed from the part of it that recalls, arranges, puts into words. I know how it went because Meryll and Tunnie told me. All I remember is that du Bellay was more skilful than I thought he would be.

Nevertheless, I got through his guard right away, laying open his cheek; he replied with a slice down my right forearm – bloody but not serious. One feels no pain until later, of course. Then came a bit of back-and-forth; he tried to force me into the trees, I retreated, grunting a bit as though tiring. Then, pretending to trip, I made him overextend on the lunge, which opened his flank. I danced away and as I passed him slashed his thigh, unfortunately just missing the hamstring. We edged around in a circle; he was limping now and I was pushing him, looking for a chance for a final strike. I feinted right, a little slow; he read the feint and lifted his sword to parry a thrust to the left. I took him on the right, slipping under his guard and deep into his abdomen. I thought I'd gone straight to the heart but he twisted and my blade caught on a rib. He seized my right hand, trapping me, and lifted his sword to strike at my neck. I raised my left hand to block it, wrenched my sword free and pulled it out. He crumpled, dead before he reached the ground.

Time began to slow. I looked down; I was soaked in blood. My right hand was numb; my sword dropped. Blood was flowing into my eyes; I tried to lift my left hand to wipe it away but couldn't make the arm work. I stared at it, willing it to obey me, and saw the long white bone exposed.

The rising sun slanted through the trees; the light broke into icy slivers. I turned, staggered, fell. A lovely calm came over me. So this is death, I thought. Meryll's face appeared, disappeared. There was a great jolting, I felt a sudden wave of nausea, then blackness.

I've become very small, weightless, untethered. Everyone is far away, their voices faint. Meryll again, and behind him the white-haired old man, looking down on me as though from a great height, smiling. Are you Death? I ask, but he doesn't answer.

They carry me to a boat and lay me on a richly hung bier. The boat has no sail, no rowers, but we glide out on to a glassy sea. Women with soft hands undress me and wash my wounds. Who are you? I ask.

Don't you know us?

The mist clears, their faces emerge. Miranda, Agnes, Lucy, Johanna, all in wimples and old-fashioned gowns. Ah, I think, I'm in *Le Morte D'Arthur*. That explains everything.

The soft swell of the ocean carries us on. Days pass, and gentle nights. It's evening when we arrive, the western sky still aglow and stars glimmering above. The Isle of Avalon is just as I'd always imagined it. I'm welcomed as an old friend, returning after long travels. They show me to a house that they tell me is mine. It's strangely familiar, like something from childhood, long forgotten. Oh, I remember this, I think, as I step out to the garden. I laid out this path, I planted that rose. The yew trees, the pyramid in the moonlight, I remember this. From somewhere in the house comes the sound of a lute. Grace is playing one of those slow, sad songs that she loves.

I stand in the doorway to watch. You shouldn't be here, I tell her. This place is only for the dead.

60

Down that Dark Road

🌿

The surgeon had been so certain that I was beyond hope, he didn't bother dressing my wounds until Meryll put a pistol to his head. Du Bellay's dying blow had lopped two fingers from my left hand, sliced open my face, removed half of my left ear and cut deep into my shoulder before ripping down my arm. I'd lost so much blood no one thought I'd survive the trip back to the house. For a fortnight I was in the grip of fever and delirium; another month passed before I could speak or sit up.

During this time I imagined many things; afterwards, I found it difficult to sort the dream from the real. Meryll had been an almost constant presence, Isabel too, and Tunnie. Many others had come and gone, the dead as well as the living; in my state I discerned no difference.

Japhet, my old dog, lay at the foot of the bed; Sebastian paid a call and upbraided me in his mocking way for getting cut up by a French son-of-a-whore. He acted out the duel, explaining where I had missed my chances. Until Meryll and Tunnie described the real duel for me, I thought Seb's version was accurate. The truly odd thing is that my hatred of him had vanished. It was not that I'd forgotten what he had done, but all that he had done, the good as well as the evil, was like smoke from a long-dead fire.

I had lengthy conversations with the stranger – the old man I'd seen in the Bois de Boulogne. He told me his name, but I forgot it immediately. It was only later, when I asked Meryll about him, that I realised he had been a dream, or a phantom, or a ghost – though of whom I had no idea. I'd constructed an entire scenario in which he, happening to have witnessed the duel, had followed us home and, being a doctor, offered his services. In fact, I'd credited him with saving my life and at first refused to believe Meryll when he said the man didn't exist. What had saved my life, Meryll thought, was the application of my own mould, astragalus and salix preparation, which Tunnie, remembering that it had been very effective when he'd cut his hand on a rusty knife, had found in my laboratory.

When I was at last able to sit up, sip broth, and stay awake for more than ten minutes, I made Meryll tell me all that had happened since I'd last been in the world.

Sandro had come; I'd been raving, but he sang to me, which had calmed me. He'd had to leave Paris for his next engagement in St Petersburg, but was writing constantly, demanding news. Du Bellay's death had been reported as a riding accident; his mother, the Marquise, grief-stricken, retired to her estate in the Loire. She had sent me a letter, which Meryll opened at my request. It said only, *'Forgive me. I have brought this on myself.'*

'What does she mean?' said Meryll. 'Forgive her for what?'

'I don't know.'

'Having an unspeakable ass of a son, I suppose.'

I'd asked for Grace at once, of course – as soon as I could speak. They said she would come; then they said she had come while I was asleep and would come again soon. At first I believed them because in my dreams, which I failed to distinguish from reality, she came often, sat on the side of the bed, played her lute and sang. She had been so glad to see Japhet again, and he to see her. I'd been relieved that she wasn't angry with me for killing du Bellay.

At last the truth came out. I asked for her again, growing irate when Meryll said she couldn't come at the moment. He sighed, left the room and returned a few minutes later with Tunnie and Isabel. They stood looking down at me; there was something in their faces that I didn't want to read. Instinctively I closed my eyes.

'Francis,' Isabel said, her tone so sad that at once I wanted it unsaid.

'No,' I said, my eyes still shut.

I could hear that she was crying. 'No,' I said again, raising my hand as though to ward off a blow, or to push the moment back into non-existence.

Even now, after almost two hundred years, I shy away. I do not want to remember; I do not want to write it. At the time, I was certain that I could will my own death if I desired it fiercely enough. I could not bear it that I had not been with her as she sickened and died, to save her, to protect her, to fight Death when he came for her, or, if that was not possible, then to go with her down that dark road. I pictured her wandering and lost, lonely and cold, but then I remembered the dream of Avalon, and I knew she was waiting for me.

61

My Secret Life

❧

I recovered my health slowly and unwillingly. I resented my body – first for becoming incapacitated when Grace needed me, then for strengthening, in its ineluctable animal way, towards life when my mind and heart yearned only for death.

I stayed in my darkened room. If I had been alone, I would gladly have let myself starve, but Tunnie pestered me to such a degree that I took sustenance to make him go away. Solitude was precious, sleep most precious of all, because every night in my dreams I died and my soul flew to Avalon. When I could not sleep I lay in bed with my eyes shut, telling myself stories about Grace, what she was doing, how she was growing, her suitors, her gowns, her *bavaroises*, her daily joys and tiny, fleeting troubles, which she confided in me and which I could always put right. It was my secret life.

I had visitors sent away, but one morning in November a letter arrived from Mme Harper, who had been rebuffed several times before. It said that she absolutely had to see me and would call at four o'clock, no reply needed.

'You can say that I am not at home,' I told Tunnie.

'But the note says it is a matter of importance.'

'Tell her I am not at home.'

'No.'

'What?'

'I cannot lie.'

'That statement is a logical contradiction, Tunnie.'

'Yes, sir. I will show her in when she comes, and this is what she will see.' He fetched a mirror. 'Look at that. Do you want her to die of fright?'

It was true that I had become rather unkempt. I didn't recognise the gaunt, bearded man in the glass.

'And I might also point out, sir, that you smell very rank.'

I had not the strength to resist. Tunnie, delighted to have an occasion at last, fussed happily with my clothes. I had lost so much weight that nothing fitted; he summoned an emergency tailor. I was bathed, shaved, manicured, coiffed, perfumed, encased in silk and lace and propelled downstairs to greet Mme Harper, her *demoiselle*, slave boy and ocelot.

I saw the shock in her eyes; Tunnie's ministrations had evidently failed to achieve the full semblance of health. The *demoiselle* settled to wait in an antechamber; I told Tunnie to take the boy and the cat to Grace's room as she would enjoy playing with it.

Tunnie clucked and Mme Harper gave me a strange look. I realised my error and almost turned to flee but Tunnie was blocking the stairs. I murmured an apology as a footman led the way to the morning room, where tea and cakes awaited. Who had arranged all this? Tunnie, I supposed, wanting to call him back so that he could partake of them with Mme Harper and let me go back to bed.

We sat. The footman poured, served, withdrew. Mme Harper spoke of ordinary things. I had learned a way of slipping out of the world, using those little cracks between words, but it was very unsatisfactory. I waited for the visit to end so that I could return to my secret life with Grace.

'It is about your ward Grace that I wanted to speak,' said Mme Harper, stitching my two lives abruptly together. 'Ah, I see that has got your attention.'

'Yes.'

'Please accept my deepest sympathies.'

I said nothing; accepting was not what I wanted to do.

'I would not consider it any of my concern,' she said, 'but for one thing that I think may be of interest to you. Knowing that your duel with du Bellay had to do with your ward's honour, I thought I should tell you. Do you remember Monsieur Gribois?'

'From the Marquise du Bellay's mystical soirée?'

'Yes. After that evening, I decided to consult him on some business matters. He gave the advice I requested – and good advice it has turned out to be. But then he guided the conversation to other services he could provide: love potions and spells to attract but also, he insinuated, poisons and curses to dispose of enemies. My doubting response had the effect of encouraging him to boast about work he had done for clients of the very best sort. He told me, among other things, that he had set a curse on behalf of Mme du Bellay, on a young and highly unsuitable girl with whom her son Etienne had, she believed, become besotted. At the time I did not take him seriously and gave the matter no further thought. I had only the vaguest idea of Etienne – he had not made much of an impression. I'm afraid I did not recall meeting your ward at all until – when we heard that she had died – my *demoiselle* reminded me that you had introduced her on the day we visited the Exhibition of Monstrosities, and that Etienne had been quite attentive to her on that occasion. And then I thought of that horrid Monsieur Gribois and his curse.'

Forgive me, the Marquise had written. *I have brought this on myself*. I began to understand.

When Mme Harper left, I sat looking out at the sunny garden. The summer had passed; it was autumn and red leaves were falling. After weeks in a shuttered bedroom, the light and colour felt like an assault. Until she had spoken, so casually it seemed, of Grace's death, no one had dared to say her name. I closed my eyes and willed myself back to Avalon, but something had happened; I could not get in. As I pushed at it with my mind, seeking the entrance, it drifted away, a mist closed over and it disappeared. I knew, as I had not let myself know before, that Grace was gone.

I went to her room; it was dim and silent, the shutters closed. As I opened them I had a moment of fear that all trace of her would have vanished. But no; when I turned, everything was as she'd left it, though far too tidy. I looked into her wardrobes, stuffed with gay silks, her chests of linen and lace, her jewellery box with the pearls I'd given her, the opal bracelet, the golden rings. The little carved Japhet, very shabby, looked out of place on her dressing table next to her silver brushes and ivory combs. Her lute leaned against a chair whose seat cushion still held her impression. I picked it up, sat in her place, touched the strings.

I told myself that the Marquise's curse had nothing to do with Grace's death. Looking back, I could see the illness's gradual approach – the fevers, bouts of lethargy, the bleeding from her nose. And yet the Marquise clearly believed not only that her curse had been effective, but that it had rebounded on her with terrible justice. In her view of the workings of fate, her act against Grace had been the true cause of the death of Etienne.

But that was nonsense. Wasn't it? Despite my efforts to ignore it, an awful symmetry arose and presented itself, in which my desire to kill Etienne had returned to me as the death of Grace. I'd wanted to kill him, I had to acknowledge, since I first met him, though I pretended I merely disliked him. And when I killed him – I remembered the sensation of my sword entering his body, probing for the heart, scraping a rib – it never occurred to me that I was taking the life of someone's child.

With sudden clarity I saw the evil in my own nature seeping into the world like poison, like curses. I had no horns on my head, no claws, no hideous deformity, but there was a monster in me. My black temper, my love of duelling, the raw pleasure of fighting for my life, the joy of hurting and, yes, the satisfaction of killing. If I had not been so consumed with the passion to kill Etienne I could have been with Grace, perhaps even saved her somehow. I'd had a choice, and I chose death over life.

I put the lute down carefully, the strings making a dissonant murmur.

Other people were not like this. Meryll, for instance – he could become angry, he could fight if necessary, but he had no craving for violence as I apparently did. When had it all started? I thought back over the people I had hated, the people I had killed or wanted to kill – du Bellay, d'Armillac. The men – faces forgotten now – I'd fought in London; I could not even remember what we had quarrelled about. Sebastian, Jack Hathaway, Purefoy. A crowd of other, smaller hates, lethal desires never spoken or acted upon, going back as far as I could remember, back to my father. As soon as I thought of him I felt my fury rising like a fire. There was something ecstatic about that sensation of pure anger; a part of me loved it, cherished it, nurtured and fed it.

I fingered the small scar on my brow where my father had struck me, and next to it the much larger scar, still swollen, given me by du Bellay. I pictured my father's face, but try as I might, I couldn't compel it to wear the look of cold contempt that had always enraged me. He insisted on regarding me quizzically, with a small smile.

Do you still want to kill me, boy? he said, but there was no hard sneer in his voice, just fond amusement.

No, I said. And, Forgive me.

And to Grace also, Please forgive me.

254

62

Remember Them

❧

I insisted on visiting her grave. Isabel, Meryll and Tunnie tried to dissuade me but I would not be put off, so they wrapped me in blankets and bundled me into the carriage.

'Where is she?' I asked.

'Quite near,' said Isabel. 'St-Anne-de-Lys. It's such a pretty spot.'

'Now you mustn't think we've converted to Rome,' Meryll said. 'The curé was very sympathetic, and found himself able to overlook the fact that we, that she . . . not baptised Catholic. Half his family had been Huguenots, he said. She had . . . it was a lovely service . . .'

'Be quiet, Edward,' Isabel said gently.

Tunnie rearranged my blankets. 'Are your feet warm? We should have brought a brick for your feet.'

Their anxious faces watched me as though I might explode or expire at any moment. The carriage proceeded at a walking pace, but even so the jolting caused me to wince.

'What is it, sir? Are you bleeding? Has the wound reopened?' Tunnie pulled at the blankets, trying to look. 'We'd better go home. I knew this was a terrible idea.'

I pushed his hand away. 'I'm not bleeding.'

The church of St-Anne-de-Lys was small and square, with narrow windows and a slender bell tower. At the side, a gate led to the graveyard. Old pear trees leaned over the walls; beyond were fields and meadows.

They took me to her grave. 'You can change the headstone,' Isabel said. 'We didn't know what you'd want to say, so we just, well, here it is.'

Grass was already growing over the mound. A plain marble stone, a few words:

> *Here Lieth the Body of Grace Brown,*
> *born December 2, 1717, died July 12th, 1733.*
> *Beloved Ward of Francis Damory.*

I asked them to leave me alone. There was some doubt about my ability to stand unaided, so Tunnie found a chair for me.

I thought about Grace, but also about my life, which had so nearly ended and in which I had achieved nothing of any worth. What, aside from killing a few people, had I done with my thirty-three years? I had dabbled at chemistry and medicine, fighting and gambling, women. If you'd asked me what my purpose was in life I would have said, to look after Grace. And in that I had singularly failed. I had failed to look after any of my children.

I made myself remember them: Christopher, to whom I'd paid so little regard. Miranda's and my baby daughter, dead of the smallpox before she was two months old. For a moment I couldn't even recall her name . . . oh yes, Margaret, for Miranda's mother. Johanna's unborn son, who never had a name or a grave.

All through the winter I went to the graveyard every day. It was the only place I wanted to be. Because I had not sat with Grace during her illness, I sat with her now. The curé stopped by occasionally. He was a homely young man with prominent ears, new to the job. He had the gift of reticence; often he would say nothing, just stand in silence at my side, then murmur a brief blessing and depart. Sometimes he would speak of everyday things, drawing my attention to a bird, the wind, new buds on the pear trees. He noticed shapes in the clouds. 'Isn't that one just like a ship,' he would say, 'no, not a ship, a woman on ice skates, see her skirts?'

Spring returned and still I lingered at the grave. I was possessed by a vague sense of waiting, though for what, I had no idea. Perhaps just for time to pass and my wounds to heal, or so I thought.

63
What I Must Do

I was not the only visitor to the graveyard. Some walked through quickly, paid their respects and hurried out; others lingered. A few came every day. Occasionally a family would bring food and wine, spread a cloth and have their dinner upon the grave of a favourite ancestor.

One day my attention was drawn to just such a group – a man in his fifties, a young woman of eighteen or so and a little girl, perhaps nine or ten. The curé had stopped to speak with them and I heard him mention my name.

The curé returned to the church; the man whispered in the little girl's ear, pointed at me and, smiling, gave her a push in my direction. She trotted up to me. 'Are you Monsieur Damory?'

I acknowledged that I was.

'My papa says to tell you,' she glanced over her shoulder and received encouraging gestures, 'that he is also Monsieur Damory.'

'And . . .' called the man.

'And,' said the little girl, 'he invites you to . . . would be pleased if you . . . would join us.'

I stood; she took my hand and led me across the graves to her father. We bowed.

'I understand your name is spelled differently,' he said, 'but perhaps we are related nonetheless. My name is Bertrand d'Amorie. This is my eldest daughter, Arlène,' the young woman curtseyed, 'and my youngest, Charlotte, whom you have met. And we are here to visit the grave of my mother.' He pointed to the headstone at his feet.

I read the inscription. *Here lieth Henriette Bréville d'Amorie, Beloved Wife of* . . . I bent to push aside a tuft of grass that obscured the bottom of the inscription . . . *Thibault Geoffroi Herbert d'Amorie*. Thibault . . . Tobias? TGHD. I looked again at Bertrand d'Amorie, recalling the portrait of Tobias that hung in the library at Farundell. Yes, the same nose and something similar, too, around the eyes, though Tobias had a pale, ascetic cast to his visage and Bertrand the flush of good living.

I recalled the eerie voice of M. Gribois's boy and felt a shiver pass over my skin; in that moment my obsession with Tobias began. I'd been fascinated by his legend, intrigued by his alchemy, but I had never believed Enderby's claims about his longevity. Now I began to wonder. It struck me with all the force of revelation that it was Tobias who had, all along, guided my destiny towards this very encounter.

'I think I may know your father,' I said.

'Truly? But he died more than forty years ago, and you cannot be so old.'

'He's dead?'

'Yes, though he is not buried here; he lies near our home in Cernay, in the Alsace. My mother is here because her family, the Brévilles, are from here and when my father died she returned to them.'

'I beg your pardon,' I said. 'I must be mistaken.' These people would conclude that I was mad if I told them what I was thinking.

But I knew that Thibault Geoffroi Herbert d'Amorie had to be Tobias Geoffrey Herbert Damory. And this was what I had been waiting for.

I joined Bertrand and his daughters on the grave of my step-great-great-grandmother; over cakes and wine we decided that we must be eighteenth cousins, forty-three times removed. Bertrand's robust good humour was a tonic and I began to shed my morose invalid ways. I talked, I smiled, once I laughed at something little Charlotte said, and the sound so startled me that I fell to coughing. I even noticed that Arlène had a beguiling dimple when she smiled.

I invited them to Les Pommiers for supper and during their stay in Paris they came often. Isabel welcomed them as long-lost cousins. She would have welcomed Satan himself and all his demons if that was required to get me interested again in life. Bertrand had come to the city to purchase Arlène's trousseau; she was to be married to a neighbouring baron in September. Isabel took Arlène and Charlotte under her wing, escorting them on the rounds of the best dressmakers, hatters, glove-makers, shoe-makers, lace-makers and so on. Bertrand was delighted to be spared the tedium; he and Meryll and I went for walks or drives, and occasionally joined the ladies for an evening at the theatre or opera.

I waited until a few days before their departure to raise the subject of Tobias. Isabel and Meryll had known of my interest in him but it was news to them that I thought he might still be alive.

'But if he really was Bertrand's father,' said Isabel, 'you are too late. Bertrand's father is dead now.'

Bertrand nodded. 'And he was not particularly old. I remember his funeral; it was the first time I wore full mourning. Awful stiff suit.'

'Do you know how he died? Was it a long illness, or quite sudden?'

'He was always travelling,' Bertrand said, 'and succumbed to a sudden, fatal illness whilst abroad, in Switzerland, or was it in Italy? I cannot recall the details. Unfortunately, because of the seasonal difficulties of transport, his body could not be returned to us, but his bones came back in a casket.'

'How remarkable,' I said. 'That is exactly what happened to him the first time.'

'What do you mean?' said Isabel, and I explained what I'd learned about Tobias's bones.

'Do you know where your father was born?' I asked Bertrand.

He thought for a long time, then shook his head. 'Not certain knowledge, no. I'd always assumed at Cernay, but I realise I have no basis for that.'

'He travelled a great deal, you say?'

'My mother used to say that she scarcely noticed the difference in him, dead or alive; he wasn't there.'

'Did he leave any books or papers?'

'That is quite possible. As a family, we are the sort who never throw things away as long as there is an attic to put them in, and our house has innumerable attics.'

I continued with the questions until Bertrand threw up his hands, laughing. 'I don't know the answers, Francis my dear. But I will help you to find them. I meant, in any case, to invite you to visit; now I insist. There may be clues in the attics, and perhaps people still alive who knew my father better than I. Come to Château Langenfeld with us, enjoy the countryside, and who knows what you may discover.'

I caught him exchanging glances with Meryll and realised they were only humouring me, but that didn't matter.

The evening before my departure I went to Grace's grave for the last time. I'd bought a rose-bush and, borrowing a spade from the curé, I planted it, then filled a bucket at the well and watered it.

I rested my hand on the earth, still warm from the day. Death ruled the darkness below and he would never release my darling girl. But if Tobias was still alive, then he had defeated death. I had to discover what he knew.

The setting sun spilled gold across the barley fields; a blackbird sang from the top of the bell tower. 'I'm going away, sweetheart,' I said. 'There's someone I have to find, or at least try to find. I believe it is what I must do.'

64
Château Langenfeld

🌺

Bertrand's carriage was very comfortable, with wide seats upholstered in blue leather. He'd had to hire another one for Arlène's new dresses and hats; Tunnie rode in that, with Arlène's maid and Bertrand's valet. We were always well-provided with food and drink; in addition to lengthy dinners at the best inns, Bertrand enjoyed nibbling at something almost continually and had food baskets prepared at every stop.

The journey took six days in easy stages. The first two, across the flat lands to the east of Paris, were swift, the roads good, but as we approached the Vosges Mountains the way became more difficult. The road followed the river valleys, with frequent fords and rickety bridges, and was not always in good repair. The reliability of the posting stations, too, deteriorated the further from the capital we progressed: horses we had ordered were not available, postilions arrived late or too drunk to ride. Bertrand took it all with good humour, regarding delays as opportunities to sample the local cuisine and buy a few bottles of the local wine.

After his father died, Bertrand's mother Henriette had taken him to live with her father in Paris. He was a prominent lawyer and, her mother having died, Henriette took over his household. Young Bertrand, it was hoped, would go into the Law as well, though he yearned to be an actor and spent several years pursuing that desire until it became clear that he would not succeed. He returned to the Law, much to his grandfather's relief, and found an outlet for his theatrical flair as an eloquent and impassioned advocate. He had recently been made a judge which, although gratifying and highly remunerative, he nevertheless regretted, for it reduced his scope for drama.

Although he came into the Cernay estates on his twentieth birthday, he had remained in Paris for several years, practising law and building a reputation. He married Constance, the illegitimate but acknowledged daughter of a marquis, and when he took her to Cernay they already had two children, a boy and a girl; both died of the smallpox soon after. Several other children followed, of whom three lived: Arlène, Charlotte and between them, a boy. Claude, now sixteen, was at school with the monks and – to Bertrand's despair – was determined to enter the priesthood.

Thibault d'Amorie's estates and investments had been left in the care of a man named Julien Pernelle, who proved an able and honest steward. When Bertrand came to Cernay and assumed control of his inheritance he found himself a wealthy man.

All this, at far greater length and with many discursive details, I learned as we travelled. Aside from exercising his natural volubility, I saw that Bertrand, in telling me about himself, hoped to engender similar candour in me. I disappointed him, though he never showed it. For a thousand reasons, not least of which was my knowledge that I had nothing to boast about, I found it hard to speak of my past; there were few good memories that were not inextricably linked to very bad ones.

Bertrand had long since asked Meryll about the obvious matter of my missing fingers, my scars and debilities – I still could not raise my left arm above the shoulder – and had learned about Grace and the duel. With extreme delicacy he made it known that although he would never presume to pry, he would welcome any confidences I cared to bestow.

Although little Charlotte, mercifully, was nothing like Grace – dark where Grace was fair, funny and sharp where Grace was kind and sweet-natured – it was not always easy to see her hug and kiss her 'dear Papa-who-stinks-of-garlic', and to watch her sleep in his arms.

Arlène presented other difficulties. Demure and decorous while her father was awake, she took advantage of his frequent naps – which I enjoyed for the silence they brought – to flirt with me. She would complain of the heat, loosen her kerchief, tug her bodice lower, then lean against me as though overcome with drowsiness. The joltings of the carriage would cause her arm to slip and her hand to drift sleepily across my thigh. Uncannily, she always managed to rouse herself just as Bertrand stirred, so that by the time he woke and opened his eyes, Arlène was upright and with her garments once more modestly arranged.

Across from me Charlotte, sometimes wakeful, watched these performances. I suspected she knew exactly what her sister was doing, but had not yet come up with a clever remark or, perhaps, the occasion to deploy it. I learned later that she was being bribed to keep silent.

My plan was to ignore Arlène. I could pretend to be asleep as well as anyone, and I succeeded very well until our next-to-last day on the road. We'd had a late start and decided to carry on for an extra stage that evening; the roads were reported to be decent, horses were available, the postilions were not too drunk. We'd been going for about an hour when a storm broke right over us, thunder and lightning and torrential, blinding rain. Our postilion and driver managed to keep the horses on the road, but the following coach, top-heavy with baggage and containing Tunnie and the other servants, ran into the ditch. No one was hurt, but the coach was thoroughly stuck. We helped to free the horses, then decided to leave the driver and postilion with the wrecked coach and its baggage and take its passengers with us to the next post, from where we would send assistance.

We made room for Tunnie and the other servants, and in the rearranging of bodies in the dark, Arlène found her way on to my lap. She had two hours in which to obtain evidence of arousal and at this, eventually, she did not fail.

Château Langenfeld was a sprawling, appealing, inelegant pile; flocks of geese and chickens inhabiting the courtyard gave it a rustic air. It was set among three hundred acres of its own vineyards above the town of Cernay. Beyond the cultivated land the wooded hills stretched for miles, home to boar, wolves, bandits and, reportedly, a unicorn.

We were expected, although two days late – that had been expected too. Madame d'Amorie – Constance as she at once insisted I address her – was exactly as I had pictured her while listening to Bertrand. She was plump, petite and cheerful, though very much in command of her household, who scurried to do her bidding almost before she spoke.

The château had received so many additions over the years, in so many architectural styles, that it was impossible to say to which period the building belonged. The governing principle seemed, in any case, to have been function rather than form. Bertrand and Constance escorted me to a chamber on the first floor, which Bertrand told me had been his father's room. 'It's much as he left it.'

'Certainly it is not,' said Constance. 'What will Cousin Francis think? The bedding is new, and the hangings; there are new curtains, a new carpet . . . It's our best guest room.'

The room was large and square, with oak wainscoting and a coffered ceiling. Deep-set windows had small leaded panes: some looked out over the valley towards the distant, slow-flowing Rhine, others framed views of the dark mountains to the west and north. A massive fireplace filled one wall, facing an equally imposing bed set into a panelled alcove and hung with forest-green brocade. It bore a distinct resemblance to certain rooms at Farundell. Had Tobias missed his home?

65
A Perpetual Traveller

The following day Constance asked her major-domo to show me around the château's attics and storerooms. I had not quite appreciated that when Bertrand spoke of his family's penchant for keeping things, he meant that they kept literally everything. Nor was there any apparent order; things had been put wherever was convenient.

I started from Tobias's room and worked outwards. The drawers of the desk were empty of all but paper, pens and ink; the chests, cupboards and shelves held only my own things. Hardly surprising after so many years, but I didn't want to overlook the obvious. A cupboard down the hall yielded nothing but some moth-eaten woollens and four pairs of extremely large shoes that might have been a hundred or even two hundred years old.

Château Langenfeld's library was modest compared with the one at Farundell, and in less than an hour I'd taken down and examined every book. None had the distinctive TGHD glyph and none had as their subject matter anything remotely related to alchemy. If Tobias had achieved what I suspected, he would have had no further need of books.

The day was hot and breezeless. I abandoned coat and waist-coat and ventured into the baking attics, working my way past broken chairs, empty picture frames, a rocking horse and crates of children's toys towards the trunks and boxes stacked in the eaves.

If he had planned this death as neatly as he'd planned his first one, Tobias would have taken pains to ensure that the event did not look in the least planned; he would not have tidied his life away. And indeed, he had not. Spread among three different attics and a number of storerooms and cupboards in remote, unused portions of the château I found dozens of boxes and trunks full of papers and miscellaneous objects dating from his time at Cernay.

I carried the first lot down to my room, rolled up my sleeves and set to work. There were bills, contracts, deeds, account books, ledgers, papers related to lawsuits, documents pertaining to taxes in several principalities, sheaves of articles cut out of newspapers, pamphlets, advertisements for bunion cures and Elixirs of Youth, sheet music, business cards from tailors, furniture makers and property agents, a yellowed piece of lace, a green kid glove in a woman's size, a red silk stocking, dried rosebuds, broken pens and an enormous number of letters.

After an hour I was sweaty, thirsty and dusty; when Arlène appeared with a bottle of chilled wine and two glasses I was almost pleased to see her. She tried to pick up where we had left off in the carriage; I tried to have a conversation about matri-mony. 'Your maidenhead belongs to your husband,' I said, as sanctimoniously as I could.

'Oh yes, part of the bargain.' She made a face. 'He doesn't deserve it.'

'Perhaps the good Baron will oblige by dying on your wedding night,' I said, thinking of Mme Harper's husband. 'Or he may be the sort who doesn't like women at all.' I thought of Reginald, who had turned out to be, in many ways, quite the most obliging husband Isabel could have hoped for.

'Your sister told me about her husband. Unfortunately, my fiancé likes women. He had two previous wives and whenever we are alone he tries to touch me with his horrid fat little hands. I can't bear it, but I'd very much like it if you touched me again.'

'I wonder where Tunnie is. He said he'd be right back.'

'I've paid Charlotte to keep him busy for an hour.'

In the end, I was forced to acknowledge that there were quite a few things one could do that did not compromise the maidenhead; we did them, on that and many other occasions during my stay.

My excavation of the life of Tobias in his incarnation as Thibault d'Amorie stretched out through the long Alsatian summer. I started with the accounts, legal documents and ledgers. He had bought the Langenfeld estate through a property broker based in Paris, and did not take up residence until some years later. The household books showed that he came and went; most entries had been made by his wife Henriette, a frugal manager of the domestic budget.

Thibault's business interests had been many and varied: he owned tin and silver mines in the west of England, a dye-works in Rotterdam, paper mills up and down the Rhine, a scientific instrument manufacturer in Antwerp, a shipping company in Genoa, a publisher in Paris, shares in dozens of other companies. Aside from the fact that in defiance of the law of averages every one of his investments seemed to prosper, there was not the slightest suggestion that Thibault d'Amorie was unusual in any way. The only thing noteworthy was that about a year before he died, he sold a number of stocks and shares, realising quite a significant profit which did not appear to have been reinvested. I turned to the letters, with more positive results.

Thibault had corresponded with people in many countries and languages, on subjects ranging from medicine, philosophy and architecture to music and mathematics. Among the ones I could read (those in English, French, Italian, German, Greek and Latin; the Russian and Hebrew were beyond me, as was something that I speculated might be Arabic), there was nothing of particular relevance, until I found the Boyle letters.

Erasmus Enderby would have been pleased to learn that Mr Boyle had indeed corresponded with the real Tobias Damory, though to judge from Boyle's end of the correspondence it was unsatisfactory. Many of his letters were pleading in tone, others expressed frustration. All were extremely respectful. Despite the fact that they used code words for every aspect of the alchemical process (anyone unfamiliar with the matter would have thought it a correspondence about viniculture), I gathered that Tobias refused to reveal the ultimate secrets because he thought Boyle too trusting of others, too open about the Great Work.

Another correspondent caught my eye: the Duchesse de Cossé-Brissac, Mme du Bellay's famous mystical mother. After numerous references to plans, building materials, the resonance of various geometric shapes, the combining of pigment with scented oils, it dawned on me that Thibault must have been 'the architect skilled in the magical arts' who had designed that tower with its cabinet of curiosities, seven temples and musical chambers. It was evident that the Duchesse was passionately in love with him; she protested continually about his coldness, his indifference, his failure to reply to her almost daily missives, which sometimes ran to a dozen closely written pages. The final letter dropped a greater revelation in my lap; it referred to 'our daughter', the newborn Marie-Louise. I checked the dates; yes, it had to be the Marie-Louise who would become the Marquise du Bellay. I'd fucked Tobias's daughter in his temple; I'd killed his grandson. Connected by fate, indeed.

I spent the days up to my elbows in dusty piles of paper and, aside from regular interludes with Arlène which began, inevitably, to ease my melancholy, I achieved nothing. Whether or not Thibault was Tobias, his life, to all appearances, had ended as Bertrand said. If he had lived on in some other guise, he had left no clue. None of the correspondence yielded any suggestion of the new life that he must have been preparing for himself elsewhere. Perhaps he had several lives going at once; if so, he had not permitted any leakage between them.

I tried to put myself in his place. By the time he came to Cernay he had lived, if I was right, for a hundred and thirty-odd years. How old did he look? He was evidently attractive (Mme de Cossé-Brissac was not the only enamoured correspondent) and not in the least feeble; he had sired children, endured the rigours of travel, managed his affairs with exceptional dexterity. The tone of the letters addressed to him suggested that he possessed a dry sense of humour and considerable joie de vivre; though firm in his opinions, he was a gracious and valued friend. I imagined him poised in the middle age of his portrait at Farundell, one of those chameleon people who look old or young, lovely or homely, seraphic or sad according as the light falls on their faces. But at some point it would be noted that he seemed not to age, questions would be raised; he would have to move on. How long could he stay in any one place, in any one life? Fifteen years? Twenty at the most. What must it be like to tear yourself away from your home time and time again? Did his wife know? Suspect? Perhaps it was to preserve some necessary rootlessness that he remained a perpetual traveller, using Cernay only as a place to rest for a brief while, replenish his coffers, attend to correspondence. Perhaps he had other such places.

Still – could I have left my young son? But what was the alternative? To stay and wait for him and everyone you love to die while you live on. The horror, the inhuman sorrow of that, was impossible to bear. I understood why he always had to leave.

66

The Order of the Rosy Cross

I asked about Julien Pernelle. Bertrand remembered him as a man already past middle age and thought he would surely be dead by now, but enquiries were sent out. In due course we learned that, though nearing ninety, he still lived. He had retired to a monastery and taken holy orders a few years after Bertrand had returned to Cernay and claimed his inheritance.

The monastery of St Anthony was a few miles away in the town of Isenheim. I set out early one morning on horseback, with Tunnie for company and a mongrel hound of Bertrand's named Schwarzie who'd taken a fancy to me. The sun rose over the river as we made our way down to the road. Pockets of mist lingered in the valley and the cool air echoed with the clang of cowbells and a child's shrill 'Hi hi hi' as she twitched her willow wand to direct a flock of geese.

The roadside crucifixes, common everywhere, were even more numerous here. I found them grotesque. What was gained by this depiction of torture and death? No one had to look beyond their own life to see suffering and death aplenty. They reminded me of the anatomy theatre, the corpse spread on the slab. The excruciating detail of the carving revealed the muscles and tendons as though the body had been flayed for exhibition. To the people of this region it was so ordinary a sight that it had no effect, but I had to avert my eyes.

I left Schwarzie and Tunnie at an inn and rode to the monastery, which was a little outside the town. It was clearly fallen from better times, with high weed-pocked walls and a dank courtyard that smelled of piss.

The Antonine Order's particular work was the care of sufferers from St. Anthony's Fire. Unfortunately, the saint's intercessions were not always effective; the monastery was home to a number of invalids in the advanced stages of the disease. They were a sad sight, taut with long-endured pain, faces blotched with fiery red patches, their fingers and toes, hands and feet blackened and rotted away. The more able hobbled or crawled; most sat unmoving, waiting for the kindness of death.

When I enquired after Brother Renatus (as Julien Pernelle was now called), the gate-keeper squinted at my missing fingers and the ugly red scar across my face and assumed that I had come seeking treatment. As well as being half blind, he was apparently half deaf; despite my attempts to explain that I was only here to see Brother Renatus, he ushered me into the chapel so that I could begin my cure by praying to St Anthony.

I shouted 'Brother Renatus!' into his ear. He smiled, nodded, said something that sounded like 'Please wait,' but could equally have meant 'Pray and wait for deliverance.' He shuffled away.

The chapel was cool, silent and so dark that I tripped over a loose paving stone and banged my knee. I cursed under my breath and groped my way forward, nearly falling over a crouching monk. He was sweeping the aisle, the same spot over and over. He glared at me as though I'd brought dog shit in on my boots as I sank into a pew and nursed my bruised knee.

'You think you suffer?' he hissed in my ear. 'Try *that* for suffering, why don't you?' He poked his broom handle at the altar, then returned to his sweeping with renewed vigour.

As my eyes adjusted to the dim light I made out a tall painted altarpiece. It depicted a Crucifixion, by far the most hideous I had yet seen. The figure of the Christ loomed disproportionately large. His ribs bulged, the spear-wound gaped in His side. His flesh was riddled with pus-filled cuts; hundreds of black splinters festered under the green-shadowed skin. His elongated arms twisted out of their shoulder sockets, knotted with pain. His head hung down, slack-jawed, grey-lipped beneath a brow crowned with suppurating sores and thorns long and vicious as knives. His gnarled feet curled around the iron spike like tree-roots, dripping thick, ropy blood; His hands clawed the sky in a beseeching, futile gesture.

I felt sick. I tore myself away from the grisly sight and fled. I sat on a stone bench in the sunny cloister, dazzling bright after the gloom of the chapel, and tried to erase the memory of that hideous Christ. I watched ants coming and going from a small, perfectly conical mound of earth. I felt a pang of envy for these creatures who, no matter their difficulties, at least had no souls to suffer the torments of sin and ignorance. They could not make wrong choices; they could not lose all that mattered to them; they could not waste their lives.

'You wished to speak with me, my son?'

I turned to see a slight, stooped figure in the Order's black habit. 'Brother Renatus?'

'That is what they call me.' He sat down beside me and tucked his hands into his sleeves. He was bright-eyed as a bird, his face seamed and sun-browned, his shiny pate bald but for a few wiry white hairs.

'And you were once Julien Pernelle?'

'That was my name.'

'I am staying with Bertrand d'Amorie at Langenfeld, and we

have been . . .' I realised that I should have worked out in advance exactly what I was going to say, but it was too late; I had started and had to prattle on in the hope that some reasonable explanation would occur to me. 'I am a cousin of his, a distant cousin, from an English branch of the family that went over with King William. I'm something of a family historian, I suppose you could say, and I'm tracking down d'Amories all over the place. We are certainly a fascinating lot! I intend writing brief biographies of as many as I can. I believe you knew Thibault d'Amorie and I was hoping that you could tell me . . .'

'He's dead.'

'Yes, so I have heard.'

He shook his head, *tsked* to himself, got up and walked away.

'Wait!' I hurried after him. 'Please don't go. I just want to ask a few questions.'

'You tell your masters in the Inquisition that I have nothing to say. Can they not leave an old monk in peace?' His voice took on a querulous tone that seemed to me not entirely genuine.

'I'm not from the Inquisition. Do I look like an inquisitor?' I had never met an inquisitor, but I'd always imagined them with hooded robes and fierce glares. I tried to appear friendly and mild, but Brother Renatus scuttled off across the courtyard and disappeared around a corner.

I followed, slowly so as not to alarm him. Surely this dumb show of idiocy, this fear of the Inquisition, which, as far as I knew, had not been active in France for many decades, were proof that he did know something about Thibault. I caught up with him in the vegetable garden, where he was energetically hoeing between rows of cabbages. When he saw me approaching he turned his back, hunched over his hoe and began edging towards a group of tall tomato plants among which he tried to hide.

I stood at a respectful distance. 'Brother Renatus, please don't run away. I promise you I'm not with the Inquisition. I'm only interested in Thibault d'Amorie because, well, he seems to have lived such a fascinating life . . .'

Brother Renatus emerged from the tomatoes, straightened and gazed up at me. 'He's dead,' he said firmly.

'Yes, you told me . . .' Something about the way he'd said it struck me; he'd used the same tone before, exactly the same words. And I'd replied – what had I said? Something insignificant, and that was when he'd shaken his head and walked off. I'd said the wrong thing. '*Dieu merci il est mort*,' I said, and repeated it in English. 'Thank God he's dead.'

Brother Renatus burst into tears and embraced me. 'You have come in answer to my prayers,' he said when he had recovered, wiped his eyes and blown his nose heartily into the sleeve of his robe. 'We in the Order are all so old, you see, and I have been so afraid that we will die before we are able to pass the teachings on to a new generation, as we are required by oath to do.'

Did he think I was seeking to become a monk? 'I'm not here to join your Order, Brother Renatus. I'm not even a Catholic. It's Thibault d'Amorie I'm interested in.' I leaned towards his ear and spoke loudly and clearly.

'Yes, yes, he is the Imperator of our Order.'

Thibault alive and an Antonine? Hiding here, a few miles from Cernay? That, I had never expected.

'He has summoned you, hasn't he?' Brother Renatus could not stop smiling. 'I never lost faith in him, never.'

'No, he hasn't summoned me, at least I don't think . . . well, yes, I suppose in a way he has.'

'I knew it.' He took my hand and pressed it warmly. 'Now, he has no doubt told you that I will give you our little Book of Rules to study. If you wait here I will fetch it.' He smiled and bustled off, humming and suddenly spry.

A book of rules? Little as I knew about the workings of Catholic monastic orders, I was fairly certain that joining them did not involve receiving rule books in the vegetable garden. What had he called Thibault? Imperator of the Order? What Order? Surely the leaders of monastic orders were called abbots.

By the time Brother Renatus returned, so many questions tangled my thoughts that I did not know where to begin.

He drew a small, crudely bound pamphlet from beneath his robe and put it in my hands with great solemnity. 'This is a momentous undertaking, my son. You will be tested but I know you will triumph. Pray only for a pure heart, and enough light to take but one more step upon the path.'

'Er, yes, thank you. I certainly will try.'

'Follow the instructions on the final page. Follow them exactly. Come tomorrow night at midnight.' He gave me directions: take the road north towards Ruffach, turn left at the gallows, go along the cow path to the brook, walk upstream to the source, then ascend to the top of the hill.

He returned to his hoeing. I collected my horse from the stables and made my way to the inn where I'd left Tunnie and Schwarzie. I bespoke rooms, ordered some dinner and sat down to read the extraordinary *Liber Regulorum vel Ordo Rosae Crucis*: The Book of Rules of the Order of the Rosy Cross.

The pamphlet was handwritten and declared itself to be '*a true and faithful copy of the original received by Greatly Honoured Frater C.R.C. from the unseen Masters of the Order and buried with him, as described in the most revered declaration, the* Fama Fraternatis, *published to the world in* Anno Domini *1614 by the Greatly Honoured Fraters whose names shall remain secret.*'

I stared at the title page for a long time. Could this be, at last, the real Rosicrucians? Was Brother Renatus' Antonine habit a disguise, a cloaking of his true nature in the costume of this time and place, as the *Fama Fraternatis*, which I recalled very well, commanded the brethren to do?

I turned the page.

RULES OF THE ORDER

¶ The Order consists of seven degrees, plus an eighth, invisible, unknowable and unnamed. The seven manifest degrees are Neophyte, Philosophus, Magister Arti, Adeptus, Magister Templi, Magus and Imperator, which last degree can only be occupied by one person at a time.

¶ The Imperator shall every fourteen years change his abode, name, and surname. Should he think it needful he may do so at shorter periods, the brethren to be informed with all possible secrecy.

¶ It is commanded that each brother, after his initiation into the Order, shall change his name and surname. Likewise, should he travel from one country to another, he shall change his name to prevent recognition.

¶ No brother should carry any written description of the Art about him, but should he do so, it must be written in an enigmatical manner.

¶ The brethren shall refrain from stirring up hatred and discord among men. They shall not discourse of the soul, whether in human beings, animals, or plants, nor of any other subject which, however natural to themselves, may appear miraculous to the common understanding. Such discourse can easily lead to their discovery. But if the brethren be alone they may speak of these secret things.

¶ No person having the Stone in his possession shall ask a favour of any one.

¶ It is not allowable to manufacture pearls or other precious stones larger than the natural size.

¶ It is forbidden to make public the sacred and secret matter, or any manipulation, coagulation, or solution thereof.

¶ The brethren shall take pains always to appear ignorant, continuously asserting that the existence of such secret arts is proclaimed only by charlatans.

It went on in this vein at some length and included long lists of brethren going back to Christian Rosenkreutz himself, represented by their Latin mottoes, such as *Perdurabo* ('I will Endure'), *Deo Non Fortuna* ('God not Fortune'), *Deo Duce Comite Ferro* ('God my Guide, my Companion a Sword'), *Sapientia Sapienti Dona Data* ('Wisdom is given to the Wise') and so on. Could these be real people who had lived and, perhaps, lived still?

I would like to say either that I wholly believed or that I was entirely sceptical from the first, but I vacillated. In the end I decided, with what I thought was an admirable application of reason, that I would rather be a fool with a chance to learn the truth than a safe sceptic who scoffs at everything he does not understand and misses his chance. So it was with calculated foolishness that I undertook the preparations.

67
The Knowledge and Conversation of My Holy Guardian Angel

Brother Renatus had drawn my particular attention to the final section of the book, entitled 'Advisements for Candidates to the First Degree'.

I sent Tunnie out to buy fresh linens; the instructions required 'raiment unworn'. If that meant an entire new coat and breeches

I would have to fail, as Isenheim had no tailor able to provide them.

From that morning I fasted, drinking only water, and ordered up three successive baths: hot, warm and cold. The innkeeper, Tunnie reported, had decided that I was mad.

The instructions said to pray to the archangels Raphael, Michael, Gabriel and Auriel, facing in turn each direction of the compass. I was unsure what I was meant to pray for and floundered about a bit, asking for mercy, guidance, forgiveness of my sins, et cetera; then I came upon a footnote giving a useful prayer *'suitable for all persons, whether Protestant, Catholic, Mussulman, Jew or any other religion'*, requesting the Knowledge and Conversation of my Holy Guardian Angel.

I had no idea of how long it would take to reach the spot to which Brother Renatus had directed me, so I set out an hour before midnight, alone as commanded, well-washed and in fresh, scratchy linen. Tunnie had imagined that he would accompany me and looked very sour when I forbade it. I made him swear the most terrible oaths that he would not follow me.

The moon had risen and the road was clearly lit. The diligence rumbled by on its way to the Isenheim post; a group of riders passed at a trot. The gibbet was about a mile out of town, but one came to the smell first. A corpse hung half rotted and crow-torn above the fetid ground. I turned away, following a cow path between fields bordered with meadowsweet towards a narrow, burbling brook. The banks were muddy and lined with brambles; the only way was to walk in the stream. Before long I'd lost my footing on the slippery rocks and had a fourth bath, falling backwards into a surprisingly deep pool.

I climbed out, emptied my boots and struggled on. The banks became steeper and rockier as I approached the source at the base of a hill. The stream was just a trickle here, emerging from the dense forest that covered the slope. I walked a little way in, but saw no path. The moonlight which had made the plain almost as bright as day did not penetrate far and I was reluctant to leave it behind. Why in God's name had I embarked on a night expedition to an unknown place without a lantern or any means of making light? The Advisements had not told me to, that was why, and I had obviously become the sort of idiot who only did what he was told.

I had been told to pray to my Holy Guardian Angel so although I thought that giving directions, in such a literal sense, was probably not worthy of the attention of such an august being, I framed a prayer that I might find my way without harm to my destination. I closed my eyes, turned round several times and set off, stepping carefully and holding my arms out in front to fend off low-hanging branches which I was not certain my Angel would take into account.

The ground rose under my feet and I seemed miraculously to avoid roots, holes and loose stones. I opened my eyes, but it made no difference; I could not see my hand in front of my face. I stopped and listened. All around me the forest breathed darkness; an owl hooted in the distance. I moved on, more confident now. There definitely was a path, and as my eyes adjusted I saw that the blackness was not quite complete; here and there, the moon sent silvery flickers down through the leaves as a breeze moved the highest branches.

As I approached the top of the hill the ground levelled off; the forest was more open here and, after the darkness of the ascent, almost bright. I made my way towards a clearing illuminated by a shaft of moonlight. There had been a chapel here once; the forest was encroaching on fragments of stone walls, an arched window, a mossy stone cross, fallen and fractured. This must be the place. There was no one else; no doubt I was early. I found a comfortable spot among the roots of a giant oak and settled down to wait.

As time passed, I heard occasional rustlings from the forest that

I thought indicated the arrival of others, but no one appeared. I recalled the tales of wolves and bandits that roamed these woods; I'd brought my dagger but left my sword and pistols behind. More idiocy.

It occurred to me that I didn't even know what I was waiting for – would I meet other members of the Order? How many were there? Might I possibly meet Tobias himself, the Imperator? If I did, would this be the time to mention that I'd killed his grandson? Would I be questioned, subjected to tests and ordeals, entrusted with secrets, made to take oaths of allegiance, sworn to silence? Would I be able to back out, or was it already too late? What had begun as mere curiosity about an ancestor seemed all at once to have brought me to the edge of a precipice. I stifled an urge to slink away.

A wind stirred the treetops; the moonlight wavered and the air turned suddenly chill. I shivered and peered into the shifting shadows. Was that a man moving among the ruins of the chapel? Two men? Three? I stood up and stepped forward, rubbing my eyes. No, there was no one, just the play of moonbeams and my fevered imagination.

From behind me came a blood-curdling howl, quickly silenced. I spun around, heart pounding. The sound of footsteps, a scuffle and a grunt, then another strangled howl and Tunnie appeared, pulled by Schwarzie on a rope.

'Damn you, Tunnie, you swore not to follow me.'

'I didn't follow you, sir, I followed Schwarzie.'

'Pedantry in servants is especially annoying,' I said, but I was very glad to see him. The light of his lantern revealed that he was armed to the teeth: his own sword and mine, two pistols in each pocket, a long dagger in his belt and, no doubt, his usual assortment of hidden knives.

'Stay here and keep that dog quiet.' I took the lantern and advanced into the clearing, walked around the chapel ruins and some distance into the surrounding woods, calling 'Halloos'. There was no sign of anyone and I returned to the oak tree. Schwarzie had calmed down and Tunnie was sipping from a flask, which he handed to me. I sniffed. Brandy. 'Not on a stomach as empty as mine,' I said.

He reached into his satchel and brought forth a chunk of bread and cheese and a wineskin. 'Also available is half a chicken, three nice venison sausages and a plum cake.'

My stomach growled. Was there any point in continuing the fast? The rules had already been broken by the presence of Tunnie and Schwarzie. I took out my watch and held it near the lantern. It was twenty minutes past midnight. Had the Order come, but withdrawn when Tunnie and Schwarzie appeared? Had they not come at all, or had I mistaken the time and the place? Or was Brother Renatus simply mad, and I, for a while, had joined in his delusion?

I ate and drank, wondering whether I was disappointed or relieved that my reckless excursion had yielded no results. After waiting another twenty minutes, we made our way down the hill and back to Isenheim. The innkeeper was extremely difficult to rouse and almost refused to let us in. Tunnie gave him some coins and, I think, a sharp twist to his arm; he cursed us for madmen, but quietly, and lit the way upstairs. Tunnie built up my fire, poured me a cup of wine and retired to his little room down the hall. Schwarzie fell asleep on the hearthrug.

I sat by the fire, stared into the flames and tried to assemble my thoughts. I took up the *Rules of the Order* and looked through them again. The whole thing was too . . . orderly to be entirely mad, but too mad to be credible without supporting evidence. Far from answering questions, Brother Renatus had led me deeper into confusion. Everything I'd taken as fact, as sign or clue, looked extremely flimsy now.

In relation to my original questions about Thibault, I had

learned nothing reliable. Julien Pernelle could easily have known about 'TGHD' – perhaps 'Thank God he's dead' was an old family joke. I had no reason to give it occult significance, ironic or otherwise. And anyway, it was only by the most convoluted logic that the exchange with Brother Renatus, in which he said 'He's dead' and I replied 'Thank God he's dead', could mean anything other than that he was, in fact, dead. That I had immediately taken it as near-certain proof that he was alive showed how far I had gone down the road to unreason.

I had to give serious consideration to the proposition that Brother Renatus was mad and his Order of the Rosy Cross a wild invention. Madmen could have notions of great apparent coherence and internal consistency. His twitchiness about the Inquisition may have been another symptom and no indication that he had anything to hide. Of course, he might be mad yet the Order was real; perhaps it was the Order that had driven him mad. Alternatively, he was not mad but the Order was nevertheless an invention, his own or another's, for reasons about which I could not begin to speculate.

I lay on the bed and, though I was sure my mind was too agitated for sleep, fell into uneasy slumber and an unusually vivid dream. I was trying to return to the meeting place on the hill. The journey was more difficult than it had been the first time, darker, the road impossible to discern; several times I became lost and realised I'd gone around in a circle. Every step was accompanied by the growing fear that I was too late, I had missed my chance. In a torment of anxiety and desperation I tried to run, but by the time I arrived at the gibbet I felt as though I was dragging my limbs through treacle. The pleasant fields and meadows were now filled with sharp rocks and invisible holes into which I stumbled. The brook had turned icy cold and was far deeper than I remembered; in several places I had to swim and was nearly drowned by the weight of my clothes. The hill, when I arrived at the base, was steeper than before and so densely packed with thorny brambles, low branches and spiky, stabbing twigs that my clothes were shredded before I reached the top and I was bruised, cut and full of splinters.

At first I thought that no one was there and I'd come too late; it was with incomparable relief that I noticed a robed figure among the ruins of the chapel. Was it Brother Renatus? I couldn't make out his face. There was an odd quality to the light; everything looked as though it was underwater. I tried to speak, to make my presence known, but paralysis seized my limbs. The figure lifted his hand and pointed at me; I gazed down at my body as though from a towering height and saw that I was naked, my flesh ripped and mauled, bleeding from a hundred wounds that were festering and dripping with pus.

I took one step forward, stumbled and fell, fell and fell towards a dark, terrifying abyss. The impact, when it finally came, was a blinding explosion of pain that I knew would last until the end of time; I had fallen to Hell. I awoke screaming.

Schwarzie leapt on to my bed, barking and yowling; Tunnie rushed in with a candle. In its wildly flickering light I thought they were demons come to torment me. I lashed out, giving Tunnie, as we discovered in due course, a magnificent black eye. He spoke soothingly to me and I came slowly to my senses. It was almost dawn.

The inn was stirring; Tunnie went down to the kitchen and by the time he'd returned with breakfast and coffee, the dream had faded, though my eyes were gritty and burning, I had a blinding headache and I ached all over.

It was Sunday, cool and overcast, with church bells tolling from every steeple as I rode to the monastery. Mass was under way in the chapel; I slipped into the back and looked for Brother Renatus, but it was too dark to discern the faces of the monks in the choirstalls. All light was focused on the altar. Against my will, my eyes were drawn up towards that ghastly Crucifixion and with a jolt I recognised the wounded, festering body as the one that had been my own in the dream.

I did not see Brother Renatus among the monks who filed out after the service. When I asked for him they told me that he had died in the night.

68

One Great Lost Love

❧

I had promised Bertrand that I'd stay for Arlène's wedding at the end of September, which in this region was still summer, dry and hot. Château Langenfeld had been mobilising for weeks; the baking, slaughtering, roasting and stewing had reached such a pitch that Bertrand and I took to the hills with Schwarzie and his other dogs, where we enjoyed the relatively peaceful activity of shooting at rabbits with pistols.

Baron Richenveir and his entourage arrived, filling the house to bursting. After the ceremony (which I did not attend, pleading toothache), a week of parties and feasting was planned. Of course I had not let myself feel anything for Arlène but her smiles and her teasing, her kisses and her ardent pleasures had comforted me amid the utter failure of my search for Tobias.

On the wedding night I took supper in my room. Fortunately, the feasting hall and the Baron's chamber where the deflowering would take place were at the opposite end of the château, though the din of merry-making echoed through the corridors. I drank several brandies, went to bed early and pressed a pillow over my ears, but I could still hear the raucous laughter, whoops and roars. I wondered if they were observing the old tradition of exhibiting the bloodstained sheet as proof that the Baron had got what he'd paid for. Poor Arlène. I hoped he had not hurt her.

When I awoke, it was silent but for the scratching of mice in the attic over my head. The window was open to the mild night and I lay watching clouds pass slowly over the bright face of the moon. I had not yet told Bertrand, but I'd decided to leave the next day. I had made a list of Thibault's regular correspondents in Europe; my plan, which I regarded as in all probability futile, was to visit them all, working my way first through France and the Low Countries, then Bohemia, Switzerland and finally Italy, where Isabel and Meryll were planning to go after their summer's tour through the south of France.

I heard a creak from the door; it opened and Arlène slipped in. She climbed into my bed.

'I'm not a virgin any more,' she said. 'But he couldn't do it with his prick, it was too feeble, so he did it with his finger first.' She shuddered. 'And then he fell asleep on top of me, snoring and drooling. I washed and washed. There is nothing of him in me now.'

No doubt a better man would have sent her back to her husband; for many reasons, I am so glad I was not a better man. I did try to tell her that adultery on one's wedding night was really very naughty, but my arguments lacked conviction.

At a certain moment she, desiring greater leverage, reached above her head to grasp at the ornate carvings of the bed. She must have pulled and twisted in just the right way because with a sudden sharp click a panel moved, opening inward. It was not the right moment to pause, but when we arrived at a natural hiatus in the proceedings we lit a candle and investigated. I had never noticed the tiny carved rose, hidden among swags of ivy and oak leaves on the ornate headboard.

'I'm sure this is what you've been looking for,' said Arlène. 'And you would never have found it if I hadn't decided to be unfaithful to my husband as soon as possible.' She smiled, vindicated. 'Aren't you going to see what's in there?'

I hesitated. Was I more afraid of discovering real evidence or of having my hopes again dashed? I reached in.

The space was about two feet deep, roughly square. I groped about with my hand, but it was empty, absolutely empty. If this had been where Tobias kept his secrets, he had taken them away with him. 'There's nothing.'

'Are you sure?' Arlène reached in and felt about. 'No, wait, I feel something. But I can't quite . . .' She tried with her other arm. 'It feels like a piece of paper has slipped into a crack at the back. There's just a corner sticking out.'

I reached in again. She was right. The wood had shrunk, leaving gaps. In the furthest corner, where the gap was greatest, a tiny triangle of paper protruded into the compartment. I tried to grasp it, but only succeeded in pushing it further into the crack.

Arlène tried with her slimmer fingers, but couldn't get a grip. 'We'll have to take the bed apart.'

'But not right this minute,' I said.

In the morning I described how, tossing and turning in the agonies of toothache, I had knocked against the secret latch, causing the compartment to open. Everyone rushed upstairs to have a turn climbing on to the bed, reaching in and groping about, pulling at the corner of paper but only pushing it further in. Constance brought tweezers and Charlotte, as the smallest and most dextrous, made a final attempt to extract it, to no avail.

Bertrand summoned his carpenter and some wine; we sat down to watch as the bed was dismantled, taking bets as to what the paper would turn out to be. Constance thought a map to a buried treasure; Arlène, a love letter from Thibault's secret mistress;

Bertrand, a copy of his pact with the Devil. Charlotte proposed a laundry list.

It took the carpenter two sweaty hours, but at last the paper was placed in my hand. It was a letter, folded small and addressed to 'T.G.H. d'Amorie, Ch. Langenfeld, Cernay, Alsace, France' in a firm, squarish hand.

'Oh, for God's sake, read it!' Bertrand was bubbling with impatience.

'It's probably nothing,' I said, but I held my breath as I opened it. There was a date, *March 22, 1688*. A year before Thibault's 'death'. And an address: *Villa degli Eremiti, Ven.* Below that, just three words: *Je suis ici* – I am here.

Bertrand, with a grunt of exasperation, plucked the paper from my hand and read it aloud.

'Does this mean anything to you?' he asked.

'No.'

'Villa degli Eremiti. House of the Hermits. Ven? Venice maybe. His bones came back from Venice, didn't they?'

I nodded. I'd found a docket from a goods transporter based in Venice, but no indication of the casket's origins. The city of Venice was a collection point for post and shipping from far and wide.

'A slightly more detailed address would have been helpful,' Charlotte said.

'The writer assumed Thibault knew the place,' said Bertrand.

'A signature would be nice.' Constance took the letter from Bertrand and studied it as though he and I might both have missed something. 'Who could it be from?'

'His secret lover, of course,' said Arlène. 'Lost through some accident of fate. And he'd been searching for her all these years.'

'Nice for his wife, I'm sure,' said Constance.

'Oh, he loved his wife,' Arlène said. 'But he had one great lost love, and now he's found her again, so off he goes.'

'What a story!' said Bertrand. 'You are making him into the hero of a romance.'

69
The Precipice

❦

I made plans to go to Venice. God knows, I had little enough to go on, but it was the best that fate seemed prepared to offer. I wrote to Isabel at her last address in Nîmes; also to Lyons, her next destination, from where she and Meryll planned to cross the Alps. For various reasons I did not set out immediately, as I'd planned; I stayed until Arlène and the Baron departed for his estates. Everyone said, in tones of some incredulity, that marriage seemed to agree with her. Seeing her leave with her husband was more difficult than I'd imagined. She'd told me that she loved me.

On the morning of my departure, Bertrand took me aside. 'Francis, my dear cousin,' he said. 'I wish you all the best in your pursuit of this man you believe to be two hundred years old. But you are going into Italy, where a very dim view is taken of such things. I have nothing to say one way or another; we Alsatians always manage to straddle the fence. If what you believe is true, it is certainly a marvel, whether the work of God or the Devil, though I do not have any envy for a man who has lived so long. What I am saying is,' he tapped my arm for emphasis, 'if he has taken pains to appear to die, he will not be grateful if you spread rumours that he lives. Search, yes, but for a man no more than ordinarily old. Say that he is an uncle, a cousin, what you will. But not your great-great-grandfather.'

I took the diligence to Lyons. The roads were good; aside from the cramped conditions in the coach and the mediocre quality of the posting inns, the journey was not unpleasant. Schwarzie had insisted on accompanying me, but proved amenable to sitting on top with Tunnie. I slept most of the way, having hardly slept at all during my last few nights in Cernay.

Isabel and Meryll joined me a week later and we set off at once. They were intrigued to learn about the cryptic letter and the Villa degli Eremiti, thought I was mad to have believed a single thing Brother Renatus said, commiserated over Arlène.

Isabel was pregnant and they hoped that the reach of her husband's family would not extend to Italy, or at least not immediately, and that they'd be able to keep the child, at least for a while.

'I thought Reginald would have died by now,' Meryll said, and although he laughed, there was a new bitterness in his tone. 'A man wants children,' he added. Isabel nudged him and glanced at me.

'I beg your pardon, Francis,' he said. 'I know . . .'

'Please don't apologise,' I said. 'I am aware that there are children in the world, and the fact that I have lost mine is no reason for everyone to avoid the subject.'

'You'll have more,' said Isabel. 'You should have married Arlène and settled down in Alsace.'

'She was already betrothed,' I reminded her.

'Oh, pooh. You could have got rid of that Baron Rich-and-Vain, whatever his name is.' She flicked Arlène's husband aside with her fan.

Meryll had designed a travelling coach with a well-padded interior, compartments for food and drink, a writing table, a cunning washstand, a bookshelf and a fold-down bed. A rented coach followed with the servants and luggage; this we left at Pont de Beauvoisin, where we hired mules and porters for the Alpine crossing. Beyond that point, there were no roads and Meryll's coach was disassembled into fourteen pieces, each strapped to its own mule. We went in sedan chairs carried by two porters, although I preferred to walk until we came to the higher paths, which were already snow-covered and slippery.

The porters, robust Savoyards, seemed indifferent to the conditions. They coated the soles of their shoes with resin and trudged along at a brisk, unvarying pace on tracks cut into the sides of the mountains. At first, I found this mode of transport rather terrifying. The paths were narrow and uneven, the precipice mere inches away. Great torrents of icy water cut across the track and in places the snow was so deep that the little mules almost vanished and the porters had to wade through drifts up to their thighs. Through all, they kept up a running banter and commentary in their guttural patois. It was barely recognisable as language, seeming instead a natural sound of the landscape, like the rush of falling water, the soughing of the wind in the vast pine forests and the distant cry of a lammergeier.

Towards sunset, we came around a bend in the path to behold a sight so extraordinary that it caused us to cry out in amazement. A snow-capped peak, higher by far than any we had yet seen, floated on a sea of pearly clouds. Mountain and clouds were tinged with rose and violet and the last golden rays of the sun touched the thin pennant of snow that blew from the summit.

We descended into a small valley and took rooms at an inn, which was awful. We didn't care. We ate the filthy stew, drank the vile wine and slept like babies on the hard, lumpy beds, protected from the many and varied vermin by our bed-sacks of deerskin lined with down.

We set out before dawn and, as we climbed to the next pass, again saw the eerie floating peak, behind us now, and touched by the rising sun. This side of the mountain had received less snow; Meryll and Tunnie and I coated the soles of our boots with the Savoyards' resin and walked behind Isabel's chair.

Schwarzie ran ahead, darting in and out of the thick woods that covered the slopes above the track. I was becoming accustomed to the precipice and strolled along just a foot or two from a sheer cliff whose bottom I could not even see. Tunnie, I noticed, kept close to the inside of the path and did not look outward, let alone down.

Our train of porters and mules was strung along the twists and turns and the leaders were out of sight when we heard shouts and barking. We hurried up the line. Schwarzie was crouching in the middle of the path facing the largest wolf I had ever seen. Both were growling and baring their teeth.

'Tunnie, my pistol, quick,' I said. He was already loading it, but by the time he had it ready the wolf had launched itself straight at Schwarzie. There was a frenzy of yelping and snarling. The wolf had his teeth in Schwarzie's throat; Schwarzie had seized the wolf's leg. I drew my dagger and tried to get near enough to strike, but they were scrabbling all over the path. Tunnie came up with the pistol, but there was no clear shot. We could only watch in horror as, with a last howl, they tumbled over the cliff, still locked together. I rushed to the edge. A trickle of loose stones marked their fall, but they had vanished.

The silence was broken by the grunts of the porters, resuming their burdens and moving off. I felt unaccountably bereft.

We passed another night in a wretched inn, where Tunnie and I got drunk and sat up past midnight talking about dogs.

Two days later we reached the top of the pass at Mont Cenis and began the descent into Italy. The fertile Susa valley was a welcome sight after the harsh monochrome of the mountains; the city's walls and church towers glowed in the afternoon sun. We were looking forward to a good hotel, hot baths and a decent supper.

Meryll and I were walking near the head of the line when we heard Isabel cry out. We hurried back to find her doubled over in

291

pain, pressing her hand to her stomach. Her maid was at her side and waved us away.

'No, no, no, no, no,' Isabel was moaning softly.

'Oh God,' said Meryll, and pushed the maid aside to kneel by Isabel's chair.

After half an hour the chief porter came to me – there was no place to shelter for the night; we had to go on. As delicately as I could, I explained the situation. As delicately as he could in thickly accented French, he indicated that he understood. Isabel already had the best of the porters; now he called them aside and instructed them that Madame must be carried '*sans déverser une larme du vin*' – without spilling a drop of wine. He even went so far as to offer gruff assurances to Meryll, who walked alongside, holding Isabel's hand. '*Tout va bien*,' he said, but it did not go well. By the time we arrived at Susa, Isabel had lost her baby.

We took rooms at the best hotel. There was an English doctor in town; we sent for him and he came at once, though there was nothing he could do but assure us that Isabel would recover with rest and a bland diet. He prescribed an elixir of capsella, vitex and valerian. This sounded reasonable to me, but I went to the apothecary myself and insisted on verifying the purity of the extracts and watching as the recipe was prepared. I had seen too many examples of the substitution of cheap or adulterated ingredients.

Meryll stayed at Isabel's bedside day and night as if by force of will he could restore her health, but he was as sad as she and they were no comfort to each other. Finally she ordered him to go for a long walk and when he'd reluctantly complied, she sent for me.

She was sitting up in bed. Her hands twitched at her shawl and she wouldn't meet my eyes. 'I have to confess something,' she said, 'and there's no one else I can tell.'

I took her hands in mine and tried to press some warmth into them.

'I think God is punishing me,' she said.

'What for?'

She looked away and pressed her lips together. 'I killed my baby. Our baby. Edward's baby.' Tears welled in her eyes. 'Soon after the Harfields took our son away I was pregnant again, though no one knew, and I was afraid the same thing would happen and I couldn't bear it so I went to Sally Bird and I killed our child and now God won't let me have another.'

'God wouldn't do that,' I said.

'Oh, you understand the mind of God, do you?'

'Yes, I saw Him just last week. He said He knew what you'd been through and He wished you well.'

I got a tiny smile. 'Blasphemer,' she said.

I passed her my handkerchief. 'If it helps.'

'It does.'

'I'm glad.'

'But it's Edward I'm concerned about, Francis. He frets so much about me it's making him ill. He deserves a good wife, and children, and I'll never be free. I'm just a burden to him.' Her voice broke and she was weeping again, crying hard now. I put my arms around her; she buried her face in my shoulder and sobbed.

The handkerchief was overwhelmed and the shawl well soaked before her tears were exhausted and she sank back on the pillows. I passed her a cup of wine; she drank and tried to smile. 'I shouldn't complain. I'm alive, Edward's alive, you're alive. I should be grateful to God, not despairing.'

'I'll be sure to tell Him when I see Him next.'

'Oh, Francis.'

'Oh, Izzy.'

'What am I going to do?'

'Go on. Go to Rome as you'd planned. Get pregnant again. Sit in the sun and eat figs.'

Isabel recovered her health and, more slowly, her spirits. I took

Meryll aside and told him to make a greater effort to be cheerful, and it was touching to see how he tried. We stayed in Susa for a fortnight, eating and drinking well, then I made arrangements to travel east to Venice and Meryll reassembled his coach for their journey south to Rome.

70

The Hermit's Cell

❧

I arrived in Venice in the carnival season (which lasted for six months in those days) when everyone, including children, was required by law to wear masks in public. The mysteries and confusions this engendered were like the water on which the city floated, the uncertain glimmer of reflected light and the disconcerting, subtle shifting under the feet that happens when one has just stepped off a boat.

I rented an apartment and sent my card round to my acquaintances among the city's many foreign visitors and residents. Most lofty of these was Mme Harper. Caroline – as she now bade me call her, since we were such dear old friends – had achieved her title, and it was a very good one indeed. She was the Duchesse du Léran; her husband, Philippe Louis François Charbrillon, Duc du Léran, a famous libertine, was the French ambassador to the Republic of Venice.

Philippe was an interesting man. He had been a sickly child whom no one expected to survive; it was his elder and more robust half-brother who had received the upbringing required for the heir to one of France's oldest titles. When their father died (some said he was poisoned by his third wife in collaboration with his mistress), Philippe was twelve, his brother fifteen. Contrary to all predictions, Philippe's health improved and it was his brother who fell victim to a mysterious wasting disease.

Philippe's childhood had for the most part been spent in bed, reading. By the time he inherited the title he was so well versed in history that he could discourse for hours on the interwoven dynasties and vacillating fortunes of all of Europe's royal houses. His other passion was classical sculpture; over the course of his life he amassed the largest collection of Greek and Roman statuary in the world (now scattered amongst the museums of Europe . . . and at Farundell).

Beneath a gentle and complaisant manner he had a sharp and penetrating intelligence and an uncanny ability to get to the heart of people's true motivations, even those of which they were themselves unaware. Once he had understood their real fears and desires, he played people like marionettes. And he always, always got his way. Often I watched him in conversation: smiling, impeccably gracious, perfectly agreeable, yet behind his mild blue eyes he measured, weighed, calculated, assessed. He took a deep, almost sensual pleasure in the conspiracies and counter-conspiracies that were the warp and weft of his life.

We became friends. I sensed that he enjoyed the company of someone who was not part of the intense, elite world of international politics and finance in which everyone he met, man or woman, was seeking to use him for some purpose of their own. I just liked him; we laughed at the same things.

Philippe and Caroline entertained in the most sumptuous manner imaginable. Their palazzo on the Grand Canal was decorated in a unique blend of Parisian and Venetian styles – grand salons with glowing frescoes by Tiepolo on walls and ceilings, shimmering tapestries, massive gilded mirrors and candelabra, serpentine columns, floors inlaid with coloured marbles and, of course, statues, as Philippe expanded his collection to include bronzes by Cellini, Antico and Giambologna.

Winter in Venice was freezing, with that damp cold that penetrates. It rained even more than in England, or perhaps it only seemed that way; rain falling on water is twice as wet. What made it worse was that the little boats in which one travels about, though occasionally equipped with a risible canopy, are open-sided so that the wind drives the rain in at the sides while whipping up the waves from below. During a particularly wet crossing of the lagoon to a party on the island of Murano, I asked the boatmen why they did not at least put down the sunblinds, which, although flimsy, would have shielded me from the worst. They puffed out their cheeks and blew. I expressed incomprehension (in sign language, for the Venetians pretended not to understand my Italian); they shrugged and lowered the blinds, whereupon we immediately found ourselves being blown sideways out to sea. I resigned myself to getting wet.

The social life was relentless. There was a pleasure-party or a ball every night in one or another grand palazzo or in one of the city's secret *casinos* – 'little houses' which could be hired for private entertainments, complete with cook, courtesans and blind musicians.

Weeks passed and I had not decided how to proceed with my search for Tobias. Bertrand had been right; for my own sake, as well as Tobias's, I must be discreet. It was not difficult to postpone the issue; there were abundant distractions. I suspected, as well, that the sooner I began making enquiries, the sooner I would be disappointed.

Caroline invited me to a party in honour of Philippe's birthday. Not the main one; that had been celebrated with a spectacular ball at their palazzo attended by hundreds. This was a private party for their closest friends; she would send a boat for me. At the appointed hour I went to the landing and found a gondola waiting. I stepped in and we moved off. It was, for once, not raining and Tunnie had dressed me in my most gorgeous suit, an ivory taffeta embroidered with garnets and pearls. I wore a half-mask which covered my scar and missing ear. I'd taken to stuffing the fingers of my left glove to conceal the missing ones, as such an obvious distinguishing mark put me at a disadvantage in a city where everyone else could disguise their identity as much or as little as they liked.

After a while I realised that we were not heading towards the palazzo but delving deeper into the small canals in the heart of the city. *'Dove andiamo?'* I asked the gondolier.

'Va'd'ermi.'

'Cosa?' The Venetian dialect shortened words and dropped vowels.

'Vil-la de-gli Er-e-mi-ti.' He enunciated with exaggerated, contemptuous clarity and spat, as though speaking comprehensible Italian left a bad taste in his mouth.

Had I heard aright? Could it be? I tried to ask him more, but he didn't answer.

He put in at a small, private landing; a door opened as I approached. I presented my invitation and was ushered in. Dimly lit rooms, thronged with maskers, were furnished in a vaguely Oriental manner: tall palms in brass pots, incense curling from the mouths of man-high Chinese porcelain dragons, latticework screens, low tables inlaid with brass and mother-of-pearl, piles of velvet cushions. Moroccan musicians played long-necked lutes, strange viols, flutes and drums; dancing girls performed with veils; serving girls circulated with exotic beverages. If this was truly the Villa degli Eremiti, the name was obviously ironic. I acquired a companion, masked but otherwise not overdressed, costumed as an houri in a few bits of transparent silk. I asked her about the name of the place, but she only smiled and suggested that we retire to a private chamber.

297

She led me up a stairway, along a passage and into a room with so many mirrors that it was some time before I felt sure of its dimensions. Where not mirrored, the wall panels were carved and painted with flowers, strange animals and exotic foliage. There was a large bed, a few tables and chairs, a sideboard with wines and food. My companion was joined by another lightly clad houri; they served me wine and oysters.

They pretended not to understand me when I tried to speak, but as their intention was clearly to seduce me, words soon became unnecessary. It was mystifying but all so enjoyable that I could not complain. We shed our masks and our clothes and things had progressed to the point of becoming very interesting when one of the wall panels swung open and another houri entered. The girls withdrew, giggling, and the new houri took their place beside me on the bed. I removed her mask. It was Caroline.

'You were watching,' I said.

'Yes. There is a little chamber. The hermit's cell, they call it. In the centre of each of those carved flowers is a hole through which one can see everything. I wished to determine what sort of a lover you were before I entered the game.'

'And your conclusion?'

'I am here, am I not?'

After a while we paused for refreshment. 'Is this how you honour your husband's birthday?' I asked.

'*Certainement*. It is my special gift for him. Philippe has refined and varied tastes; this we share. He is watching us now.' She gestured towards the wall. 'Does that discomfit you?'

'If it doesn't discomfit him, it doesn't discomfit me.'

'Would it discomfit you if he joined us?'

It did not.

71

Never Without Consequences

Winter passed into spring; by March the air was mild, most days sunny. I continued to postpone taking any concrete steps in my search for Tobias because I could not think of any. The Villa degli Eremiti turned out to be an extremely exclusive brothel that had been in existence for only a year or two. I made casual enquiries about 'a relation' of mine who might have come to Venice a 'few' years ago, but no one had heard of any other Damory or d'Amorie. I had begun to feel that fate was teasing me: offering a Rosicrucian Brotherhood that turned out to be a figment of the imagination of a mad monk, then luring me all the way to Venice in search of a Villa of the Hermits that turned out to be a brothel. Things I had taken to be signposts led nowhere, or only to greater uncertainties. It occurred to me that every-thing I considered a more or less genuine clue – the 'message' at Mme du Bellay's soirée, Thibault's name on the tombstone of his wife, the letter in the secret compartment of his bed – had come to me by chance, not through any effort on my part. I concluded that I should wait for fate to show me the way forward, if there was one.

Caroline and Philippe bought a villa just north of the city. For the last two hundred years the great families of Venice had built their summer houses on the verdant banks of the Brenta – a canal made from a series of linked rivers joining Venice to Padua. Some of the houses were truly stupendous, with hundreds of rooms; others more rustic, with only forty or fifty. Caroline and Philippe's was called La Fontana; it had been built for the famous Bragolo family who had poisoned, stabbed, drowned and strangled each other into extinction by the end of the last century. Although of only moderate size, it was exquisite. Designed by Palladio, its facade was an elegant composition of warm yellow stucco and creamy marble columns, with portico, pediments and a tympanum adorned with statues of the Graces. The ground-floor salons, tall-ceilinged and many-windowed, had glorious frescoes by Veronese of idyllic family scenes, in which children, dogs, cats, ducks and rabbits gambolled on flower-strewn, emerald lawns beneath trees heavy with ripening fruit. The garden was designed around a natural spring which emerged from a grotto and flowed into a grand fountain of Neptune among leaping dolphins. Arbours and colonnades led to topiary labyrinths, each concealing a little garden room dedicated to a different flower: roses, lilies, tulips and irises.

Philippe's mania for collecting expanded to fill the space. He had buying agents everywhere and received a steady stream of antiquities from Greece, Egypt and further afield. Six columns from a temple of Aphrodite on Cyprus. The Seven Arts from a Roman villa on Ischia. A wall mosaic from Crete. The owners of the house next door to La Fontana, finding themselves in straitened circumstances, sold off their collections. Philippe bought nine statues of Hermes – three large marbles and half a dozen smaller bronzes. The garden began to look a bit overcrowded.

We discovered a shared pleasure in fishing; his most treasured book was Izaak Walton's *The Compleat Angler, Or, The Contemplative Man's Recreation*, of which he possessed a rare first edition, as well as the more useful revised edition which he carried in his pocket. At every opportunity we would put on shabby clothes, evade Caroline and the servants, and set out in a small rowing boat with a few bottles of wine in a net bag which we towed behind to keep cool.

The Brenta teemed with fish. Philippe was a fly man, while I favoured worms; about these and related matters we had many delightful disputes. One of the things about which we disagreed was location; he favoured an open area with a good-flowing current, while I thought quiet pools overhung with trees were best. In search of such a spot I had rowed us into one of the wide river loops that made occasional islands in the canal, in whose lee I hoped to find a sheltered cove. And, indeed, I found an excellent spot: the bank hollowed around the roots of an old willow, which leaned over the water creating just the sort of speckled shade in which trout like to bask. The island, a hectare or two in size, seemed a wilderness, densely covered with trees and rampant vines. We tied up the boat; I settled under the willow while Philippe walked out on to a pebbly shoal from where he could cast into the current, such as it was.

I caught three lovely trout, one straight after another; Philippe caught nothing. I put another worm on my hook in the secure manner recommended by Mr Walton, on which it is impossible to improve, and tossed it in again. Philippe cursed mildly, reeled in his line and retrieved the cooking apparatus from the boat. I caught one more fish and cleaned them while he made a fire and heated oil in the skillet. I tossed the fish into the pan, then hauled up the wine and opened a bottle as he completed the cooking. The wine was the perfect temperature; the fish golden and succulent. We ate with our fingers, straight from the pan.

A cat appeared, sniffed at us cautiously, then seized one of the fish heads, dragged it under a shrub and began gnawing. Soon another cat appeared, and another, twelve in all. When every scrap of fish was gone, they washed themselves, then sat staring at us. The first cat, a skinny black female, came and rubbed her head against my knee. I scratched behind her ears; she climbed on to my lap and began chewing the leather buttons of my coat. When I tried to lift her off she dug her claws into my arm.

'You have made her love you,' Philippe said. 'That is never without consequences.'

72

Fate, Is This You Again?

✤

The next day Philippe was called into the city – some international crisis required his delicate intervention – and I returned to the island alone. The little black cat seemed to have been waiting for me. As soon as I climbed out of the boat she emerged from the trees and twined herself so devotedly around my ankles that she nearly made me fall into the water. Within a few minutes the other cats had joined us.

I fished; they ate.

After about an hour I became aware of the sound of singing coming from somewhere on the island. I strained to hear. It was a woman's voice. One by one, as though summoned, the cats disappeared.

I followed, pushing through the undergrowth, and after a few minutes' struggle emerged into a garden, now reclaimed by nature and filled with saplings and brambles. Creeping vines covered what might once have been statues and fountains with rounded, immobile waves; a small villa was half submerged. The voice was coming from the far side. I waded towards it, using my dagger to slice a path through the tangled green sea.

I peered around the corner of the house. A woman stood on a broad, paved terrace, with her back to me and her face lifted to the sky. Red-gold hair, unbound, flowed to her waist. She was dressed like a classical statue of a goddess, in a sleeveless, pleated tunic girded over a trailing skirt, a long shawl draped over one shoulder. She was singing to the cats, who had gathered in a semi-circle at her feet. Several joined in, lifting their faces and yowling melodically. The words of her song were Latin, a hymn, it seemed to be, in praise of Isis. She raised her arms above her head, shook a silver sistrum and moved her feet in a slow dance. She turned round and round and I glimpsed her face between the falling curtains of her hair, eyes closed as though in a trance.

I thought I was dreaming, or had been somehow transported two thousand years into the past. I was holding my breath so as not to disturb the vision, which I was certain would shatter or dissolve at any moment. It did not. She continued her dance, singing and swaying. Her face was serene and very beautiful, her body lithe and graceful. I noticed, then, the stains on her skirt, the dirt under her fingernails, the tangles in her hair. This was a real woman, which, in a way, made her even stranger and more bewitching.

There was a sharp click as a pistol was placed against the back of my head and cocked. 'Don't move,' said a man's voice in rough Italian. He removed the dagger from my belt.

The woman stopped her dance abruptly and opened her eyes.

'I mean no harm,' I said. 'I was only fishing.'

'I apologise, Altezza,' said the man. 'I will get rid of this man at once.' He addressed her as Highness – was this strange woman a princess? Perhaps, after all, I was dreaming.

'How did you find me?' she asked me in Latin.

'I followed the cats,' I replied in the same tongue.

'You had better leave right away,' said the man. His pistol remained firmly pressed to the back of my head.

'I know him, Bortolin. He may stay,' said the woman, reverting to Italian.

'Altezza, is that wise?' said Bortolin, but he lowered his pistol, uncocked it and stepped away from me, though he kept my dagger. I exhaled in relief and turned to look at him. He was a short, grizzled fellow of fifty or so, with a countryman's rough skin but a city man's sharp eyes.

'He will stay for dinner,' she said. 'Tell Besina.'

'Altezza . . .'

The woman frowned and her voice became imperious. 'He will stay. Bring wine.' And to me, in a lighter tone and once more in Latin, 'I am pleased that you have come. Will you take some wine while my servants prepare a repast?'

She led the way to a table and chairs at the far end of the terrace.

When we had seated ourselves, I introduced myself and asked her name.

'They call me Myrionymos,' she said. The word was Greek; it meant 'of many names' and was a common epithet of Isis.

From within the house I heard Bortolin's voice raised in argument, and a woman responding. He appeared bearing a tray with a bottle of wine and two glasses. Shaking his head and sighing dramatically, he served us; he failed to catch the woman's eye and departed, scowling.

I tried to make conversation. I began an explanation of my presence, mentioned fishing, Philippe and Caroline, La Fontana. She made no response, though she smiled once or twice. I let it drop. I began to formulate questions but they faded in the face of her compelling silence. She looked at me; I looked at her. She could stare at a man for ever, it seemed, without becoming flustered.

Although I had at first taken her for a woman in her twenties, I realised that had been because of the assurance with which she moved and spoke. Her skin was smooth and unmarked as a child's: pale, with a hint of rose on her cheeks and lips. Her throat and arms, too, had a child's marble purity. I revised my estimate; she might be as young as sixteen. Her hands, with their dirty nails, lay in her lap, though occasionally she would press them together as though in prayer, then release them with a brief washing movement. It was the only break in her composure.

Bortolin returned, accompanied by a woman of similar age and demeanour; Besina, no doubt. I surmised that they were husband and wife. They set the table and served dinner: salad, cooked vegetables, rabbit stew. I made a few more attempts at conversation, but gave up. The food was not good, the meal obviously stretched at the last minute to accommodate the unexpected guest. Below the terrace Bortolin was feeding the cats, tossing down chunks of raw meat, over which they squabbled.

My hostess ate little. 'They are the souls of my dead companions,' she said suddenly.

'The cats?'

She nodded. 'Everyone I have ever loved is dead. Or departed, never to return.'

'I am so sorry to hear that. I too have lost many that I loved.' I found myself slipping into her strangely stilted manner of speaking.

'Yes,' she said. 'You understand.'

I ventured a question. 'What did you mean when you said you knew me?'

'I said that?'

'Yes.'

For the first time a troubled look crossed her face. 'And I do not?'

That was as much conversation as I got from her that day. I asked if I could return the next day and was given a gracious nod. I took my leave and retraced my steps towards the back of the villa. As I approached the corner of the building, I overheard Bortolin and Besina in the midst of an argument. I paused to listen, since the dispute was about me.

'We must speak with him,' Besina was saying, her tone pleading and urgent.

'You are a fool. What makes you think we can trust him?'

'She does, doesn't she? What other sign could you want? We can't go on for ever. Surely *they* wouldn't have wanted us to leave her uncared for. And we don't have to tell him everything. Let us ask if he will help.'

I stepped around the corner of the house. Besina made as if to speak to me, but Bortolin pushed her towards the house and stood in my path, hands on hips. He had my dagger in his belt.

'I'm coming back tomorrow,' I said.

'You should not,' he said.

I stared him down. He scowled, sighed and gave me my dagger. 'As you will, Signore.' His look said, I can always kill you later. 'There is a landing. I will show you.'

He took me around the house to the front, where a colonnaded path led down to the Brenta. It was now as overgrown as the rest of the garden but for a narrow trampled track. We descended a flight of steps and pushed through a clump of oleander to a cracked and tilted stone landing where a rowing boat was tied. From the canal, it would be all but invisible.

Back at La Fontana I told Caroline about my encounter. She thought I was inventing a story to entertain her; indeed, it sounded so much like a dream, or a tale from the *Arabian Nights*, that I half doubted it myself. We sent for the steward and asked if he knew of a villa on an overgrown island a mile or so upstream. He did not, but had only been in the job for a few years and was not a local man. He went off to make enquiries of the head gardener, who had worked at La Fontana all his life. The steward returned, eventually, with the information that there was a villa, though it had been inhabited only by caretakers for as long as anyone could remember. It had a bad reputation: there was a demon, or a ghost, or a witch, or an evil sorcerer. Many years ago a man who attempted to visit the island was found drowned, several miles downstream. Others, it was rumoured, had simply vanished.

Naturally, I was more fascinated than ever, and returned the following morning. I rowed past the old landing twice before I spotted it behind the oleander. The mooring posts had rotted away and there was no place to tie up my boat. Broken chunks of masonry lay about, the remains of fallen gateposts. Bortolin's boat was moored to one of these, but none were quite within reach of my rope. They were too big to lift, so I set to work rolling the nearest one closer to the edge. When I heaved it over, I noticed some carved letters, worn and cracked, on the face now upturned:

L A
L I
I T I

The name, perhaps, of the villa. I looked more closely. Was that the foot of an M in front of I T I? I gazed around at the water, the trees, the sky. Everything looked ordinary, but I felt a shiver pass over my skin. Fate, I said, is this you again?

73
An Odd Little Girl

🌿

I moored my boat and walked up to the villa. A few cats were sleeping in the sun on the steps of the terrace, but there was no sign of the girl. I found Bortolin at the back of the house.

He greeted me with a grunt.

'Does this villa have a name?' I asked him.

'Yes, Signore, it is called the Villa degli Eremiti, though no one remembers that name any more.'

'Does anyone remember the name Damory? Or d'Amorie, or . . .'

'Yes, Signore!' Besina emerged from the house. 'I told you so,' she said to Bortolin. 'You never listen.' She seized my hand and kissed it. 'Thank God you have come. And you were going to kill him, you idiot.' She turned on her husband, who was still regarding me with suspicion.

'I was not going to kill him,' he said. 'I only wanted to frighten him.'

'You did.' I recalled the deaths and vanishings of previous visitors to the island. I could well believe Bortolin had 'frightened' them all.

Besina went into the house to fetch some wine; Bortolin, with grudging courtesy, pointed me to a bench beneath a grape arbour. The area around what was evidently the kitchen door had been converted from just discernible parterres to something very like a farmyard. There were chickens, ducks, rabbits in a pen, two teth-ered goats and a kid, several pigs and numerous piglets rooting at the edge of the woods, an extensive vegetable patch, fruit trees, raspberry bushes and strawberry beds.

I was debating how to broach the subject of Tobias when Besina returned with the wine and three glasses. 'My name,' I began, 'is Damory . . .'

Besina nudged her husband and smiled broadly at me. 'You're the grand-nephew, aren't you?'

'Er, yes . . .' I followed her lead. I was, without doubt, some-one's grand-nephew.

'We are so glad you have come. An answer to our prayers, isn't it?'

'Yes, it is,' Bortolin said. 'As you see, Signore, we're not growing any younger,'

'We could die any time, and then what would become of her?' Besina lifted her hands in a despairing gesture.

'I hurt my back last year, can't carry things,' said Bortolin. 'And chopping wood, well, it's hard. Never used to be, but it is now.'

'I can't see so well,' said Besina, rubbing her eyes. 'I can't clean properly.'

'So we decided that we had to ask for someone to help . . .'

'Who could take over when we . . .'

'When we can't manage any more.'

'I have been planning to go into the city to speak with Signore Malipiero.'

'You said you'd go last month . . .'

'I was going to, but then you . . .'

'You always blame me.'

I let them talk on and on; there was a great deal they had obvi-ously been wanting to say for some time. I pieced together their story.

Bortolin and Besina were newly married when, thirty years ago (ten years after Tobias-Thibault had been summoned to the Villa degli Eremiti), they came to work as gardener and cook at the villa. Their employers, the Conte and Contessa d'Amori, had a young daughter of about nine years, named Rosmarina. They were a reclusive family and never entertained, dedicating themselves to Rosmarina's education.

'Music, all kinds of instruments,' said Besina.

'And painting, and languages,' said Bortolin.

'How many languages?' Besina asked him.

'Oh, many, many. She could read when she was only two, they said.'

'Always with her nose in a book.'

Bortolin and Besina grew very fond of the child and, when it became clear that they would have none of their own, took her to their hearts.

'She was such an odd little girl,' said Bortolin.

There was a pause; they looked at each other and Bortolin shook his head slightly. Besina seemed flustered. I wondered what could have happened to Rosmarina.

'Time passed and all was well,' said Bortolin firmly. 'The Conte and Contessa had to go away for a while, and left us in charge.'

'The other servants quit, one by one,' said Besina.

'But all was well,' insisted Bortolin. 'We could manage. We were content. Weren't we?'

'Yes,' Besina said. 'Yes, we were.'

'The Conte had left money for us, for the household.'

'And it was enough.'

'Then we heard that he and the Contessa had perished at sea . . .'

'And we didn't know what would happen.'

'But then the lawyer came, Signore Malipiero . . .'

'The Conte had left instructions, the money was to continue.'

'And if more was needed, we were to tell him . . .'

'And he would write to ask the Conte's heir, his grand-nephew. You, that is, Signore.' Besina beamed at me.

'And you always agreed. So we are very grateful.'

'Very grateful.'

'And now . . .'

'You've come.'

They went on at length, describing how the house had gradually slipped into disrepair, the garden surrendered to nature or adapted to an increasingly isolated life. These days they rarely left the island.

One thing not explained was the identity of the girl I'd seen yesterday. Could she be Rosmarina's daughter, Tobias's grand-daughter? And who was Tobias's Contessa? The fact that they were reported to have perished together at sea suggested that they had gone on together into another life. The grand-nephew and heir had to be Tobias himself, in his next identity. As long as he did not return to a place where he had been known, as long as he dealt with matters by correspondence, there was no reason why he could not keep his affairs going indefinitely. When anyone who had known him was certain to have died, it occurred to me, he could even return and take up the life again, as his own heir.

We were on our second glass of wine when the girl appeared. Her manner was very different today; she was playful, gay and, if not garrulous, certainly more talkative than before. She spoke French and greeted me with a modest curtsey. Bortolin addressed her as Mademoiselle, not Altezza as yesterday.

She took my arm and we strolled around the vegetable beds and chicken coops as though they were the fine gravelled paths and fountains of Versailles. She stopped to greet the animals and introduced each one by name, down to the smallest piglet.

There was a swing at the bottom of the garden. She sat on it and asked me to push her. I obliged, gently, but she urged me to push harder, to send her higher and higher. When eventually I became tired and wanted to stop, she grew sulky, then angry, then stormed back into the house.

She would not see me again that day. I had dinner with Bortolin and Besina and, later, when Besina had gone inside, Bortolin walked me to my boat.

'There is just one thing I do not understand,' he said.

Only one? I thought. Lucky man.

'Why did you not say who you were from the first?'

That was a good question. I played for time while contriving a plausible explanation. 'As I recall, you greeted me with a pistol to my head.'

'I apologise, Signore. If I had known . . .'

When on shaky ground, it is often best to assume an attitude of arrogance and superiority. I glared at him. 'But you did not know. That is the point, Bortolin. I was interested to see how you treated a stranger. And how you have carried out my great-uncle's instructions.'

He bristled. 'We have done our best, Signore.'

I clapped him on the shoulder. 'Indeed you have, Bortolin. I am satisfied with your conduct.'

'*Grazie*, Signore, *grazie*.'

74
Not a Ghost

I returned the next day with one of La Fontana's junior kitchen-maids, a girl named Almira, to help Besina, an under-gardener by the name of Giancarlo to assist Bortolin and Tunnie to keep an eye on all of them. I'd taken him aside, explained about 'my great-uncle Conte d'Amori', and instructed him to make friends with Bortolin and Besina. He was to evade all enquiries about me while discovering everything he could about the situation at the villa. I was sure there was something – perhaps many things – they had not told me.

We rowed over to the island in a larger boat. I took Tunnie and the servants round to the back of the house and introduced them to Bortolin and Besina, who were astonished, pleased and a little uneasy at the sudden appearance of three further strangers.

I found the girl on the terrace, reading Ovid. We conversed in a mix of Latin, French, Greek and Italian about the *Metamorphoses*. Sometimes she would stop in the middle of a sentence and gaze off into the trees, then resume after a minute or two. I found this disconcerting at first but soon became accustomed, and then began to enjoy the silences, during which I could mull over my growing list of questions.

I asked about her parents, her memories of childhood and so on, but were it not for her utterly guileless manner I would have said she was expert in the art of evasion, for she managed to answer without telling me anything.

In the afternoon I returned to La Fontana with Tunnie and the servants, promising to bring them back the following day.

'What did you learn?' I asked Tunnie when we were alone.

'They are definitely hiding something,' he said. 'I don't know what it is, but I'm fairly certain it has to do with Signorina Rosmarina.'

'Rosmarina? Is there another person in the household then, an older woman?'

'No, not as far as I know, though I have not yet been through the entire house. Most of it is closed off, looks as though it's been uninhabited for years. Rosmarina is the girl.'

'The girl I was with? You are sure?'

'Yes, I'm given to understand that's her name, though it was explained to me that on different days she was to be addressed by different titles. We were told to refrain from addressing her at all if we encountered her and were unsure of the correct form.'

Of course, I thought. Rosmarina was the daughter of Tobias and this Contessa of his, two people who might very well be immortal, or at any rate enjoying a relationship to age and death quite other than is usual. No wonder she was a bit odd. If Bortolin and Besina were right about her age when they first came to the villa, she was now at least forty years old. This was undoubtedly what they were trying to conceal, unsure of what I, as Tobias's heir, might already know.

It can be difficult to get information when one must simultaneously conceal that one lacks it. I chose a middle path, of general knowledge that was nevertheless deficient in specifics, and sat down for a long talk with Bortolin and Besina the next day. I could see, I said, that Rosmarina suffered from a strange condition, which was why my great-uncle had been so careful to provide for her care.

'She, she . . . well, as you see, Signore, she is not like other people . . .'

'It took us a while to realise it . . .'

'When one sees someone every day, one does not notice . . .'

'That they do not change.'

'She has not changed for twenty-five years.'

'In many ways, she is still a child.'

'Sometimes.'

'Mostly.'

'But not really.'

There was another of those uneasy pauses, in which something was conspicuously unsaid.

'She has no idea of the world,' Bortolin said. 'She has never left this island.'

'She will not set foot in a boat.'

'She's terrified of the water.'

'She drowned, you see. It was before we came, but the other servants told us.'

'She lay dead all day, they said.'

'But then she came back to life as they were laying her in her little coffin. And since that day she has not gone near the shore.'

Their faces wore similar expressions of fond confusion and deep disquiet. There was a long pause. 'Now that you have come . . .' said Besina.

'We hope you can . . .'

'Help her, or . . .'

They fell silent again.

Bortolin and Besina, I realised, assumed that I was intending to move in to the villa. I was, after all, the heir; it was my house. Well, why not?

With the help of Almira and Giancarlo, the villa was soon cleaned and aired, carpets beaten, linen scrubbed. I settled into rooms on the first floor, across from Rosmarina's. Tunnie had a small chamber adjacent, Giancarlo a room off the kitchen near Bortolin and Besina's, and Almira a place in the attic. In the morning she announced, quite proudly, that she had seen a ghost.

'Is there a ghost?' I asked Bortolin and Besina. They shifted uneasily.

'I have never seen one,' said Bortolin. He glanced at Besina.

'But we have felt something,' she said.

'I saw him perfectly clearly,' said Almira. 'From my window.'

They stared at her. 'What did he look like, then?' said Bortolin.

'He was an old man with white hair and spectacles, wearing a long black coat.'

'Ghosts do not wear spectacles,' Besina said. 'You are a silly girl. You were dreaming.'

'I was not dreaming. He was in the garden with the Signorina. Then he disappeared into the moonlight. That is how I know he was a ghost.'

'Did they converse?' I asked.

'I could not hear any words, but they stood near to each other for some time.'

The sky had darkened and showed signs of rain. I left Besina and Bortolin to deal with Almira and sought out Rosmarina. I found her standing by a window in a long, dim salon, gazing out over the terrace. Rain began to fall, slowly at first, then harder. She watched the drops strike the glass and roll down, tracing their tracks with her finger.

I stood beside her, though she seemed not to see me. 'Rosmarina?'

A tear rolled down her cheek. Before I could stop myself, my hand moved to brush it away. 'I beg your pardon,' I said.

She glanced up at me, and the look in her eyes was at once so pure and so knowingly erotic that I was thrown into confusion.

I strolled about the room to regain my composure. The furnishings were of the best quality, though very worn. Dozens of paintings hung on the walls, all done by the same highly skilled yet idiosyncratic hand. Most were portraits and I was not surprised to recognise Tobias. In many of them he was with a woman and I lit a candle to examine her more closely.

The shock of recognition lifted the hairs on the back of my neck. Tobias's companion was my Contessa.

I heard the girl's soft step behind me. She reached out and touched the Contessa's face.

'Did you paint these?' I asked.

She nodded. 'Lost,' she said. Another tear rolled down her cheek.

'Your mother and your father?'

'Yes.'

'Who were lost at sea?'

'That is what they say.'

'But you do not believe it.'

'Sometimes I see them in dreams, and I know they're alive.'

'And you paint your dreams?'

She nodded.

I took the candle slowly from painting to painting: the Contessa and Tobias together or alone, standing or sitting, walking or riding, against many different backgrounds: a wooded hillside, snow-capped peaks, a garden surrounded by high walls, a pavilion by a lake, a boat on a brilliant blue sea, a desert beneath a cloudless sky, a tiled courtyard with a fountain. I almost dropped the candle when I recognised the garden in Highgate, with the Contessa by the pyramid.

Rosmarina followed me round the room. 'In the dreams I see them so clearly,' she pressed a hand to her eyes, 'but they never see me. They must have forgotten me by now. I used to think they would come back, that we could live together for ever, but now I know they never will.'

'How can you be sure?'

'My friend told me.'

'Who is your friend?'

'He is your friend too. He told me long ago that you would come.'

'Is he the old gentleman you were with last night?'

She nodded.

'Is he a ghost?'

She laughed. 'He is not a ghost.'

'What is his name?'

'Do you not know? He is Mr Pym.'

75

The Conundrum

❧

Days passed into weeks, spring into summer, hot and humid. A torpor lay over the Villa degli Eremiti to which everyone succumbed. In the afternoons Bortolin and Besina, their most onerous tasks taken over by Almira and Giancarlo, dozed in garden chairs in the shade. Tunnie and I swam in the Brenta while Rosmarina painted or played one of the many instruments at which she was skilled. In the evenings we entertained ourselves with cards or chess.

Philippe visited and we fished. I introduced him to Rosmarina. I could see that he was simultaneously charmed and disconcerted, though his polished imperturbability never wavered. He did not come again, and although I occasionally rowed over to La Fontana for dinner with him and Caroline, I found that I had no wish to speak of Rosmarina or our life at the villa, and longed to return to my little island.

Rosmarina and I had late suppers on the terrace by moon- and candlelight. She seemed never to sleep. I tried many times to stay awake, hoping for a glimpse of Mr Pym, but if he came again, I did not see him.

Rosmarina was consistently inconsistent – sombre and sad one day, frivolous the next; a serious scholar one minute, playful and giggling the next. Some days she seemed to be sunk in mourning and hardly spoke, on others she chattered like a giddy young girl.

I struggled to read her, but she was maddeningly elusive. Her moods changed like light on water and it was impossible to tell if she was childlike or mad, a bit simple or a genius, profoundly naive or extremely canny. Occasionally I caught her watching me with a strange smile. She mystified and fascinated me; I did not know how to help her, or whether I should even try. It was easy to let the long days and languid nights slide by.

Every once in a while I would think about Tobias, and make plans to find out where he was. But having taken on his own false identity as his grand-nephew I'd complicated things enormously. So, like Odysseus beguiled by Circe, I let myself linger. Had not fate, after all, led me here? In the strange person of their daughter I felt that I was touching both Tobias and the Contessa, figures more mythical than real to me at that time.

One day Rosmarina told me – without fuss, and as though it was a fact long acknowledged – that the following night would be our wedding. She kissed me for the first time on the lips.

I went for a long swim and then sat on the riverbank, wondering what to do. She was beautiful, desirable – of course I was attracted to her and had often to repress my physical response. In so many ways she is still a child, one part of me said sternly. And in many more, a woman, said another part, persuasively. There was something fitting about marriage; without doubt I felt very strongly connected to her. She needed a protector, and who better?

But what did she mean by marriage? Surely not what ordinary people meant. The thought of Rosmarina in a church was ludicrous.

Was she a virgin? On some days I would have said yes, without a doubt; on other days, when her mood changed, I fancied her not inexperienced. She was, after all, a woman past forty. Had other men courted her over the years? Had she, perhaps, 'married' them? What about those dead or vanished ones? Perhaps they had transgressed and Bortolin had got rid of them. Was that one of the instructions Tobias had left? When I caught myself arguing that those instructions would surely not apply to Tobias's heir, I realised I had already decided to marry Rosmarina. Who was I to defy what I could not help but recognise as destiny?

When I returned to the house in the late afternoon I did not see Rosmarina; Almira told me she'd had to prepare a bath for the Signorina, with rose petals and jasmine, and lay out fresh clothes.

I ordered a bath as well and had Tunnie set out a lightweight linen suit; it was far too warm for silk. I looked through my jewellery and found an emerald ring, the clear, perfect stone engraved with a serpent. I'd worn it on my smallest finger, which I no longer possessed; it might fit Rosmarina. I summoned Almira and told her to deliver it with my salutations and return to tell me the Signorina's response. She returned in a few minutes: Rosmarina had accepted the ring, put it on the middle finger of her left hand and smiled.

I instructed Tunnie to arm himself, stay awake and keep watch for Bortolin, just in case.

At dusk I heard Rosmarina's voice in the garden below my window. She was singing her hymn to Isis, shaking her sistrum and dancing her slow dance. The sun was setting as the moon rose over the treetops opposite. I went downstairs and stood in the doorway watching her. She was wearing the ring I had given her.

When she finished her song she came to me, walking slowly, her face solemn. She lifted a golden chain from her neck and placed it around mine. 'This belonged to my mother.' It was made of heavy, twisted links and ended in an ornate knot. She traced it with her finger. 'The knot of Isis.'

That was as much ceremony as we had; she led me to a table laid with silver and linen and decked with flowers. Besina had spent all day cooking her best approximation of a wedding feast. There were fresh cheeses and salads, roast duck stuffed with walnuts and grapes, stewed kid with parsnips, carrots in butter sauce, sweet wine and a peach tart. Bortolin served with a carefully neutral expression and would not meet my eyes.

As darkness closed in and stars appeared overhead, Rosmarina took my hand and led me to her room. Moonlight lay across the bed; an owl called from a nearby tree. She was not a virgin.

I must have fallen asleep for a few minutes; when I opened my eyes she was bending over me, a dagger in her hand. I stared at it in fascination, sure that I was dreaming. The hilt was gold, inlaid with opals; the blade was shimmering silver and wavy as a snake. She lowered it to my chest; the tip pricked my skin and I woke fully. I had been dreaming but the knife was real, though it was an ordinary kitchen knife.

I tried to sit up.

'Do not move,' she said, and pressed the blade a little deeper, probing expertly between the fourth and fifth ribs. A trickle of blood ran down my side.

'What are you doing?' I tried to keep my voice steady.

'But you know. It's why you came. So we can live together for ever.' She began to whisper the words of her hymn to Isis. The part about the death and rebirth of Osiris, Isis's brother and husband, suddenly took on a new significance. For a few moments I almost believed that she could kill me into immortality.

I was startled out of my trance by the sounds of a violent scuffle in the corridor, then a great thud as the door burst open and Tunnie and Bortolin crashed in. Tunnie had one of Bortolin's arms twisted behind his back and was trying to stab at his eyes with the fingers of the other hand. Bortolin kneed Tunnie viciously in the balls and when Tunnie fell back gasping, jumped on him and held him down by the throat. 'I am here to save him, you idiot!' he shouted, and both of them turned to look at me.

Bortolin leapt to his feet and lunged for Rosmarina.

'Stop!' she said, and so commanding was her tone that he stopped at once.

'Wait,' said Tunnie. 'If you move suddenly she might kill him.' He climbed slowly to his feet, edging away from Bortolin so that by the time he was upright they were several yards apart. Rosmarina's eyes flicked from one to the other.

Besina appeared in the doorway, her mouth wide; Almira and Giancarlo peered over her shoulder. Tunnie closed the door in their faces, then strolled casually around the room lighting the candles. The moonlight faded in the golden glow. Rosmarina's hand trembled.

'Please put the knife down.' I spoke very softly.

She gazed at me, confusion in her eyes, her certainty of purpose wavering. 'But this is what we must do. We cannot turn back.' She tightened her hand on the knife and leaned forward to press it in. Strangely, there was no pain. I just had time to notice one of Tunnie's slender throwing knives protruding from her arm before she released her grip with a cry. Bortolin dived forward and pulled her back.

Besina burst in and screamed. Tunnie retrieved his knife, Besina recovered her composure and pushed us out of the room. We retreated across the passage to my room, where Bortolin poured himself a glass of brandy from the sideboard and drained it in one gulp. Tunnie raised his eyebrows, poured a glass for me, then, at my gesture, one for himself as well. Bortolin refilled his own glass.

'How many have there been?' I asked him.

He shrugged.

'Anyone else survive?'

He shook his head.

It occurred to me that even if others had survived Rosmarina, they could scarcely be allowed to leave the island with tales to tell of madness and attempted murder. Bortolin had been a very able protector, and it was possible that he had further plans for me.

'Will I survive?'

He spoke with heartfelt candour. 'Yes, Signore. You must survive. Who else will protect her, keep her secret safe?'

Who indeed? I fingered the chain around my neck, the golden knot; I saw the conundrum into which fate had led me. 'Will she try to kill me again?'

'I do not know.'

76

A Paralysis of the Soul

❧

Against the most urgent advice of Tunnie, Bortolin and Besina, I went to see Rosmarina alone, in her chamber, after breakfast. 'I know that you will listen at the door,' I told them, 'but be quiet about it.'

Rosmarina sat on a chair by the open window. I kissed her cheek, brought another chair near. She did not look at me. I took her hand; she was still wearing my ring. I showed her that I was wearing her golden chain. She ignored me for an hour, after which I rose, kissed her hand and left. The listeners at the door had been sorely disappointed.

I returned in the afternoon and again in the evening; it was the same. She did not leave her room. Besina put her to bed at night, got her up in the morning, washed her, dressed her, combed her hair, moved her to this chair or that to catch a breeze, to listen to the birds, to avoid the midday sun. She chattered to her incessantly and cooked all her favourite dishes. Rosmarina would eat if food was brought to her mouth, drink if a cup was placed against her lips. She seemed neither happy nor sad; her mood did not change; there was no mood. She blinked, she breathed. That was all.

'Has she ever been like this before?' I asked Besina on the third day.

'Yes, Signore, but not so bad.'

'And how long did it last?'

'A few days, a week.'

After ten days with no change, I insisted that Rosmarina come out. With me on one side and Besina on the other, we guided her downstairs to the terrace. She went where we led her, unresisting, indifferent. It was as though she was sleepwalking.

I made her come out with me every day, morning and evening, round and round the farmyard and garden. I couldn't remember the names of the animals she had told me, so I made up new ones for every rabbit and piglet and chicken. I sat her on the swing and pushed, but gently as she was not really holding on. I plucked flowers and held them to her nose, cupped her hands around warm brown eggs and furry peaches, picked berries and put them in her mouth. I kissed her.

I took her to the music room and sat with her at the harpsichord, placed her hands on the keys and, when she didn't respond, put my hands over hers and moved her fingers to play a simple tune. We did this every day. Sometimes I thought I felt her fingers make tiny movements of their own, but I could never be sure. I led her to her easel, where a primed board awaited. I mixed paint, filled a brush, put it in her hand, guided it to stroke the surface. We painted a face, blotchy and indistinct. I hoped she would be inspired to bring it into a likeness – of Tobias perhaps, or the Contessa – but it didn't work. Nothing worked.

One night I woke to hear her calling me. By the time I had lit a candle and crossed the passage to her room all was silent, and I wondered if I'd dreamed it. She was in her bed, but awake. I sat beside her and took her hand, then lay beside her. I touched her face. 'Rosmarina,' I said, but she didn't look at me. I held her for a while and spoke quietly about unimportant things. I think she fell asleep; at any rate, her eyes closed. I returned to my room.

Weeks passed; Rosmarina did not change. Whereas before I had been exasperated by her relentless changeability, this stasis was unendurable. From my travelling medicine chest I prepared elixirs designed to stimulate various organs and functions of the body; none had any effect. I went to an apothecary in Venice to obtain certain rarer ingredients: no effect.

Autumn came, with fog and damp and chill winds. The villa was draughty, the chimneys smoked. Philippe and Caroline had shut up La Fontana and returned to their palazzo, where I had dinner with them a few times. They thought I was mad to stay on the Brenta, but I liked the stillness that the season brought. The steady parade of party boats had ceased, leaving only the taciturn watermen with their laden barges, plying the canal to and from Padua. The shuttered facades of the great houses loomed out of the low-lying mist, guarded by vigilant herons.

But the real reason I stayed, of course, was Rosmarina. I was chained to her, and she to the island. Thinking that perhaps I could take advantage of her passivity to induce her to come with me in the boat, I led her, on one of our morning walks, towards the landing. At the first sight of the water she began trembling so violently that she could not stand. Her face turned grey, her lips blue. I carried her back to the house as fast as I could, calling for Besina. We sat her by the fire, wrapped her in blankets, chafed her hands, poured brandy, a few drops at a time, into her mouth. Slowly she recovered; that is, she returned to her blank and vacant state.

I despaired. Mistrustful of doctors as I was, I felt I had to seek medical advice. I had told Philippe and Caroline little about Rosmarina, letting them assume that she was just a mistress to whom I was excessively attached. Of her parentage and eccentricities they knew nothing; I had not mentioned our 'marriage' or its aftermath. Now I told them only that she was ill and would not leave the island.

They summoned Venice's most celebrated doctors for me to interview. I was not about to bring a flood of strangers to the island; I would describe 'my wife's' condition and choose the one, if there was one, whose diagnosis seemed right, whose treatments were sane and wholesome – no bleeders or dosers with mercury. But none impressed me and I went home to fret and concoct further ineffective elixirs. A week later, Caroline sent word that the Dutch ambassador had acquired a marvellous new personal physician and graciously agreed to lend him. She had arranged for him to call the next day, so without any expectations I went into the city to meet him.

Augustijn van der Veer was a wiry, energetic man with a long nose and a short beard. He had been a student of Georg Ernst Stahl – of whom, I recalled, both Purefoy and Bayliss had spoken with respect – at the University of Halle. Unwillingly, as I listened to him, I had to acknowledge that he made some sense. His manner was modest but he asserted his theories with clarity. He had treated a number of cases similar to Rosmarina's, he said, cases which other practitioners had abandoned as hopeless. 'Because,' he waved a bony finger, 'they are ignorant of first principles. They rely on dogma and superstition, they invent forces and spirits and humours to embellish their ignorance and never penetrate to the true cause of disease.'

'And what is the true cause of disease?'

He hesitated. 'To understand the true cause of disease, sir, requires a certain metaphysics.'

'Do not be concerned,' I said. 'It is understood that we are speaking here of medical matters, where there can be no heresy.'

He made a small bow. 'I will speak as plainly as I can. Man is a transient, material mixture that is congealed or, as it were, coagulated and brought into activity by an immortal and immaterial soul. The soul is the vital principle of life itself, and it maintains its connection to the body through an act of will. God's will, that is to say, of course. We need no nonsense of hierarchies, elements or correspondences. No intermediaries: the willed activity of the soul is all. The body's changes, which we call diseases if they seem unpleasant, are merely the effects of changes in this vital principle. In essence, what your wife suffers is a paralysis of the soul. Tell me, sir, did her condition come on gradually or suddenly?'

'Rather suddenly.'

'I see. Can you recall any particular event that may have brought it on?'

'She . . . had a shock.'

'Yes, a sudden shock can result in such a condition. I have seen it before.'

'And what treatment would you propose?'

'That is impossible to say without examining the sufferer.'

I took him and his reassuringly large medical bag to the villa, though I would not permit his assistant to accompany us. I brought him to Rosmarina. Anticipating a lengthy wait I settled in the salon, but the doctor, followed by Besina, reappeared after only a few minutes.

'Your wife is with child,' the doctor said.

I looked at Besina, who evaded my eyes. 'You knew this?'

'I suspected.'

'And you did not see fit to tell me?'

'I was waiting another week to be sure.'

'Does she know? Does she understand?'

'I do not know.'

'Have you spoken to her?'

'I have tried, but . . .' she shrugged.

327

I turned to the doctor. 'In her state, can she bear a child?'

'There is no reason why not. I have further examinations to make, but her body is responding as it should to her condition. It is, as I said, a question of the activity of her soul.' He went back upstairs, trailed by Besina.

I put another log on the fire but it was damp and the flames sank away. The log hissed and steamed. I watched as the fire died. Bortolin came in with a basket of firewood, grunted disapprovingly and relaid it. I found that I had a cup of wine in my hand and took a long drink.

Of course I wanted a child; I couldn't deny that. But what would it do to Rosmarina? What awful luck, what terrible timing.

The doctor came down after an hour and accepted a chair and a glass of wine. 'I am afraid I may have caused your wife some discomfort,' he said. 'I needed to examine her blood under my microscope, and had to prick her finger. I apologise.' He sipped his wine. 'Her blood is healthy.'

'So what is the matter with her? And what is the treatment?' I saw now how people were so easily taken in by false doctors – reason was overrun by hope, the desire to believe in a cure, the longing for someone to explain and put things right. Somehow I had invested all my trust in this man.

'This is her first child?'

'Yes,' I said, realising that I did not know.

'If I may ask, sir, your wife's age?'

Only an outright lie would do. 'Twenty.'

He frowned, then seemed to put his thoughts aside. 'It may be,' he said, 'that no treatment is required. There is a natural instinct in some women to withdraw from the world at this time, to turn all their strength within. She may emerge slowly as the child quickens, or it may be that the crisis of birth will be what awakens her. Remedies directed at her body alone will have no effect, but any remedy that stimulates your wife's soul too violently risks damage to the delicate soul of the child. I recommend a quiet life and plain food. Whatever seems to please your wife is what she should be given and anything distressing to her should be avoided.'

Dr van der Veer pledged to come at once if sent for and took his leave, refusing an invitation to stay for dinner. I returned to my seat by the fire. It was not easy to accept that there was nothing I could do; nothing, in fact, to be done. But perhaps the doctor was right and my fears had been misplaced. Rosmarina was not ailing, only extremely still. It made a kind of sense that the growth of a new life in her womb would bring about the reawakening of her soul; it might be exactly what she needed. Maybe it was what she had wanted all along. My mind filled with a rosy vision: Rosmarina healed, come home to herself, finding her true life's purpose in motherhood. Our child – the grandchild of Tobias and the Contessa – growing up happy and strong, endowed with who knew what marvellous qualities, what powers, what gifts? He, or she – I pictured beautiful boys and girls in rapid alternation – would have a perfect childhood in this island paradise, thriving among the rabbits and piglets. We would live here together for ever, Rosmarina and I, just as she wanted, or if not for ever, then for as long as fate would allow. We would have more children, many children, and I would protect them all. They would be our immortality; they would be the golden children. When I began to hear echoes of Meryll's Hymn to the Sun I gave myself a shake. New Eden's golden children had been a dream, a bright delusion. Life was dark, difficult and uncertain.

I found Rosmarina in her room, tucked up with blankets by the fire. Besina sat in a corner. 'Has the Signorina ever been in this condition before?' I asked her.

'No, Signore.'

I took Rosmarina's hand and placed it on her belly. There was a well-defined roundness there.

'You are with child,' I said. 'Do you understand?'

It was impossible to say whether she comprehended my words or not.

'It is my child. You are pregnant with my child.' I looked to Besina for help.

'It is true, Signorina, you are with child,' she said. 'But do not fear, we will care for you.'

Rosmarina made no response. I thought I saw the corner of her mouth move, but it may have been the flickering firelight. I kissed her hand and returned to the salon, where the fire had gone out again.

77

The Absence of Will

As the autumn passed with no change in Rosmarina except the swelling of her belly, our island paradise came to seem a prison. My fears returned and proliferated. I summoned Dr van der Veer every few weeks, though he refused to administer any treatments. He said that the birth of the child would be her rebirth as well and there was nothing to do but wait. I was not certain he still believed it himself, but at least he did not suggest spurious remedies merely to have something to do.

It caused me the greatest imaginable anxiety to know that even if he was found at once and able to set off at once, it would take several hours for him to get here. If only I could bring Rosmarina into the city and establish her in a nice warm palazzo, with doctors and apothecaries a few minutes away, but the attempt to intro-duce her to a boat had nearly killed her and I didn't dare try again.

I toyed with the idea of dosing her with laudanum and carrying her off, but it was too risky for the child.

By December I knew that I had to find Tobias. He and the Contessa were the only people capable of understanding whatever was happening to Rosmarina. Bortolin and Besina had communicated with Tobias's heir – that is, Tobias himself – through his lawyer. I recalled the name: Signore Malipiero. I asked Philippe about him.

'Oh, very old family,' he told me. 'A bit stubborn. Likes things done by the book. No scandals, I regret to say. What do you want with him? If you need something done, you have but to say the word and I will . . .' he waved his hand.

'No need, no need. I only want to get in touch with a client of his.'

The next day, dressed in sober finery and once more in the persona of the enthusiastic family historian, I presented my card at his office. After a delay of almost an hour I was told that Signore Malipiero was not available. I returned the following day and the procedure was repeated. At last, on the third day, I was grudgingly escorted up the stairs, along a dark passage and into a grand but faded room overlooking the Canale di San Marco. Portraits of grim old men lined the walls and an enormous desk kept visitors at a distance from the grim old man hunched in a crimson chair, his chin sunk into his chest like an immensely ancient tortoise.

I was writing a history of my far-flung and fascinating family, I began, and while researching among the archives of the Alsatian branch had learned about the Conte and Contessa who had vanished, so tragically, at sea. I waited to see if this would generate any response from Signore Malipiero. I think he may have blinked.

What was the least I could reveal? 'I understand that you were the executor of the Conte's will and may be in touch with his grand-nephew, his heir . . .'

Signore Malipiero drew his chin a little further into his chest.

'. . . whom I would like to meet. I would be deeply obliged if you could tell me where I might find him.'

Signore Malipiero lifted his hand and a shadow detached itself from the wall and edged closer. A diminutive black-clad clerk had been here all along, so discreet I hadn't noticed him. He bent and placed his ear next to Signore Malipiero's mouth, paused, nodded, straightened and turned to me.

'Signore Malipiero wishes you good day,' he said.

'But . . .'

He crossed to the door, opened it and bowed. I left and sought Philippe.

'I think I may need your help after all,' I said when I found him. 'I do not seem to know how things are done here.'

He smiled.

After a week of string-pulling, favour-trading, arm-twisting and some outright bribery, I learned that the Conte d'Amori's heir was named Tibaldo d'Amori and received correspondence care of the Venetian consul in Alexandria, Egypt. My hopes of immediate rescue faded.

It took me several days to compose a letter. Philippe had warned me that correspondence to the Ottoman Empire, indeed to and from all other principalities, was routinely read by any number of agents and officials before it arrived at its destination, so I had to be careful of what I said. I needed to tell 'Tibaldo' that I knew who he was without revealing it to other readers; I had to explain, without incriminating myself, that I was currently posing as the same fictitious grand-nephew that he was himself pretending to be; that I had taken over his household; that I had married, or at any rate bedded, his daughter; that I knew her secret. In the most guarded possible terms, I had to describe our wedding night. I had to tell him about her illness and her pregnancy and, most difficult of all, to ask for help. At the end, I could not resist adding a postscript sending my regards to the

Contessa and mentioning how much I had enjoyed our last meeting in Highgate.

By the most optimistic calculations, given the uncertain weather of the Mediterranean in winter, it would take at least six to eight weeks for my letter to reach Alexandria and his reply, if written at once, to reach me. Pessimistic scenarios were far more numerous: contrary winds, delays, storms, pirates, shipwreck. A letter might spend weeks or months in a dusty office waiting to be collected. It might very easily be lost.

February passed with no reply, and March. In April I was seized by the hope that he was on his way and would arrive at any moment, but he did not come and I was forced to conclude that my letter had very likely never reached him.

In May, a fortnight before the baby was due, I hired midwives, not one but two, and installed them in rooms near Rosmarina's; Besina had been sleeping on a couch in her room for some time. The household seethed with tension; the atmosphere was intolerable. Bortolin was so gruff that Giancarlo became surly. Almira had crying fits; Besina boxed her ears. Tunnie gritted his teeth and kept me well-dressed and impeccably groomed. I rowed about on the canal just to get off the island, but returned every half-hour in case something had occurred.

Finally, one night, Besina woke me to say that Rosmarina's waters had broken. I got up and dressed, drank a brandy, paced the room from door to window and back. I went out into the passage and stood for some minutes outside Rosmarina's room but heard only indistinct voices as the women spoke quietly to each other. Would Rosmarina scream as Agnes had? I hoped so. It would show that she was coming back to life. I thought about what Dr van der Veer had said – the paralysis of her soul, the absence of will, the withdrawal of the vital principle. Surely if anything could reawaken her soul it would be the birth of this child.

Down in the salon I drank another brandy and waited for

morning. I could hear people passing on the stairs, doors opening and closing, but no one came to tell me anything. At first light I went and stood outside Rosmarina's room again, heard nothing, went away.

In the kitchen I found Tunnie, Bortolin and Giancarlo. They offered me breakfast, but I couldn't eat. I went back to the salon and tried to read a book. I paced, sat, drank another brandy. Tunnie looked in occasionally, brought plates of food, took them away uneaten. I watched the clock, each minute like an hour. Somehow, time passed. It grew dark. I went upstairs and listened at Rosmarina's door. There was the sound of voices, perhaps even an argument, though I couldn't distinguish the words. I knocked, waited, knocked again.

Besina opened the door.

'What . . .' I began.

She shook her head. 'Nothing yet,' and closed the door in my face.

The night passed; though I was sure I could not sleep, I dozed fitfully in my chair. In the grey morning I woke full of dread but didn't dare go upstairs. I summoned Tunnie and told him to bring Besina to me at once.

She came, looking drawn and afraid. I expect I looked the same, for I didn't have to ask.

'The child is ready,' she said, 'but the Signorina . . . she will not do what only she can do.'

I cursed her and sent Tunnie and Bortolin to fetch Dr van der Veer with the greatest possible speed, but even so it was past midday when he arrived. I said nothing, merely gestured him towards Rosmarina's room. I drank another brandy.

Two hours later Dr van der Veer clattered down the stairs and entered the salon with an air of urgency. 'There is not time to speak delicately,' he said. 'Your wife is dead. I can save the child if I operate in the next few minutes. Do I have your permission?'

'Operate?'

'The child is trapped in the womb. If I do not cut open your wife's body to remove it, it will die very soon. You have lost her already. Choose now if you will save your child.' He folded his arms and waited.

The horror of what he proposed, when I had grasped it, shook me to my core. I stared at him, speechless.

'Well?' he said. 'You must tell me now.'

'Yes,' I said, and as he ran from the room I ran to the window and vomited.

We buried Rosmarina beneath an old apple tree in the garden. In attendance were Tunnie, Bortolin, Besina, Almira, Giancarlo and Providenza, the wet-nurse, with the infant wide-eyed and silent in her arms. Philippe and Caroline came with Dr van der Veer, who was moved to speak a few words about the immortality of the soul as white blossom drifted down. Everyone wore black which, amid the wild verdure of the island, gave the scene a theatrical aura. No one remarked upon the absence of a priest. I recited the hymn to Isis, which I'd heard so often I discovered that I knew it by heart. The cats watched from a distance.

I picked some flowers to put in the coffin before it was closed. Besina had dressed Rosmarina in her wedding finery, combed her hair neatly and folded her hands over her heart. She was wearing my ring. Beneath the smooth linen folds of her robe I pictured her body as it had been on our wedding night, its beauty, its perfection. I pictured the long incision, the gaping womb.

335

78

His Glorious, Immortal Life

Philippe and Caroline were once again in residence at La Fontana and they insisted that I stay with them. Something of Rosmarina's paralysis of the soul came over me and I was unable to make decisions. The island had become an awful place to me, yet I could not bear to leave. They dragged me away, with Tunnie's help and to his immense relief. Caroline had, with her usual ease and panache, given birth to her own first child a few months earlier, and now she sent her second assistant nursemaid to the villa to supervise the care of the infant.

I named my son Tobias. He thrived from the first, sucking lustily, sleeping well, rarely fretful. Or so I was told.

I had received no reply from 'Tibaldo' and had no way of knowing whether my letter had ever reached him. There was nothing to do but go and find him myself. It was what I should have done long ago, instead of entangling myself in the life of the Villa degli Eremiti. But now, with such tidings, it was no longer a meeting to anticipate with pleasure. What a strange, sad road my search for him had taken, wreaking death and suffering among his children.

I could not bear to go to the island; I did not want to see the child. Of course it was unreasonable, but I blamed him for murdering his mother. It was preferable to blaming myself. I sent Tunnie to bring Bortolin and Besina to me at La Fontana to receive my instructions. They came and listened in unhappy silence. I was going away for a while, I told them, but would return. They were to maintain the household and look after the child. I introduced La Fontana's steward; they were to consult him if any problems arose and he would provide whatever funds were needed, thus bypassing Malipiero.

Besina sniffled. 'I promise you I will return,' I said, 'but if anything should happen to me there are provisions in my will for you and the house to be maintained.' As I spoke, it occurred to me that Tobias must have spoken to them along similar lines before he vanished. 'And the child will go to my sister, so the burden will not fall upon you.'

Isabel and Meryll had rented a villa in Rome. They'd planned to come to Venice to meet Rosmarina and celebrate the birth of my child, but when Isabel herself was discovered to be pregnant they decided that travel was unwise. Her last letter had been full of happy news; she was healthy and blooming, Meryll inspired and adoring. She closed with a series of excited questions about my imminent joyful event. I wrote to her the day before I left so that she would have to send her reply to Alexandria; it would be weeks before I had to read it.

Philippe provided me with letters of introduction to every person of importance anywhere in the Ottoman Empire; I secured letters of credit from my Venetian banker to his associates in Alexandria. Tunnie packed, unpacked and repacked, a process fraught with the most terrible dilemmas as the vast majority of my wardrobe had to be left behind. I planned to take only one trunk, but that, he declared, was out of the question. I ended up with two large trunks, a waterproof box for those books I could not live without, a chest with a hundred drawers and compartments for medicines, a strongbox for my jewellery and important papers and several smaller cases.

We set out one evening in late June on a Venetian merchant

ship with a cargo of paper, glass, wine, fox pelts, clocks and, lashed to the deck, a diving bell. The device had been ordered by an Alexandrine Pasha, a passionate excavator of ancient monuments, who had conceived the notion that the lost city of Atlantis was hidden beneath the waters of Alexandria's harbour. It was escorted by its German builder, a voluble man named Mecklenberg, with whom I shared a cramped cabin. He had learned the science of the diving bell in England from Edmond Halley, the famous inventor and explorer. Halley's device utilised a remarkable technique for refreshing the atmosphere in the bell by means of two weighted barrels of air which, raised and lowered continuously by assistants in tethered boats, enabled the operator to descend to depths of a hundred feet and remain in perfect comfort for an hour and a half. He offered to take me down in it when we reached Alexandria, but I demurred. No matter how often he explained the sound scientific principles of the thing, it still looked like an oversized coffin to me, and undersea exploration a particularly unappealing way to die. If I wished to drown myself, I told him, I would do so in a more straightforward manner.

Tunnie was happy to be at sea and began to shed the disquiet that, I realised, had lain over him since we first took up residence at the Villa degli Eremiti. For me, never having been to sea (crossing the English Channel did not count), everything was fascinating, from the creaking songs of the rigging to the *lingua franca* spoken by the crew; the strong, strange scents of tar and brine; the hypnotic pattern of waves beneath our bow and the constant motion of the deck. I was relieved to discover that I did not suffer seasickness (or so I thought on this, the most pleasant and uneventful sea voyage I ever made). The weather was perfect, the winds propitious, the sea kind and dazzling blue. There came an exhilarating moment when the land was lost to sight and I was, as it seemed, alone beneath an empty sky.

I was not, of course, alone; in fact, never have I been in a more crowded place. But no one knew me, no one knew my past, what I was fleeing or what I was seeking. There is a sort of shipboard etiquette that allows one's fellow travellers to preserve a cloak of anonymity if they choose. During the voyage I pretended to be carefree, footloose, travelling for the sake of the adventure, the new, the unknown. I wished it were true, but beneath this mask my determination to find Tobias only deepened. I could imagine no other purpose for my life; if I did not accomplish it, I had better not lived at all.

Sometimes, when staring out to sea with what I thought was a blank mind, I caught myself talking to him. The Tobias whom I addressed was a godlike figure: all-wise, all-knowing, free from human limitations, from suffering, from death. Fabulously wealthy, he moved through the world with consummate skill, getting what he wanted, slipping away, remaking himself time and time again, executing grand plans I could not begin to comprehend, moving towards unfathomable ends. I thought about the Contessa. Was she with him? The idea of seeing her again aroused feelings I could not easily define.

It dawned on me that I was jealous of Tobias; then, that I was furious with him. He'd had children, many children, and deserted them all for the sake of his glorious immortal life.

79

A Very Strange Englishman

✣

The voyage took two weeks. We hugged the Istrian coast, putting in overnight at Orsara to take on ballast, sheltering during a brief squall in the lee of Curzola, one of a hundred rocky islands strung along the coast. We passed a whole day at Aulon, purchasing supplies, then sailed on to Missolonghi, where the shore is edged with fishermen's huts built of reeds and teetering on salt-crusted stilts. Our last port was Heraklion, before we set out across the open sea towards the distant coast of North Africa. With good wind and no pirates, we made it in two and a half days; I did not know how lucky we were.

Alexandria appeared at dawn. I had been awake all night and was watching from the bow. At the first sight of that distant smudge on the horizon a strange shiver passed over me, as though I was shedding a skin.

A mile or two out we were joined by the harbour pilot who guided the ship between the two forts, Little Pharillon and Great Pharillon. Linked by long moles to the land, they guarded a bustling waterfront with hundreds of vessels at anchor, flying flags of every nation. The town rose behind: an untidy jumble of houses, some whitewashed, some pink or dull ochre, with flat roofs shaded by striped awnings; tall, graceful minarets; the occasional green of a palm tree. A broken obelisk, ruined walls and fallen towers were reminders of the ancient glory of the city, though the great column of Pompey still dominated the vista. The long arc of the quayside was crowded with warehouses and taverns, thronged with people in the brightly coloured costumes of a dozen different lands.

Officials came on board to check passports, others to search for contraband or taxable items. I saw a number of bribes change hands quite openly, then everyone sat down and had coffee together. Eventually we were allowed to disembark.

It was without difficulty that I located a representative of the English consul; he was cursing loudly in that language, directing a gaggle of porters who were carrying cases of claret from the ship to a waiting cart. I introduced myself. Englishmen were, at the time, such a rarity in those parts that he greeted me with wonder and delight. The Englishmen then resident in Alexandria could be counted on the fingers of one hand; a new face was a great event.

His name was Henry Harvey-Austin and it turned out that he'd been at St Asher's College a few years before me. He'd arrived in Alexandria – 'best city in the world, my dear fellow' – five years ago after service in Aleppo, Smyrna and Damascus. His porters piled my luggage on top of his wine and he took me to the consul's house, where he insisted I must stay.

'The first thing you need,' he said after seeing me installed in a commodious apartment on the first floor, 'is a dragoman.' He moved his hands in a weaving gesture. 'To translate, go-between, arrange. Without one, you are a little lamb among wolves. I will find you one for you tomorrow.'

News of my arrival spread fast, and the entirety of Alexandria's English community arrived within a few hours, soon followed by most of the other Europeans. It became a party with musicians and Greek dancing girls (and boys) summoned from the brothel next door.

The next morning Harvey-Austin introduced me to Nikolaos Demetriades, a Greek from Crete. He was about fifty, I thought, an imposing figure in a tall white turban, his glossy black beard threaded with silver. He wore scarlet boots, loose trousers and an embroidered coat belted beneath a sleeveless robe. A scimitar hung at his side. His rather fierce gaze suggested arrogance until he smiled, revealing a row of large brown teeth with a gap in the middle.

He bowed, sweeping his outer robe aside with a graceful gesture. 'I am honoured to serve the most noble and greatly esteemed Francis effendi,' he said, in only slightly accented English.

Nikolaos proposed an itinerary beginning with the Obelisk of Cleopatra and the pillar of Pompey, then a special dinner at his cousin's restaurant; tomorrow the catacombs, followed by a leisurely few hours at the bathhouse. The list of attractions might have gone on, but I stopped him.

'I hope that I shall have the opportunity to visit all of these places,' I said, 'but today I wish to call on the Venetian consul.'

He made an effort to overcome his disappointment and with a gesture indicated the house across the road.

I went in and was greeted warmly by several of the men who'd been at last night's party. They introduced me to the consul, who regretted that he had not been able to attend the previous evening, owing to a digestive indisposition. He offered me a glass of excellent Barolo and I presented the relevant letter from Philippe, whereupon he regarded me with a different sort of interest and discernibly greater circumspection.

'Our poor outpost is honoured by your visit,' he said. 'In what way may I assist you?'

I produced the 'family historian' explanation, and although he clearly thought me eccentric in the extreme to have come all this way for such a purpose, he nodded solemnly as though it was quite the usual thing. He rang a bell which summoned a clerk, to whom he put my enquiry.

'Tibaldo d'Amori, yes, we occasionally receive letters for him. Very occasionally.'

'And he collects his letters? Does he live here in Alexandria?' I could not quite believe that I had found him so easily, and indeed, I had not.

'No,' the clerk said. 'We send them on to the Cairo office.'

The consul gave me a letter of introduction to his colleague in Cairo and reiterated his extreme pleasure at making my acquaintance. I returned to Nikolaos. 'Take me to Cairo,' I said.

'To Cairo?'

'At once.'

'It is quite some distance, effendi, and such a journey requires a great many preparations.'

'Make as many preparations as you like, but we leave tomorrow.'

'It is not possible, effendi. Tomorrow is Friday, the holy day. No one works.'

'Very well, we will leave on Saturday.'

He grumbled into his beard but went off to 'make arrangements'. I half expected him to appear on Saturday to demand more time but was pleasantly surprised to be called down to the courtyard first thing in the morning. Nikolaos bowed and indicated his preparations: a bullock cart for the luggage and gaily caparisoned donkeys for us to ride – Europeans, he explained, were not permitted to ride horses.

I introduced Tunnie to Nikolaos, and was not surprised to see both swell and bristle and begin what would be a protracted jousting for position. Nikolaos led me to inspect the Janissaries he had hired, without whom it was unsafe to travel. They seemed satisfactory: two brawny, moustachioed Armenians armed with swords, daggers and pistols.

'If I may also suggest, effendi, it would be wise, outside Alexandria, to dress in our manner. And you may find it suits you to grow your beard, which will ensure that you receive the respect that is your due.'

'My lord prefers to be clean-shaven,' said Tunnie.

'I have taken the liberty of bringing some garments for you, effendi,' Nikolaos said, ignoring Tunnie. He snapped his fingers and a slender, pretty boy appeared with a pile of clothes in his arms. Nikolaos held up a flowing robe of flowered silk that shimmered in the sun.

'Such attire is more appropriate for ladies,' said Tunnie, but I had been admiring the native dress, which was routinely worn by many of the Europeans, the French in particular, who cut quite a dash.

'When in Rome, Tunnie,' I said. 'And you as well.' I balanced this diminishment of Tunnie by ordering Nikolaos to get him some appropriate garments of his own.

As we left Alexandria we passed beneath Pompey's huge red granite column. Nikolaos proposed a pause to examine and admire it, but I was interested in only one thing: finding Tobias. I'd wasted enough time in my life. When I insisted that we press on, he seemed truly downcast and was silent for several miles.

Tunnie whistled a jaunty tune. He had consented to a striped tunic and brass-studded belt, but kept his good English breeches and hat. I had indulged in a complete transfiguration from turban to boots, and immediately felt more at home. The new mode of dress suited my new, purposeful mode of being, and if it were not for the inherent absurdity of a man of my height riding a donkey, I would have felt every inch the noble knight.

The donkeys took us as far as Lake Madiah, where the baggage was loaded on to a flat-bottomed boat. In this we crossed the lake and entered the Canopic branch of the Nile. The water was extremely low, it being just before the inundation, and, shallow as was our draught, the boatmen frequently had to pole us off hidden mudbanks. It was blazing noon by the

344

time we reached Aboukir Bay, and the cool sea breeze was very welcome. We coasted along for a mile or so to the entrance of Lake Edko, which we traversed, landing finally at a village where we mounted donkeys once more and rode to Rosetta, arriving at the Nile quay at dusk.

Once again, I was impressed with Nikolaos's arrangements. He had sent ahead by horse-messenger, and a dahabeah awaited us – a broad, shallow-bottomed boat with two lateen sails, ubiquitous on the Nile, Nikolaos told me, since the time of the Pharaohs.

He introduced the captain, or *reis*, a rotund Arab named Mohammed, who showed us to our cabins. With lanterns lit at bow and stern, we set off, a gentle north wind filling the sails. Men with ten-yard poles stood ready to fend off sandbanks and mud bars as Mohammed watched anxiously from the tiller.

We were served dinner on the foredeck, where cushions and low tables had been arranged beneath an awning. The food was edible. Goat stew, I think, though I didn't enquire. Henry Harvey-Austin had given me a case of claret as a travelling gift and I shared a bottle with Tunnie and Nikolaos; Mohammed, being a Muslim, only drank one glass.

The sky blazed with stars. Nikolaos and Mohammed introduced Tunnie and me to the *nargila* – an elaborate tobacco pipe with multiple ivory-tipped tubes and a water chamber through which the smoke is drawn with a pleasant bubbling sound. Tunnie found it unsatisfactory but I enjoyed it; it was a cooler smoke than the English clay pipe, and more sociable.

Reis Mohammed excused himself to take charge of the tiller and Tunnie went to bed. Nikolaos turned to me with a smile. 'So, Francis effendi,' he said, 'I think you are not here to visit our magnificent antiquities.'

'No.'

'For the boys?'

'No.'

'At the Venetian consulate they think you are a spy for the English. Or perhaps for the Russians.'

'If I was, do you think I would tell you, Nikolaos?'

'You should tell me. I will help you.'

'I am not a spy.'

He glared at me. 'What, then?'

'I am looking for a relative of mine.'

'You have come all the way from England for this?'

'Yes.'

'A very important man, your relative?'

'Important to me.'

'Ah. He owes you money, a great deal of money.'

'He doesn't owe me anything.'

He slapped his hands on his knees in exasperation. 'You are a very strange Englishman, effendi.'

At dawn there was a great clamour from the crew that brought me running on to the deck. The first floodwater had been seen; the inundation had begun. We stood at the rail and Nikolaos pointed ahead to where the green-brown water changed colour abruptly to red. A long red tongue was lapping at the eastern bank and spreading steadily. As we sailed towards it, it grew towards us until we crossed the line and a cheer broke out. The rising sun touched the red water and seemed to set it afire; the men started a rhythmic song. I stood entranced; a thousand years, two thousand, might never have passed: the sun, the river, the earth and sky had not changed.

It is impossible to make haste on a river, especially when the current and the winds are opposed. My impatience was gradually eroded by the slow, dreamy slipping past of the muddy, undulating riverbank. The rising water crawled across the parched land along the network of irrigation ditches, making a glistening web. Every few hours we would pass a cluster of mud-brick huts on a patch of high ground. Halloos would be called and children in little boats with eggs and vegetables to sell would paddle out and shriek their wares.

The river widened day by day. Ever informative, Nikolaos told me that the level, rising now by four or five inches a day, would soon be rising by a foot or more. At the height of the inundation the Nile would have risen by about thirty feet and spread to ten miles wide.

No one knew what caused the river to rise, but Nikolaos related with amusement some of the popular theories: an invisible dew that falls from the Moon to his sister the Nile, whom it impregnates, thus bringing fertility to the land; the sudden breaking open of a cavern, far to the south, in which the water had accumulated and which gradually silts up again, thus causing the cycle to repeat; or the oldest story, which he told in a whisper, that it was the prodigious ejaculation of an immense and ancient god.

'And what do you think, Nikolaos?' I asked.

He stroked his beard. 'The people here hardly ever see rain,' he said, 'but I have been in places where many inches of rain may fall in a single day. I think that when the north wind begins to blow, as it does every year about a month before the flood, it brings moisture from the sea. When this strikes the mountains in the south it falls as a great rain, which causes this flood.' He smiled, pleased with his explanation, but I rather liked the story of the ejaculating god.

Sailing day and night, we reached Cairo on the afternoon of the sixth day. Nikolaos took me straight to the English consulate where I presented my letters and was given rooms and a welcome party, much as in Alexandria. In the morning, resisting Nikolaos's plaintive entreaties to visit this or that famous site ('the Pyramids, effendi, symbols of eternity, the greatest wonder of the world'), I had him take me straight to the Venetian consulate. Yes, I was told, they did occasionally receive post for Tibaldo d'Amori, although nothing had come for over a year.

So my letter had been lost, as I feared. Perhaps it was better, after all, that I should come unheralded. But come where?

Further questioning revealed that, in an arrangement predating the tenure of any current clerks, a servant of Signore d'Amori's called every couple of months with letters to be sent on, and collected any that had arrived.

'Does he have a name, this servant?' I asked.

One clerk thought he was called Rasul; another said Abdul-Hakim; another said Abdul-Malik.

I left, uncertain of how to proceed, other than sitting at the Venetians' door every day until this many-named servant reappeared. I told Nikolaos what I had learned.

He laughed. 'All those names tell us nothing. Rasul means messenger, Abdul-Hakim means servant of the wise man and Abdul-Malik is simply servant of the master. No doubt he is all those things. Go back to the English house and leave this with me. I will find out who knows, I will smoke and drink coffee and talk of families, and eventually I will discover who this man is.'

He came back in three hours, having befriended the Venetians' Greek doorkeeper; it turned out that they were distant cousins. The man we sought was named Rashid Ibn Abdullah al-Misri and he came from Sakkara, a village twenty miles upstream. 'So we go at once to Sakkara, effendi?'

'Yes.'

'Forgive me, effendi, if the arrangements have not yet been made. I learned of your desire to be there only one second ago, but all will certainly be ready by the day before yesterday.'

80

Something Had Gone Terribly Wrong

At dawn the next morning we returned to our dahabeah. As we left the Cairo quayside, already bustling and noisy, Nikolaos stood at the rail and pointed mutely to the west. Across the wide waters of the Nile the pyramids caught the light of the sun. Even at a distance of several miles they were staggeringly large; what must it be like to stand at their base and confront those awesome blank facades?

'We could go there now, effendi. On the way to Sakkara.' Nikolaos said.

'Sakkara first, Nikolaos,' I said. If I found Tobias – and I was a long way from allowing myself to believe it – I would perhaps have time to take in the sights.

After a few hours Nikolaos pointed to a village of mud-brick huts on a low, rocky plateau about a mile away: Sakkara. Beyond the village more pyramids loomed, but they held no interest for me.

Reis Mohammed brought the boat as near to the shore as he could and we climbed into a skiff, to be poled the rest of the way. This took two trips: Tunnie, one of the Janissaries and one of our boatmen, who was from Sakkara and wished to visit his mother; then Nikolaos, the other Janissary and me. Although the village was only a quarter of a mile away, Nikolaos insisted that it was beneath our dignity to walk. He hired three scrawny donkeys from the boatman's uncle; we mounted and set off with Janissaries marching at front and rear.

Word of our arrival had gone before and we found a delegation of elders awaiting us at the village well. Gesturing to me to remain on my donkey, Nikolaos dismounted and began a lengthy conversation. I could tell from the tone that it was full of compliments, polite phrases and circumlocutions. I coughed a few times. Soon I heard the name of the man we sought, followed by much nodding as everyone turned and pointed north, beyond the village, to a high white wall that shone in the sun.

Declining repeated invitations to stay for coffee, we rode along the edge of the plateau. On our right, the river valley with its spreading water; on the left, the barren desert stretching to the horizon, pyramids half buried in the sand. The midday sun beat down.

Nikolaos had learned that Rashid Ibn Abdullah al-Misri was a highly respected man, a scholar in his own right, who was the steward of a very great scholar and doctor, Sheikh Tabib al-Damcari – the owner of the vast estate whose walls we were approaching. 'Perhaps your relation is a guest of this Sheikh Tabib,' he said.

'Perhaps.' Or maybe . . . 'Tabib – is that a common name?'

'Not so common as a name, effendi. More as a title. It means doctor.'

'And al-Damcari – what does that mean?'

'It means "from Damcar".'

Damcar? Now why did that sound familiar? 'Where is Damcar?'

'I do not know, effendi. Somewhere east of here, I think. In Arabia, perhaps. Not in Egypt.'

Then I remembered. Damcar was the city in the desert to which Christian Rosenkreutz had journeyed, the city of adepts where he studied the secrets of nature. This sheikh had to be Tobias. He had been English, French, Italian and who knew what else? That he lived as an Arab was no surprise; I recalled seeing correspondence in Arabic among his papers in Alsace.

We had been riding along the high white wall for several minutes before we came to a gate, but it was such a small and insignificant gate, moreover with no bell, that Nikolaos decided the main entrance must be yet further on. Our donkey's hooves kicked up the dust; it grew hotter by the minute. Palm trees showed over the wall; I could hear water splashing within. We plodded on.

'If we ever find the gate, Nikolaos, will they let us in?'

'Of course they will, effendi. We are well-dressed travellers, not brigands or beggars. We are owed hospitality wherever we go.'

At length we arrived at a tall gate, with a grille at eye-height and a bell-pull. We rang and at once a face appeared at the grille. Nikolaos asked for Rashid Ibn Abdullah al-Misri, the gates opened and we entered a courtyard. Servants came running to take our donkeys to the stables; others brought water in basins so that we could rinse off the dust of the road. The Janissaries were shown into the guardroom to wait as Nikolaos, Tunnie and I followed yet another servant, this one with gold brocade on his turban, along a shaded path between sweet-scented shrubs. We passed through a series of gardens laid out like rooms, with fountains, arbours, pergolas and many flowers whose names I did not know. The air was full of birdsong and I glimpsed brief flashes of bright colour flitting among the trees.

A long pool lay in front of the house, filled with floating blue lilies which gave off a marvellous scent. Another servant stood at the open door. He bowed and ushered us through a cool, dim anteroom to an interior courtyard. A tiled fountain splashed at the centre, divans ranged about the walls in the shade beneath the overhanging first floor. The place looked oddly familiar; I searched my memory and realised that it was the setting of one of Rosmarina's paintings of Tobias and the Contessa.

A tall, thin man emerged from a room at the side. He was well, if simply, dressed in dark blue robes, with a pristine white turban and a somewhat straggling black beard. He wore spectacles and clutched a scroll in an inkstained hand. He squinted at us, removed his spectacles, noticed the scroll in his hand, glanced around and put it on a table, then hastened forward, bowing deeply and uttering a greeting in Arabic. When Nikolaos began to translate, he interrupted him with a smile and addressed me, to my astonishment, in English.

'The visit of strangers is a blessing from Allah, good sirs. I am Rashid Ibn Abdullah al-Misri, humble steward to Sheikh Tabib. It is my very great honour to welcome you to his house. Please rest and take refreshment.' He gestured us to a divan.

Servants entered; first with more water, this time jasmine-scented, for our hands, then a pipe of tobacco, then coffee and a variety of sweetmeats, then sherbet, then a sort of tea with fragrant herbs, then a basin of lemon water to rinse our fingers. During all this I controlled my impatience and took my cue from Nikolaos, who spoke only of inconsequential matters and indicated his appreciation of the food and drink with polite murmurs. Lengthy courtesies and interminable exchanges of small talk, I was learning, were the Eastern way. Tunnie had declined to sit; he stood, silent and alert, just behind me.

An hour, perhaps more, passed in this way before the servants withdrew to the edges of the room; the business of the visit could begin. I took a deep breath, but the thought that I might at last be near Tobias momentarily stopped my tongue and I was at a loss as to how to proceed. I had grown accustomed to presenting a carefully crafted web of lies, but our welcome had been so generous and open that I could see no point in being anything other than straightforward. More or less.

'My name,' I said, 'is Francis Damory, and I have come from England to find a relative of mine, Tibaldo d'Amori. Do you know him?'

Rashid smiled. 'Yes, of course, effendi. That was my master's name many years ago. Now everyone calls him Sheikh Tabib because he is a great doctor and a very wise man.'

'Is he . . . is he here?' I hardly dared breathe.

'I regret to have to tell you, effendi, he is not here, but I know that he would wish you to be at home in his home.'

'When will he return?'

'I am not certain.'

'Where has he gone?'

'He is in Constantinople, effendi.'

I had come so close; it was maddening to feel him sliding through my fingers. Was he arranging to 'die while abroad' again? The slippery bastard. 'How long has he been gone?'

'He has been gone for three months, effendi. He went in order to seek the advice of an old friend of his, a doctor, because . . .'

We were interrupted by the sound of a child's voice. An enormous spotted cat ran in, chased by what at first I took to be a skinny boy of perhaps six, then realised was a tiny little old man who was running and shouting like a child. He caught the cat and picked it up; it hung limp and uncomplaining in his arms, almost as big as he was. Staggering under its weight, he went up to Rashid, who smiled at him.

They spoke in Arabic, then Rashid said, 'Here is a chance to practise your English, Jamal. This noble guest has come all the way from England.'

I was profoundly confused. Rashid had spoken as though to a child, yet I saw a man more wizened and ancient than I would have thought possible. He was bald but for a few white hairs, his skin so transparent that the veins stood out like ropes. His arms and hands were scrawny, the joints swollen and knobbed. Lashless eyes protruded from a shrunken and oddly distorted face.

I met Rashid's eyes and saw deep sorrow. 'This is Jamal Ibn Tabib,' he said, 'my master's son. He is twelve years old.'

353

Still holding the cat, the boy inclined his head graciously. 'I bid you welcome to my father's house,' he said in a thin, piping voice. 'This is Ptolemy. Would you like to hold him?'

'Thank you,' I said. 'I would be honoured.' I took the cat, who was even heavier than he looked. He dug his claws into my knees and began to purr, a loud rumble. 'He is a very handsome cat.'

'He is a very bad cat,' Jamal said. 'He killed and ate a bird in the garden.'

'That is his nature,' I said.

'Yes, I know. But my father says that we can be more than nature, and I am trying to teach Ptolemy to be more than just a cat.'

Ptolemy leapt from my lap and pounced on the trailing end of Jamal's sash; the two resumed their chase around the courtyard. 'Slowly, Jamal, slowly,' Rashid called, but was ignored.

He sighed deeply, clapped his hands for coffee and summoned another pipe. I was full of questions; would it be outrageously rude to ask them? I glanced at Nikolaos, who raised his eyebrows and tilted his head ever so slightly in my direction. I understood that, as the highest-ranking person present, it was up to me to speak, or not.

After I had smoked and sipped my coffee, which I commended at length, I addressed Rashid. 'As you were saying, Sheikh Tabib has gone to Constantinople to consult a doctor . . . about Jamal?'

Rashid nodded. 'He made many attempts himself to understand the disease, to find a cure. He worked day and night; I assisted him in the laboratory. But we failed. It was apparent from soon after his birth that all was not right with Jamal. It seemed that he was ageing before our eyes, though as you see, inside he is an ordinary boy. An intelligent boy.'

'And what of his mother?'

'She died when he was two, a boating accident on the river.'

Could the Contessa possibly have given birth to such a catastrophe? 'And I suppose,' I said, 'that her body was never found.'

'Yes, that is so.' Rashid gave me a curious look. 'We searched for days.'

Had she vanished into another life, leaving Tobias to care for the child?

Rashid had been keeping a worried eye on Jamal and when the boy collapsed, panting, to the floor he was at his side in an instant. He picked him up and carried him, protesting feebly, from the room. Ptolemy trotted after them.

Rashid returned in a few minutes and sat down heavily, summoning another pot of coffee with a weary wave. 'He is sleeping. He tires so easily, and his little heart pounds and pounds. It frightens me. Should I forbid him to run and play?'

I could not answer.

Although Rashid pleaded with us to stay for as long as we liked, I would not even stay the night. He had told me the name of his master's friend in Constantinople, Salih bin Nasrallah Ibn Sallum, and written a letter of introduction. As far as he knew, Sheikh Tabib had no immediate plans to leave Constantinople. This information made me more impatient than ever. For the first time, I knew with some certainty where Tobias was. I was tormented by the fear that he would have died again and disappeared into a new identity before I could pin him down. Just stay there, damn you, I thought at him. Just stay there for a few more weeks and I'll have you.

Nikolaos clearly considered my haste to be the height of incivility. To compensate, he made an elaborate speech about the unsurpassed magnificence of the house and our utter unworthiness to pass even a single night in such a sublime paradise. It was dusk when we finally boarded the dahabeah.

The moon rose, casting water and land in silver as we drifted downstream towards Cairo. I sat on the deck and smoked a pipe.

I felt as though an earthquake had shifted the ground under my feet. Tobias was not as I had thought: all-wise, all-knowing, free from human misery. His long life was not the parade of triumphs and achievements I had imagined. If he'd ever had a master plan, it might not be working out. He, like the rest of us, had reeled from mistake to mistake, failure to failure. Rosmarina – preserved in perfect youth, but quite mad. Jamal, an old man at twelve. And who knew how many others? Something had gone terribly wrong.

81

The Persephone

🌿

Ten days later I was back in Alexandria, looking for passage to Constantinople. Ships set off in that direction every day but most hugged the shore, stopping and trading at every port from Ashkelon to Iskenderun and taking a month or more. Also, Harvey-Austin pointed out, they were prey to the petty brigands who lurked in every bay. Far better to wait for a large, well-armed ship that could cross the open sea. Tunnie, too, made it known that he strongly favoured large vessels. I agreed to wait. An English galleon, the *Persephone*, had just put in to port and was expected to depart in a few days for Antalya, from where it would be easy to find passage to Constantinople.

Those few days in Alexandria seemed interminable. Nikolaos showed me all the interesting ancient sites, but our visits had to be completed by mid-morning, when streets and stones and the ever-present dust reached oven-like temperatures. He took me to the bathhouse every afternoon, where I was steamed, scrubbed and pummelled, not emerging until the cool of the evening. The German engineer Mecklenberg had, with his Pasha, begun an exploration of the harbour. I went down to watch, joining a considerable crowd on the quay. Once again he invited me to make a descent in the diving bell; again I declined. I passed most nights at the brothel next door to the English consul's house and learned how to smoke hashish, which helped to pass the time.

Letters had arrived from Isabel and Meryll. My sister berated me for everything from cowardice to arrogance, calculating selfishness to senseless self-abnegation. I was deranged by grief; I had fallen into occult delusions; I had gone mad, as Father had always feared. (I hadn't known he'd told her of his concerns for my sanity.) There was no hope, she was washing her hands of me; alternatively, I must be rescued at once and she, being unable to come herself due to her condition, was sending Meryll forthwith. I had a moment of panic until I read the next sentence: '*He refuses to go.*' She enclosed a small, sealed note for Tunnie, which made him laugh. He wouldn't tell me what it said.

Meryll's letter, in pleasant contrast, was calm if bemused. He had cultivated a very soothing manner. He spoke with cautious optimism about Isabel's well-advanced pregnancy; the baby, I realised, had perhaps already been born. I wrote to both of them and to Caroline and Philippe before I left Alexandria, saying nothing about myself but giving my next address as the English embassy in Constantinople.

We finally departed on the 7th of August and it was with indescribable relief that I felt the coolness of the sea air as we left the harbour. The sails snapped in the breeze; the ship surged forward. Constantinople was a matter of days away, a couple of weeks at the most. Tobias was within reach, and I felt as though I could propel the ship through the water by the force of my will alone.

I shared a cabin with a fat, blond Englishman named

Minchington, a Levant Company merchant, and a sallow, taciturn Pole called Laski, like me on his way to Constantinople. For the first day and night the *Persephone* made good progress but on the afternoon of the second day the winds died. The sun blazed in a white-hot sky; the sea was like glass. Some sails were lowered, others raised, to no avail. We were becalmed.

The captain, a jovial Kentishman named Pardoe, seemed more anxious than I thought was warranted by what was surely a temporary delay. I joined him at the rail, where he was scanning the empty horizon with a long spyglass.

'See any wind?' I asked, and he gave a short laugh.

'No, nor anything else, so far, thank God.'

Before I could ask what he meant, he had crossed to the opposite rail to scan the other side. I found Tunnie at the stern, similarly engaged with a borrowed spyglass. I asked him why he looked so worried.

'We are fish in a barrel, sir, and I don't like being a fish in a barrel.' He gazed up at the slack sails. 'He should get those damn sails down,' he said. A moment later an order was called, men clambered up into the rigging and the sails came down.

'Why?' I said. 'Surely we want to catch any breeze there is.'

'Too conspicuous. If a wind comes, you can be sure he'll have the sails back up in less time than it took to get them down. Much harder for them to spot bare masts than an acre of white canvas.'

'Them?'

'Pirates, sir. Slavers. I don't fancy ending my days chained to an oar in a galley.'

'No, nor do I.'

'Oh, you'd be held for ransom. For me and the rest of these poor sods,' he gestured at the crew, whose expressions shared a certain grimness, 'there's no way out of the galleys once they get you. You're shackled to the bench in a row, hundreds in all in some of the big boats. You sleep there, you shit there, you eat there if they feed you. And you die there.'

'You wouldn't die there, Tunnie. I'd ransom you.'

He looked away, coughed and swallowed. 'That is uncommonly kind of you, sir.'

He went off to sharpen our swords, prime our pistols and, no doubt, conceal half a dozen throwing knives in his boots and up his sleeves. I paced the deck. The sailors moved about with quiet purpose; the smith was busy at his wheel, putting razor edges on swords, cutlasses and long-handled spears for repelling boarders. The swivel guns, mounted on the rail and capable of firing in all directions, were oiled and trays of ammunition prepared. From below the deck came a muffled rumbling as the 24-pounders rolled out.

I was joined by Minchington, whose round face was streaming with sweat. He had bitten his nails to the quick and was working his way towards the knuckles.

'My first voyage,' he said. 'Invested everything. Red Sea pearls. A sure thing, thirty-per-cent profit guaranteed. Now what? No damn wind. In the middle of nowhere. Pirates, too? Just my luck.' The rest was unintelligible as he gnawed on his bleeding fingers. I excused myself and went to my cabin.

Laski was sitting on his bunk, bent over, and at first I thought he was ill. Then I saw that he was unstitching the sole of his boot. He made a quick gesture as though to conceal it, saw that I had seen and gave me a hard look instead. He inserted something into the gap, then took up a stout shoemaker's needle and waxed string and restitched it. When he had finished he left without saying a word.

Although I was not inclined to undertake any cobbling, it seemed like a good idea to keep important papers on one's person. I opened my strongbox and looked through my letters, selected the most important – those from Philippe, Rashid and, of course, from my banker – and strapped them securely under my shirt in an oilcloth pouch. Rosmarina's chain had never left my neck and I disposed the rest of my jewellery as best I could: rings on every finger, watches in my waistcoat pockets, brooches pinned inside my sleeves.

Tunnie appeared with our arsenal, buckled on my sword and handed me my pistols. 'If you have a shot at a pirate, sir, take it right away. Shoot him in the back if you can. Don't call out warnings, as you might be inclined to do, being a gentleman, and honourable. There is no honour here, just survival.'

As the afternoon faded into twilight with no sign of pirates, the tension increased. 'But surely we'll be safe at night,' I said to Tunnie. 'If we can't see them, they can't see us.'

'Not so simple, sir. If they've been careful to keep a distance, they might have been watching us without us ever knowing.'

'How so?'

'The earth is curved, sir, and this ship stands very tall and conspicuous. The pirates in these parts go about in galleys, which are low to the water and much harder to spot. They might have been lurking for hours just below our horizon. They'll take their bearings and come after us when it's dark. If we don't spot them before they're alongside, all those big guns are useless.'

I turned slowly around, the empty dusk suddenly filled with menace.

Night fell, sultry and close. Strict silence was maintained; even a whisper would carry far across still water. There was no moon. The flat, glimmering black sea blended into the starry sky; it was impossible to discern the horizon.

Tunnie leaned over the rail, cupping his hands behind his ears; I copied him and found that it amplified the smallest sounds. I strained my eyes to discern any movement and held my breath as I listened for the telltale splash of oars.

I noticed that it was getting darker; a bank of cloud had

appeared, low in the north-west. Did this mean that a wind was on the way? I pointed it out to Tunnie. He studied it for a moment, licked his finger and held it high, then shook his head and shrugged. Whatever promise the cloud held, it was not yet of any use. We returned to our watching and listening. Agonising minutes passed. The harder I stared into the darkness, the more it teemed with creeping shadows.

I felt Tunnie catch his breath, then I too heard a faint splash, and another, in a slow and ominous rhythm. You cannot imagine the terror aroused by that sound. It was drawing closer, though I could not tell the distance or the precise direction. For a long moment I stood paralysed by fear.

The night was shattered by an immense crack of thunder; the deck jumped beneath my feet. The *Persephone*'s 24-pounders had fired. Smoke roiled from the gunports, obscuring the view – had they hit it? My eyes were burning, my ears were ringing and I was completely unprepared for the grappling hook that seemed to drop out of nowhere and attach itself to the railing between me and Tunnie. As I stared blankly at it, Tunnie fired his pistol along the line of its rope and severed it with his dagger. Shouting filled the night as hand-to-hand combat broke out all up and down the ship. The broadside had missed them completely; they'd already been under our bow. For no good reason, the big guns fired again.

I could not see more than a few feet into the darkness, rapidly thickening with smoke from the cannons and the swivel guns. Fear heightened my senses and some kind of instinct took over. I cannot say I enjoyed it as I enjoyed duelling, but I took pleasure in fighting efficiently and, for the first time, side-by-side with Tunnie. His ruthless calm steadied me, and we set about killing as many of our fellow men as we could.

We seemed to be getting the upper hand; no more grappling hooks were landing in our immediate vicinity. We reloaded our pistols and as we made our way aft, where the fighting was still intense, we heard a shout from the opposite side of the ship. We rushed to the rail. Two more galleys had slipped in under the guns and dozens of men were swarming up the ropes. We emptied our pistols at them, but as soon as one man fell, another took his place. We were retreating towards the stern, where a small group of officers was about to be overwhelmed, when something erupted under my feet and I was flung into the sea.

I came up dazed and gasping as Tunnie dived in after me. The water was full of blazing debris; he seized my collar and swam strongly away from the ship. When he saw that I had recovered my senses he stopped and we looked back.

'What happened?' I said, when I'd caught my breath.

'Powder keg must have exploded on the gun deck. Some idiot threw a grenade into the gunport, or a gunner dropped a taper, or maybe it was just a spark.'

Flames were visible at the gunports; another blast sent more burning fragments arcing into the sea.

'I suggest we swim a little further away, sir,' Tunnie said. 'They may not be able to put the fire out in time.'

'In time?'

'Swim, sir, if you please, now.'

We retreated a further fifty yards, turned and trod water. A clump of debris floated by; Tunnie caught hold of it and we rested our arms across it. I repeated the question. 'In time, Tunnie?'

'Before the fire burns through the floor of the gun deck and ignites the powder store, which is directly below it.'

As we watched in horrified fascination, the fire spread. Men were silhouetted against the flames as they ran to and fro, trying to extinguish the blaze. The red light reflected off the water and made the figures fighting on the deck look like demons dancing in Hell. It was evident that the battle was nearly over; the pirates had subdued all the sailors except for the small band of officers, who had retreated to the poop deck. The galleys were tied on near the bow and already loading prisoners.

My attention was drawn to movement at the stern; several men were climbing down a rope ladder from the overhanging gallery of the captain's cabin into a small boat, which pushed off and began to row rapidly away from the ship. Tunnie saw them too; when they drew near I called out and we swam to meet them.

The boat contained Captain Pardoe, Laski, Minchington, a large iron-banded chest which Minchington held protectively between his feet and a single sailor at the oars, who hauled me in. I pulled myself upright and reached down for Tunnie.

'Not him,' said Laski. 'No room.'

In an instant I had my arm around his neck and my dagger at his throat. 'You are mistaken,' I said. 'There is plenty of room.' I was still in a killing frame of mind and restrained myself with difficulty from the obvious solution to the overcrowding problem, which was slitting his throat and tossing him overboard as I'd been doing to pirates.

He made a strangled sound. Pardoe grunted and waved his hand at the sailor, who pulled Tunnie in and then resumed rowing as fast as he could. I released Laski, though not before giving him a small but bloody nick quite close to his jugular.

At that moment a huge explosion lit the sky and rocked our little boat. The fire had found the powder store. The *Persephone* was obscured by a billowing cloud of smoke. When it cleared we saw that the blast had holed her below the water-line; within seconds she began to list. Pirates and sailors alike were jumping overboard; the galleys cut their mooring ropes and rowed away, leaving the water full of desperate men.

'Row faster, damn you,' said Captain Pardoe, and the sailor redoubled his efforts. Tunnie sat beside him and took one of the oars.

In far less time than I thought possible the *Persephone* began to sink, stern-first. At the very last the bow made a feeble surge upwards as though for a final gasp of air before it was pulled under.

One imagines such a thing happening in silence, but the noise that accompanied this nightmare vision was more horrible even than the sight. A great creaking and groaning as the ship's huge timbers warped and snapped; the roar of the flames and the hiss as fire met water; the screaming of many men; the hideous sucking sound as the ship vanished beneath the sea.

82

The Sea

❧

The darkness was sudden and silent but for the fading cries of drowning men. The stars were half hidden by the approaching clouds and I could barely make out the pale faces of my companions. We sat in silence as Tunnie and the sailor rowed. They had settled into a steady rhythm, and though there were no visual markers to indicate our speed, we seemed to be making rapid progress. But towards what destination?

Captain Pardoe stood up in the bow and gazed ahead. He peered at an enormous pocket watch, then tapped the sailor and Tunnie on their shoulders and pointed to a bright star that hung a few degrees above the still-clear eastern horizon. A small correction to our course was made.

'Where are we going?' I asked.

'Away from the pirates, may they rot in Hell,' said Pardoe. 'They headed for the mainland; we shall head for Cyprus, which is about

364

fifty miles east-south-east.' He turned to study the looming clouds. In the meagre light it was impossible to make out his expression, but he did not look overjoyed.

A slender moon rose and cast an oily sheen over the black water. The dense, humid air was charged with tension, the stillness somehow unnatural. The cloud bank was about a mile away when the first cold gust of wind hit us and the sea became choppy. The leading edge of the storm was riven with lightning and marked by a line of undulating waterspouts. Thunder cracked and boomed.

And then it was upon us: tearing wind, lashing rain, hailstones like musket shot. Tunnie and the sailor had all they could do to keep the boat from slewing sideways between the rising waves. The wind was whipping the sea and driving water into the boat from every direction.

Already low in the water, we were in danger of being swamped. I could see no bucket or pail, so I began bailing as fast as I could with my hands. Pardoe and Laski took off their hats and began to help, but we were losing the struggle. The boat was too heavy, and it wasn't Tunnie who had to go.

Laski was bailing hard at my side. I nudged him and jerked my thumb at Minchington and his iron-bound chest. 'Him or it?'

He gave a grunt that may have been a laugh. I seized one handle of the chest, he the other, and we heaved it overboard. It had weighed, I reckon, over two hundred pounds and the boat now rode considerably higher in the water. Minchington howled and cursed us; Laski and I resumed bailing without a further word.

At first I hoped that the storm would blow over fast, but it did not. For hours we rode the waves, bailed, prayed and vomited. At last, I knew what seasickness was. It makes one long for death, but I had to keep bailing. To distract myself, I tried to picture a map of the Mediterranean Sea; how big was Cyprus, how easy to miss? And if we missed it, where was the next landfall? Or would we be taken by pirates after all? I bailed blindly in the dark.

It seemed that the night would never end, but a dull dawn finally came. The wind had slackened, but the sky was full of heavy clouds and it was raining hard. The waves were monstrous long rollers in the lead-grey sea, with steep peaks and terrifying troughs. They went on and on and on.

I considered the possibility that I had died and gone to Hell. I strove to recollect my Dante; surely this was the seventh circle, for those who had led violent lives. Or no, perhaps the second circle, for the lustful. To console myself, I tried to remember lust, but felt only nausea.

At the crest of the next wave Captain Pardoe cried out – had he sighted land? He was screaming at Tunnie and the sailor to turn the boat. When we topped the next wave I saw it too. Land indeed, and close. Another trough to be endured before I could look again; I glimpsed jagged black rocks and a tumult of white foam.

As the rowers struggled to turn the boat away from the rocks we failed to reach the top of the wave and instead slid sideways back down the trough, swamped beyond any hope of bailing. The next wave would sink us.

'Swim for it!' yelled Pardoe, setting an example by diving into the sea, followed by the sailor. That was the last I saw of them.

'I can't swim,' Minchington wailed, wrapping his arms around my leg.

Laski kicked him hard in the gut and Minchington released his hold; Laski dived overboard. Tunnie and I leapt together and in seconds the sea had carried us some distance away. I looked back to see the boat tipping over, Minchington's mouth wide with terror, his scream lost in the crash of the surf. When I turned around Tunnie had disappeared. I caught one glimpse of him thirty yards off and called out, but the gap between us was rapidly widening and he could not have heard me in any case. I thought I saw him raise his arm and wave, then he vanished.

I swam for shore, aiming for a pale gap between the rocks that I hoped was a sandy cove. In the deep water I was able to ride the waves and, to some extent, control my direction, but when I came to the surf I was utterly helpless. A huge wave flung me against a hidden rock, which knocked the wind out of me. I was tumbled on to my back and sucked out to sea by the receding wave. I struggled up gasping, having swallowed a considerable quantity of water. When the next wave brought me close to the shore I swam for it with the last of my strength. My feet had just touched the bottom when the ebbing wave spun me around and slammed me down. I was tumbled through a maelstrom of pebbles and coarse sand that filled my mouth and nose and scoured my skin, then lifted up and hurled down again. I dug in my hands and feet and hung on for my life. The sea flattened me on to the shingle and dragged me backwards. I clung to the land and, as each wave abated, crawled a little further up the sliding shore.

83

My Cherished Friend

I woke to the tinkling of little bells. I was half buried in storm wrack, I couldn't move and my eyes felt like they'd been cemented shut. I forced them open a crack and saw many bare feet, adorned with silver toe rings and ankle bells, edging closer. Someone poked me with a stick. I tried to sit up.

I'd been surrounded by twenty or thirty women and girls, who now fled giggling and squealing. All except one, who stared at me with wide grey-green eyes.

I croaked a greeting; she said nothing. The other women reached the top of the beach, where a striped pavilion was being erected by a troop of blackamoors. As soon as I was pointed out they raced down the beach, shouting in curiously high-pitched voices. They surrounded me and pulled me to my feet, which caused such pain that I screamed.

My clothes were torn and I was covered with cuts and bruises; the skin had been flayed from my hands, elbows and knees; I had a broken nose, a black eye and, as it would turn out, a broken collarbone and several broken ribs.

They dragged me away; mercifully, I fainted.

Of the next hours I remember little. I later learned that the doctor had given me laudanum to keep me unconscious as he cleaned and dressed my cuts and bandaged my shoulder and chest. I slept until the afternoon of the following day, deep in lovely opium dreams about a mysterious beauty with grey-green eyes who rose from the Cyprian sea like Aphrodite and healed me with her kisses.

I woke to a throbbing headache and dull pain all over my body. As soon as I opened my eyes, a young man who had been sitting by the bed stood, smiled, bowed and left. His soft footsteps receded. I was in a cool, white-walled room with an ornate wooden ceiling and rich carpets on the floor. Carved screens at the windows filtered the sunlight into a thousand golden rays.

My attendant returned with an older, bearded man, who smiled warmly and greeted me in halting English. He spoke French and Italian almost as badly so we conversed in Latin, in which he was proficient, with words from other languages as needed.

My pouch of letters had survived; they, and the jewels I wore, had convinced him that I was no mere vagabond sailor or ship-wrecked pirate. He introduced himself: Moses Hamon, personal physician to Prince Ibrahim Ismail Heyreddin, the cousin of Sultan Mahmud, may he be a thousand times blessed. He told me that I had indeed landed on Cyprus, on a stretch of coast belonging to the summer palace of the Sultana Safiya Zuhal, Prince Ibrahim's mother and the Sultan's revered aunt.

I began to tell him about the pirates and the sinking of the *Persephone* but he already knew; another survivor had been found walking, apparently unharmed, along the coast not far from where I had washed up. He had not needed the attentions of a doctor so Dr Hamon had not seen him, but he thought he was a European.

'Do you know his name? Where is he? I was with another man, and we were separated near the shore.' I was desperate for news of Tunnie.

Dr Hamon sensed my urgency; he made soothing sounds. 'I do not know, effendi. I will make enquiries, but you must eat, drink and then sleep again. We will find your cherished friend, have no fear.' He clapped his hands and as he rose to go, servants entered with food and drink.

I had planned to get up immediately after eating, to search for Tunnie, but sleep overcame me. I dreamed that the woman with the grey-green eyes came into my room. The little oil lamp she carried illuminated her face with a dim golden glow and scented the air with roses. When I awoke, the room was empty, but I was filled with the most ardent desire I had ever known. I sat up until dawn, wondering how a woman I'd glimpsed for a minute could so inflame me, and how I could contrive to meet her.

In the morning the doctor returned, smiling as before. The other European was here; did I wish to see him?

My heart rose, but it was not Tunnie who appeared at the door. It was Laski. He looked remarkably fit, and but for a torn cuff even his attire was unscathed. He saw me looking at his boots – salt-stained but intact – and made a small bow.

'What of the others?' I asked. He said he hadn't seen anyone after he dived off the boat. The waves had washed him up on a wide, smooth beach about half a mile to the south; he'd been able to walk out of the sea, having suffered no more than a soaking. I was glad to see him, though we had hardly been friends; it gave me hope for Tunnie. Laski was leaving the next day, having already arranged passage to Constantinople.

There was no word of any other survivors, although Dr Hamon assured me that the coastline for miles in both directions was being meticulously searched. He allowed me to walk about my rooms and the adjoining courtyard, which eased my stiffness. I was in an apartment in the wing of the palace reserved for foreigners, which had its own separate gate, its own baths, kitchens, laundry and servants, mainly Greeks, who were deemed less likely to be offended by foreign ways.

When I expressed a desire to search the shoreline myself, it caused some consternation and necessitated elaborate arrangements. A person of my standing, apparently, could not go about without a considerable retinue, though whether they were to protect me from others or others from me, to ensure that I behaved properly or just to keep an eye on me, I did not know. My procession comprised a sedan chair with two bearers, four Greek footmen with necessaries such as fans, food and beverages, six Janissaries, a Circassian dragoman and a Turk with an enormous moustache whose function I could not guess because he never spoke.

The palace compound, as I learned during my sojourn there, covered sixty hectares: a sprawl of low buildings in stone, marble or painted stucco, with shaded balconies, towers and quaint turrets, set like islands among lush gardens and tiled courtyards. The air was filled with the chitter of many birds and cooled by the splashing of innumerable fountains. Four hundred people lived and worked here, divided into separate though intersecting tribes of courtiers and slaves, soldiers and servants; men, women, children and eunuchs; true believers and infidels; tradesmen, artisans, bureaucrats; clerks and scholars; cooks and gardeners and foreigners.

Of course that first day I saw only a bewildering and rapid progression of corridors, courtyards and walled paths as I was carried in the sedan chair towards the foreigners' gate. The beach on which I had been found was just below the palace; I directed my bearers along the shore to the north, for the current had been carrying Tunnie in that direction when I had last seen him. The coastline alternated between rocky cliffs whose jagged teeth extended into the water and sheltered, sandy bays. The sky was translucent blue, the sun was hot but not unpleasantly so and the slight breeze scarcely ruffled the surface of the sea. Tender wavelets lapped at the shore. It was impossible to imagine that this same sea had been a raging, murderous monster.

I had myself carried into every cove, where I limped along the tideline while the Janissaries and footmen scrambled over the rocks. Everyone was instructed to shout 'Tunnie' at the top of their lungs at regular intervals.

After a couple of hours, when we were about a mile along the coast, one of the footmen called out. He'd seen a body, the dragoman reported, all but hidden by overhanging rocks. There followed an awful wait as the men climbed down and hauled it up. As they carried it over the rocks towards me I saw with immense relief that it was Minchington. His fat form was unmistakable, though the sea had stripped him naked and battered him black and blue.

Two of the Janissaries went back to the palace with the body and the rest of us returned to the search. I asked the dragoman if there were any houses or villages nearby to which Tunnie might have gone or been taken, and was informed that the Sultana owned the land for miles in all directions; there were no other inhabitants.

By mid-afternoon the heat had become oppressive, the bearers dragged their feet and the Janissaries muttered. The dragoman advised a return to the palace; I insisted that we continue. We had a little battle of wills; I gave him one of my rings and we continued until sundown. I had a marker set at the point where we turned back; we would resume the next morning.

The activity had caused my cuts to reopen and I had to submit to much tut-tutting from the doctor and a painful reapplication of myrrh salve and linen bandages. I was dining by the fountain in my courtyard when word came that an injured man had been brought to the infirmary; Dr Hamon had been summoned and was on his way.

I arrived a moment after the doctor. An unconscious man lay limply on a bed. It was Tunnie, and though they assured me that he was alive he looked more than half dead. He was bruised and scraped, as I had been, with a particularly ugly gash to his shoulder. There was something seriously wrong with his right leg: the thigh was bent at an unnatural angle and hugely swollen. Dr Hamon sucked his teeth and probed at it with delicate fingers.

'The bone has not broken through the skin,' he said, 'which is good. I will try to reset it, but if gangrene has begun . . .' He didn't finish. In a calm voice he issued orders to his assistants, who scurried off and returned with basins and towels, splints and bandages and medications. Tunnie's cuts were washed and the myrrh salve applied, then he was securely strapped down to the bed. One of the assistants held Tunnie's right calf as the doctor slipped wedges beneath the broken thigh to brace it, but as soon as he applied pressure Tunnie woke with a scream. Another assistant had been standing by with a cloth soaked in laudanum; he applied this and Tunnie subsided with a moan.

At Dr Hamon's signal, the man at the calf pulled hard as the doctor, with one swift, precise movement, aligned the thigh. Drugged as he was, Tunnie groaned. More laudanum was administered and the leg was splinted and bandaged.

Dr Hamon stepped back, wiping the sweat from his brow. He was white and shaken. 'He has the laudanum, but I imagine the pain,' he said. 'I wish I did not, but I do. I always have. A disadvantage in my profession.'

'Will he survive?' I asked.

'I will pray to Allah, and you pray to your Jesu. We will know soon enough. If he makes it through the night without fever, he has a good chance.'

I sat by Tunnie's bed all night, checking every few minutes for signs of fever and dripping water into his mouth. He breathed, he swallowed, from time to time he murmured or twitched and when, gritty-eyed, I welcomed the dawn he was sleeping peacefully. He slept until mid-morning. When he woke and saw me, tears filled his eyes, and perhaps mine as well.

He'd been carried for several miles by the current, finally coming to shore in a rocky area. While trying to scramble up the cliff, his leg had become wedged in a narrow crevice; it saved him from being pulled back out to sea, but the battering waves had tossed him around so violently that the leg had snapped. He struggled to free himself, to no avail, and had all but given up hope when some fishermen, passing in their boat, heard his fading cries.

Tunnie improved steadily over the next two days, but on the third day it was apparent that, although his leg seemed to be doing well – the swelling had gone down and the bruises were receding – the gash on his shoulder was not healing.

Dr Hamon studied it closely and shook his head. 'This is very deep, my friend, and the flesh is not knitting as it should.'

'Pity we lost your medicine chest, sir,' Tunnie said to me. 'I could do with some of that magic powder of yours.'

'What magic powder?'

'The one that saved you when that Frenchman cut you up so bad.'

I remembered – my salix, astragalus and mould preparation. 'Perhaps I can make some more.'

I learned from the doctor that the palace had a fully stocked apothecary; he took me there and I was duly impressed. They had several varieties of astragalus and of salix; the quality was excellent. Mould was easily obtained from the kitchens. Dr Hamon watched with interest as I compounded the recipe. He knew, of course, of the various properties of salix and astragalus, but had never heard of mould being used in this way and was politely sceptical. When I explained that I had learned about the use of mould in an ancient book translated from the Chinese, he was somewhat reassured.

The 'magic powder' brought an immediate improvement to Tunnie's wound, abetted, no doubt, by his fervent belief in its efficacy. Within a day, the inflammation and redness abated and the wound began to close.

It became apparent that it would be weeks before Tunnie could walk without crutches and considerable pain, which he tried to hide. At first he insisted that he would be fit in no time; then, that I should go on to Constantinople without him. I refused, though not without a twinge, which I am certain I concealed.

My obsession with Tobias had dragged Tunnie on this dangerous and so far futile quest. He had been unfailingly loyal, often wise, usually cheerful, always extremely useful. We had fought side-by-side; he had risked his life for me and saved me more than once. Tobias, on the other hand, was as much myth as man, and I'm not sure I truly believed that I would ever find him. Beneath my fervour and determination, I harboured a strong suspicion that he would remain one step ahead of me, no matter how diligently I pursued him. I wondered whether he was not, perhaps, elusive by his very nature, and if I ever found him, he would not be the Tobias I sought.

84

An English Drawing Room

❧

'Prince Ibrahim wishes to meet you.' Dr Hamon was unable to contain his pride and pleasure. 'I have spoken of you. He has a fondness for all things English.'

'That would be a great honour.' I felt like a rare object about to be offered to a discerning collector by a hopeful dealer.

I had been given a modest wardrobe of linen shirts, loose trousers and long sleeveless robes; slaves now trotted in with a selection of sumptuous silks and I was quickly transformed into near-princely splendour. I donned all my jewels and allowed my now substantial beard to be combed and oiled. Dr Hamon asked me to bring the jar of 'magic powder', though he did not say why.

Escorted by my retinue of Greek footmen, the doctor led me through courtyards and gardens of steadily increasing opulence towards the royal residences. The footmen stayed at the outer gate; at each of three subsequent gates I was courteously but very thoroughly searched before being allowed to proceed. Well-armed Janissaries patrolled the corridors and guarded every doorway. It seemed rather excessive to me, and while we waited in an anteroom I asked Dr Hamon if the Prince lived in fear, even here in the heart of the palace.

He spoke rapidly, in a low voice. 'There has been a recent attempt on his life.' He glanced around; there was no one within earshot. 'During a fencing lesson he received a wound to his side.

His fencing master was a Frenchman.' The word, as he articulated it, was laden with implications of untrustworthiness and duplicity. 'He insisted that it was an accident, that the Prince's servant had failed to fasten his protective breastplate properly. Both were tortured, of course, but died without revealing any details of the plot or accomplices. That was about a month ago. Then, a week later, the Prince's most beloved friend and tutor, like you an Englishman, died suddenly. We believe it was poison, though I could not determine what sort. We found no one to blame, so the entire kitchen staff was executed. Prince Ibrahim has been deeply disturbed by these events, and his wound has not healed. It is possible that the Frenchman's blade was poisoned. My skills, I am ashamed to admit, have not been sufficient, and when I saw the effect of your powder on the wound of your friend, I spoke of it to the Prince. He did not say he would try it but neither did he refuse. He has quite lost faith, I regret to say, in the efficacy of salves and powders. I think it is more your Englishness that interests him. Do you know Mr Milton? He is very fond of Mr Milton.'

I assured him that all Englishmen knew Mr Milton, and he breathed a sigh of relief. 'I am counting on you, my friend,' he said.

Prince Ibrahim was a slight, handsome youth with a wispy moustache and delicate, well-manicured hands. We entered his presence with many bows and it was not until we had drawn quite close that I looked up and met his eyes. They were warm, intelligent and somewhat wary, with a tight whiteness around the lids that told of suppressed pain. He was reclining on silk pillows beneath a window screened by exquisitely carved panels set with coloured glass and inlaid with mother-of-pearl. A tawny gazelle with dainty gilded hooves nibbled at some grapes from a low table; another lay at the Prince's side. He stroked its head absent-mindedly. Behind the Prince, watching me with a cold, mistrustful gaze, stood a richly dressed elderly man.

'Zurnazen Bey,' Dr Hamon whispered. 'Prince Ibrahim's adviser.'

With a graceful gesture the Prince indicated that I should sit near him on the divan. 'Please call me Ibrahim,' he said in excellent English. I could see that the effort of speaking caused him pain. 'And I will call you Francis. I so enjoy the English informality.'

During the lengthy parade of pipe, coffee, sweets, sherbets and various other delicacies, we spoke about England. He mourned the loss of his tutor, a Cambridge man named Matthew Singleton, who had come to Cyprus some years ago to study the Roman ruins and never left. I wondered if they had perhaps been more than just tutor and student, or prince and subject. Ibrahim was delighted to learn that I had attended Oxford; he hoped to attend an English university himself one day. 'Cambridge, or even your Oxford, which is very good also,' although his family was unlikely to allow it, especially now. Everything he ate or drank was tasted first by a slave.

After an hour or so of pleasantries, Dr Hamon, who had stood politely to one side, coughed.

'Yes, my dear doctor,' Ibrahim said. 'You are impatient to tell me about the medicine that my new friend Francis has brought.' He spoke as though I'd come all the way from England solely for that purpose.

I brought forth the jar of powder, explained its formula and its use. Dr Hamon nodded encouragement, and added a testimonial to its effect on Tunnie's wound.

Zurnazen Bey bent close and studied the jar without touching it. He beckoned to the taster slave, who picked it up and opened it carefully. The bey made a further inspection and addressed me for the first time, in bad English. 'He eat?'

'No,' I said. 'It is applied directly to the wound.'

He said a few words to the taster and Dr Hamon in Turkish.

The slave held out his left arm, Dr Hamon made a long incision with his dagger and applied the powder.

'We wait now. You may go,' Zurnazen Bey said to me.

'Dear friend Francis,' Ibrahim said, 'you will come back tomorrow and we will continue our delightful colloquy. I am so glad that you are here.' He smiled sweetly, ignoring the grim-faced bey and the bleeding slave. We might have been in an English drawing room; perhaps that is where he was pretending to be.

85
Politics, Spies, Assassinations, Factions, Conspiracies

The slave survived. When I returned the following day the powder had been applied to the Prince's wound and he declared he could feel it working already. At his request I visited him every day for pipe and coffee, sweets, sherbet and decorous conversation. He was desperately eager to hear about my travels: London, Paris, Venice, crossing the Alps, riding in a public diligence, meeting strangers, staying at terrible inns. I told him stories of my university days, too; skirting, of course, around many subjects. He loved hearing about the escapades of the Isis Society and the poets of Wykeham's coffee house, though I was careful to omit mention of the significant part played by drink and drugs. He adored chess and was hugely delighted when I beat him.

'Everyone wants only to please me,' he said. 'They let me win, they praise me when I know I have little skill. Oh, how I wish . . .'

'What do you wish?'

'That I could be like you,' he said with a small laugh. 'That I could be an ordinary man, not that you are ordinary, my dear Francis, I know you are not. Dear Mr Singleton, my friend Matthew, was an ordinary man. But I would so love not to be Prince Ibrahim. Well, I am not Prince Ibrahim. Prince Ibrahim is a creature of my mother and Zurnazen Bey. I am . . . someone else.'

Quite late one evening during the second week of my stay I received a visit from one of the black eunuchs who bowed and said, in English clearly learned phonetically, 'She see you now. Come.'

'Who?' I said, but he made no reply. Intrigued, I followed him through a maze of side rooms and minor passages. I could tell that we were going in the general direction of the royal apartments, though he avoided the main rooms and busy public courtyards which were my usual route.

Who had summoned me, and why so surreptitiously? I speculated that it might be my Aphrodite, though it seemed extremely unlikely that a harem girl, for that is what I assumed she was, would dare such a thing. Nevertheless, the thought of her sent a strange, painful pleasure racing along my nerves.

We passed through several gardens, keeping to the small, unlit paths used by the gardeners rather than the paved promenades which glowed with lamplight. A winding track led into a denser part of the garden; my guide stopped at an unprepossessing wooden gate in a high wall, scratched, waited, scratched again. The gate was opened and a whispered word exchanged. A woman's hand reached out and drew me in; the eunuch stayed at the gate.

The woman set off along a colonnade overhung with roses. Although a long scarf covered her hair, she wasn't veiled. I caught up with her and tried to see her face. Could it be my Aphrodite?

'Wait,' I said. '*Aspetti, Signorina, attendez un moment, Mademoiselle. Qui êtes-vous?*'

She whispered a few unintelligible words and hurried on, but I'd recognised her eyes and my heart jolted.

A marble pavilion stood in the centre of the garden, with latticed windows and slender columns glowing in the moonlight. My guide led me into a tiny room, lit with many lamps and unfurnished save for a single stool which faced a wall with a small screened window. She gave me the briefest of smiles before passing through a door into the unlit room behind the screen, from which I heard movement and whispers. I sat on the stool facing the screen and felt myself being closely observed.

A woman's voice addressed me in fluent Italian. The voice was low, a bit harsh, not a young voice. She thanked me for coming and apologised for the irregularity of the manner in which I had been brought. She paused; I heard the sound of a pipe being lit, then a cloud of sweet hashish smoke drifted through the screen.

'Can you guess who I am?' she said, with a rasping laugh.

The dangers of guessing wrong, of causing some dreadful insult, tied my tongue. 'Er,' I said.

'My name, though I can barely remember it, was Cecilia Mocenigo-Contarini, and I was born to a noble family of Venice. Tell me, how is Venice?' Her voice took on a melancholy lilt, as though she was remembering a sad song.

'Venice is as she always is, Signora,' I said, hoping that was a sufficiently diplomatic reply. Was this some grande dame of the harem, indulging in illicit flirtation with the visiting foreigner? And how did she know I had been to Venice?

Another suck at the pipe, another cloud of smoke. 'And how is Philippe du Léran?'

She could only know of my acquaintance with Philippe if she had read his letters of introduction. Of course, anyone could have done that; they were in an unlocked chest by my bed. 'The last I heard he was well.'

'I am glad. His father was ambassador to the Porte many years ago when I was young. I hear that the son is like him: beautiful and devious.'

A few minutes of silence followed as she smoked her pipe, then she sighed. 'What was your business in Alexandria, Signore Damory?' Her voice had lost its dreamy tone.

'I was looking for a relation of mine.'

'Who is he and why did you seek him?'

I was quite unprepared for this line of questioning and fell back upon the family historian story, although it seemed, even to my ears, unconvincing. I tried not to squirm on the stool and wished I had a brandy.

More questions followed about my intentions in Constantinople. If she had read my letters, she would have seen the one to Salih bin Nasrallah Ibn Sallum, so I mentioned his name in order to appear entirely open.

'But surely Ibn Sallum is dead by now. He's even older than I.' She laughed her rough laugh.

Her next question took me by surprise: she wanted to know about the other passengers on the *Persephone*, their characters and occupations.

Naturally I thought at once of Laski, and whatever it was he had hidden in his boot. I realised, somewhat belatedly, that I had better choose my words with exceeding care. I glimpsed a shadowy world of politics, spies, assassinations, factions, conspiracies. It seemed unlikely that my questioner was merely a lady of the harem. This had to be the Sultana Safiya Zuhal herself, wishing to determine if I really was just a hapless stranger washed up on her shore.

Laski had left the palace extremely quickly; was it possible that she did not know he'd been here? No, best to assume that she knew everything. I told her the truth, omitting only the mysterious item in his boot. She could not possibly know I'd seen that, and until I knew who was on whose side, and to what end, I didn't want to give him away.

She changed tack again and began a series of questions about my medical expertise. I was quick to deny that I had any, insisting that my 'magic powder' was the result of a lucky experiment. She seemed nonplussed by my self-deprecation, and I wondered if, by stressing my ignorance and innocence, I was not creating the opposite impression in a mind as conditioned to subterfuge as hers.

There followed questions about my family and education, my home and my travels. I answered with winsome candour; at least I tried to. I either convinced her or bored her; the interview finally came to an end. I heard the rustle of cloth and felt a slight draught as a door on the far side of the pavilion opened and closed. A moment later my Aphrodite appeared. I tried to speak to her, but she led me back through the rose garden without a word. The eunuch was waiting at the gate and escorted me to my rooms by a different and equally circuitous route.

Tunnie's leg would never be quite straight, but he was regaining the use of it and took longer walks every day. He had, in his perambulations, come across the palace's resident smith and showed me proudly the set of six shiny new throwing knives he'd had made. He practised with them every day, getting his arm back, as he said.

I spent much time with Ibrahim, whose wound was healing well. The vizier was usually present, his mistrust of me ill concealed. I maintained an innocuous persona as if my life depended on it, which perhaps it did. I was preparing to broach the subject of my desire to continue on my journey when Ibrahim announced that we would all be going to Constantinople in a few days. It was September, the change of season; the Sultana and her entire household left the summer palace to return to her main residence on the Bosphorus.

'I hope, dear Francis, and my mother most sincerely hopes as well, that you will come with us and continue as our honoured guest.'

'That is most kind,' I said. For some reason, the Sultana's presence in this invitation made it seem more like a command than a friendly offer. Although I might have liked to establish myself independently in Constantinople, I did not wish to make an enemy of the Sultana. 'I would be honoured and delighted,' I said. I could always leave later.

86

Constantinople

🌿

Two ships of the Ottoman navy came to take us to Constantinople: one for the Sultana, her ladies and eunuchs, another for Ibrahim and his household. I stood at the rail of the Prince's ship with Dr Hamon while the crew made final preparations for departure. The Sultana was being rowed to her ship and as they passed I searched for my Aphrodite among her ladies. I spotted her at once; she was the only one who was not fully veiled.

'Who is that unveiled woman?' I asked Dr Hamon.

'The Sultana's new *kira*,' he said.

'Kira? Is that her name?'

'No, no. Her name, I think, is Esther. A *kira* is a Jewess who serves as an intermediary. Our Sultana has many dealings with the world, and since she cannot go about herself, and may not wish to entrust certain matters to the eunuchs or palace officials, the *kira* goes about at her bidding.'

Tunnie joined me on deck after stowing my luggage, which consisted entirely of gifts from Ibrahim and the Sultana: clothing, a jewelled sword, a few beautifully bound books, a portable writing table inlaid with ivory and turquoise, a silver coffee set. I had a cabin to myself, far more luxurious and spacious than on a European ship. The anchor was raised, the sails filled with wind, Cyprus receded and we were once more upon the open sea. Although I was never able to undertake sea voyages without some anxiety, especially during the nights when I imagined pirates swarming in from all directions, Tunnie pointed out that we were as safe as it was possible to be. No one in these waters would attack the Ottoman navy.

And no one did. There was one storm, not very large, as we passed Lesbos one evening but we rode it out and by morning had entered the Dardanelles. That night was spent crossing the Sea of Marmara beneath a velvet sky, blazing with more stars than I had ever seen. Ibrahim and I stayed on deck, smoking and talking. We would come to Constantinople at daybreak and it was imperative, he said, that I should not miss the first glimpse of it. His tone, when he spoke of the city, mingled awe and pride.

As dawn approached, however, a thick fog hid the horizon. The ship seemed to slide through utter stillness; a steady breeze filled the sails, though on deck we could not feel it. The sun rose above the fog bank and the sky glowed clear and blue. I peered ahead through my spyglass, trying to make out a shoreline.

'Just wait,' said Ibrahim, then, 'Look!'

I could see nothing.

'Look up,' he said.

I lifted my gaze and gasped. There, floating above the mist, was an enormous golden dome, surrounded by four gleaming silver-tipped minarets.

'The Hagia Sofia,' said Ibrahim. 'And look,' he waved his hand as the fog melted away from the hillside to reveal layer upon layer of buildings, an intricate jumble of red-roofed houses with abundant patches of green where trees clustered and lush vines sprawled over walls.

The ship moved steadily on as the fog receded. On our left, Ibrahim pointed out the Hill of the Seraglio, with its gardens and pavilions, pines and terebinths overtopping the crenellated walls. The vast palace glowed in the light of the rising sun. 'The house of my honoured cousin,' he said. 'May he be a thousand times blessed. But we don't live there, Allah be praised. Mother has a palace of her own.'

The Sultana's ship sailed ahead of us, trumpeters in her bow blaring her arrival. The water was filled with hundreds of boats, large and small, which crowded around, their occupants cheering and calling out. A pair of galleys, with bright red oars and gilded prows, came racing to meet us; one went to the Sultana's ship, the other came to ours. Salutes were exchanged; we furled our sails as towing lines were attached. The galleys, each manned by twenty-six rowers in skullcaps with blue tassels, pulled us up the narrowing strait.

As we entered the Bosphorus the hill of Scutari, on the Asian side, became visible, crowned with tall cypress and what appeared to be a cemetery. Through the spyglass I could make out tombstones, ancient and tilted. The curtain of mist dropped, revealing narrow streets of purple and yellow houses, kiosks and galleries and gardens.

Ibrahim tapped my shoulder and bade me turn around: the Golden Horn appeared, snaking inland. No wider than a river, it was covered with little boats darting among the larger ships that sheltered in its deep anchorage. The six hills of the old walled city of Stamboul rose on the left, the minarets of countless mosques piercing the mist. The cosmopolitan city of Galata climbed the opposite shore, with its straight streets and stone houses, open squares and Catholic churches.

The Sultana's palace was a mile or so further on, set in terraced gardens. I was shown to a magnificent set of rooms overlooking the Bosphorus where I discovered that the Sultana had provided me with a dragoman. He was a Greek Orthodox Christian named Theodosius who took obsequiousness to new depths. As I'd thought, the Sultana's hospitality was motivated not so much by affection as by the desire to keep me where she could see me.

Theodosius's family, he told me with pride, had served as dragomans to the Sublime Porte for five generations. He was a creature of the court; it had been so long since he had presumed to speak his own mind that I think he'd forgotten he had one.

Tunnie was determined to attend me; he limped vigorously with the assistance of a stout walking stick that Dr Hamon had given him. Thus accompanied, I went first to the bank, where I deposited my letter of credit and received some local currency, then to the English and French embassies and the Venetian bailo, leaving at each the appropriate letter of introduction from Philippe. The ambassadorial residences were more like palaces, clustered together on a hill above Galata. The district, called Pera, was so given over to the Europeans that it seemed, somehow, more European than any single European city could be. There were Frenchmen and Swedes, Wallachians and Moldavians, Venetians, Genoese and Florentines, Dutch, English, Hungarians and Germans, all mingling with Persians and Greeks, Egyptians and Armenians, Russians, Arabs, Scythians, Jews and, of course, Turks, who swaggered like the overlords they were.

I asked Theodosius how many languages he spoke; he had to stop and think. 'Eleven, effendi, I both speak and write. Turkish and Ottoman of course, Arabic, Persian, English, French, Italian, Latin, Greek, Hungarian and Hebrew.'

At each of the embassies I had to undergo time-consuming rituals of welcome that combined, sometimes awkwardly and sometimes with grace, the customs of the host nation with those of the Orient. I learned that although Ottoman robes were considered wise when visiting the Old City of Stamboul, where richly dressed Europeans might encounter abuse, most wore European dress in Pera. Tunnie and I had only the clothes that Ibrahim had given us. Theodosius suggested we pay a visit to one of Pera's many French tailors so that I could obtain more appropriate attire. I ordered two or three suits with reluctance, though Tunnie was undisguisedly relieved to see a pair of breeches again. Wigs, too, were *de rigueur*, as were gloves, handkerchiefs, silk stockings, brocade shoes and walking sticks. It was all tedious beyond belief, with the exception of the walking stick. I found a fine old one from Samarkand: an ebony shaft topped by a crystal egg entwined with a silver serpent that the merchant assured me had once belonged to a great magician.

It was late afternoon by the time we'd finished these chores and I showed Theodosius my last letter, the one from Rashid to Salih bin Nasrallah Ibn Sallum.

'I do not know this person, effendi,' he said. 'It says "near the mosque of Atik Mustafa Pasha". That is in the district of Ayvansaray in the Old City.'

'So take me there.'

'May I suggest we wait until tomorrow, effendi? It is almost time for the afternoon prayers.' As he spoke, the first calls of the muezzins rang out from the minarets.

Out of the corner of my eye I noticed Tunnie brighten; he'd been sagging. 'Very well, Theodosius. First thing tomorrow.'

There had been letters waiting for me at the English embassy – one from Isabel and Meryll and one from Caroline, passing on the news that all was well at the Villa degli Eremiti, my son was healthy, strong and growing. I'd put Isabel and Meryll's aside to read later, dreading to learn of some mishap, but when I turned to it that evening there was good news. Isabel had been delivered of twins, to everyone's astonishment but her own: a girl called

Catherine Bella and a boy named Francis Edward, already being called Freddie to distinguish him from me. Isabel sounded healthy and complacent, her great work achieved. Her talk was all of details: their eyes, the colour still murky and undetermined, their eyelashes, their fingernails, their toes, their squawks and burps.

Meryll was more succinct, but his relief and joy were undisguised. Not wishing, I suppose, to gloat, he moved on quickly to other subjects: their life in Rome; the eccentric characters they'd befriended; his study of the ruins; the course in fresco painting he was attending; news of mutual friends and relations. He enclosed a clipping from a newspaper that everyone apparently knew referred to my brother Andrew. It suggested that scandalous revelations involving a militaristically inclined Lord D—— and his very fond friendship with a certain neighbour were soon to explode upon the O——shire county scene.

Andrew the Virtuous, caught playing about with someone else's wife? Too good to be true. I wrote back, demanding verification and details. I gave Meryll a brief account of the pirates and shipwreck, but commanded him not to tell Isabel. To her, I merely sent congratulations and good wishes, and said I'd bring presents for the twins when I returned.

87

Fabula

In the morning Tunnie and I, dressed in plain and inconspicuous Ottoman robes, found Theodosius waiting with four Janissaries and the silent, luxuriantly moustachioed Turk who had accompanied me in Cyprus. Such an entourage seemed unconducive to tracking down the elusive, ephemeral Tobias.

'I will not take the Janissaries, Theodosius,' I said. 'You and Tunnie are sufficient.'

'But, effendi, the Janissaries are there for your good, to protect you and ensure that you are shown the respect you deserve.'

'No Janissaries, Theodosius.'

'That is most unwise, effendi.'

Moustache spoke rapidly in Turkish; Theodosius nodded. 'The Sultana has ordered that you be protected, effendi. The Janissaries cannot disobey her order.'

'Who is this discourteous person, Theodosius, who speaks without introducing himself?'

Theodosius and Moustache exchanged further words.

'Let's go,' I said to Tunnie, and we walked briskly towards the door. Behind us I heard sounds of consternation. Would anyone dare to stop us?

I felt a touch on my shoulder and turned. It was Moustache. This, I had a feeling, was a man who understood only force. I seized his wrist, twisted it behind his back and kicked his knees out from under him. He sprawled to the floor; I put my foot on his neck and pressed hard. Throwing knives had materialised in Tunnie's hands.

'No Janissaries,' I said.

Moustache flapped his hands feebly. I lifted my foot a fraction and he croaked a few words. The Janissaries turned and marched away.

Theodosius, looking pale, hastened to my side. 'As you wish, effendi. I will be honoured to accompany you alone.' He gazed down at the prostrate Turk. 'It is evident that you can protect yourself,' he added. Something in his voice told me that he loathed Moustache and was experiencing a rare, private satisfaction.

We descended the terraces to the waterside. 'Who is that man?'

I asked, on the principle that it was wise to know one's enemy's name.

'Hamza Fâkih.' His tone was careful not to betray his contempt, but it was there.

'And who is Hamza Fâkih?'

'He is the Sultana's . . . I am not sure of the term in English. He deals with spies, informers, people like that. Also, some say, he kills people when she decides it is necessary.' He shuddered. 'I beg of you, tell no one what I have said. I should not have spoken.'

A number of boats were moored at the quay. Theodosius indicated a narrow, high-prowed vessel with six rowers in the Sultana's livery. We climbed in and set off at a very rapid rate, considering that the waterway was crowded with hundreds of other vessels. All seemed miraculously to melt away as we approached.

We put in to a wharf about two miles up the Horn. On one side of us, porters were carrying bales of fragrant cinnamon and cloves from a line of kneeling camels to a waiting ship; on the other side, an Algerian slaver was unloading his chained and even more fragrant human cargo. We were jostled from all sides by people in the attire of a dozen nations and immersed in a babble of voices. Theodosius pushed ahead, trying to clear a path. The Janissaries would have been useful.

Theodosius took us inland, up and down winding streets and unexpected steps, along wide, cobbled thoroughfares lined with prosperous shops and dirt streets of ramshackle houses. We arrived at the Atik Mustafa Pasha mosque, a low, plain structure that, Theodosius told me, had originally been a Christian church dedicated to St Thekla. A bustling market spread around the mosque and here Theodosius asked directions to the house of Salih bin Nasrallah Ibn Sallum. It took him four tries before he found an old Jewish bookseller who knew the name.

We climbed a steep street that zigzagged up the hillside. At some point the paving ran out and we picked our way over rubble and rubbish and chickens. There were no signs of humans, although occasionally as we passed under a window I heard women's voices, quickly hushed at our approach, and once caught a glimpse of dark eyes watching us from behind the lattice. Cooking smells wafted across our path: onions, roasting meat, pungent spices that I couldn't identify.

Theodosius led the way into a courtyard with a cracked fountain. Men squatting in front of a dingy coffee house smoked their pipes and watched us through the haze. We crossed the courtyard, dodging a few goats, and ascended a tilted, weed-cracked stair between two buildings. It led us into a narrow alley that ended in a high wall.

'The last house on the right.' Theodosius pointed to an ancient wooden building whose upper storeys sagged alarmingly over its low doorway. I was sure that we had been misdirected. I could not imagine Tobias, or any friend of his, inhabiting such a hovel.

Theodosius tugged at a ratty rope hanging beside the door; we heard a bell ring somewhere within and, eventually, the sound of approaching footsteps. The door was opened by a young man in a white turban and black robe, plain but cleaner than I expected. He and Theodosius conversed briefly in Turkish and we were shown into a room somewhat better furnished than the exterior had suggested.

'Yes,' Theodosius told me, 'this is the house of Salih Ibn Sallum.'

'Is the master at home?' I asked. The answer came back that he was. I handed over Rashid's letter; the man bowed and disappeared, returning about ten minutes later to indicate that his master would see me. He led us through a series of passages, rooms and courtyards; the house was much larger than it had seemed. I tried to keep my sense of direction and realised that it must extend behind the facades of every house along the alley.

We emerged into a garden. To the right, a breathtaking vista appeared: the whole of the Old City, the Golden Horn, Galata, Pera and the distant hills. I had no time to take it in; we were ushered down a gravelled path lined with fruit trees and vegetable beds. A gardener, hoeing between rows of purple brassica, looked up as we passed. A little stream ran in a tiled channel alongside the path; its soft burbling blended with the purring and cooing of a flock of white doves inhabiting an elegant dovecote. Bees buzzed and from somewhere came the sound of a flute playing a low, lilting melody, rising and falling, eerie and sad. I found that I'd stopped, transfixed; the others had turned and were waiting for me. The flute song ceased and was replaced by the sound of approaching laughter and playful shrieks. A group of children ran across the path. They appeared and disappeared so quickly that it was not until they were gone and their laughter had receded that I realised they were all dwarves.

We emerged between clumps of myrtle and bay to an open area with a fountain which spilled into eight channels that radiated through the garden: the source of the little stream we'd walked along. Other paths followed the streams outward towards arbours, pavilions, bowers.

The garden, like the house, was larger than seemed possible; I was craning my neck this way and that like a gawping boy. I glanced at Tunnie. He shrugged and tapped his sleeve, which I took to mean that he was glad to be well armed. Theodosius's face was inscrutable.

We ascended a series of terraces and, under the pretext of wishing to catch my breath, I stopped and sat on a bench beneath a spreading pine tree. The whole garden was laid out below; beyond it, that incomparable view.

I allowed myself to wonder whether I might, at last, be within reach of Tobias. No, probably not, I told myself. Far more likely I shall learn that he has once again vanished, been lost at sea, died while abroad, escaped into another life. I sighed and stood. Well, it would be interesting to meet this Salih Ibn Sallum whom the Sultana, I recalled, had thought long dead.

At the top of the terraces was a pavilion, screened on three sides by trellises covered with late-blooming jasmine. The young man led us up a set of marble steps. As my eyes adjusted to the dimness I took in divans and rich carpets, a table with pipe, coffee, fruit, a servant waiting with rosewater for my hands and a man in austere grey kaftan and turban who rose and greeted me in Latin.

'I am Salih Ibn Sallum,' he said. 'Please be welcome to my home.'

I replied in the same language and he smiled. 'It is good. We have no need of a dragoman.' He turned to Theodosius. 'You are a son of Peter Theodosius, are you not? Yes, I thought I recognised you. Perhaps you will take some refreshment with my son, Yusuf.'

Neatly done, I thought, as the young man took Theodosius's arm in a firm but friendly manner and led him back down the path through the garden.

I caught Tunnie's eye and glanced outside; he withdrew to the bottom of the steps.

Ibn Sallum waved me to a seat on the adjacent divan. The servant lit the pipe and served coffee; we smoked and sipped and I studied my host. The Sultana's comment had led me to expect a very old man, but although Ibn Sallum's beard was white, his brows were still black and his skin, though lined, was taut. While certainly not a young man, he was no ancient.

I praised the garden; he said he had read a book about English gardens which he had found quite inspiring. I praised the weather; he agreed that September was the perfect time to visit Constantinople.

Once again, neatly done, I thought, as he steered the conversation, after the obligatory pleasantries, to the purpose of my visit.

The further I had travelled in pursuit of Tobias, the more

improbable seemed the family historian story, so I presented it as secondary to my main purpose which was just to see the world. I described how I'd found traces of my far-flung and fascinating family here and there on my travels.

'And then,' I said, 'when I learned that Sheikh Tabib, that is, Tibaldo d'Amori, was here, I thought why not? I'd always wanted to visit Constantinople and I am so interested, of course, to learn his story, and anything he might know about other members of our family.' I paused and swallowed hard, having come sooner than I'd expected to the very goal and purpose of my life. 'So, er. Do you know . . . is he, that is . . . Rashid al-Misri believed you might know where I could find him.'

I steeled myself for news of his recent tragic death and the regrettable absence of remains.

'Ah,' said Ibn Sallum, 'here he is now.'

I turned and my heart jumped into my throat. The man coming up the steps of the pavilion, an expression of friendly curiosity on his face, was unquestionably Tobias.

'We are speaking Latin, Tibaldo,' Ibn Sallum said, as the servant stepped forward with the rosewater. 'Come and meet a distant cousin of yours. This is Francis Damory from England, by way of Venice and Egypt.'

I could not take my eyes from Tobias as he washed his hands and sat beside Ibn Sallum. He was clean-shaven, his features lean and pale as in his portrait at Farundell, neither old nor young. He wore a dark-red turban and a brown surcoat over a white shirt and loose trousers.

Ibn Sallum showed him Rashid's letter as the servant fussed with the pipe and coffee. I ate some grapes and recollected who we were meant to be: I the travelling family historian; he Tibaldo d'Amori. I would no more blurt out the true nature of my quest than he would admit to a stranger that he was two hundred years old.

'Cousin Francis,' he said. 'I join my friend in welcoming you.'

'It is an inestimable pleasure to meet another member of our family,' I said. The dance had begun.

'Have you determined in what way we are related?'

'Not precisely, no. I have traced our mutual ancestry as far back as a certain Tobias Geoffrey Herbert Damory, who . . . died in 1620.'

'How fascinating,' he said. 'I have never heard of him. I regret to say I did not even know there was an English branch of my family. We are Venetian and Greek, though I was raised in Aleppo.'

'How fascinating,' I said. 'I would be so interested to hear more.'

'Yes, Tibaldo,' said Ibn Sallum. 'You must tell your story, and then your cousin will tell his. I do so love a good story.' He used the Latin word *fabula*, which could mean a personal account, or equally a fiction.

Tobias – Tibaldo! I reminded myself forcefully – smiled, though the smile did not reach his eyes. 'I will be happy to tell my story, uninteresting though it is, if you do not mind hearing what you already know. But first, if I may ask, Cousin Francis – you have come recently from Sakkara. Did you see my son Jamal?'

Whatever elaborate fictions he had woven about himself, there was a father's true care in his voice.

'Yes, I saw him.'

'And he was well? Rashid writes to me, of course, but you have seen him. And spoken with him?'

I sensed that he so craved contact with his son that he barely restrained himself from seizing my hand. I told him everything that had occurred during my visit, with the exception of Jamal's collapse and Rashid's concern. He smiled when I recounted Ptolemy's misdemeanour.

'And your son said the most remarkable thing,' I added as

though it was an afterthought. 'He said he was quoting you, in fact. What was it? Let me try to recall.' I pretended to search my memory. 'Ah yes, I have it. He said, "My father says we can be more than nature, and I am training Ptolemy to be more than just a cat." I think that is quite the most remarkable thing I have ever heard from a child.'

'Yes, remarkable,' said Ibn Sallum.

'He is a remarkable child,' said Tibaldo. I sensed the curtains being drawn, the subject closed.

The servant brought more coffee and some sherbet. The sun beat down on the garden, though the pavilion was pleasantly cool. In the distance, boats bobbed on the Golden Horn and the waters of the Bosphorus sparkled sapphire blue. The midday call to prayer began, moving in a wave from east to west across the city. Tibaldo and Ibn Sallum ignored it; whatever else they were, they were not devout Muslims.

'I fear my story is quite dull,' said Tibaldo. 'But I am happy to tell it to you nonetheless. I was born in Aleppo, as I said. My father was from Venice, though he left as a young man for reasons about which he never spoke. He worked on ships all over the Mediterranean, settling finally in Aleppo where he built up a business as an intermediary between Venetian merchants and the caravans from Persia and India. He married the daughter of one of his competitors, a Greek from Chios, and eventually took over his father-in-law's business. I was their only child and my parents died of the plague when I was quite young. But they left me well provided for, and I was able to pursue my dream of studying medicine. I received my degree in Aleppo, which is where I met my dear friend Salih Ibn Sallum. We both then came to Constantinople for further studies.' The two men smiled at each other.

'I entered the service of a Pasha,' Tibaldo continued. 'When the Sultan sent him to Cairo as deputy governor, I accompanied him.

He unwisely involved himself in conspiracies, and died after two years. In the meantime I had married the daughter of a local Mamluk sheikh; when in due course he died, his property in Sakkara came to her, and to me. Sadly, she died before we were able to have children. Some years later I took another wife. Jamal is our only child; my wife drowned in the river when he was very young. There, you have it all. As I said, quite dull.'

'So how did you come to be the heir of Conte and Contessa d'Amori of Venice?' I watched closely as I released this hitherto unmentioned detail and thought I noticed a quick reordering going on behind his eyes, though he replied without hesitation.

'It can only be because I was the last of the line. The Conte d'Amori was the brother – or was it the cousin? – of my father's father. I did not even know of his existence until – oh, it must be over thirty years ago – I heard from a Venetian lawyer that I was the beneficiary of his will.'

'So you have never been to Venice yourself?'

'I have been meaning to visit, but you know how it is. One is so busy.'

I nodded sympathetically. Tobias was doing a very good job of being Tibaldo d'Amori; I had found no chink. Ibn Sallum had a small smile on his face that made me believe that he knew, if not who Tibaldo really was, then certainly that this *fabula* was at least in part a fabrication. The servant appeared with mint tea and sweet pastries; we paused for refreshment and prepared for the second round.

88

The Beautiful Hand

'And now we shall have the story of this brave young traveller,' said Ibn Sallum, sucking on the pipe and settling into his cushions with the air of someone who anticipates an entertaining afternoon.

'It all started,' I said, 'in Paris, with a woman named Marie-Louise de la Rochefoucauld Derain, the Marquise du Bellay. She is the daughter of the Duchesse de Cossé-Brissac.' I was sure I detected a momentary flicker in Tobias's eyes as I mentioned his daughter and his lover.

'Through a regrettable series of events, it happened that I killed her son in a duel.' Your grandson, I thought. 'And he nearly killed me.' I gestured towards my scarred face and missing ear with the three fingers of my left hand. 'During my convalescence I spent much time in a certain cemetery on the outskirts of Paris – I will not bore you with the reason – but it was there that, quite by chance, I met a man named Bertrand d'Amorie. He had come to visit the grave of his mother, Henriette Bréville.' As I named his wife and his son a tiny frown flitted across Tobias's brow.

'We fell to talking, and though we never quite decided just what degree of cousins we were, we became good friends.' I wondered if Tobias hungered for news of Bertrand as he had of Jamal. 'Bertrand is a happy and successful man,' I said, 'with a wonderful family. He has a charming wife, a son who is entering the Church, and two daughters. He invited me to his home in Alsace, Château Langenfeld, a very handsome and prosperous estate.' A look of satisfaction passed over Tobias's face, almost too fast to see.

'I spent a summer there, researching in the family archives. They never throw anything out; the attics were full of every sort of document, correspondence, bills, account books. All terribly fascinating to an amateur historian like myself, though no doubt quite boring to you, so I will not go into detail about what I found.' Let him wonder, I thought.

'I became quite intrigued by Bertrand's father, Thibault d'Amorie.' You, that is, I said with my eyes.

Tobias blinked; I continued. 'Thibault was long dead, but his correspondence had been kept and I managed to piece together much of his rather unusual life, though there are some considerable gaps. Perhaps one day I will write a brief biography.'

I paused to sip my tea, and asked that some refreshment be taken to Tunnie. Somewhat to my surprise, I realised that I was enjoying myself. This was like a duel, but slower and not so bloody. I considered what to deploy next.

'Thibault d'Amorie,' I said, 'had many interests. Do you know, he corresponded about viniculture with the great English chemist, Robert Boyle? I had no idea he'd been interested in wine-making. The English climate is so unsuited, it can't have gone well, but evidently he regarded Thibault as quite an expert and was continually writing for advice.'

At what point, I wondered, would Tobias begin to suspect that I was not mentioning all these things in innocence and by chance?

'Even more curiously, I met an old man named Julien Pernelle who had known Thibault quite well. Of course he may have been mad, but he told me that Thibault was some sort of Rosicrucian, who went about the world changing his name every few years.'

'What is a Rosicrucian?' Tobias's tone was perplexed.

'I wonder that as well,' I said.

I allowed a moment's silence as I beckoned the servant to light the pipe for me. So far, unlike Tobias, I had told the exact if not the entire truth, which I felt had both shielded and strengthened me in this battle. It was a battle, no doubt about it, and the outcome far from certain. Some part of me, I realised, had hoped that Tobias would recognise me as I had recognised him, would welcome me, if not as a son, then at least as a kindred spirit. I would become his student, his disciple even. He would initiate me to a higher wisdom, impart his secrets . . . and so on. But why should he? I'd been deluded to imagine that I had any value to him. I began to consider that even having found Tibaldo, I might never penetrate to Tobias.

'And then,' said Ibn Sallum, after allowing a polite interval for me to smoke in peace, 'you went to Venice?'

I put the pipe aside. I was not finished yet; there were more weapons to deploy, powerful ones.

'Yes,' I said. 'Among Thibault d'Amorie's papers I came across mention of a place near Venice called the Villa degli Eremiti, which I realised must be the home of another branch of the family.'

The flute was playing again and fragments of melody drifted up to the pavilion on a warm breeze. I had a sudden desire to back out, to stop here, to retreat into ignorance. The temptation to lie my way out of this situation was strong. But I didn't dare. Only the truth, I told myself, and this time the entire truth.

'May I say, Cousin Tibaldo, that I wish I did not have to tell the next chapter of the story. It is very sad, and I am not proud of my part in it.' Tobias remained expressionless, but a momentary look of concern crossed Ibn Sallum's face and he shifted against his cushions. Was he merely worried that the afternoon might not prove as amusing as he'd thought, or was he beginning to suspect that I was not the guileless traveller I'd seemed?

'The Villa degli Eremiti was the home of the Conte and

Contessa d'Amori,' I said. 'But I think, as his heir, you must know this.' I paused, hoping at least for a nod, but Tobias seemed frozen.

I continued. 'You will be pleased to hear that Bortolin and Besina have proved completely loyal and dedicated to carrying out your . . . great-uncle's instructions, and I hope you forgive them for not killing me as perhaps they should have done. You see, they thought I was you. By "you", of course, I mean Tibaldo d'Amori, their master's grand-nephew and heir. I'm afraid I allowed them to continue in this assumption.'

Although he did not move, there was an edgy alertness in Tobias's body that had not been there before. It occurred to me, astonishingly for the first time, that he might simply kill me. Too late to stop now. I took a deep breath. 'Pretending to be him – that is, you – I took up residence at the villa.'

Tobias stared at me. 'There was a daughter, was there not?'

'There was a strange and beautiful woman.'

'You met her.'

'Yes.' I loosened the neck of my shirt and lifted Rosmarina's golden chain into view. 'I married her.'

Finally, a reaction. Tobias stood abruptly and went to the doorway, where he gazed out over the garden and the city below. Ibn Sallum sat up very straight, looking from his friend to me and back again.

Tobias turned and in one swift movement had crossed the room to my side. He seized the necklace; I thought he was going to strangle me with it. I felt no desire to resist. I was, instead, fascinated by his hand, so near to my face. A two-hundred-year-old hand. It was smooth and pale, with long, strong fingers; muscles, veins and tendons clearly defined beneath skin like marble. I wanted to kiss it. I was so entranced that I took little notice of the silver flash that whistled past my face.

The beautiful hand withdrew. 'All well, sir?' said Tunnie,

retrieving his knife from the cushion next to Ibn Sallum, who was gazing at it with a puzzled expression.

I returned to my senses. 'Yes, thank you, Tunnie.'

Tobias resumed his seat, Tunnie retreated to the bottom of the steps and Ibn Sallum summoned more coffee and a fresh pipe.

Tobias studied me with new interest, but I had no idea whether he was planning my murder or my initiation. At last he spoke. 'What happened?'

I told him about the summer spent coming to know Rosmarina's many faces, my gradual acceptance of my role as her protector, the sudden yet inevitable, as it now seemed, marriage. I told him about the wedding night, the knife, Rosmarina's lapse into mute lassitude.

'And?' He knew there was more.

I told him about the pregnancy, the diagnosis of Dr van der Veer, the long and terrible labour, the death and the birth.

'The birth?'

'A son. I have named him Tobias.'

He exhaled a long, harsh breath. 'Tell me, how does the child?'

'I hear that he thrives.'

'And what will become of him?'

'I will look after him.'

'You are not travelling for pleasure, cousin.'

'Not entirely.'

'Nor are you interested in family history.'

'Not particularly.'

'How long?'

I understood the question, though the words made little sense. 'Since my eleventh birthday,' I said. 'I was walking in my sleep and you spoke to me from your portrait. You said, "I have a gift for you if you can find it." You showed me a book, with a rose on a cross. The rose was alive; it was the most alive thing I had ever seen. And then on my seventeenth birthday I saw that book again, and I met a woman who knew of you. I thought you had led me to her. She said that the book I sought could not be written . . .'

'Ah, you met *her*.'

Something in his tone aroused my jealousy. 'I did more than just meet her.'

'You have more than just met quite a few people.'

'In my few years.'

Our battle was flaring up again, on new fronts. I pressed on. 'My father tried to destroy your books, but a man named Trevelyan saved them by stealing them. I started finding your glyph, TGHD, in books, real books. *Fama Fraternitatis*, Hermes Chrysotum. In Oxford your books led me to Erasmus Enderby. Thank God He's Dead, he called you. Boyle's assistant, do you remember him? You should; no one was more dedicated to the Great Work than he.'

'You studied with Enderby?' Tobias's tone was mild and affectionate.

'Yes. So it *was* you at Boyle's laboratory that night?'

He didn't answer.

I could feel my heart beating faster. 'At St Asher's I joined your Isis Society before I knew it was yours.' I rushed on, desperate to convince him that none other than Fate herself had drawn me to him across centuries and continents. 'Your daughter Marie-Louise told me we were connected by fate, before I knew who she was. She read the cards for me: Horus, the Child of Dawn. Death. And the Stone of the Wise, a strange black card with a hole in the middle. I knew somehow that was my card. She showed me your cabinet of curiosities, your seven temples. "*Rosa Æterna Clavis*", you wrote; I read it and understood. I found the key, the rose, and I opened those doors.'

'And then you killed her son?'

'I have done many things I wish with all my heart I had not done.'

'So have I,' he said quietly, and gazed at me for a long time as though reading my soul.

Then he got up, said a few words in Turkish to Ibn Sallum, and left. I started to follow.

'Stay, friend,' said Ibn Sallum.

I watched Tobias's figure recede down the garden. 'Stay, friend,' repeated Ibn Sallum. I returned to my divan and found that I was trembling.

'I couldn't bear to lose him now,' I said, not realising I spoke aloud until Ibn Sallum said, 'You have not lost him. He said you could return tomorrow.'

I wanted to laugh, to weep, to shout, all at once. I felt the most extraordinary elation and utter exhaustion. I was exhilarated and terrified. It was like love, but a thousand times worse. I looked down the garden to the point where he had disappeared beneath the trees. Already my whole being was longing for him to return.

I looked up and met Ibn Sallum's eyes. 'I've been searching for him my whole life.'

'So was I,' he said. 'Many years ago.'

The pipe was refreshed; we smoked in silence for a time. Never had I more appreciated the decorum and reticence of Ottoman social customs. The flute began to play, joined now by a second flute.

'Shall we walk in the garden?' said Ibn Sallum.

We descended the terraces. Tunnie followed at a polite distance as Ibn Sallum pointed out this and that rare plant from India, or China, or Japan – plants with purple berries, yellow berries, red thorns on black stems. The largest bees I had ever seen wandered indolently among trumpet-shaped orange flowers cascading over a wall.

'I have bred these bees,' said Ibn Sallum, 'for thirty generations, each time allowing only the largest to reproduce. I had another type that made exceptionally sweet honey; I was going to mix the two strains, but the sweet honey ones turned out to have such a vicious temperament that I had to destroy them all.'

He drew my attention to a tree that was loaded with ripe fruit of a kind I'd never seen. 'Have you ever considered the nature of perfection? Or the perfection of nature?' He selected one and handed it to me. 'Taste. And see if you can guess what it is.'

I bit into the fruit and although it was delicious, sweet and juicy, I could not identify it.

He smiled, pleased at my bafflement. 'It is not any fruit you have ever tasted because it is a new fruit that I have created. *Malum persicum* mated with *Armeniaca*.'

I took another bite. Yes, now I could taste the peach, the apricot. 'It's wonderful,' I said. 'I didn't know it was possible to combine two fruits in a single tree.'

'Oh yes, possible. Many things are possible, if one has the time.'

We stopped in the doorway of a small wooden pavilion. Within, the dwarf children sat in a circle around Yusuf. Ibn Sallum watched with the smile of a proud parent.

The children were of different ages but none were more than two feet tall. Some had pale skin, some black. A few were a middle-brown colour and two were piebald, with patches of black and white. Even more oddly, none were deformed in any way, ugly and distorted as dwarves usually are.

Yusuf was reciting from a book; the children repeated the words after him.

'Are they learning the Koran?' I asked.

Ibn Sallum listened for a moment. 'No, not the Koran. An old Persian poem; I will translate it for you, but Latin cannot convey the poetry. It says: "*My beloved walks at my side; he rises with the sun and sets with the moon. His name is beauty; his name is death.*"'

He took my arm and led me on. I was dazzled by strangeness; I felt like a child in a new world, drinking it all in. As we approached the source of the flute music I paused, transfixed as before.

Ibn Sallum smiled that proud father's smile again. 'They make the most exquisite music, do they not?'

I nodded, picturing two beautiful girls playing while others danced a slow dance, sensual and sad.

'Would you like to meet them?' He gestured towards a low building set among fig trees.

The interior was dim and I couldn't make out how many people were within. When my eyes adjusted I thought at first that there were two, then four. I gazed for a long time before my mind was able to give words to what I saw. There were two two-headed girls, each with four arms. One girl played flutes with her two heads while the other danced, waving her arms gracefully.

I thought of Polypus, the twisted, cowed creature I'd seen at the Exhibition of Monstrosities in Paris. These girls were nothing like that. One was fifteen or sixteen, the other a bit older. They seemed healthy and happy; they were even pretty. Their hair was carefully dressed; they wore gay clothes and tinkled with bracelets and bells.

'Gülbahar, Gülben, Gülpah, Gülsun,' said Ibn Sallum. 'Here is someone who would like to meet you.'

The girls stopped their playing and dancing and made little obeisances, touching their joined hands to their foreheads. I realised then that they were both, or all, pregnant.

'Hürmuz and Hümeyra, their mother,' Ibn Sallum turned and gestured to someone I had not noticed. A woman – or two – reclined on a divan. One of her heads appeared to be asleep, the other was eating grapes.

'It is a pleasure to meet all of you,' I said. Ibn Sallum translated for me and everyone except the sleeping one smiled.

I recall little of my return to the Sultana's palace. I was in such a daze that I could not speak. Tunnie knew when I needed silence;

Theodosius was far too well trained to express his curiosity. I went to bed and slept; when I awoke it was the middle of the night. The silk curtains stirred in a mild breeze as I stepped out on to the balcony. The Bosphorus glinted with the lanterns of many little boats. Voices called gaily across the water, laughing, singing. Someone in the garden just below began to play a lute, the pliant notes rising through the darkness.

89

A Coat of Perpetual Pain

🌱

I returned to Ibn Sallum's house alone, eluding both Theodosius and Tunnie by slipping out before dawn. I walked through Pera and Galata by moonlight and made my way down to the Horn as the eastern sky turned from black to blue to rose and the call to prayer echoed across the water. I bought coffee and a sweet roll from a stall at the quayside and boarded a crowded ferry to Stamboul. Pleased with my invisibility, I climbed through the Old City, past the mosque of Atik Mustafa Pasha and up the crooked streets.

I don't know what I expected, but certainly not what happened. Ibn Sallum's son Yusuf escorted me to the garden as before, though not to the pavilion. Instead, with a small smile, he took me to a shed in an out-of-the-way corner and introduced me to an old man: Kökcü, the head gardener. Kökcü spoke only Turkish, but managed to demonstrate what I was to do. First, clean the shit from the henhouse; then from the dovecote and the rabbit pens. A drainage channel had become blocked; I dug it out. I weeded the vegetable beds and chopped wood until Yusuf came at dusk to tell me to leave. I found Tunnie and Theodosius in the outer chamber, their annoyance cooled to glum acceptance by the long wait.

I returned the next day, and the next. I shovelled shit, I dug in the dirt. I knew that this was a test and even if I had wanted to complain, as my hands blistered and my back ached, not a murmur would have passed my lips. But I did not want to complain. I was where I was meant to be.

Along one wall of the garden was a building that contained a hospital and a laboratory where Ibn Sallum and Tobias worked. Sometimes the inmates were brought out to the garden. They were a sad sight. The peach-apricots and the bees, the dwarves and the two-headed girls were Ibn Sallum's successes; among these poor creatures were the failed results of his own experiments as well as oddities that he had collected. There were humans and animals and those that seemed both human and animal. They would have been exhibited in cages in Europe; here, at least, they were clean and well fed, their sufferings alleviated as much as was possible. Among them I saw two aged and wizened children like Jamal, and I understood why Tobias had come here to search for a cure for his son.

After a few days Tunnie and Theodosius stopped coming after me, but I began to notice the same nondescript man in a dun-coloured robe, never far behind me as I walked through the city, always on the same ferry, always lounging in the café by the cracked fountain and just getting up to leave as I passed when I left Ibn Sallum's.

I lived a double life. When I returned to the palace in the evenings, I bathed and donned a turban and a silk kaftan to dine with Ibrahim, or a wig and a French suit to attend this or that ambassador's soirée. I speculated about how I could contrive a graceful exit from the Sultana's hospitality, but decided it would only invite suspicion and closer scrutiny. I told Ibrahim that my long-lost relation was an eccentric old man who spent all day working in his little garden.

I saw Esther once, as I passed the Egyptian market. She didn't see me, and I spent a few moments watching her. She had begun to seem like a character from a vaguely remembered dream. My life in Ibn Sallum's garden was everything to me, and I imagined that I had already transcended worldly desires.

The post between Venice and Constantinople was fast, regular and reliable; I received further letters from Isabel and Meryll. Isabel's was just two inky blotches accompanied by a scribble that identified them as Freddie's and Catherine's footprints.

In response to my plea for further information about my brother, Meryll reported that Andrew's wife was said to have launched a divorce suit in the ecclesiastical court, a rather drastic action suggestive of considerable animosity. I tried to picture her and came up with a vague image of a tight-mouthed, mousy woman; I couldn't remember her name. As far as I knew, they had no children. Evidently Andrew had done something to make her very angry. It seemed distant and unreal, like the sham tribulations of characters in a play.

As I worked in the garden I glimpsed Tobias from time to time; he would look at me but never speak. At last one day he beckoned; we sat on a bench in an arbour. He gazed off into the distance, hands folded in his lap, and although he seemed to ignore me, I sensed that he was listening intently.

For some reason I found that I was remembering the child who'd drowned in the frozen lake at Farundell. I started to tell him about that, and then I was on my knees at his feet, blind with tears, scoured by weeping.

From then on we sat together for an hour or two on most days. Each time I thought, today I will ask him questions and he will begin to teach me, but he only listened as I poured out my whole life for him: events and people tumbled together, overlapping, returning on themselves, connecting, plaiting, weaving. It was death, I came to see, death that had always been with me, close as a twin. Death in that icy lake, death in the filthy Fleet, death by drowning, death by hanging, death by poison, death by knife and scalpel, sword and gun. Death in anger, death in sorrow; death from disease, from starvation, from ignorance, fear, stupidity, greed. Death in birth, death before birth. Death had its tentacles in every moment, in every thought; it was the worm in the heart of every fruit. The life I had known was death, not life. It sickened me; it was like a coat of perpetual pain.

90

This Is Not Your Road

✿

Early one morning Tobias came by as I was pruning a rampant climbing rose. 'I am leaving now,' he said. 'God be with you.' He turned and walked away.

I stared after him for a moment, uncomprehending, then ran, catching him at the garden gate. 'What do you mean, leaving? Why?'

'There is no reason to stay. I have learned that Jamal is dead.' His tone was neutral, distant, but carried an echo of unspeakable sorrow.

He was walking fast and I trotted down the street after him. 'Where are you going?'

'East.'

'East? Where in the East? I'll come with you.'

'Go back, Francis. Go home.'

'Home? What home? I want to be wherever you are. I won't hold you back. I can help. Shall I arrange transport? How much luggage will you bring? I hardly need any. We should take Tunnie, don't you think?'

I carried on gibbering in this manner as I followed him down to the Horn. Was he here to book passage on a ship? I wasn't letting him out of my sight. He boarded a ferry for Scutari. Was that where one went to arrange passage east? Eventually I ran out of questions and just stayed mutely at his side as we disembarked. He walked briskly to the end of the wharves and up to the road, along the road to the edge of the town, out of town past cemeteries and farms. I was perplexed, but followed doggedly. It was not until we came to the main road and joined a steady stream of men and camels, donkeys and horses, carts and carriages that I began to wonder if he was simply walking east.

We walked all day without pause. I grabbed a quick drink of water as we passed a well, then had to run to catch up with him. Night fell and we left yet another caravanserai behind. He showed no sign of flagging, but I could not keep on much longer without rest and food. Had he no need of these things?

A bright moon rose and the air turned chill. I could no longer feel my legs; I walked numbly, by habit. When I stumbled and almost fell, I realised I'd fallen asleep on my feet. I trudged on, falling further and further behind. Time passed but the road did not change: a pale line across the silent grey land. I woke from a nightmare in which I walked for ever, towards something I could never reach, to see that Tobias was almost out of sight. With the last of my strength I ran after him and caught hold of his robe.

He stopped. His face in the cold moonlight was remote; I'm not sure he recognised me at first. He was already gone but I didn't know it.

'Great-great-grandfather.' I sank to my knees.

He seemed to drag himself back from a vast distance. 'Go home, Francis,' he said. 'This is not your road.'

'Please take me with you.'

'You have a son.' He extricated his robe gently from my hands and walked away.

I knelt in the road and watched until he disappeared into the night. I slept where I was, curled in the dust. At dawn I was woken by gruff voices. Taking me for a mendicant, someone tossed me a few coins; someone else half a loaf of bread. I sat up and ate the bread as a caravan passed, plodding eastward into the rising sun. I turned back towards Constantinople.

My absence had caused considerable trouble. Tunnie was beside himself with aggravation; he and Theodosius had made huge nuisances of themselves at Ibn Sallum's house. The nondescript man who'd followed me every day was about to be executed for dereliction of duty – he'd not seen me leave by the garden gate, which gave on to a street some distance from the square with the cracked fountain where he had lurked. The English embassy had been notified; they'd written to the Porte demanding an investigation. In order to be seen to be doing something, the Janissaries had arrested a number of known criminals and were torturing them to find out where they had hidden my body. Prince Ibrahim greeted me with exclamations of relief and a vigorous scolding.

I placated everyone and went to Ibn Sallum's house. Tunnie and Theodosius insisted on accompanying me and only by swearing that I would not disappear again did I persuade them to wait in the outer room.

Yusuf escorted me to the pavilion where Ibn Sallum greeted me with pipe and coffee and companionable silence. I could not find words for my desolation, but I think he understood.

'He left something for you.' Ibn Sallum handed me a small, plain wooden box. It contained an intricately made iron key on a

412

red silk cord. I turned it over and over in my hands but it told me nothing.

'He said that if fate should lead you to the door, open it with his blessing.'

'What does that mean? What door?'

Ibn Sallum smiled and shrugged. 'I do not know, my friend, but he wore that key around his neck all the years I've known him.'

I put it around my neck; it clanked against Rosmarina's chain. 'He'll come back, won't he? A new life, another name?'

'I don't think so. Not this time. He has tidied his affairs; there is nothing to bind him.'

'Where has he gone? All he said was that he was going east.'

'He told me once about a land of vast mountains and eternal snow, thousands of miles to the east. There was such longing in his voice when he spoke of it. It may be that is where he is going.'

'Is he going there to die?'

'I do not know if he can die. But I think he has no great will to live any longer. Jamal . . . Jamal was everything to him. His name means beauty, you know.'

91

A Damsel in Distress

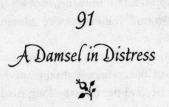

I lingered for two months in Constantinople as though it was my departure rather than Tobias's that would be the final severance of my hopes. At last I booked passage to Venice on a Dutch merchant vessel, one of six in convoy with two warships. Dreading the thought of unavoidable proximity to other travellers, I secured a tiny cabin to myself by paying several times the usual rate.

Ibn Sallum said goodbye with many expressions of sorrow and regret. He had invited me to stay and offered me the chance to work in his laboratory, but although I think he was a good man, there was something about his work that disturbed me. For all his talk of nature and perfection, I do not know what he believed in. Was he a Rosicrucian? Immortal, as Tobias perhaps was, or merely very long-lived? If he possessed a Stone or an Elixir, he did not tell me. Perhaps I will never know.

Prince Ibrahim was inconsolable; also petulant. It was evident that he wished he could order me to stay. All at once he decided to accompany me and sent slaves scurrying to pack; the next day he reported bitterly that his mother had forbidden it. About to mention that it was possible to disobey one's mother, I held my tongue. For him, it was not.

At last came the day of my departure. The Sultana loaded me with gifts: three enormous trunks full of embroidered silks, fur-lined coats, sumptuous carpets, inlaid furniture, jewelled boxes of precious resins and so on. Each required four porters to bring on board; once in the cabin, there was barely space to get to the bed. I am sure she was grateful for the efficacy of my 'magic powder' in healing her son's wound, but even more grateful, I think, to see me leave.

We got under way about noon on a rainy day in December. I stood at the rail as Constantinople disappeared beneath the low clouds, picturing, beyond the city, the long road east on which a solitary figure walked. I stayed on deck until I was soaked, then went to my cabin where Tunnie was laying out dry clothes. He'd set out shirt and coat and breeches; I waved them aside. 'A kaftan, Tunnie, and a fur coat. And my head feels cold without a turban. I suppose you know where my pipe is? And the opium.' I had decided how I would pass the time on the voyage.

Tunnie opened one of the trunks and lifted out a sable-lined coat. He was about to close it when he stopped and looked again, then beckoned to me. A small bare foot showed under the edge of another garment. Silver toe rings: a woman's foot. Could this be one of the Sultana's gifts? I reached down and tickled it.

There was a muffled shriek, the furs flew aside and a girl sat up. Her hair was tumbled over her face; she pushed it back and looked wildly around. It was my Aphrodite.

'Miss Esther!' exclaimed Tunnie.

'You know her?' I turned to him.

'From the palace,' he said. 'She . . . she . . .'

'She needs your help,' she said, climbing out of the trunk and kneeling at my feet. She gazed up at me with those grey-green eyes. I deduced that I was dreaming; I had smoked my pipe and was already adrift on soft seas of phantasy.

'Please, you must help me.' She wrapped her lovely arms around my legs. This opium is really excellent, I thought.

'I throw myself on your mercy, noble English lord.' She spoke fluent Italian and sounded like the helpless damsel in an Oriental romance.

The sound of halloos and thuds from the deck roused me from the dream, but the girl was still there. I looked at Tunnie in alarm. 'Surely not pirates?'

'Couldn't be pirates, sir. We've barely left the harbour. More likely someone forgot to pay their export duty.'

There was a knock at the door. In a flurry of panic, Esther dived back into the trunk and pulled the lid down.

Tunnie opened the door. It was the captain, who informed me in exasperated tones that half a dozen galleys of the Ottoman navy had blockaded the Dutch convoy. A platoon of Janissaries and innumerable officials had boarded and would not allow us to proceed until they had searched the ship – all the ships of the convoy – from top to bottom.

415

'What are they searching for?' I asked, fearing that I already knew the answer.

'A woman, apparently. Who the hell cares? All I know is we're going to lose the damned wind and have to lay over until tomorrow.' He stomped off.

I locked the door and leaned against it, thinking hard. It now seemed unlikely that Esther was here with the Sultana's knowledge or permission, let alone as one of her gifts. I was unsure what the position of *kira* entailed – was she servant or slave? In either case, stealing or abducting the Sultana's *kira* was undoubtedly a serious crime.

I opened the trunk. 'Is it you they're looking for?'

'Please, you must help me. I'll explain everything later.'

Those wide, grey-green eyes. 'All right, stay there,' I said, cursing myself for a fool. 'Cover her over, Tunnie.'

'If they're searching, sir,' he said, 'they'll look in the trunks first thing.'

I gazed around the cabin. There was nowhere to conceal her. Sounds from the passage indicated that the search had begun; they would be here in minutes.

'Quick, Tunnie, give her a pair of breeches and a shirt. Yours, not mine, mine are too big. Shoes and stockings.' We scrambled madly from trunk to trunk, flinging their contents everywhere. 'A wig!' I said, shoving one on her head. 'Tuck your hair up under that.'

Tunnie dropped his hat on top of the wig. I wiped my fingers around the inside of a lamp to collect some soot, which I smeared over her cheeks and throat. In the dim light it might resemble the shadow of a beard.

Tunnie opened the door to the soldiers' knock, revealing Esther poised in the act of pouring me a glass of wine. She bowed and stepped back to the edge of the room, keeping her head down.

The Janissaries were accompanied by a dragoman who begged pardon for the intrusion. 'Have you or your servants seen a woman on board?'

'We have been here in my cabin since we left port,' I said. 'There has been no opportunity to see anyone at all.'

'Of course, effendi. However, unlikely as it is that such a person could be hidden, the Janissaries have their orders: a thorough search must be made.' He stepped back and three soldiers entered. The cabin was now too full for anyone to move; two soldiers withdrew. The remaining one opened each trunk and poked around inside, peered under the table and left.

Tunnie shut the door. We waited in tense silence as the search moved through the other cabins, gun decks and holds; then the sounds indicated that the soldiers had disembarked. The ship got under way again, having not lost the wind after all.

Esther sat on the edge of the bed. We studied each other. There was no longer any trace of the damsel in distress, no more kneeling at the feet of her lord and saviour. It had worked; I had done what she wanted. And I was now complicit.

The ridiculous wig, Tunnie's ill-fitting clothes, the soot on her face all conspired to enhance her appeal. If I was in her power, so too was she in mine. But why was she here?

'So,' I said. 'The explanation?'

'Could I have a glass of wine? I'm very thirsty.'

I gestured to Tunnie; he poured her a glass and she sipped decorously. She'd had plenty of time to assemble a story, or amend one to take into account the possibly unexpected discovery of her absence; the delay had to be just for effect. Or perhaps she really was thirsty.

'I need to get to Venice,' she said, which was not at all what I'd expected to hear.

'Why?'

'My family come from there and I wish to visit my relations.'

I repressed my growing irritation. The conversation reminded me of ones I used to have with Grace, when I was questioning her about some naughtiness: she would give me little titbits of true but irrelevant information while pretending she did not know exactly what I was asking about. The best tactic in those situations was to glare at her in silence until she was so discomfited that she confessed all. I tried it with Esther but it didn't work. She sipped her wine, entirely composed and at home. I began to feel like an intruder in her cabin. I gritted my teeth. 'Why are the Janissaries looking for you?'

She shook her head sadly. 'A misunderstanding.'

'About what?'

'Marriage.'

'Whose marriage?'

'Mine.'

'You are married?' Wonderful. I was now abducting someone's wife.

'I was to be married.'

No, only someone's betrothed, though that might make him even more annoyed with me, whoever he was. 'To whom were you to be married?'

'Hamza Fâkih, the Sultana's chief assassin.'

I remembered him – the charming Moustache. 'And you did not wish to marry him?'

'No, I did not.'

'That is understandable.'

'Nevertheless, the Sultana wished it.'

And the Sultana was not a woman one would lightly disobey. I began to see how flight may have seemed the only option.

'I saw the trunks being packed with gifts for you and I just jumped in. I thought I'd slip out and hide on the ship, but I fell asleep. And then you found me. And saved me. I haven't thanked you, it's all been such a shock. But I'm very grateful.' She was the

418

damsel in distress once more, beautiful grey-green eyes brimming with well-timed tears of gratitude.

The unprompted effusion made me suspicious; the spurious information was surely intended to deflect my attention from something. 'And the Sultana was so angry when she discovered her match-making had been thwarted that she sent a battalion of Janissaries to stop and search eight ships of another sovereign nation, just to fetch you back?'

She shrugged.

Tunnie coughed in the particular way that indicated he had something to say.

Esther yawned prettily. 'I'm so tired. Would you mind if I rested for a while?'

'You have a nice little nap,' I said. 'Tunnie, come with me.' He followed me out of the cabin and I locked the door behind us, pocketing the key. We found a spot on deck, in the shelter of the gunwale, where we would not be overheard.

'Out with it,' I said. 'Everything you know about Miss Esther.'

'You were away from the palace a good deal, sir, and even when you were there, if I may say, you did not notice much.' He shook his head. 'These people, sir, these Turks – well, I've never known people so devious. After a while they became accustomed to seeing me about the place; then they didn't notice me at all. One hears things and sees things. They're so used to having slaves, sir, and even the servants are treated like slaves. It doesn't occur to them that someone like me could think for himself, could have a mind of his own and put things together. Everybody, I reckon, was playing a double game – at least. There's the Russians. And the English, the Dutch, the Venetians, the French. Oh my, the French. They are playing everybody against everybody else. I don't know how they keep it straight. Perhaps they don't. You remember Laski, who was on the boat with us?'

'I remember Laski.'

'He was around the palace quite a lot, thought never at the front door, if you know what I mean. I think he was working for the Russians while pretending to work for the French. He had dealings with our friend Hamza Fâkih and with that fellow Zurnazen. I even saw him meeting the good Doctor Hamon once. But the person he met most often was Miss Esther. He was murdered two days ago, poisoned they say, and dumped in the Bosphorus. His body washed up at the palace quayside, next to the Sultana's galley. Fully dressed, but barefoot. People took it to mean . . . well, who knows? And last night Hamza Fâkih was found dead. He'd been stabbed in the eye with a long needle. While he slept.'

This cast a new light on things. It might not have been the Sultana who had sent the Janissaries after Esther – the Sultana might have hidden Esther in my trunk herself, to help her escape. Had Esther murdered one or both of those men on the Sultana's orders? In which case the soldiers had been acting on the orders of . . . who? The Sultan himself? I shuddered. What had I got myself into?

But I could not imagine Esther committing cold-blooded murder. Not my Aphrodite. No, not possible. The threat of a forced marriage to an odious man was sufficient reason for flight. The deaths of Laski and Hamza Fâkih had nothing to do with her. No doubt these spies were always killing each other.

'If I may suggest, sir . . .'

'Yes, Tunnie?'

'We should keep her locked in the trunk. After all, that's where she chose to be.'

'That is undoubtedly the wisest option.'

She was sound asleep when we returned to the cabin; she slept all afternoon and woke hungry. Tunnie brought some supper from the officers' mess. I knew he wanted to remain on guard, but whatever Esther had done – and there was no proof that she had killed anyone – I was sure she meant me no harm. I sent him off to his hammock in the crew's quarters.

Esther and I ate by the light of the swaying oil lamp, sitting cross-legged on the bed. She dispatched her food with delicacy and avidity, wiped her fingers on the sheet, leaned back with a satisfied sigh and fell asleep. She looked so innocent and lovely that I hadn't the heart to wake her; I tucked her in and made myself a bed of coats and cushions on the floor.

I watched her sleep and tried to think very carefully. Of course she would not tell me everything; why should she? From what Tunnie had told me of her milieu, she was rightly suspicious of everyone. Maybe she assumed that I too was a spy; perhaps she even imagined she knew for whom I worked while pretending to work for someone else. Hard to prove what one is not, and my behaviour had undeniably lent itself to multiple interpretations. It was so convoluted that it made my head hurt. I looked longingly at my pipe and wished that all this had been an opium dream.

The voyage lasted for twelve rainy days; I slept on the floor for twelve lonely nights. Once Esther was sure I would not betray her, there was no flirtation. She was cool and courteous, requiring me to leave the cabin whenever she wanted to relieve herself, wash or change her clothes. She wore one of Tunnie's shirts belted over a pair of his breeches which she requested he take in for her at the waist. She showed him how much. He was somewhat piqued but I laughed at her imperious ways and asked him to oblige her.

Gradually, as we spent time in close proximity, I learned her story. Her father had been an apothecary, a Venetian Jew who'd moved his business to Constantinople a few years ago, as that city was far more tolerant of Jews than any in Europe. Esther was his only child; her mother had died when she was small, so she alone accompanied him and helped him in the shop. He had done well until debts and illness ruined him; he'd died last year. Esther, suddenly having to fend for herself, put her knowledge of the apothecary's art to use by making cosmetics and beauty treatments, which she sold to ladies of quality. They were so good that she came to the attention of the Sultana who, recognising a fellow Venetian, doted on her, entrusting her with various little tasks. All very innocent. To the Sultana, Esther explained, the marriage to Hamza Fâkih – in which, after converting to Islam, she would have become his fourth wife – was a great honour and an elevation for a Jewess with no money, no dowry, no position.

It was not until the evening before our arrival in Venice that I realised I was utterly and agonisingly in love.

92

A Thousand Strings

I made plans. I would rent a house for her, hire servants, give her clothes and jewellery. I debated over the best approach – how could I manage to give her money without offending her? Of course I desired her – more intensely, in those first chaste days, than I have ever desired any woman. But I also felt an overpowering urge to protect her, to smooth her path in the world, to give her a good life, whether or not that life included me in any role whatsoever. This was not easy to explain, so I wrote it all out in a letter which I planned to present to her when we arrived in Venice.

After we docked, one thing and another delayed me on deck; when I returned to the cabin she was gone. The lock had been picked from within. She had taken shirt and breeches, the wig and Tunnie's hat. Knowing it was futile, I ran to the rail and scanned the crowded wharves. There were dozens of similarly dressed people.

I made my way to Philippe and Caroline's palazzo in a dark mood. Venice was cold and gloomy. I felt like a dog coming home with his tail between his legs, a failure in every way. The boat, laden with my possessions, rode low in the murky water of the lagoon.

The palazzo was buzzing with activity; there was to be a masked ball that evening. Caroline was the still centre of the whirlwind. She greeted me with genuine delight and a rather lascivious kiss, followed by a grimace of distaste directed at my beard. I had my old suite of rooms on the second floor, overlooking the Grand Canal. The view did nothing to comfort me; I missed Constantinople, I missed Ibn Sallum and Kökcü and the garden, I missed Tobias and my lost chance of knowledge, but most of all I missed Esther. I made plans to track her down the next day. She had never told me her surname, but I was sure I'd be able to find her. The Jewish ghetto was not large; everyone would know her family and her return would surely have been noted.

I got drunk early and stayed drunk all night. Philippe lent me a mask; for costume, I wore my most lavishly embroidered kaftan, a fur-trimmed surcoat, a turban with a ruby aigrette. With my full beard – which I had refused Tunnie's offer to shave or 'Please, sir, just trim a little' – I was often mistaken for a genuine Turk. Surprisingly, or perhaps not, this seemed to have an aphrodisiacal effect on women and a few men; I received a number of quite forthright propositions.

I was curious to learn what Philippe might know of the Sultana Safiya Zuhal. I looked for a chance to catch him alone; not easy, but eventually I spotted him in the shadows of a narrow colonnade outside the ballroom. He was speaking with a masked woman; I stood aside and waited for them to finish.

They laughed together; he kissed her hand and gave her what

looked like a heavy purse, which she slipped into her pocket. As she left him, she brushed past me and I caught a glimpse of grey-green eyes behind the mask. It was Esther, I was sure of it. She had to have recognised me – the clothes which she'd seen on the ship, the beard. She smiled and dipped the briefest of curtseys. I stared, momentarily paralysed, then ran after her into the ball-room. She had vanished into the swirl of dancing maskers.

Philippe appeared at my side, laughing softly to himself. 'You know, Francis, I am more and more convinced that woman is superior to man.'

'You will not get an argument from me,' I said. 'Who was that you were talking to?'

'One of those superior women of whom I was thinking. She has been doing some work for me this last year and was just reporting the successful – the more than successful – outcome of her under-takings. A remarkable young woman.'

'What is her name?'

'Jeanne-Colette Vauregard du Mellisant-Plessis.'

'French?'

'I believe so, though she is vague about her ancestry. Issue of the finest loins, they say, but the wrong side of the bed.'

'You gave her money.'

'Not money. Diamonds. She wished to be paid in diamonds.'

'Paid for what?'

He raised an eyebrow. 'Services to France.'

'She serves the State?'

'She serves, I believe, the sovereign state of herself. Why are you so interested?'

'I think I may have met her in Cyprus.'

Philippe compressed his lips.

I did not take the hint. 'Where does she live?'

'Paris. Prague. London. Amsterdam. She travels a great deal.'

'Where might she be travelling tonight?'

'She did not tell me her plans.'

Was Philippe's evasiveness due to politics and the delicate nature of her work, or . . . 'Is she a lover of yours?'

He laughed. 'What are you after, Francis? She's an adventuress, a very high-flying one. I know you, *mon cher*. It's domesticity you truly crave.'

I thought he was probably right, but for some reason I craved Esther, or Jeanne-Colette Vauregard du Mellisant-Plessis, or whatever her damned name was, despite the fact that she had played me for a fool. I thought over everything she had told me and concluded that it had contained not one iota of truth.

I prowled among the revellers for an hour, staring into every woman's eyes and garnering yet more, and more lubricious, propositions. She was not there. When I returned to my rooms, Tunnie received the news of Esther's revised identity with a complete lack of surprise.

'So she was working for the French all along,' he said. 'I told you, sir. Everyone against everyone else. D'you suppose she found out that Laski was really a Russian agent? Or did he find out who she really was and threaten to expose her? Was she working for or against the Sultana? The old lady was truly fond of her, I'd heard. Should have locked her in the trunk, sir.'

'Opium pipe please, Tunnie.'

I slept until midday when an altercation among boatmen beneath my window roused me from dreams of a diamond-bedecked woman who danced with me before stabbing me through the eye with a needle. After Tunnie supplied me with coffee, brandy, more coffee and hashish, the pain in my head eased. I got out of bed, donned my slippers and a fur-lined coat against the Venetian chill and went in search of Philippe, intending to pester him further about Esther-Jeanne-Colette.

On the way downstairs I encountered Caroline, who marched

me smartly back up to my rooms. 'You are to shave him at once,' she told Tunnie. 'I simply cannot bear to see a handsome man with fur all over his face. I shall stay to make sure he does not resist.'

She watched, smiling sweetly and maliciously, as I was shaved, combed, lightly powdered, perfumed and inserted into an elegant but confining suit and high-heeled shoes that pinched my toes. I recognised this as a necessary adaptation to the life I had to live and the world in which I was compelled to live it, but since then I have always changed into Ottoman attire at home.

Caroline released me; I found Philippe in his study. He was in full flow, dictating to a secretary, but he waved me over, rummaged about on his desk and handed me a letter.

Addressed to me (care of Philippe), it was from Signore Malipiero, Tobias-Tibaldo's lawyer, inviting me to call on him at my convenience on a matter to my benefit. Not wanting to waste so much appropriate attire, I went straight away.

My reception was almost cordial. Although he did not speak to me himself, the clerk conveyed his greetings; I conveyed my own. Malipiero looked even more reptilian than before, all sagging jowls and scaly skin. In what was, for him, a positive frenzy of activity, he reached out one clawed hand and pushed a stack of papers an inch or two across his desk towards me. The clerk pushed them the rest of the way.

I picked up the top document, an elaborately scribed vellum adorned with stamps, seals, ribbons and multiple signatures.

'The last will and testament of Tibaldo d'Amori,' said the clerk. 'Who has perished at sea. Signore Malipiero wishes me to tell you of his most sincere condolences. The will names you, Francis Damory of Farundell, Oxfordshire, England, as his sole heir with a single exception, to wit: a certain property at Sakkara, in Egypt, and an income for life, to one Rashid Ibn Abdullah al-Misri.' The clerk mangled the pronunciation dreadfully.

There was more, but I didn't hear. I thought about my great-great-grandfather walking into the night. He had left the world behind; he had left it to me.

That evening I worked my way through the documents: deeds and stock certificates, investments, deposits, holdings. After a while I lost count. Tobias had made me an extremely wealthy man and tied me to the world by a thousand strings.

The next morning I hired a boat and boatmen to take me up the Brenta to the Villa degli Eremiti. The air was still and cold. The oars creaked in a sluggish rhythm; a heron flapped low over the marshes and fine drizzle blurred the surface of the water.

The landing had been repaired, with painted mooring posts and new steps. The garden, too, had been cared for, the encroaching trees cut back, parterres revealed, a fountain uncovered and splashing into a stone basin.

I went first to Rosmarina's grave beneath the old apple tree. Its branches were black and bare, mottled with lichen. Grass grew over the mound and someone had planted a myrtle.

'I saw your father,' I said. 'You were wrong. He never forgot you.'

At the house, Bortolin and Besina greeted me with joy and relief; Almira and Giancarlo came running. Naturally everyone had feared the worst.

'We hear about pirates, Signore, Barbary corsairs . . .'

'And storms, and shipwrecks . . .'

'We were so worried about you, Signore.'

'Among foreigners, those Turks . . .'

'We Venetians know you can't trust a Turk . . .'

'But you survived, Signore, and you've come home and that's all that matters.'

'And you will want to see your son. Almira, fetch Providenza and the boy.' Bortolin brought me a glass of wine while we waited.

The wet-nurse appeared with my son. Toby was a sturdy lad with a head full of golden curls. He regarded me with interest from Providenza's ample arms as Besina looked on proudly. I had the uncanny sensation that Tobias was watching me through his grandson's young-old eyes. I offered him my finger; he seized it with a strong grip and chortled.

'Yes, you have me, don't you?' I said. He found that hilarious and laughed even more, squeezing harder.

Providenza laughed; so did Besina. 'He makes everyone laugh,' she said. A cloud passed over her face. 'Will you be taking him away, Signore?' She fussed with his wrapping gown, tugging it over his legs. He laughed at her and kicked it off at once.

I had not decided what to do. I spent the day at the villa, catching up with everything and going over the place from top to bottom, searching for a door whose lock fitted Tobias's key. No luck, and I was no closer to any decisions. Evening was approaching; I said I would come back in a few days and returned to my boat. Almira was waiting for me at the landing.

'Excuse me, Signore, I wanted to tell you, but Besina said I shouldn't, then Giancarlo said I should, and Bortolin told me to do whatever I wanted, so here I am and if you don't mind I think I had better tell you.'

'Yes, Almira, I'm sure that's the right decision. Tell me what?'

'That the ghost comes and speaks to Master Toby.'

'The same old man you saw before?'

She nodded.

'What does he say?'

'I do not know. He does not speak Italian.'

'Does he come often?'

'No, only sometimes. But maybe other times I don't see. Providenza does not notice him.'

'It is good that you told me, Almira.' I gave her a coin. 'If you see the ghost again, would you tell him I'd like to speak to him?'

93

Home

❧

My deliberations about 'what to do' were brought to a head by news that awaited me at the English embassy, where I went the next day to check for letters. I was greeted with servility mixed with something I couldn't identify at first, though later I recognised it as firmly suppressed embarrassed amusement. The servility I put down to news of my sudden wealth having preceded me; given what I knew of the speed with which such information travelled along unofficial channels, this seemed likely. But the source of the amusement and embarrassment was only made known to me when a secretary showed me the newspaper.

It was dated two weeks earlier; the article was on the front page. The headline ran: *Oxfordshire Peers in Double Suicide*.

I had to read it three times. As I'd heard, my brother Andrew's wife had filed a divorce suit against him in the ecclesiastical court. The only admissible grounds for this were really heinous behaviour – ordinary meanness and infidelity insufficient – so I'd already guessed that he'd done something quite exceptionally annoying. The clipping Meryll had sent me had been correct in alluding to indiscretions with a neighbour, but I'd been entirely wrong to imagine Andrew with someone else's wife. For the last several years he had been having an affair with our neighbour at Harfield: Isabel's husband, Reginald.

I left the embassy speechless, the newspaper clutched in my hand.

The secretary ran after me. 'Lord Damory!' He was holding a bundle of letters that had come for me; I took them blindly and staggered back to Caroline and Philippe's palazzo. The whole business only began to seem real after I had told them about it and shown them the article. Of course, as soon as it became real it became farcical, and we spent the evening in hilarity at my poor brother's expense.

It was not until I saw his grave at Farundell, so conspicuously outside the wall of the graveyard and with such a mean stone, uninscribed even with his name, that I wondered about the sad, hard, painful life he must have led. I felt pity for him at last, and perhaps even loved him a little. I had a proper stone made and, after a couple of years, moved the wall.

I wrote to Isabel who, having heard the news a few days before, had written to me in Constantinople. Letters flew back and forth between Venice and Rome. We both urgently needed to be in England, she to look after her (and Meryll's) son Gerald, the new Earl of Harfield, I to deal with lawyers, managers, bankers and tax collectors, but neither of us wished to leave Italy. Our various children were too young for such a journey, especially in winter. Having inherited vast wealth and a title in the space of a few days, I was immediately confronted with a situation in which neither was of any use.

Eventually it was agreed that the children should for the time being remain where they were – Freddy and Cathy with Meryll in Rome and Toby in Venice. Besina *et al* at the Villa degli Eremiti were the only people who were happy with the plan. In the summer, when the journey could most safely be made, I would return to Italy and, with Meryll, bring the children home.

I spent a good part of my last days in Venice searching for

Esther-Jeanne-Colette. The fact that she had turned out to be deceitful and manipulative had done nothing to dampen my feelings; if anything, the increased complexity of her character heightened my interest. On the chance that the story she'd told me was closer to the truth than the one she'd told Philippe, I made enquiries in the ghetto. No young woman had recently returned; no apothecary had left for Constantinople in living memory.

I made enquiries in society. A few people knew her, or of her. She had a reputation as an adventuress, as Philippe had said. Accounts of her supposed parentage varied: royal and illegitimate or a common harlot with airs and graces. English, French, Polish or Venetian. Raised in a convent; seduced by her mother's lover; an Arabian princess; a man in disguise. Of the woman herself there was no trace.

I set out for England. Isabel and I would have to go partly by sea as the Alpine passes were closed for the winter, so we met at Leghorn and booked passage to Marseilles on a small, well-armed galleon, scheduled to travel in convoy with a dozen other vessels and three French ships of the line.

The day before our departure we went to the English Cemetery to visit Agnes's grave. It was a suitably English day, damp and melancholy. The cemetery was on the outskirts of town, guarded by tall cypresses. There was no one about. We wandered for half an hour among marble monuments and headstones, some new and well cared for, others aged to illegibility and overgrown with moss, before we found her stone. I was touched to see the care that Jack had taken. The stone was carved with a relief of the Roman Forum and simply inscribed:

Agnes Beatrice Enderby Damory
25 August 1698–3 October 1730
Beloved Daughter, Mother, Wife and Companion

Isabel burst into tears. I stared hard at the grave, willing myself to remember Agnes. She seemed like someone from another life, or from a novel so skilfully written that its characters become real for the brief time that they inhabit one's mind. One mourns when they are gone, but soon forgets.

I wished I'd brought something to leave. I thought of the figurine of the dancer I'd given her those aeons ago, that she'd left behind at New Eden. After escorting Isabel back to our hotel I searched every shop in town until I found one as like as possible and took it to the grave, where I stood it upright and piled some pebbles around its base. I pictured Agnes dancing in Heaven and the image made me smile. I wasn't sure she'd approve of a Heaven with dancing.

The voyage from Leghorn to Marseilles was stormy; Isabel was seasick and miserable. She pined for her children and felt sure that this torment was her punishment for abandoning them.

'Seasickness induces morbid phantasies,' I told her, but I don't think she took much comfort. She was pregnant again, but didn't realise it until some weeks later. I read to her, to keep her mind occupied, and we played cards when the seas were calmer.

Tunnie reported that pirates had twice been sighted prowling like wolves on the horizon but had not approached, deterred by the size of our flotilla.

Once in France we made good time on the roads, where money can buy speed, and arrived in London in early February. The city was drab, filthy, muddy, stinking, dark and ugly. I loathed it, I loathed the armies of lawyers and clerks, I loathed the house in St. James's Square, cold and uninhabited for the last few years, with a staff of servants so creaky and moribund that they were flummoxed by the simplest requirements, such as a hot bath.

I went almost at once to Lytton's Bookshop in Cecil Court, thinking to send another missive to Mr Pym, whoever the hell he was – ghost, mysterious landlord or Rosicrucian. The shop was no longer there, the premises occupied by a wig-maker who knew nothing of any previous tenant. I enquired up and down the Court; no one knew. Eventually I learned from another antiquarian bookseller that Mr Lytton had sold off his stock and retired to Scotland, or Wales, or Yorkshire. It seemed to me that I had been cast out into a cold and meaningless world, with nothing to remind me of the realities I had sought but an enigmatic key to an unknown door.

And then I went to Farundell. It was raining when I left London but the skies slowly lightened and the sun emerged, low in the west, as we crossed the River Isis and turned on to the road that meanders up through the hills. I opened the carriage window. A man was ploughing a field; I leaned out and sniffed the rich fragrance of the turned earth. When he looked up I recognised a Butterfield and waved.

He snatched his hat from his head, grinning widely. 'Welcome home, m'lord,' he called out.

We turned into the drive and passed through the oak woods. Swelling buds tipped the bare branches and snowdrops lay in drifts beneath. The drive curved, then came the view of the lake, the island . . . and then the house, long facade of golden stone and ivy, smoke rising from the chimneys, tall windows reflecting the sky. The years dropped away; I was coming home to Farundell as I had a thousand times before.

94

Everything the World Can Give a Man

❧

It was early morning but the sun was already strong in a clear blue sky. The children raced up the track, splashing in the puddles left by last night's rain. Jezebel and Jacinta, Japhet's granddaughters, bounded after them. Two hapless footmen, whose duty it was to keep them all out of mortal peril, trudged behind like patient donkeys. Gerald walked at my side, though I could tell that part of him wanted to run and splash with the others. He was sixteen now and about half of the time he remembered that he was too dignified for such things.

'Do you think I'm too young for university, Uncle Francis? My tutors are so boring. I want to go to Oxford, like you.'

Isabel would not appreciate my meddling in her eldest son's upbringing. 'What does your mother say?'

'She says I'm too young. But if you told her I was quite mature for my age she might consider it.'

'What do your Harfield relations say?'

He snorted. 'They say an earl has no need of so much education.'

I wondered, not for the first time, whether he might have preferred to be Isabel and Meryll's bastard rather than Gerald Bythesea Mortimer Gathorne-Gordy, 8th Earl of Harfield. He was the very image of Meryll – same pale skin that flushed red

434

when he was excited, same dark hair and eyes. Everyone, including Gerald, knew the truth; no one spoke it.

The smallest child, my daughter Izzy, had fallen behind the others. Gerald scooped her up, swung her around and tossed her to me. She screamed with glee and demanded more. We tossed her back and forth as we walked, until we grew tired and put her down. She wailed for a few seconds, then trotted after us as fast as her little legs could carry her.

Toby, Freddy and Cathy had stopped by the old chapel to pick blackberries. They looked like a tribe of pygmy savages, their hands and faces stained with juice. Izzy ran to join them, hanging on to Toby's breeches and begging for berries, which he dropped into her mouth after making her jump for them. 'Don't give her too many,' I told him.

Even Gerald could not resist. I winced as his clothes acquired indelible stains; unlike the others, who looked like peasants, he was decently dressed in fine cambric and lace. He'd ridden from Harfield yesterday without telling anyone; I'd had to send a groom galloping over there with the news. He always returned from Farundell with his clothes ruined, prompting complaining letters which we ignored.

I continued to the top of the hill. We had chosen this site for the Temple of Hermes because it was the most awkward and inconvenient place imaginable to build a large edifice with twenty-foot columns and hundreds of tons of stone which had to be hauled up on oxcarts, requiring the cutting of a new road, a mile in length, that ascended in a spiral at a sufficiently gentle gradient. The trees we'd chopped down would keep us in firewood for years; we'd had to build a new shed to store it.

The last part of the ascent was by a stair cut into the rock, a flourish which Meryll had required on aesthetic grounds, but which had greatly aggravated the builders, who'd had to construct a crane to lift the materials up the final few yards. A natural spring, uncovered when the steps were cut, trickled into a basin. The Farundell hills are full of such springs; their water is the purest and most delicious in the world. I stopped to drink, then climbed to the top.

The temple leaps into view very suddenly, hidden by the steepness of the steps until one is right in front of it. The columns appear even taller than they are and the dome seems to float, a trick of cornicing or something like that which Meryll had more than once explained at length.

A marble obelisk with a golden tip stood in the middle of the small paved area in front of the temple. It was our tribute to Philippe, who'd died five years ago and whose statues of Hermes the temple had been built to house. It was inscribed with an account of his life and triumphs, not neglecting his most famous amorous exploits and the time he had caught eighteen trout in one hour on the Brenta.

I saw Meryll and Isabel making their way up the hill with little Roma. They stopped at the chapel and Roma ran to join the other children, who were still among the blackberries. If they had been eating berries all this time . . . 'Tell the children no more berries,' I called down.

'The great god Hermes speaks from on high,' Meryll shouted back. 'We hear and obey.' Isabel stayed to enforce the prohibition; she waved Meryll off, pressing her hand to her swollen belly to indicate that she didn't fancy the climb. He disappeared from view as the road curved around the back of the hill.

He and Isabel had been living at Farundell for the last few months while their new residence was completed. They had bought Turton Park, the former Plachard estate a couple of miles away; Lavinia and Cornelia's family had been brought to ruin by having too many daughters. Meryll was remodelling the old house. He'd acquired a reputation as an architect especially adept at translating the new fashion for all things classical into buildings that sat well in the English landscape, and had received a number of commissions for country houses and follies. He'd modelled my temple on an elegant Roman design: circular, about sixty feet in diameter and surrounded by a deep colonnade.

I lit my pipe and sat on a bench, resisting the urge to peek inside. He had just completed the frescoes and wanted to show me himself. He arrived a bit out of breath; he'd put on a few pounds. He sat down and wiped the sweat from his brow. We looked out over the valley, the house, the gardens, the lake. The view went on for miles; this was, of course, the reason we had chosen this spot.

He pointed to the island in the lake. 'And that is where we'll put your Temple of Aphrodite.'

'You're joking.'

'Not at all.'

'As if it wasn't enough to build this one on a mountaintop, you want to build the next one on a remote island. How will we get the columns out there?'

'We'll build a barge. They got here from Venice by ship, didn't they? And before that they came from Cyprus. So what more appropriate than that they should end up on another island? Now come and see my paintings. Your paintings.'

He had divided the interior of the temple into eight panels separated by tall doors, which he opened one by one, flooding the space with light. Each panel showed Hermes in one of his many guises: Hermes Logios, god of language; Hermes Psychopompus, guide of souls; Hermes of the Crossroads and so on. The colours were subtle and glowing, the figures graceful. Each panel was set in a *trompe l'œil* niche and captioned by a *trompe l'œil* chiselled inscription. The influence of Raphael was clear, but Meryll's style was his own.

I moved slowly about the room, taking it in. The three large marble statues – Hermes with caduceus, Hermes with moon-topped staff, Hermes playing the lyre, a nymph at his feet – had not been easy to bring up the hill, but now looked as if they had always been here. The six bronzes stood around the edge, each on a simple onyx pedestal. As I looked from different angles, new juxtapositions of paintings and statues were revealed, giving them a changeable, lifelike quality. 'It's absolutely marvellous,' I said.

Meryll grinned like a boy. 'I've enjoyed this job; I'm only sorry it's over.'

We went back outside and sat in the sun beneath the colonnade. The children were coming, preceded by yells, laughter and dogs. Toby and Freddy appeared, tripping over each other in a race to the top; they fell in a tangle of limbs as each tried to prevent the other from reaching us. It became a wrestling match until Gerald intervened, hauling them apart by the scruffs of their necks like puppies. Next came Cathy and Roma and the footmen, one of whom carried Izzy, who, seeing me, demanded to be put down. She ran to me and presented me with a handful of squashed blackberries.

Meryll's face, as he watched the children, was radiant with contentment. 'You are the very image of the happy paterfamilias,' I said.

'I am, thank the gods.' He studied me for a moment. 'But you are not.'

'What makes you think that?' Izzy was chewing on a button of my coat, reminding me of the little black cat from the Villa degli Eremiti, which reminded me of fishing with Philippe. I gazed at his obelisk, missing him and those free-hearted days before Rosmarina . . . before Tobias.

'Oh, just one or two small things,' Meryll said. 'You smoke hashish all day, you drink all evening and smoke opium all night.'

'I had no idea you paid such close attention to my schedule.'

'Don't get prickly with me, Damory. I know you too well.'

He was right. I knew I ought to be happy; I knew I was not. I even knew why, but there was nothing I could do about it. I had everything the world can give a man, but not what I wanted. Every worldly gain served only to enhance my awareness of what I lacked.

I had searched Farundell for a door to fit Tobias's key immediately upon my return, and regularly thereafter. It had become something of a habit. I also checked the doors of any house I visited, just in case. 'If fate should lead you to the door,' Tobias had said, which meant that it could be anywhere. I had the odd feeling that this searching somehow pushed the discovery, if there was to be a discovery, further into the future or perhaps out of reach altogether, but I couldn't stop myself. 'If fate should lead you': that 'If' tormented me. If I should die without ever finding it I would die hating my life. No matter how full of good things it had been, it would have been empty.

'For example,' said Meryll, 'at this very moment, while your beautiful daughter is frolicking in the most charming manner at your feet, you are grinding your teeth as though undergoing torture.'

I had told Meryll and Isabel that I'd found Tobias and lost him, but even if I had comprehended how immense the loss would be, how it would grow with time, not diminish, I could not have expressed it and they could not have understood. Although they never said anything, preferring to avoid the subject altogether, it was clear that they regarded my obsession with the key and its unknown door as bordering on the insane. They had never believed that Tobias was immortal; I could not doubt it. Doubt was a refuge no longer available to me. I knew. I knew, and that knowledge was why my existence was a torture, why I was grinding my teeth. I made myself stop.

I picked up Izzy and held her close, kissing her sweet-smelling hair.

'Come with me over to Turton this afternoon,' Meryll said. 'I've redesigned the west face – more symmetrical. You'll like it. And I've decided to dig a lake. I need your advice about the best site.'

'Can't. It's the drive-round. We're going to display Edward Philip George to his future subjects.' My son and heir had been born four months ago; the annual September drive around the estate was to be his first venture into the world.

'Is Caroline up to it?'

'She insists. She says that all she has to do is sit in the carriage and wave.' Unlike her other children – Louis, Duc du Léran, who lived with Philippe's family in France, and our Izzy – Edward had given Caroline a difficult pregnancy and a long, hard labour. That women had to suffer so outrageously in this perpetual reproductive endeavour made me angry, but since that was pointless, and I, useless, I despaired instead. Surely only some kind of idiotic, merciful forgetting permitted them to repeat the experience willingly.

We had married two years after Philippe died, the summer I returned to Venice to fetch Toby. I'm sure he would have preferred a more romantic death, one better matched to his life: poisoned in some intricate political conspiracy perhaps, or shot by a jealous husband. In the end it was fishing. I was staying with them at La Fontana while tidying matters at the Villa degli Eremiti. We'd gone out on the Brenta. A hook became caught in his hand; he pulled it out and carried on fishing all day. By evening it was swollen, but he refused attention. The next morning, though feverish, he insisted on attending an important meeting in the city. They brought him home shivering and unable to stand. Doctors could do nothing, the fever raged through the night and by dawn he was dead.

The repercussions were international. Philippe had been entangled in so many complex conspiracies whose details were known only to him that his departure caused chaos throughout the embassies of Europe and beyond. I was devastated by the suddenness. I had loved him as a friend, and more than that: I had looked upon him as an exemplar of the life skilfully lived. He had seemed so perfectly in control; I had never known him to hesitate, to make a mistake, to doubt himself, to fret. He had everything: wealth, beauty, breeding, education, the finest intelligence and an inexhaustible capacity for pleasure. He had moved through the world with such impeccable elegance that I had thought he would be there for ever.

Caroline and I were at his bedside when he died, and we knew he would have been glad for us to comfort each other. Woven into the fabric of our marriage was both mourning and memorial.

After an early dinner we set out in the open landau, with Izzy in her best frock and Edward, swathed in yards of lace, in the arms of his nursemaid. I tucked a blanket around Caroline's legs.

She pushed it off. 'I am not an invalid, Francis.' Her tone was testy, but she softened it with a smile. In fact she looked very well, and I told her so. There was colour in her cheeks and her eyes sparkled. The bright sun showed the lines on her face, deepened this last, hard year, and the new silver hairs at her temples.

Toby, scrubbed and dressed like a proper little gentleman in a velvet suit, followed on his pony. He was old enough now to have a role in the drive-round: he carried the purses with coins that we would give to each of our tenants. Freddy followed Toby, as he did everywhere. Although he was only two months younger, there was never any question about who was leader. Toby was taller and stronger and cleverer, but it was his natural air of authority that Freddy could not help but recognise. I wondered what it would be like for Edward, growing up in the shadow of such a brother, over whom he would eventually take precedence. Toby kicked his pony to a canter and passed the landau, causing the driver to *tsk* and the footman to smother a laugh. Freddy followed, waving an apology up at the box.

Caroline saw me smile. 'Do you wish he . . . ?'

She meant, did I wish he was the legitimate one. I couldn't answer that, so I kissed her hand and shrugged.

I had thought Caroline would find Farundell dull and prefer to spend most of her time in London, but she'd surprised me. She'd grown up on a large estate and, as the only child, had been taken everywhere by her doting father, from whom she had learned quite a bit about farming and estate management. I did not enquire too deeply into that father of hers, remembering the rumours that had circulated about her in Paris.

She had made herself well-loved at Farundell. Knowing, from her marriage into an old and insular French family, that an outsider is not easily welcomed, she made a special effort. Relentless dinners for the local gentry; endless good works among the poor. She 'adored' the old house, but that had not stopped her from building a new wing and redecorating from attic to cellars. She improved conditions for the servants, too, replacing the old kitchens and adding a dormitory for the maids.

The inactivity of the last year had been a huge frustration for her; she was a person, I discovered, who always had to be doing something. She was baffled by my ability to sit and think for hours while doing, to all appearances, nothing whatsoever. 'Are you well?' she would ask, and 'What are you doing?' Eventually I took to holding a book open in my lap although, to her, reading was not really doing, rather something one did when one could not be out doing things. During the enforced languor of her pregnancy I tried to show her how reading could be as much of an adventure as any that one could have out in the world – more so, in fact, because one could go anywhere, do anything. I offered *Robinson Crusoe*, which amused her 'a little', though she didn't finish it. 'It's not real,' she said, 'so it doesn't really matter what happens to him.'

The first stop on the drive-round was Henry Butterfield's farm.

Henry was standing by his gate, where the boys' ponies were tied. When we pulled up they came running out of the cottage, hands full of sweets. Providenza followed, wiping her hands on her apron. Toby was chattering to her in Italian.

She curtseyed. 'Welcoming great sir and great lady on the passing-by,' she said. 'I am wishing for you all nice thing and for the son also.' She gave Caroline a small, neatly stitched pouch. 'I am giving you this for to help you with all.'

She had produced five children in four years; they squabbled about in the dirt of the front yard like piglets. By my calculation, she and Henry had to have started within a week or two of her arrival at Farundell with Toby; they'd married a few months later.

Toby and Freddy had already remounted and were trotting ahead; Providenza and Henry waved as we set off. Caroline opened the pouch and smiled when she saw what it contained. 'How sweet of her. Isn't it hideous?' She showed me the garish painted statuette, 'La Madonna' inscribed on its base.

Halfway down the hill was Farundell hamlet – twenty or so houses clustered around a bridge. Here were many retired servants whose families had worked at Farundell for generations, and here lived Bortolin and Besina. When I sold the Villa degli Eremiti I had thought they would enjoy a retirement somewhere nearby. I could not imagine that, at their age, they would want to live in a foreign land, let alone endure the hardships of travel. But they were desperately unhappy at the thought of being parted from Toby and overjoyed when I offered to take them to England with us. They had adapted well to English life; everyone called them 'Nonno' and 'Nonna' and they were great favourites with the children. Their flair for growing vegetables had made them well liked by all, since they produced far too much for themselves. Besina made preserves and jams and gave these out at every opportunity.

Bortolin had acquired something of a reputation as a breeder of chickens and had recently acquired a flock of geese. He still came up to the house and did a few hours' work every day in the garden. He was especially adept at pruning the topiary, which he would allow no one else to touch.

They were sitting on the bench in front of their cottage as Toby and Freddy demonstrated an acrobatic trick. A circle of muddy children watched, open-mouthed in amazement, as Toby ran at Freddy, leapt on to his shoulders and somersaulted off with a whoop.

Besina ducked into the house and came out with a jar of some preserved fruit which she gave Caroline with a shy smile. Bortolin produced a bottle and poured us each a small glass of golden liquid.

'*Fiori di sambuco*,' he said. 'What is that in English?'

'Elderflower,' said Toby.

'*Grazie, bello*. Is kind of *vino*. I make myself. You like?' He looked hopefully from me to Caroline.

'It's delicious, Bortolin,' she said.

'Ah, *mi piace*, *Signora*.' He recorked the bottle and gave it to me. 'You drink more. Very good for love.' He grinned as Besina hit him.

The drive-round took all afternoon and it was dusk when we returned to the house, where supper was waiting. Caroline was unusually silent at the meal. 'Are you feeling quite well?' I asked. 'Was the drive-round too tiring?'

'Not at all,' she said. 'I enjoyed it. I enjoyed it very much.'

'So . . .'

'So I enjoyed it. That is all.'

Meryll and Isabel glanced at each other and began to talk about the weather.

'I suppose you will return to London now,' Caroline said later, when I walked her up to her rooms.

'I was planning to, yes. The opera . . .'

'Shall I come?'

'Would you like to?'

'Not really.'

'Would you like some new gowns? I'll send Monsieur Duplis out with the latest materials.'

'Yes, that would be nice. He always cheers me up.'

'Do you need cheering?'

'Oh, I don't know.'

I made a mental note to buy her some new jewels.

She yawned, sighed, turned away and sat at her dressing table. We looked at each other in the mirror; I kissed her cheek and left as her maid stepped forward to unpin her hair.

Downstairs I sought out Isabel. 'Is something the matter with Caroline that she is not telling me?'

'Oh, Francis,' Isabel said. 'Really, for such an intelligent man you are astoundingly stupid.'

'I am?'

'Without a doubt.'

'Are you going to tell me where my stupidity resides?'

'Should I?'

'Oh, for God's sake. Is this some kind of woman thing that a man cannot possibly understand? Because if it is, I'm glad. I'll just stay stupid, thank you very much, and I'm sure you women are clever enough to deal with it.'

I retreated to the library. I had acquired about thirty of Tobias's books on magic and alchemy; I read and reread them, studied them, scrutinised them, but, although I found a great many references to doors and keys, objects whose metaphoric pliability made them susceptible to innumerable symbolic interpretations, I found no clue to the nature or location of the door whose key hung so heavily around my neck, next to that other weighty chain.

The matter of alchemy itself, as a practical undertaking rather than a metaphysical proposition, was one I had not settled. I built

445

a laboratory at Farundell and equipped it with the latest apparatus. I made a list of formulae I wished to test, from Tobias's books and from others. I assembled ingredients and spent a lot of time making neat labels for my jars. I had even stoked the ovens and prepared a bain-marie, but an awful sense of futility paralysed me and I could not proceed with the first experiment. I thought about Erasmus Enderby, with his twenty-eight attempts at the Great Work, all failures that he never fully understood. He just tried and tried and tried until he died. The thought of spending my life like him filled me with dread, so I had the equipment packed away and abandoned the laboratory.

Tobias had ruined everything for me with his pronouncement about fate. He had condemned me to the knowledge that there was nothing I could do that would bring me what I sought: it would happen, or not. I suppose this might have led some men to a light-hearted attitude towards life, but only, I think, if they did not know what they were missing. I have never been able to decide which is the greater torment: hope, or the absence of hope.

95
The Nightingale

I spent the rest of the autumn in London. My little novel, *The Rosicrucian*, had finally achieved realisation as an opera. Several librettists had come and gone over the years; I had tinkered with it as well, and it was no longer the naive adventure it had been. Maestro Handel's health had wavered and funding had repeatedly fallen through, but Sandro's commitment to the project had kept it alive. They had turned it into a bit of an epic, with horses, chariots, fireworks and a flying dragon, but that is what audiences expect. Something of the spirit of the original, however, was preserved in Sandro's final bittersweet aria about the sorrows of immortality, as he walks off into the East. It had been a triumph, and was held over for a further six performances.

Sandro announced his retirement during his fifth curtain call after the final performance. It was a shock to everyone, even to me, waiting backstage; the audience responded with disbelieving silence, followed by wails and cries of 'No! No!'

I had detected not the slightest flaw in his voice, his presence, his power, but afterwards, when we were for a brief moment alone in his dressing room, he turned to the basin and vomited a stream of blood.

'My God, Sandro, how long has this been going on?'

'A few weeks.' He emptied his pockets of bloodstained handkerchiefs. 'Francesco, I . . .' He lowered himself gingerly to a chair. 'I do not know what to do. I am afraid.'

'What do the doctors say?'

'Nothing. Everything. Anything.'

'You are coming home with me.'

At Farundell I made up a suite of ground-floor rooms for him in the new wing: a sitting room with french doors looking out over the gardens and lake; on one side a bedroom and associated *cabinets*, on the other a salon where we installed his harpsichord.

I worried that he would suffer from the cold and damp. We talked about going to Italy for the winter, but we both knew that he had not the strength for the journey. I had the fires in his rooms kept going day and night, and the warm bricks at his feet regularly replaced. Oddly enough, none of the servants minded the extra work. The Nightingale, they called him, and clustered at the keyhole to hear him sing, which he could no longer do every day.

447

He was very ill through December and January, but as the days grew longer and the sun strengthened I began to hope that he would recover. We opened the doors of his room; he sat on the terrace with a blanket over his legs. The white rose, Madame Alfred Carrière, that covered the side of the house bloomed with astonishing profusion that year, filling the air with fragrance. It was a spring of exceptional sweetness, followed by a gentle, balmy summer.

I read to him in the long evenings, with the doors open to the night and moths fluttering around the lamp: Dante, though he would have only the *Paradiso*; D'Urfé's *L'Astrée*, which had the virtue of being endless.

An owl frequented the tall beech tree near the house and Sandro took great pleasure in duetting with him. It so confused the poor bird that he would fly down in a sudden silent swoop to perch on the open door and peer, perplexed, into the room.

'Do you have any idea what you are saying to him?' I whispered, trying to suppress my laughter.

'I am saying . . .' and he began to put words to his melodious hoots, '*tu, tu, tu, tu mi, tu mi, tu mi, tu mi chiama caro, caroooo . . .*'

People had discovered where he was; there were sacks of letters and a steady stream of hopeful callers. He saw no one; he answered no letters. After a life spent pleasing and performing, he shut everyone out as completely as he had once served them. The exception was Maestro Handel, who came often, played the harpsichord and talked with him late into the night while I sat quietly in a corner.

I had to admit that he was not getting any better, and against his wishes I sent for doctors from London. One said consumption; one said retention of the putrid humours; another drew up his astrological chart and reported that he would improve when Saturn had ceased to occlude his Venus. Sandro took no medicines, would submit to no treatments and refused to allow any of them to touch him. He weakened steadily and one day he could no longer walk. We cut down the legs of his harpsichord and carried him to it, but soon he could not raise his arms to play, so I played for him.

His voice was fading, but still pure and clear as water. He could no longer sing the huge, complex arias that had made him famous; instead he returned to the sad, devout music of his childhood: Lotti, Vivaldi – the *Stabat Mater* – which reminded me of the Contessa and her garden. I told him stories, spinning out my encounter with her into a long, many-chaptered romance because he didn't want it to end.

The children visited him every day and he sang with them on those days when he was feeling strong. I commended him for his tolerance of their lack of ability.

'I love to see them,' he said. 'Francesco, I have a confession.'

'What, *caro*?'

'Sometimes I pretend that they are mine.' There were tears in his eyes.

'Would you have chosen differently?'

'Yes! No. I do not know.'

'You have touched perfection. And given a taste of it to thousands.'

'But I am not natural, and I wonder if that itself is not a sin? If I am not a living, breathing sin, here in my unnatural body?'

I sat on the bed and put my arm around him. He leaned against me with a sigh. Was nature incompatible with perfection, I wondered, and was it wrong, then, to alter nature if one could?

His fox-trimmed dressing gown hung loosely from his thin shoulders, the lavish red and gold accentuating the pallor of his face. One day he could not sit up unaided; soon he could barely speak. I asked if I should send for a Catholic priest. He shook his head, but requested that the harpsichord be brought close to his bed and that I should play. 'Music is my only god,' he whispered. It was the last time he spoke. He died just before dawn, while I was playing Purcell's 'Fairest Isle'.

England and all the courts of Europe went into mourning as if for the death of royalty. Official people came with an immense gilded coffin and elaborate equipage to carry him to London, where he was to lie in state before being interred with all pomp and ceremony. I walked with him to the gates of Farundell. A large and silent crowd had gathered; I read in the papers, later, that hundreds of his devotees walked behind his coffin all the way to London.

96

Belwood

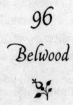

I stayed in town after the funeral, reluctant to bring my dismal mood to Farundell. With Sandro's death, the world had lost the only fragment of perfection I had ever found in it. It opened a chasm into which all other good things were inexorably sliding. Colour, beauty, joy, pleasure – all draining away, leaving a world of grey and darker grey.

I went home, of course, for a few days now and then, but the semblance of family life only served to accentuate my isolation. Isabel and Meryll tried to draw me out, but I had nothing to say. Even the children stopped coming to me, repelled by the black cloud that enveloped me. My gloom was compounded by the sad news that my brother Clarence had perished of some horrid tropical disease on his sugar plantation in Barbados.

One day, as I was about to return to London, Caroline told me that she had taken a lover.

The only person whose company I could bear was Eliza Quill. She had no illusions about the world. Her memoirs had been a great success and she was now a celebrated author, under her nom de plume Stylus Curvus: the bent pen. She still kept her salon, but it was very refined these days, more literary than licentious, though there were certain upstairs rooms accessible only to a few.

I passed the time gambling at her faro table, and though I wagered recklessly, not caring whether I won or lost, I usually won. No matter what I did, the world accrued around me, encrusting me with possessions and obligations. Sometimes I wished I had followed Tobias into the East, even though I would have died of starvation on the way.

Although I did not pick quarrels as I once had, from time to time a quarrel came my way. In the past, my spirits would have leapt at the thought of a duel but now I backed down. The first time this happened I could not understand my own response. I was not in the wrong, therefore I should welcome the fight. But I realised with a shock that I was afraid to die. If somewhere in my fate was the possibility of immortality, I dared not risk my life in some wanton, pointless duel. What was at stake was so much greater than it had been before, when my death was an inevitability. And so, although I did not enjoy life, I clung to it.

Ever since my return to England, I had been buying houses. Bonnerby – the agent I'd met in Highgate all those years ago, and who'd helped with the purchase of the New Eden land – had prospered and was now a prominent man of business. He managed my properties with both competence and honesty, a rare combination.

As I acquired each new building I would search it from top to bottom for a door to fit Tobias's key; after that, I left it to Bonnerby to install tenants, renovate, tear down or sell on as he saw fit. I was, of course, only interested in buildings of a certain age. I'd had the key examined by an expert, who said it was characteristic of English mid-sixteenth-century work, so the door was almost certainly in existence during what I assumed was Tobias's original lifetime. It troubled me that fate had not only to lead me to the door, but also preserve the building in which it stood until I should happen upon it. I saw old buildings being torn down every day, and only with an effort did I prevent myself from interrupting the demolition to run through them trying all the locks.

Once a month Bonnerby would present the previous month's accounts and a list of potential new purchases. It is to such a small thing as an item on Bonnerby's list for November 1743 that I date the first indication that my life had turned in a new direction, though I did not recognise it at the time. Indeed, I did not recognise the item on the list until he drew my attention to it.

'Do you remember that old house, my lord?'

'Which old house?'

'That one on Highgate Hill, where I met you, oh, what was it, twenty-five years ago. It's called Belwood.' He pointed it out on the list. 'It's a bit run down. Hasn't been lived in for some time, apparently. Just a caretaker, ancient fellow.'

'Buy it. I'll go and take a look at it now. Meet me there with the papers.'

How odd it felt, to be riding out of London on the road north, past the church, up the steep hill, just as muddy and crowded with oxcarts and cattle for the market, on a chilly day not unlike the first, with the sun breaking through the clouds and a brisk north wind.

I had made such a myth of the place in my own mind and, lately, in stories for Sandro, that it was a shock to see it in material form. It was, as Bonnerby had said, a bit run down. Moss grew on the roof, a few slates were missing. Several windows were broken and weeds clustered around the front door. I paused and touched the weathered oak lightly with one finger.

The door was opened before I knocked by an old man, bent, bespectacled and unkempt. I explained that I had just bought the house, gave him a shilling and told him to leave me alone.

'Eh?' he said.

Perhaps he was deaf. I made gentle shooing motions; he shuffled off towards the stables, clutching the shilling and laughing to himself. Perhaps he was a bit mad.

I went first to the garden. Of course there was no pyramid, but the yews were still here, and the fishpond, although it was dry and cracked. The garden had all but reverted to nature, but I recognised rose-bushes beneath a smothering honeysuckle.

In the house I walked slowly from room to room, wondering at the mingling of past and present, real and imagined. It was empty, shabby, cobwebbed. Floorboards creaked. Weak sun slanted through the dirty windowpanes and the cold air smelled of old fires and mould. I went over it three times but there was no door whose lock fitted my key.

I was curious to find out who had owned the house, but when Bonnerby arrived with the deeds there was nothing of interest. It had been in the hands of a succession of investors and tenants for the last seventy-five years. Before that, it had been owned by the Crown, seized for non-payment of taxes from . . . and that was where the documentation ended, but for a brief note stating that earlier records had been destroyed in the Great Fire of 1666. The names of the various tenants who had lived at Belwood over the years were not recorded, only the annual income and expenditures. When I sought out the caretaker to ask what he might know of previous inhabitants, he was not to be found.

I instructed Bonnerby to have the place repaired and renovated, but gently, so as not to disturb the patina of memory. I didn't yet know what I wanted to do with it, but I took it as a good sign that fate had made it mine.

In the following weeks I found myself often drawn to Belwood to check on the builders' progress. Once the chimneys had been cleaned and jointed, I ordered that fires be kept going in all the rooms to drive out the damp. I had the stables extended, a new kitchen added. I hired gardeners to restore the parterres and rebuild the fishpond; I bought ten golden tench and took them up myself, in a barrel, in my carriage. I even had a little wooden summer-house built in the shape of a pyramid.

It was only half an hour's drive from the centre of town, or a bit more if the roads were very busy, but so peaceful and quiet that it might have been in the middle of the countryside. I stood in the garden one evening after the builders had gone. It was silent but for the wind in the trees and the churr of a nightjar; the air was full of the scent of fallen leaves. My ears had become accustomed to the din of London; my nose to the stench. I breathed deeply; a small wave of happiness passed through me. It had never occurred to me that I could feel so at home anywhere but Farundell. I knew, then, that I would live at Belwood.

From Farundell and St James's Square I brought only a few paintings and several hundred books. Having lived my entire life with inherited or rented furniture, I found unexpected pleasure in buying and arranging it. I had a large house to furnish: I needed beds and chairs, tables and couches; armoires, commodes, *torchères*; dressing tables, *secrétaires*, bureaux and cabinets, vases and mirrors and lamps, china, silver, linen and glass. I became a connoisseur of silky mahoganies, of ebonies and ivories, glowing rosewood, kingwood and calamander; finely turned legs and sinuous carvings; ormolus, inlays and marquetries. I had the rooms painted in sumptuous colours, with the paint scented according to Tobias's recipes that I'd found at Château Langenfeld.

I bought rugs, gorgeous rugs, to remind me of the East. This would be my little Ottoman palace. I considered hiring turbaned Orientals but settled for a good English housekeeper, Mrs Jessom – cousin of my housekeeper at Farundell – and left it to her to hire cooks and maids and footmen. Tunnie was at last showing his age, though he would never admit it. I arranged for an assistant – a bright young Butterfield who'd been a junior footman at St James's Square. He drove the poor lad mercilessly, but one night I caught him teaching the boy to read.

I went to Farundell to fulfil my Christmas duties, of course, but the atmosphere was strained. Meryll and Isabel had moved into Turton Park, and though we visited constantly back and forth, Caroline and I were alone with each other more than was comfortable. She wanted to be with her lover, I wanted to be at Belwood, the children wanted to be with their cousins. Thank God it only lasted a fortnight; by Epiphany I was back in London. Soon afterwards, Caroline wrote to say that she was going to Paris.

97
A Long, Slowly Unfolding Story

❦

March 1744

The woman turned heads as Eliza escorted her to the faro table and introduced her as the Baroness de St Germain, adding sotto voce in my ear that she was very wealthy and recently widowed. The Baroness was dressed in mournful black bombazine, displaying a very unmournful décolletage adorned by a glittering diamond necklace.

I rose and bowed. 'Is it Baroness Esther de St Germain or Baroness Jeanne-Colette de St Germain?'

'Baroness . . . Esmeralda de St Germain.' I caught the shadow of a smile as she took her seat across from me and placed her bet. I put my guinea on the same card; we won. For about an hour I followed her bets across the board and our run of luck continued. Then I started playing other cards; luck stayed with me but deserted her. She lost all she had won, and more. She was admirably composed but I noticed that her hand trembled as she placed her last guineas on the nine and the seven. I played eight and won.

She unfastened her necklace and laid it on the board across the high cards. There was a sudden hush.

'Too much,' the dealer said. 'No one will play with you, Madame.'

'I will.' I pushed my pile of guineas forward on to the low cards and added my rings, pocket watch, a sapphire pin.

'Is Madame satisfied?' he asked her. She nodded.

The banker tapped the shoe and laid out his card: a seven, just in the middle. If the next card was higher, she won; if lower, I won. The odds were slightly in her favour; by my count, more low cards had been played than high ones, but I trusted my luck. It was a four.

She recoiled as if struck, then stood and left the table. I stuffed my winnings into my pockets and hurried down the stairs after her. I found her in the entry hall.

'Would you care to join me for supper, Baroness?' I asked as we waited for a footman to bring our cloaks and hats.

'No, thank you, Lord Damory.'

'Or a drink, perhaps? Champagne, or coffee?'

'No, thank you.'

The footman appeared, helped her into her cloak and opened the door. It was raining, a sleety, freezing rain; the street was a mire of frozen mud. She began walking away.

I put on my cloak and hat and followed. 'Is your carriage not here?'

She didn't answer.

'May I offer you a ride?'

'That is very kind,' she called over her shoulder, 'but I would not wish to trouble you.'

I got into my carriage and instructed my driver to follow her. Within a few steps her skirts were soaked and dragging. She struggled on for several streets, then she stopped, as did we. I opened the door. She climbed in.

'Where are you going?' I asked her.

She shrugged.

'Where do you live?'

'I have no lodgings at present.'

She was shivering; I wrapped her in a fur, poured her a brandy, lifted her legs on to my lap, took off her wet shoes and chafed her icy feet. There were holes in her stockings.

'Esmeralda isn't my real name,' she said.

'Of course it's not.'

'Neither is St Germain.'

'And neither, I'm sure, is Esther or Jeanne-Colette.'

'No.'

There was a pause. Was she going to tell me her real name or was she hastily inventing a new false one?

'It's Rosalba,' she said. 'Rosalba de Witt.'

'It is a pleasure to meet you, Miss or is it Mrs de Witt?'

'Mrs de Witt. I really am a widow.'

At Belwood I turned her over to Mrs Jessom, with instructions to put her in the guest wing, provide food and a bath and anything else she wished. Tempting as it was to lock her in, I resisted. If she did not wish to stay I did not wish to keep her. Anyway, she could probably pick the lock.

Tunnie, who'd caught sight of her as she passed on the stairs, raised his eyebrows but said nothing.

In the morning I knocked on the door of her room and was

457

pleasantly surprised to hear her voice bid me enter. She was sitting in bed with a tray of coffee, rolls, butter and jam. There was a crumb on her upper lip, but I didn't tell her. She was wearing only her chemise and a fringed shawl that had been draped over a table.

I took the diamond necklace from my pocket and gave it to her. 'It's a fake,' she said. 'I suppose I should apologise. I would have cheated you if I could. I sold all the real ones long ago. But thank you. It reminds me of better times.' She fastened it around her neck, then let the shawl drop from her shoulders and loosened her chemise. The implication was plain: I had bought her.

Leaving that room without touching her was very possibly the most difficult thing I have ever done.

I told Mrs Jessom to find a lady's maid for Mrs de Witt, then I summoned a carriage and went into town. First stop, Monsieur Duplis. I ordered dresses for day and for evening, caracos, mantuas, capes, redingotes and so on, and sent him up to the house with fabrics for her to choose. Then on to the lace maker, the shoemaker, the glove maker, the hosier, the *corsetière*, the hatter – all dispatched to Belwood at my command, while I trawled through London's best jewellers. I wanted to cover her with gems, real ones: diamonds and rubies, sapphires and emeralds, pearls, opals and amethysts. I bought her rings and bracelets, necklaces and brooches, an enamelled watch and a music box with a singing bird that opened and closed its golden beak while flapping its garnet and tourmaline wings. At last I had something on which to spend all the money that had been piling up. I tore through the shops avidly, joyfully and very, very extravagantly.

I had my presents sent up to her room, but left her alone for a week while I went to Farundell. I had business to attend to there, and I loved to spend time with my children, but I could not stop thinking of Rosalba de Witt. I'd departed without seeing her

458

because I didn't trust myself to resist her a second time; also I didn't know what to say. She assumed that I wanted her as my mistress and I had showered her with expensive gifts as though she were, yet I most acutely did not wish to purchase her favours. I could not bear to lose her again, but neither could I bear to think that she stayed with me only because she had no choice. If she took the clothes and jewels, she could go away a free woman, with enough to live on for years. If she was still there when I returned . . .

Meryll had started work on the Temple of Aphrodite. We'd agreed that what was wanted was not so much an edifice as a picturesque ruin. The columns would be arranged as though they were the remains of a long-abandoned temple, some standing, others fallen. He had just finished building a barge; we watched from the shore as, one by one, the ancient columns were ferried across the water to their new home. In the meantime, the top of the island was being cleared and levelled.

There was a natural cave beneath the cliff at the island's western end; as I child I'd thought it was inhabited by bears. We were going to turn it into a magical grotto like the one I remembered from La Fontana. Meryll had purchased a hundred thousand shells from all corners of the world to decorate the walls according to a design based on an ancient Roman mosaic.

The island would be ideal for summer entertainments; we planned a pavilion overlooking the ruined temple where guests could sit and admire the views. I'd had the idea of building a resonating chamber beneath the pavilion, such as Tobias had designed for Madame du Bellay's mother, so that guests could experience ghostly music as they watched the moon rise over the lake. This was to be hollowed out of the limestone at the back of the grotto.

When I returned to Belwood Mrs Jessom reported that Mrs de

Witt had explored the house, selected a number of books from the library, requested meals in her own room and shown no sign of wishing to leave. She had asked to play the harpsichord and did so, with great skill, for an hour every day. She had many questions that Mrs Jessom couldn't answer, particularly about me. I sent word that if she permitted, I would call on her the following day. She permitted.

I went to her room shortly before midday, after spending a ridiculously long time deciding what to wear. She had been sitting by the window reading, but stood when I entered.

'Are you comfortable, Mrs de Witt?' I asked. 'Have you everything you need?'

'Yes, thank you.'

'The dresses please you?'

'Oh yes.' Her eyes brightened like a child's. 'They're beautiful.' She stroked the russet brocade of her skirt. 'This one is my favourite, but they're all lovely, the loveliest things I've had for a long time. And the jewels . . .' her hand moved to the triple rope of pearls around her neck. 'Thank you so much. But . . .'

'But?'

'But I wish I knew what I was being paid for.'

I shrugged, feeling suddenly shy and awkward. It was no easier to explain now than it had been five years ago. Somehow the fact that she was living in my house and wearing my gifts restrained rather than emboldened me. 'The weather is quite fine today,' I said at last. 'Would you like to come out for a drive?'

'Yes, I'd like that very much.'

'Oh. Excellent. Very good. So, then, you'll excuse me while I go down and order the carriage. Will you enjoy an open one, or is it too cold?'

'It's not too cold at all. I will enjoy a ride in an open carriage.'

I backed out. My God, I hadn't behaved like such an idiot around a woman since I was sixteen. If then. I ran down the stairs, very much like a sixteen-year-old, to order the phaeton brought round. As I paced the hall waiting, I reminded myself that she had agreed to go for a drive, not sworn undying love.

We drove north through the spring woods. She sat at my side; when I glanced at her, she smiled. The seat was not wide; on the turns she swayed against my shoulder and thigh.

We talked about the weather; so nice to have sun after all that rain. We talked about the birds; the air was full of their tweets and trills. She seemed to know all their names and habits and revealed an astonishing and very entertaining facility for imitating their calls.

I was trying to think of a courteous way to ask the many questions that were in my mind.

'I suppose you are wondering about me,' she said, with the air of someone steeling themselves to face an unpleasant task.

'Yes . . .'

'Just ask whatever you want.' She straightened her back and gazed straight ahead.

'I don't wish to be discourteous . . .'

'But you are naturally curious.'

'Yes, of course . . .'

'I've told you many lies.'

'Yes.'

'I wouldn't blame you if you never believe me.'

I had no reply. It was true that I was disinclined to believe anything she said, although that caused not the slightest diminution in my feelings for her.

'I will tell you the truth,' she said. 'I don't know why, but I don't want to lie to you. And it's not because of this.' She indicated her clothes and jewellery. 'So do please ask anything.'

'Very well, if you insist.' But where on earth to start? 'Who was Mr de Witt?'

'An extremely kind man who married me. He was old. He died

461

soon after. I didn't kill him but his son thought I did, so I had to leave Amsterdam in a hurry.'

I had planned to ask her about the mysterious deaths in Constantinople at the time of her hasty departure from that city, but suddenly I didn't want to know. The fact that she had thought it necessary to tell me that she had not killed Mr de Witt was in itself a bit disconcerting. 'Where are you from?' I asked instead.

'I grew up in France, near Orléans.'

'You are French, then? You speak English so well I could not have guessed. Of course you spoke Italian equally well, as I recall.'

'My mother was half English and half French, my stepfather Italian. I had a half-sister and a half-brother and three older step-brothers. I hated them all, except for my mother.'

'What about your father?'

She coloured. 'I do not know.'

I recalled the stories about her that I'd heard in Venice: a royal bastard, some had insinuated, though which royal no one seemed to know. I wondered whether all that was not a fiction she'd invented, to seem more interesting.

'I imagine that you heard stories about me,' she said. 'Philippe du Léran . . .'

'Philippe had only the kindest and most respectful things to say about you. He considered you a superior being.'

She laughed. 'I considered him one as well. You married his widow, I heard.'

'Yes. How did you know him?'

'I met him at a duel: his and mine. Needless to say, it never took place; we became friends instead. For various reasons I was travelling as a man at the time. I called myself the Chevalier d'Aragon.'

'You were the Chevalier d'Aragon?' I had heard of him, of course – the best swordsman in Paris.

'Yes.' She smiled modestly. 'It all came about by accident, really – a misunderstanding.'

'But wasn't he – you – killed by a masked stranger in the Bois de Boulogne?'

'Philippe helped me to arrange that, and I became Jeanne-Colette Vauregard du Mellisant-Plessis.'

Despite what she'd said about telling the truth, I was still unsure whether to believe her. Was this disarming show of honesty yet another layer of dissimulation?

'I heard that you were with Philippe when he died,' she said in a more sombre tone. 'I hope you do not mind my asking. I did care for him . . . I hope he did not suffer.'

'No. A swift fever.'

'Thank you. I am glad.'

'I still miss him,' I said, surprising myself with the confidence.

'He was so alive, wasn't he? He enjoyed everything so much, women and clothes and . . .'

'And conspiring with everyone against everyone else . . .'

'Playing grand games . . .'

'And winning.'

'No one can win against death.'

I didn't tell her she was wrong about that, and the conversation shifted to mundane matters.

We stopped for dinner at an inn. I wanted to ask her more about her life but she turned the tables neatly, drawing me out about myself instead. Before I knew it, I was telling her about Grace and Johanna, Agnes and Miranda; even about Rosmarina.

It had always been painful for me to speak of my past, but somehow, talking to her, things seemed to fall into place. For the first time, I saw my life as a series of loves rather than a series of losses. By her lively listening she gave me the sense that my knotted and aleatory life was neither random chaos nor punishment for my own flaws but a long, slowly unfolding story in which everything that now seemed so tangled and confused would, in the end, be combed out and understood.

We trotted home in the dusk, not talking, just listening to the evening birdsong. Back at Belwood I escorted her to her rooms. At the door I paused, studying her face for a clue to what she wanted.

Her expression did not change, but her eyes slowly filled with tears and overflowed. I kissed her hand and left her at the door. In the drawing room I drank a large glass of brandy, and another. If she sent for me now . . . but she didn't. I went to Eliza Quill's.

98

The Mystery in My Pocket

❧

The following afternoon I was jolted from my opium slumber by loud knocking. A too-soon awakening can lead to considerable disorientation as dream overlaps with reality; I had no idea where I was. The dim rumbling of passing carriages told me I was in a city. I was naked. A sleeping girl, also naked, lay at my side. She had honey-coloured skin; I remembered her name: Honeysuckle. I was in an upstairs room at Eliza's and someone was at the door.

I pulled a sheet over us and called out, 'Enter.'

It was Tunnie. 'I'm sorry to bother you, sir,' he said, 'but this came to Belwood. A groom rode all night from Farundell to bring it.' He gave me a letter, on which I recognised Meryll's handwriting.

It said: *Come at once. We have found something very interesting.*

There are few things more annoying than such a summons: cryptic yet imperative, requiring immediate action yet entirely uninformative as to the reasons one must act.

We went briefly up to Belwood so that I could change clothes and swap carriages. I left a note for Mrs de Witt, saying that I regretted having once again to absent myself, but I most sincerely desired her to make free of my house and all it contained, and if she wished to go anywhere, to consider my carriages at her disposal. It sounded unbearably pompous; I almost tore it up and went to see her instead, but feared I would sound even more so in person.

I arrived at Farundell the next morning, having slept – badly – in the carriage most of the way.

Meryll greeted me at the door. 'At last! You certainly took your time.'

'And good morning to you, too. Not another word until I've had some coffee.'

Coffee was brought. Meryll tapped his foot impatiently; I took my time. At last I drained my cup and stood. 'All right, what is this interesting thing you've found? It had better be worth it.'

'It might be, it might be,' he said, smiling mysteriously. 'I did say *very* interesting.'

'And I came as fast as I could, so what the hell is it?'

'Follow me.'

He led the way down to the lake, ignoring my questions. The shore was bustling with workers going to and from the island; we rowed over with the head carpenter and a huge sack of nails. He and Meryll discussed the corbelling for the pavilion roof.

We climbed to the top of the island, now mostly levelled. Meryll paused to instruct the team of builders who were erecting one of the columns. I could stand it no longer. 'Meryll, damn it, show me this thing at once.'

'Oh my goodness, Damory; I almost forgot about it.' He grinned as I raised my fist. 'Of course it might not be as interesting as I thought. Perhaps you have wasted a journey after all. Shall we go back to the house and have some breakfast first?'

I glared at him.

'So you do want to see it?'

'Yes, if you please, Meryll.'

'Well, if you insist. Oh, by the way, you have that key with you, don't you?'

'Key?'

'Your famous mystery key.'

'Yes, of course I have it.' I touched it beneath my shirt. 'What the hell have you found? It's not . . . is it a door?'

'Why yes, as a matter of fact it is.'

'Here on the island?'

'No, in Kathmandu. Of course here on the island.'

'What kind of a door?' It was probably the door to a well-house or a forgotten shed or something similarly mundane.

'An old door, a locked door. A door that someone went to considerable trouble to conceal.'

My heart had stopped; now it was pounding hard. '"If fate should lead you to the door . . ."' I could almost hear Tobias whispering in my ear. And though I'd lived for it, had I ever really believed it? And yet what else could this be?

At the western end of the island, where the pavilion was being built, a set of steps led down to the cave that was to become my grotto. It had been cleaned out and now a man was at work with hammer and chisel smoothing the walls in preparation for the shell mosaic. The noise was deafening; the man, I saw, had stuffed his ears with wool.

Meryll tapped him on the shoulder and gestured for him to leave, then took up a lantern and led me towards the back of the cave. 'When we started to excavate for your little music room,' he said, 'we found not the solid limestone we expected but a pile of boulders. We removed them and discovered . . . this.' He raised the lantern.

Instead of ending where I recalled, the cave continued for

several yards, converging towards a descending stair cut into the rock. The steps, narrow and well-worn, disappeared into shadow. Meryll led the way. The stair bent to the right, then bent again. At the bottom was a landing with several alcoves; in one of them was a door. I seized the lantern and examined it. Old oak, ornate iron hinges and, yes, a lock with a keyhole of the right size.

'I took the liberty of oiling it,' said Meryll, 'just in case your key should fit. How annoying it would be if it then could not turn.'

Scarcely daring to breathe, I lifted the key from my neck. My hand was shaking so badly I had to try three times before I managed to insert it into the lock. It fitted.

Meryll let out his breath with a hiss. 'Does it turn?'

I gave him the lantern to hold – I needed both hands to steady my grip. A rusty grating sound, a small further effort, then the key turned with a resounding click.

There was a rushing in my ears and at first I thought my heart would give out, then that I was going to faint. Neither happened. Instead I started laughing and couldn't stop. I laughed so hard I cried. It was infectious; soon Meryll was laughing too.

Eventually we had to pause for breath. 'What are we laughing about?' he said.

'Tobias.' I pointed to the door. 'It's all Tobias. He made the door, he made the key; he hid it and he led me to it while letting fate do all the work. He set me on course to find this place before I ever met him.'

'What do you mean?'

'His idea – the resonating chamber. When I first saw them at Madame du Bellay's house in Paris I decided I would build one. So I would have found this door, but lacked the key.'

'One could always break it down.'

'Yes.' But I had more than just the key. Open it with my blessing, Tobias had said.

'So are you going to open the damned door or are we just going to look at it and laugh?'

I opened it.

The air was old, cold and stale. Meryll held up the lantern, revealing a room with a mosaic floor and a low ceiling supported by two square columns. The light flickered wildly as he stepped forward; I glimpsed statues in niches and painted walls. At the far end of the room, the shifting shadows revealed a tall figure with an animal's head.

'My God, Damory, I think this is a temple – a Roman temple. Look at that statue – it's Hermanubis, with his jackal head, and here's Isis, and another Isis. This floor – the pattern is just like one I saw at Corfinium. How could such a place have remained hidden for so long? And why hide it?'

Why indeed?

Meryll moved to the end of the room to study the Hermanubis, leaving me in near-darkness. I shivered. I could feel Tobias's presence, as though he'd left an imprint in the chilly air.

'There's an inscription, Damory. It says *"Thesaurum non aurum intra celatum."* A treasure not gold is hidden within. Within what? Oh, I see. There's another room back here, come and look.'

Behind the statue was an opening framed by a pair of carved stone serpents; beyond it a passage into which Meryll was disappearing. I followed, banged my head on the low ceiling and stumbled, cursing, into a second room. In the centre stood a stone sarcophagus with a massive carved lid.

'I know what this place is,' Meryll said, 'and so do you. Don't you remember? Tobias Damory's Isis Society – the Book of Records said that the initiation involved spending the night in a sarcophagus in an underground chamber on an island somewhere up the Isis from Oxford. It was here, this is it!'

So fate had connected me to this place as far back as my university days. And at our first meeting Mme du Bellay had told me that I was an initiate of Isis – I had dismissed it as nonsense, but I'd thought of my island burial.

'And do you remember what he wrote about St Asher?' Meryll was shining his lantern here and there, revealing strange figures painted on the walls. 'That he wasn't Christian at all, but rather a priest in a temple of Isis.'

'Stop waving the lantern around, Meryll. It's making my head hurt.'

He put it on the lid of the sarcophagus. 'Who – or what – do you suppose is in here?'

'A good question.' There had to be more here than just an old temple, fascinating though it was. 'Shall we find out?'

'Let's.' Meryll put the lantern on the floor and we pushed with all our strength. The lid moved half an inch. We tried again, and again, and eventually shifted it a few inches at one corner.

At first I thought the sarcophagus was empty, then, as I moved the lantern about, scraps of bone were revealed.

Meryll peered over my shoulder. 'A foot, I think,' he said. 'That's hardly a treasure, is it?'

'I'm sure that's not all there is. Come on, let's get the lid off.'

'It's too damned heavy. I'll get some help.'

'No. Just us.' Whatever Tobias had hidden here, it was not likely to be something he or I would want the world to know about.

Meryll groaned, but planted himself next to me and put his back into it. We pushed and pushed, stopped to rest, then pushed some more until, with a thud, the lid tipped on to the floor and came to rest leaning against the side of the sarcophagus.

Meryll raised the lantern. A skeleton lay amid scraps of rotted cloth that turned to dust when I touched them. The skull was tipped to the side, the jaw fallen open, the ribcage collapsed.

'Who could it be?' Meryll said.

'I don't know,' I said, though a candidate had sprung

immediately to mind – Tobias's unnamed 'second wife' who, according to the legend recounted by Sally Bird, had vanished without a trace.

The corpse's hands had been folded on its breast. Beneath the pile of little bones I glimpsed a corner of something. I reached in and laid the bones aside, revealing a rectangular box of some black material – tarnished silver, as it turned out to be – about ten inches long, perhaps eight wide and four deep. I lifted it out and rested it on the rim of the sarcophagus. It was surprisingly heavy. I ran my fingers around the edges, discerning a clasp and hinges.

'We need more light,' Meryll said. 'This candle is about to expire. Let's take that thing up to the house where we can examine it properly. What shall we do about our friend here?' Meryll pointed to the skeleton.

'Treat it with all due respect, of course. Hold the lantern closer, please.' I picked carefully through the bones, stacking them neatly at one end of the sarcophagus. I wanted to be sure I had found everything Tobias had hidden. There was nothing more.

I locked the chamber behind us and we returned to the house. In the library Meryll went to the sideboard and poured us each a large brandy. I put the box on my desk; we drank and stared at it.

Why would fate have led me to this, if not to reveal some great mystery? And if the box turned out to contain nothing of any importance? Or if its contents had disintegrated with time, like the hands that had clasped it? I didn't think I could bear it.

'Are you at all considering opening that box, Damory? Because if you don't want to, I do.'

Did I want to? Yes and no. Unopened, it contained every possibility, even immortality. Opened, it might contain nothing but the end of hope.

I took a deep breath, opened the clasp and lifted the lid. Inside the box was a slender book, vellum-bound and tawny with age. It was very like the one I'd seen Tobias holding in the dream all those years ago, except that where the astonishing living rose had been there was only a faint stain that might have been blood, or simply the natural discoloration of the skin.

I lifted it out of the box, opened it and recognised Tobias's handwriting at once. First came a title page: *Liber Lapis*: the Book of the Stone. Below, the TGHD glyph. On the next page was an epigraph from Pico della Mirandola's *Oration on the Dignity of Man*: *Poteris in inferiora quae sunt bruta degenerare; poteris in superiora quae sunt divina ex tui animi sententia regenerari.* Yours is the power to degenerate to the lowest, the brutish; yours is the power, out of your mind and will, to ascend to the divine and be reborn.

I closed the book and returned it to the box. 'You never believed me, did you?' I said to Meryll. 'You thought I was mad.'

'I have to admit I entertained the possibility.'

'And now? Now that my key has found its door?'

'I don't know what to think.'

In all the time we had been friends Meryll and I had never quarrelled, though in recent years our paths had diverged. The distance between us had steadily widened but never been acknowledged, our friendship so full of habits and common memories that the gaps could easily be ignored. Until now. I'd known for some time that fate was leading me where few wished to go. I felt that I stood on a lonely hillside, looking across the valley to a man I used to know.

From the passage came the sound of scuffling and laughter, then Toby and Freddy burst in.

'We're sent to ask . . .' said Freddy.

'Say it properly,' said Toby. 'We beg leave to enquire, my lord, whether you will be so kind as to grace our dinner table with your presence.'

I stayed for dinner and supper and a demonstration of knife-throwing. Tunnie had taught the children his arcane skill and they'd been practising every day; Toby in particular had become quite good at it. After the children had gone to bed I spent a long time watching them sleep, then I summoned my carriage and returned to Belwood with the mystery in my pocket.

99

The Book of the Stone

❧

'*To Whomever in Whatsoever Age shall find this Book, Greetings. You have been led here by Fate, in which I have played a part, but I beg you to remember that the Choice to proceed is yours.*' So began Tobias's book.

There followed an account of how he came by the Stone, but as this was accompanied by the strictest injunctions that the story was not for the ears of the ignorant, I cannot repeat it here. In any case it does not matter; the Stone is what it is, a unique substance. It has passed, no doubt, through many hands and will pass through many more before anyone comprehends it. Of its origins – whether it is of this world; whether it is art or nature; whether it was made or found – he had nothing to say and I believe he was as ignorant as I.

Next came warnings, disclaimers and caveats. Tobias reiterated that although he had taken this path himself, he did not recommend it to anyone. His motive in providing this account was not to encourage but merely to inform. I brushed past this at the time; I had already set my heart on following him. I came to understand his ambivalence very well indeed.

The pages that followed, he said, contained secrets for which

472

men had killed and died. Only a fool would expect these to be spelled out in common language, yet the meaning would be discernible to those with 'ears of wisdom'. Those with 'asses' ears' might think they understood, but would waste their lives in vain pursuits.

All this had been written in English but when I turned the page I was confronted with a mass of indecipherable shapes and squiggles. At first I thought that Tobias's handwriting had become exceptionally cramped, then I realised with a sinking heart that it was a cipher. I leafed through the remaining pages – all in code. I was evidently one of those fools who had expected the secrets to be spelled out for me. Nevertheless, I did not believe that he would have used a code I could not crack, so I set to work.

I transcribed a few pages of the scribbles as best I could. By careful examination with a magnifying glass and a lot of guessing, I came up with a list of letters. Some were simple geometric shapes: upward- and downward-pointing triangles, a circle with a dot at the centre, a cross, a star. Others suggested objects: an eye, a serpent, a fish. Among them were symbols familiar to me from my alchemical studies; I noted that those for mercury sublimate and rectified pitchblende were particularly prevalent.

I attempted the usual analyses: which letters were most common, which appeared always or never together. I made no progress; I could not even tell if the original language was English, Latin, Greek, or, for all I knew, Chaldean or Armenian. I had not realised how absorbed I was until I felt a light touch on my shoulder and looked up to see Rosalba.

'You'll ruin your eyes reading in the dark.' She set a candle on the desk.

The whole day had passed; it was evening. I put down my pen. 'Thank you.'

There was something so natural about the way she moved around the room lighting more candles – a graceful, proprietary way – as though we had long been companions. A strange glow of happiness filled me as the candles' light filled the dark room. 'Thank you,' I said again.

'You must be hungry,' she said, and I realised I was ravenous. She went to the door and returned with a tray. 'I asked Tunnie what were your favourite foods and – in consultation with Mrs Jessom, of course – asked the cook to prepare them.'

She tidied the papers out of the way, pulled up a chair and served me herself, watching me eat with a small smile.

'What are you working on?' she asked when I had finished eating and leaned back in my chair with a sigh of satisfaction.

Accustomed as I was to deflecting questions that touched on my occult pursuits, I was astonished to hear myself answer with complete honesty. I told her about Tobias and the book I'd seen in a dream; I told her how I'd chased him all over the world; how I'd found and lost him. I showed her the key and recounted the discovery of the door, the underground chamber, the sarcophagus.

She listened, eyes aglow, interrupting every so often to exclaim softly or ask about some detail. 'And so this is the book.' She touched it reverently. 'May I look at it?'

'Of course.'

She opened it and read out the epigraph. 'Ah, from Pico,' she said. '*Oration on the Dignity of Man*. I do for the most part agree with him, but he should have said *Man and Woman*.'

'He should indeed.' Surprised to note her fluent Latin, I was even more astonished at her familiarity with that rather obscure two-hundred-and-fifty-year-old writer. 'How do you come to know Pico?'

'Oh, I don't know. One comes across these things, does one not?'

'Generally not unless one is looking for them.'

She leafed through the pages. 'But this is in cipher.'

'Yes, I noticed that as well.' I showed her my list of letters.

She drew the candle closer and scrutinised them. 'I love ciphers.'

No doubt her career as a spy had required knowledge of such things.

'Have you noticed,' she tapped my list with her finger, 'that quite a few of these symbols depict objects that are letters of the Hebrew alphabet?'

'No, I haven't. My Hebrew is a little rusty. Or non-existent.' I could not conceal my astonishment. I'd known several women who'd acquired some Latin, though it was far from common. But Hebrew? 'How do you come to know Hebrew?'

'My family were great believers in education. I'm told I showed an interest in languages at a very early age, so lessons were arranged. Don't you think,' she pointed, 'that this one is clearly suggestive of a fish?'

'Yes, it could be . . .'

'In Hebrew, the letter *Nun* means fish, so let us say . . .' she drew up a blank sheet of paper and dipped a pen, '. . . fish equals N. And this one could be a door, which is *Daleth*, D; this one perhaps a house, *Beth*, B.' She went through my list, accounting for almost all of the letters.

'That is astonishing,' I said. 'You are astonishing.'

'Oh, not really. This is a cipher, if I may say, that was intended to be read.' She put her chin in her hands and studied the book intently. 'What language do you suppose the original is? If Latin, this word could be . . . no, that doesn't work. Perhaps, like Hebrew, he's omitting the vowels. What are these little dots and dashes?'

'I've no idea. I thought they were ink blots.'

'No, they must be vowel points. In Hebrew, the points tell you how to pronounce the word. See, you have one dot, two dots or a dash, above or below the letter. That gives you six possibilities: a, e, i, o, u, y.'

We pored over the book for hours. The cipher was not going to yield so easily; the original, we deduced, had been written in English and Latin, with some Greek. The spelling was inconsistent. Certain words could be decoded into more than one language, certain complex notions seemed to be represented by single symbols. It was past midnight when we turned to the last page. It contained only four words, in Latin: *Scire, Velle, Audere, Tacere*. Know, Will, Dare, Keep Silence.

A log crumbled to embers in the fireplace, a candle sputtered and died. The room was almost dark. Rosalba stood, paused at my side, laid her hand on mine. We went upstairs together.

Towards dawn we fell asleep in each other's arms. I dreamed about the garden again, the same dream I'd had the first night I'd slept in the house. Rosalba and I went out into the night, naked in a garden fragrant with lilies and roses. We followed the avenue of yews to the pyramid; the door opened to my key and we entered.

100
Anything that Anyone Has Ever Said About It Is a Metaphor

I woke with the memory of the dream lingering in my mind, but try as I might, I couldn't remember what had happened inside the pyramid. Maybe, I thought, that is where we are now. I looked at the sleeping Rosalba, and the feeling of having come home to her, irrational as it was, filled me with peace and contentment. I had to laugh at myself; I'd always imagined that these were boring sentiments, proper to old men, or men who had resigned themselves to an ordinary life and no longer quested for the dreams of their youth. But the peace and contentment I felt was anything but boring.

She opened her eyes.

'Were you really the Chevalier D'Aragon?' I asked.

She laughed. 'Yes. Shall I prove it?'

'Later.'

I left her sleeping, pulled on one of my Ottoman robes and went downstairs. The book lay where we'd left it, surrounded by piles of paper with our transcriptions and translations. I rang for coffee and started to try to make sense of it.

The book was cryptic not only because written in code; Tobias's language, like that of every alchemist I have ever read, was oblique, elliptical, ambiguous, paradoxical. Even when all the words were spelled out, those with asses' ears could very easily be misled. Deciphering the code was only the beginning.

The text contained, without a doubt, the formula for an Elixir. The terminology, for the most part, I could comprehend: ingredients, processes, time. Asses would have been utterly lost in thickets of confusion, but I understood. Three terms, however, remained coded: *Prima Materia*, *Lapis Philosophicus* and *Soror Mystica*.

Since many alchemical operations involve the combining of opposites – often referred to as King and Queen, white and red, sun and moon and so on – it is not difficult to guess what is meant by the *Soror Mystica*.

The *Prima Materia* – well, no term could be more obscure. What the 'first matter' truly is has been the subject of dispute for millennia. Enderby had died laughing about it after spending his entire life testing every conceivable thing. Bayliss, and even Purefoy in his way, had searched for it, pondered it, speculated about it.

Tobias referred to it as *hyle* – a Greek word for the fundamental undifferentiated substance out of which the cosmos was formed – and as *alpha et omega*: the beginning and the end. He also called it the *Infans Purus*, the Pure Child, which I assumed was a metaphor, like the instructions that the child must die when it was three days old, be buried and reborn.

His references to the Stone of the Wise confused me. It was clear that the Stone was the crucial ingredient of the Elixir, the one required to ferment, as it were, the others, yet its nature was never even hinted at. I realised with a growing sense of despair that Tobias assumed whoever was reading his book was already in possession of it.

Rosalba came in. It made me smile just to see her; my despair vanished like a shadow erased by the sun. We rang for more coffee and I explained the dilemma.

'From what I've learned of your Tobias,' she said, 'I don't believe he made a mistake. If he says you have it, perhaps you do.'

She had to be right. What had Tobias known I possessed? I took the key and Rosalba's chain from my neck and we scrutinised them minutely. Neither had anything like a stone, unless it was very tiny indeed. Rosalba picked up the book, turned it this way and that. She reached for a penknife. 'Do you mind if I . . .?'

'Not at all,' I said.

She slit open the binding; there was nothing.

'Perhaps he intends fate to lead me to it, like it did to the book,' I said. 'If that's the case, it could be anywhere, searching is pointless and I'm back to where I started before I found the door.'

'But what does it look like? How big is it?'

I shrugged. 'I have heard it described in so many ways. It may not resemble a stone; it may not even be a physical object. It's possible that anything that anyone has ever said about it is a metaphor. One can only hope one recognises it when one sees it.'

Rosalba took up the silver box and examined it closely. 'This box seems quite heavy for its size. Unless it's solid silver, which I don't think it is.'

She passed it to me and I turned it over in my hands. I'd noted its weight when I first lifted it from the sarcophagus. I peeled back the silk lining to reveal a wooden base. Tapped, it didn't sound hollow, but it was thicker than it needed to be, more than twice as thick as the sides and top. This was surely where the weight originated. I tried to prise it up, but its edges were set under the side panels. In the end I had to take the whole box apart, peeling away the silver skin and separating the mortised joints.

The base appeared at first to be a solid piece of wood but close inspection showed a faint seam that ran all around the sides. I inserted the tip of the penknife and, very carefully, eased it open.

I understand why the Stone is often called Mercurius. It has something of quicksilver's iridescent mutability, though it is far heavier. The Stone that was hidden in Tobias's box was no larger than the end of my thumb, but it weighed twenty-nine troy ounces, three hundred and eighty-three grains. At least, that is what it weighed the first time; the figure changed. I believe the Stone is in a constant state of change, but to be certain, one would have to observe it for much longer than I was able.

Once the Stone was in our possession, the rest of the formula began to make sense, and after a few false starts, I knew I had understood it aright. The behaviour of the ingredients themselves showed the way; Tobias's book turned out to be somewhat less metaphorical than I'd thought.

Detailed accounts of laboratory work are of interest only to fellow chemists, and I have published these elsewhere, under another name. As Canon Ripley said, and truly one cannot say it plainer, 'The body is made spiritual, and the spirit corporeal, and fixed with the body and consubstantial with it.'

Like Tobias, I speak not to encourage but merely to inform. Let him who has ears of wisdom hear what I have said, for I have in these pages said quite enough. Let those with asses' ears hear what they will, or complain that they hear nothing at all.

101

Perhaps I Always Knew

❧

There came a morning, when the garden was full of the scent of lilies and roses, that we stood in the sun and changed for ever, my *Soror Mystica* and I and our pure child, dead and reborn in the Elixir of Life.

'Are you certain?'

'Yes, I am. Are you?'

'With all my heart.'

The transformation was instantaneous, but the full realisation of it took much longer and the ramifications have not ceased to this day. Yes, I can speak of it in a few words, but words can never convey the utter strangeness and the perfect rightness of the experience. Like ink dropped into a glass of water, and just as impossible to undo, the Elixir dissolved into us and united with our substance.

I felt the effects immediately and could see in Rosalba's eyes that she did too. An effervescence, a tingling, an ecstasy permeated every part of our bodies simultaneously and rose to an almost painful pitch. Certain activities suggested themselves; we retired to the bedroom. The sensations flowed in waves of all but unbearable intensity for three days and nights, then began slowly to fade.

Although it was gratifying to know that our Elixir had an effect, and not a fatal one (which had always been a risk, given that the

Elixir, by its very nature, could not be tested on anyone other than ourselves), I wondered how long we'd have to wait to find out if it had any more significant consequences. How long need one live before concluding one is immortal? We both felt exceptionally well, and noticed in each other a lively bloom. But that was hardly proof.

My first indication of a profound change began as an itch at the stumps of my missing fingers. My scars were next and within a few hours I was mad with itching. I tried every salve I'd ever heard of, but nothing gave any relief until Rosalba sent for a bucket of ice. I plunged my hand into it while she pressed rapidly melting chunks to various parts of my body. I itched for weeks as my scars disappeared, my ear regrew and my fingers began budding. It took a year for them fully to regrow.

When we realised that Rosalba was pregnant we were certain that this child, conceived in the bliss of the Elixir, would be special, unique, a manifestation of our transcended state. We speculated: a holy hermaphrodite, a pair of divine twins, a Herakles, a Horus, a saviour. The epitome of beauty, of intelligence, of wisdom; the final achievement of humanity, the golden child, the fruition of God's plan. We imagined that we stood as Adam and Eve to a new race of men. There had been strange portents in the sky – a six-rayed comet had blazed for weeks in the North. People said it signified something remarkable and we, in our infatuation with ourselves and our glorious enterprise, dared to wonder – though we pretended to joke about it – whether it had heralded our accomplishment of the Great Work.

Rosalba thrived and though I fretted when she insisted on continuing an active life, it was obvious that she was in perfect health. I did, however, beg that she forsake riding; she consented, but only on condition that I fenced with her every day.

She had indeed been the famous Chevalier D'Aragon. Along with language lessons, her obliging parents had provided instruction in every subject or activity in which she showed any interest: fencing, horse-riding, chariot-racing, archery, pistol-shooting, mathematics, astronomy. She'd thought this was the usual thing and, when she left her sheltered home at the tender age of fifteen, was shocked to learn what narrow lives most children led.

I asked her about that time in her life, but it took much cajoling to get the story. She had run off with her music tutor, who had abandoned her in Naples. That was all she would say. I can only imagine how she survived, alone and friendless in a strange city. Her parents must have been in agonies. I wanted to track down and kill the man who'd seduced her, but she wouldn't tell me his name.

'Why didn't you go back home?' I asked.

She looked away and didn't answer.

'Were you pregnant?'

She nodded. 'And I had my pride, if nothing else. I did what I had to do.'

'Have you never returned?'

'Why would I? To beg forgiveness? No. I made my choice and I took the consequences. I do not even know if they still live. I prefer to look ahead.'

I thought about how that time had shaped her, turned her from a pampered, sheltered child into an adventuress, a duellist, a spy. She was courageous, resourceful, daring – I could only admire her, but such a life was exhausting. With me, she found surcease from the constant strain of having to make her way in the world by her wits alone. Gradually she let go of her masks, her weapons and her shields.

I could not marry her, but in order to ensure that she need never again live such a precarious existence I gave her property that provided an income of three thousand pounds a year. She chose the properties from my portfolio, more by name, I think, than by any careful assessment of their worth. She liked Green Dragon Court, White Hart Yard, Red Lion Square, Black Bear Lane and Blue Bird Alley, some fifty buildings in all. I had Bonnerby set up a separate account for her.

The child was vigorous in the womb, and when the time came he emerged quickly and with little fuss. I'd had platoons of mid-wives and doctors standing by, but none were needed. Our son flopped out, Rosalba said, laughing, 'like a fat wet fish'.

His skin was not blotchy and red as babies' often are but perfect white and rose. He opened his eyes – wide grey-green eyes like hers – and emitted one piercing shriek.

Thereafter he was a serene baby, nursing placidly and moving on to proper food at an unusually early age. His hair grew long, golden and curly, and his features soon emerged from infantile, amorphous roundness. He was beautiful. And clever. Before long he was speaking, not just baby babble but words, new ones every day. We made lists of them. Rosalba started teaching him Latin.

The subject of his name had been the source of endless debate. No ordinary name would do. Rosalba chose Raphael (from the Hebrew, meaning 'the God who heals', because we intended him to heal all mankind), Prometheus, for the bringer of fire, and Apollo, the god of the sun. More modestly, I added Perceval, for the grail-seeker in Arthurian legends, and Andrew, for my brother.

Perhaps we burdened his tiny being with too many names.

When he was a little more than a year old he began to change. His hair, which I loved to stroke and twine around my fingers, fell out in my hand. His skin developed taut, rough patches – but this was normal, we were assured. Babies had rashes, baby hair fell out and would soon grow back. But he was no longer thriving. He grew thin and frail.

The following months were full of unspoken dread. I watched him closely, but said nothing to Rosalba. She, too, was troubled, but said nothing to me. I think we both felt that to speak of it would make it unavoidably real. So we hoped in silence that Raphael would come through this odd stage in his growth and resume course for the perfection we had foreseen.

By the time of his second birthday I thought I recognised the signs; a year later he was scarcely half an inch taller and I was certain. I had seen this before. Raphael was like Jamal.

If Tobias and Ibn Sallum had found no cure for this condition, I had little hope that I could, but I tried. Raphael was of course too young for an Elixir of the sort I had achieved with Rosalba, but I made various attempts using his blood and his urine. The Stone, I found, would not dissolve.

I continued to hope. His intelligence was not affected by the progressive wasting of his body. He showed a keen interest in everything around him and had a vocabulary of hundreds of words. He was fond of animals, the cook's big orange cat in particular. I tried to keep them apart because it reminded me of Jamal and Ptolemy, but Raphael cried – one of his few displays of temper – and I relented.

It would have been better if Rosalba and I had spoken of our fears from the beginning. By the time the truth was inescapable there was a barrier between us. She had begun leaving the room whenever Raphael was brought in. The sick despair that filled me poisoned everything and at last I had to tell her what I feared.

I cannot bear to remember the look on her face.

Raphael was found dead in his bed a week later. It was like a sword to my heart, but within the pain was a tiny seed of relief, swamped at once with remorse. I turned to Rosalba, certain that, in sharing this grief, we would be together again. But she took it differently, with a brisk air of putting an unpleasantness behind her. I became ashamed of my sorrow, which made me silent. She took my silence for blame. I assured her that it had never occurred to me that the fault was hers, but in that perverse female way, she took my denials as signifying the opposite. The thought flashed through my mind that she might have hastened Raphael's death herself – a small effort with a pillow in the night – but I pushed it aside.

No matter what I said or did, she drifted further away. She grew angry over small things; she tried to draw me into quarrels. At night in her sleep she ground her teeth, clenched her hands and muttered incomprehensibly. She said that it hurt when I touched her.

At last came the explosion. I don't know how the argument began, but within a very short time we were shouting. I left the room, then returned when I heard her weeping. I evidently said the wrong things because soon she was in a rage.

. It is still, after all these years, painful to remember that night; I have as many reasons to wish to forget it as there are reasons why I never will. Words were soon insufficient; she began throwing things: her slippers, a vase, several books. I made the mistake of laughing as I dodged this way and that. Candlesticks, a clock, a bronze of Aphrodite – I caught that, one-handed; the music box, whose singing bird emitted a final diminuendo, squawked and died. Her jewellery casket landed at my feet, spilling its glittering contents. Not wishing to tread on their sharp edges, I stooped to gather them up while Rosalba searched for further ammunition.

A china elephant struck my back and shattered; I didn't notice. Among the many jewels I'd given Rosalba was one that I had not: a small and rather unimposing brooch, a cabochon ruby surrounded by pearls, set in rosy old gold. I turned it over. There was the inscription: *Gemma Ultra Pretium*. The jewel beyond price.

'How came you by this?'

She stopped, arm raised to fling the second elephant. 'My mother gave it to me. It's the one thing I've kept, no matter what happened. She said it was from my father.'

I did the calculations. Her birthday, just past, was the 8th of

August. She was twenty-seven, which meant she'd been born in 1718. She was my daughter.

Should I have been – as Rosalba was when I told her – filled with horror at what we had done? I tried, later, but couldn't feel it. Did I believe, as she claimed to, that Raphael's death was a punishment for our sin? Again, I tried on the notion but it did not fit. Who or what would kill a child because two people . . . well, I cannot believe it.

The truth is that all I ever felt for her was love, the most perfect and complete love it is possible to feel, love entirely free of conditions and regrets.

And, perhaps, I always knew.

Rosalba left Belwood with her clothes, her jewels and as I realised in due course, the Stone and Tobias's book. I thought she would return within a week or two at the most; then, surely, within a month or two, but she did not. It was incomprehensible. How could she live without me? With whom could she possibly prefer to be? She was my *Soror Mystica*; she could be no one else's.

We'd imagined an eternal life together; I'd couldn't imagine eternity without her. There were to be more children, further experiments with the Stone, other Elixirs, new discoveries. I had decades of work mapped out, and she had shared my every enthusiasm. Neither of us had sought immortality for its own sake, or merely to prolong the pleasures of the world. Perfection was possible, a way had been shown to us and it was our duty to follow it. There was another destiny for mankind, beyond the ceaseless grinding misery of suffering, disease, death; we stood on the cusp of a new way of being. The only possible choice was to go forward. Together. If she wanted to live as father and daughter, that is what we would do, though it seemed a waste. When she came home we would discuss it.

These thoughts spiralled round and round in my mind for

over a year as I awaited her return. I know she travelled because Bonnerby kept me informed as he arranged letters of credit for her in Amsterdam, Paris, Leipzig, Basel, Strasbourg, Vienna. I wrote many letters to her, care of her bankers in these various places; some, I know, were received but she never replied. When she instructed Bonnerby to sell everything and disappeared, it was as though I had been severed from my soul.

I spent three futile years ricocheting around the capitals of Europe searching for her. I looked for linguists, fencers, spies, apothecaries, Jews. I made extensive enquiries among the hordes of charlatan alchemists in Paris, Prague and Geneva and heard many rumours of transmutation, none of which led to anything other than fraud and sleight of hand. In 1751, disheartened beyond words, I returned to England.

102

No Natural Destiny

1767

For all that I had lost the heart of my life, there remained the satisfactions of the ordinary world. Perhaps fate had decided that I'd paid enough; my other children thrived. Caroline came home to Farundell at about the same time as I did, both of us bruised by our adventures. We were blessed with two more daughters, Flora and Amelia, whose births were miraculously easy. Caroline grew somewhat stout and developed a passion for quadrille. She died six years ago, peacefully in her sleep. After that, I let it be known that I had become a recluse; I was not ageing, and people had begun to remark upon it. The fewer people I saw, the safer I felt.

Tunnie certainly knew something had happened although he never asked for, or received, a word of explanation. He'd witnessed the erasure of my scars and the regrowth of my fingers, which I concealed from most people by wearing a glove on my left hand, ostensibly to hide the unsightly stumps: real fingers pretending to be false fingers pretending to be real fingers. Instead of arranging my hair to hide the scar on my face and my missing ear, he now arranged it to conceal the absence of scar, the presence of ear.

Any number of times I offered him retirement, a cottage of his own, but he refused. He had two assistants and ruled them with an iron fist; although he could barely walk, he supervised the care of my clothes with undiminished rigour. He was polishing the silver buttons of a new coat when he died.

I passed the years in reading and study; I made some translations of medical texts. I observed myself closely for the effects of the Elixir and last year published my findings – under my other name, of course. As far as anyone knew, Francis Damory, after his wild youth, settled down to a quiet life in the country. I kept mistresses, but just one at a time. I had five children by them, all of whom I acknowledged, educated and maintained.

Toby was twice-married, with three children of his own. To everyone's astonishment he'd run off to sea when he was seventeen, made a fortune and came home with tattoos. Tunnie's knife-throwing lessons had, he said, proved very useful. Freddy, his shadow, had tried to follow him but suffered so badly from seasickness that he went to university instead.

My eldest daughter Izzy married a politician and became a celebrated hostess in London. I tried to show an interest, but nothing bores me so much as politics, and I'm afraid I was constantly forgetting her illustrious husband's name. She thought I did this deliberately to slight him but I swear I did not. They had one child; another died soon after birth.

Amelia and Flora, my youngest, were charming and, if I may say, rather beautiful young ladies whose interests did not extend beyond fashion and matrimony. I paid their bills at the shops and offered dowries sufficient to enable them to be very particular in their choice of suitors.

Edward, my heir – soon to become Lord Damory – was steady, open-hearted and kind. Fortunately he married a very clever woman; they had two healthy sons and looked set to produce more.

Meryll prospered and was justly celebrated as architect and aesthetic arbiter. He was made a baronet a few years ago, which both satisfied and embarrassed him. He grew portly and a trifle pompous. He never referred to the day we entered the underground chamber; it was as though the whole episode had occurred in a dream. That is what people do with things that do not fit within the presumed pattern of their world.

Not long after we'd found the chamber, someone broke down the door. They were looking, no doubt, for treasure. We never knew for certain who it was, but Hermanubis evidently gave them a good fright; stories of monsters and demons began to circulate. I abandoned the idea of a resonating chamber on the island (though I did build one elsewhere) and eventually had the place bricked up. The bones in the sarcophagus were buried in our graveyard. Knowing no name, I had them carve a rose and a cross on the headstone.

Isabel's health was poor, and as she retreated from the world her youthful idealism returned. She founded hospitals and schools and collected, at Turton Park, a sisterhood not unlike the nunnery she'd imagined at sixteen. She rescued syphilitic whores and pregnant serving girls, derelict crones, the simple, the deformed, the wounded and the frightened. They occupied themselves with pursuits intended to bring peace to the soul: needlework, gardening, music.

Last year it became apparent that Isabel was dying of consumption, though Meryll found it impossible to accept. His optimism was an annoyance to her; she liked being with me because I acknowledged the truth. I stayed with her until she died. I stayed, too, to comfort Meryll, but I have never seen a man fade as quickly. He followed her within a few months.

We had one last conversation. I knew he was remembering the sarcophagus, the book – the startling moment when something beyond his understanding had occurred. It was like a secret that he'd folded away and only now, when all that he had been was dissolving, it came again to his hand.

'Everything changed then, didn't it?' he said.

'For me, yes.'

'You . . .'

'What?'

He shook his head. 'I do not know what you are.'

When he was gone I felt curiously alone in the world, though it had been decades since we'd been close. It was time for me to arrange my death and move on, though even then I sensed the encroaching malaise of pointlessness.

For twenty years I'd lived the life of a family man as though it was my last, my only. After all, wasn't it hubris to assume that I was immortal? With Rosalba it had seemed obvious. We were certain that it was our fate, the destiny of mankind, et cetera. Glorious ideas. But so far, all that had happened was that an ear and a couple of fingers had regrown and I looked remarkably well for my age. No, said my mirror. Not remarkably well 'for my age'. Slightly younger, in fact, than twenty years ago. And I'd had none of the agues and aches that trouble ordinary men, no infections, no gripe, no fevers. I'd tested myself every two months on an identical set of physical and mental exercises; my performance only improved. Cuts and burns healed very quickly; I was able to go for longer and longer without food or sleep. It could not be natural. I, perhaps, was no longer natural.

And yet ideas are harder to step out of than clothes. For most of my life I, like everyone else, had lived by certain large assumptions: I was trapped in suffering, limited in every dimension, hemmed in on all sides by forces beyond my control, hurtling towards an end that I could not begin to comprehend. My rational mind, if I had one, was entirely incapable of seeing beyond its own nose. I was dependent upon the good offices and kind intentions of God, or the gods, or whatever name one chose to give to the immensity beyond one's immediate field of vision.

If I was not natural, then I had to consider that I had no natural destiny, my life no preordained shape. What other creature could do what I had done? Everywhere in nature things can only become what they were born to be: the acorn becomes an oak, not a birch or an elm. I had stepped outside of all that. I'd been born human, but now? Whatever I knew of the rules of human existence might not apply. I was free of mortal fetters; I could choose my path, or so it seemed. The one thing, of course, that I could not so easily choose was not to have this choice, but that didn't occur to me.

103

Days and Nights, Sky and Earth

🌿

Time stretched before me: years, decades, centuries perhaps. What (other than wait and hope that somehow, somewhere, I would find Rosalba) to do with it all? There was no point in living a series of ordinary lives. I believed in the grand design; I believed that mine was no ordinary fate. One would be insane to covet immortality for its own sake, but the chance of knowledge, real knowledge – that was surely what I was meant for. I felt that I was uniquely placed to penetrate nature's secrets, to discover how things worked: what life was, and death, what God was, and man. And that is still true. Scientific endeavour requires nothing if not patience, a virtue I have perforce perfected.

I said farewell to my children and grandchildren as though I was setting out on an ordinary jaunt around Europe – an old man's fancy to revisit the fields of his youth. I would, of course, never return. I wondered if this was exactly what Tobias had done two hundred years ago, and who knew how often since? I wondered how often I would have to do it.

Edward, or rather, his excellent wife, arranged a grand going-away party for me. It was bizarrely like attending my own funeral – a strange experience, so strange, in fact, that the sadness did not strike me until later, and then it had plenty of time to grow and spread. It was as though I suffered each of their bereavements at my death; paradoxically, it was also as though I had to watch help-lessly as each of them died before my eyes. I began to consider the merits of a celibate life.

Everywhere I went I made enquiries and was told of women who could have been Rosalba. Some turned out to be other people, but some turned out to be people who had disappeared. I knew she was alive, somewhere.

I made my way eastward. In Constantinople I looked for Ibn Sallum. I'd corresponded with him for several years, hoping that he might have heard from Tobias, but he had not. We never, of course, spoke openly about anything of importance and eventu-ally I ceased to get replies to my letters. When I climbed the hill in the Old City I found the district in which he'd lived changed beyond all recognition. He had vanished and no one would admit to having heard of him. He had either died, I concluded, or pretended to die and moved on.

I spent some time with my old friend Prince Ibrahim who had, against all the odds, survived the decades of intrigues. I heard that he'd killed his mother. He had grown fat and abandoned hope of travel. Instead, he'd had England brought to him: an entire Jacobean country house, purchased, taken apart, shipped across the sea and reconstructed in the palace compound on Cyprus. He was curious about my youthful appearance but accepted my evasions with good grace. I was, after all, a great doctor in his eyes, and the possessor, no doubt, of more than one 'magic powder'.

At Constantinople I finally shed my first life and set out for the East under a new name, taking the role of a merchant. For fourteen years I followed the caravans as far as China to the east, north into Kashmir, south to Ceylon. Everywhere I went I enquired about local medicines, paying particular attention to substances reputed to confer longevity. I was looking for a Stone; I was looking, as well, for Tobias. I heard stories of strange gems that could transport the user to other realms or to endow them with miraculous powers, such as the ability to run for hundreds of miles without stopping, to tolerate immense cold, to breathe underwater, to be in two places at once, even to return from the dead. Stories, as well, of men who lived in the high mountains, needing no food, communing with the gods. I never saw a Stone, however, or met a man with any power other than that of persuading gullible people – including, not infrequently, himself – that what they longed to believe was true.

My ambitions for mankind began to seem absurd. What if I was just a freakish anomaly, a monstrosity, not the forerunner of a future race of men but the sad, meaningless and solitary result of a pointless experiment? Hoping to elevate everyone to a new heaven on earth, had I instead condemned myself to an eternal hell of futility?

I even questioned the Stone. Yes, something quite unusual had happened to me, but how certain could I be of its exact nature or purpose? The grand ideas that had marched like gods through my mind gradually wandered off into the immense mundanity of days and nights, sky and earth.

104

Another Life

❧

I returned to Venice, uncertain what to do next. What had I learned on my travels? Only that men are men and will do as men have always done: fuck and fight, live and die in wilful ignorance. They will be lifted to the heights of joy by petty triumphs, driven to the depths of despair by petty loss. Deluded and deluding, trapped in conundrums of their own devising, they wantonly abandon mind and will and declare themselves to be mere flotsam on an incomprehensible sea.

About myself I had learned that I was damned near indestructible.

While I considered my future and attended to financial matters, I rented a villa on the Brenta. It was oddly restful. Memories there were aplenty, but they did not torment me. I rowed back and forth past La Fontana and the Villa degli Eremiti, now occupied, it became apparent, by a family with a great many children. I watched them playing on lawns that had been a tangled jungle, splashing in the canal, fishing. One day they spotted me – I was fishing, too, near the spot I'd fished with Philippe all those years ago – and waved me over. I showed them Mr Walton's method of attaching worms to the hook and they were duly impressed. When they were summoned to the house for supper they insisted that I join them, and I had one of the strangest, most poignant evenings of my long, long life.

It was then that loneliness struck me like a blow. In the East, I had been a perpetual stranger. It was never a surprise that I had no close friends, never a disappointment. I had the sort of friendship one makes at the caravanserai: the friendship of a few nights telling stories, grappling with each other's languages, listening to each other's snores. I had not realised how alone I was.

In the autumn I left Venice and headed north before the passes closed. I found it most pleasant to travel light, with one horse and no servants. I lived out of my saddlebags and didn't even wear a sword. Bandits never troubled me; I suppose I looked too poor to be worth their while. I slept at inns when I found them, in barns or under trees. From time to time a farmer or a woodsman offered me a few days' work and a bed. In this way I drifted through Austria and Moravia, Bohemia, Saxony, Bamberg, Württemberg, deferring decisions about what to do with my life and hoping for some news of Rosalba.

Decades of experience had reduced my pharmacopeia to only forty-odd medicines, but these were truly effective and wherever I went I was able to help people with some, at least, of the ills that assailed them. Solitude, I accepted, was my nature as much as it was my fate. The life of the wandering doctor suited me. I did not even dream of women or family, of home or contentment. Time was seasons; time was weather.

I came upon the monastery of St Anthony at Isenheim at dusk one day in the spring of 1787. I approached from the east by unfamiliar roads and didn't recognise the place until I rang the bell at the gate, seeking a night's bed and board. It was even more weedy and shabby than it had been fifty years ago, the brothers indistinguishable from their predecessors but greatly reduced in number.

The poor Antonines no longer even existed; the Order had some years ago been subsumed into the Knights of Malta. And yet the place was not unpleasant; the ancient buildings had a kind of peace about them as they crumbled slowly to ruin.

I had not realised that it was Easter until, in the morning, I was roused from the guest dormitory to attend Mass. As I entered the dim, cold chapel and shuffled into a pew, I averted my eyes from the hideous Christ that writhed on the altarpiece. I remembered it well from my last visit. Even having seen as much human suffering as I had, it made me shudder.

In the middle of the service, amid much chanting and clouds of frankincense, a transformation occurred as dramatic, in its way, as my own. The image of the Crucifixion that both repelled and fascinated me was but the outer panel of the altarpiece. Two monks stepped forward and opened it, folding back the panels to reveal the Resurrection. There were gasps and murmurs; I think no matter how often one sees it, it takes one's breath away.

I was dazzled. The same hand, the same mind, had painted the tortured, grotesque flesh of the dying man and this awesome, incandescent god. Whoever he was, he understood something; of that I was certain.

The figure floats above its sarcophagus, whose lid has been flung to the ground. The guards lie tumbled like chessmen, shielding their eyes from a light too bright to bear. The risen Christ is smiling, holding up His hands with their wounds bleeding gold as if to say, 'See? I am alive!' His graceful white feet dance among the unfurling clouds of his winding sheet; His head dissolves in a spreading halo against the black sky. His whole being, and the space around him, is suffused with an unearthly radiance.

I knew how He felt. The painting depicted the experience of the Elixir as exactly as the Crucifixion depicted the true state of mortal man, nailed to the cross of matter, condemned to suffer and die.

Long after the service ended I stayed to gaze at it. I was not alone; most of the congregation lingered. The painting, I learned, would remain exposed until vespers, when it would be hidden once more behind the Crucifixion until the following Easter.

When, the next day, I made known my availability to treat ailments, the monks begged me to stay. Their infirmarian, Brother Jerome, had died a few weeks before. Although known as a hospital order, it had been some time since they'd been able to provide proper medical care. Brother Jerome's mind had been less than sound for years and few had dared to take the remedies he concocted.

They showed me his herbarium, his workshop. They looked at me with hope and trust and I thought, why not? I'll stay for a few weeks. It turned into months and, before I knew it, six years passed.

I'd brought seeds from the East and found much pleasure in attempting to grow them in European soil. Some successes; rather more disasters. One of the younger men, Brother Abelard, showed an interest in herbs and some skill at chemistry. I taught him my recipes and hoped that he would take my place when I moved on, which would surely be in the spring, in the summer, next spring . . .

I had scrupulously refrained from going to look at Château Langenfeld and heard no mention of the d'Amorie name. But one day I was crossing the yard when I saw myself dismount from a horse. No, I realised at once, not myself exactly. This man was perhaps sixty and I still looked about forty. But he was hale and lean and he had my face.

I'd stopped so abruptly that Brother Abelard ran into my heels. He looked from me to the man and back at me.

'That man looks like you,' he said. One could always count on him to state the obvious. 'Or more like your father,' he added, then took in my silent stare. '*Is* that your father?'

497

'No, of course not. I've never seen him before.'

'You must be related. I wonder who he is. Brother Augustine,' the gatekeeper was just passing, 'who is that?'

'Baron Richenveir,' said Brother Augustine, and the name rang a distant bell. 'He's here for the christening of his grandson. And look, that's his mother, the old Baroness.' The man was helping a very old woman out of a carriage. 'She must be a hundred.'

No, I thought, Arlène isn't a hundred; she's not even eighty. She was evidently rather blind, for she moved carefully, reaching out with her hands, but once standing on the ground she held herself proudly. A maid followed her from the carriage and arranged a velvet mantle over her shoulders.

A second carriage drew up and the Baron – my son! – turned away to attend another woman; his wife, I assumed, for she was near his age. She was followed from the carriage by a young woman and a nursemaid with an infant. I was transfixed; it was as though decades of family life were unrolling before my eyes. Here was another life that might have been mine: wife and son, granddaughter, great-grandson.

Arlène, left on her own, made a small, uncertain gesture to the empty air. I found that I was at her side. 'May I offer you my arm, Baroness?'

She turned her head sharply and peered at me. 'Do I know you, sir?'

It was an unexpectedly difficult question. I could not bring myself to lie outright, but . . .

'Forgive me,' she said. 'An old woman's fancy. It is only that I thought I recognised your voice, but it cannot be. I can tell that you are a man of middle years. Am I not correct?' She smiled up at me. There was that dimple, still beguiling. 'Are you one of the monks here? I used to know one or two of you, and my brother was Prior.'

'I'm not a monk but I serve here as Infirmarian.'

'Ah, a doctor. You must speak with my son. He studied medicine in his youth, but my husband died before he could complete his studies and he had to come home.'

I escorted her into the chapel for the christening. My son gave me a speculative look when I took a seat beside her, and I realised with a shake of inward laughter that he was wondering if I was a bastard son of his.

During the service, as we sat almost touching in the dark pew, I felt the question brimming in Arlène's mind. A silent tear trickled down her cheek and I took her hand.

'It's you, isn't it?' she whispered.

I squeezed her hand.

105

The Natural Dignity of Man and Woman

Even I, disinterested in politics as I have always been, could not fail to notice that France was heading for trouble, though no one could have guessed how much trouble, how bloody and prolonged. At the time, the remote obscurity of Isenheim seemed a safe place to wait out the Revolution.

There was much, in fact, about which one might be inclined to feel encouraged. The ideals of human liberty, of a new sort of state that reflected the rights of man, were appealing. Various pamphlets of the Philosophes came our way, brought by travellers and shared, surreptitiously, among the brothers. One in particular gave me a jolt. Based on Pico della Mirandola's *Oration on the*

Dignity of Man, and setting forth a series of declarations about the rights and duties of a new, higher form of humanity that it was our shared destiny to become, it was entitled *On the Natural Dignity of Man and Woman*.

In an analogy of my own step outside of natural destiny, it proposed that there was no natural social order. A slave was not born to be a slave; the masses of poor were not born to be poor. One man was not born to eat from golden plates while another was born to starve. Men and women were free to choose their fate, if they but cast off the illusory shackles of false beliefs. These ideas were so daring and dangerous that the author used a nom de plume, or perhaps I should say *nom de guerre*, as did all those writers of incendiary tracts. She, and it was obviously a woman, called herself La Rose Blanche: the White Rose. I was certain that she was Rosalba. I carried the pamphlet with me until it disintegrated; it was the only glimpse I ever had of her.

We heard rumours of uprisings, massacres, executions: the distant, tumultuous ending of the old order, now seen to have been nothing but a gilded charade. Some people were interested in overturning the charade; others in the gilding, which could be melted down and sold. Some were interested only in destruction for its own sake. Inspired by the highest ideals, men became beasts, sinking to the lowest extremes of brutality. Civilisation, it turned out, had been a paper-thin lid on a seething mass of violence and cruelty, held in place by shared delusions. Pico had said it truly: man has the power to ascend or descend. I have learned that most prefer the latter.

Still, it seemed that the chaos would pass Isenheim by, until a December night in 1793. I'd been sleeping in my workshop in the garden so I could tend to my potions through the night and was awakened by shouts and screams. I rushed out. With a full moon above and a fresh layer of snow underfoot, it was almost as bright as day. Something was afire; red reflections danced across the white ground from beyond the garden wall. When I got to the yard I saw that the dormitory was ablaze.

A mob had broken down the gate and was rampaging through the monastery. As the monks escaped from their cells they were set upon and slaughtered, their tonsures and black robes marking them as prey. In my shabby breeches and old coat, I evaded notice as I ran towards the chapel, whose windows were being smashed.

The looting was in full flow – the chapel had been stuffed with gold and silver and jewels, reliquaries, statues, crucifixes. Men swarmed over the altar, tossing down pyx, paten and calyx. Two of them had begun dismantling the altarpiece; they were wrenching off the outer panels and I glimpsed the luminous, smiling face of the god.

I was overwhelmed by fury at the thought that their crass eyes should behold Him, their filthy hands touch Him. Seizing a tall brass candle stand I laid about me like an avenging angel. Rage such as I had never known howled through my veins and I became a ravaging whirlwind. I saw nothing, heard nothing, felt nothing but the ecstasy of violence. The rages of my human life and the raw pleasure I'd taken in fighting other men were dim presentiments of what I felt now: the real thing, the pure thing, the absolute thing of which all particular instances are pallid imitations.

I do not know how long it lasted; I came to myself in the woods behind the monastery. While I held off the looters, a few lay brothers and servants had bundled the precious altarpiece into blankets and hidden it in a hay wagon which trundled away into the night.

I was alone. The moon shone through the bare branches, casting sharp shadows across the snow. There was a ringing in my ears as though a very great noise had suddenly ceased. My throat hurt and I realised the noise had come from me; I'd been roaring. I turned to look behind me. Flames rose from the buildings and the smell of burning filled the air.

The candle stand was covered with blood; I let it fall. At my feet lay a man with a shattered skull, fragments of bone gleaming white amid the red pulp of his brain. Blood was spreading, black in the cold light. A few paces on, another corpse, and another. I followed my bloody trail back to the chapel. I'd killed more than a dozen men, all by single blows to the head, some so savage that their skulls had completely disintegrated. I knelt in the snow and was violently sick.

I fled north via Luxembourg and Liège with nothing but the blood-soaked clothes I wore. Everywhere were signs of burning and looting, deserted farms, villages of ghosts and crying children. Corpses rotted in ditches, gnawed by starving dogs. I travelled at night and hid during the day as gangs of sans-culottes roved the roads, preserving the purity of the Revolution.

If this was the dignity of Man, there was no hope, no possibility of a golden future for a higher form of humanity, certainly no point to my life. We were not on our way to becoming more perfect beings; on the contrary, we were quite obviously heading in the opposite direction. The Golden Age, if it had ever existed, was a thing of the past, not the future; it would not come again. No great destiny awaited us; existence was not a glorious ascending spiral to godhood but a dead-straight line to well-deserved extinction.

Nevertheless the animal urge to survive, fractionally stronger than the despair, kept me going, applying all my intelligence and experience, my strength and endurance to the simple, primal task of living through another day. But even as I hid and ran, I wondered why I bothered. I had nothing but loathing for mankind; God was a joke; I was a killer, not a healer. What I had done appalled and revolted me, but at least I had learned the truth about myself and the atrocities of which I was capable. I swore that I would never again raise a hand against anyone, and I have kept my oath.

No doubt I should have ended it then, but across the ocean was the so-called New World. I had travelled as far east as I could; I would not give up on humanity without seeing what lay to the west. I cannot say that I felt in any way optimistic, I had lived too long for that, but I suppose there must have been an ember of hope burning somewhere. It was soon extinguished.

Though the nation on that side of the ocean has swelled in power, it is now what it was then: a trumpery of grandiose notions thinly spread over the crudest and most short-sighted self-interest the world has ever seen. Their own strength insufficient to the task of exploitation on the scale required by the sheer size of the place, they imported slaves by the million in order to spread their contamination further and faster. There was something, I think, about the vast and pristine beauty of the land and the relative helplessness of the native inhabitants that brought out the worst in people. At home in Europe, hundreds of years of custom and law had – usually – constrained them; in America, Man's natural brutality had free rein and a convenient ideological cloak. Leaders were valued for their ignorance; anyone with even the smallest pretensions of learning was shouted down, tarred and feathered.

I returned to England as yet another pointless war got under way, over what scrap of land or pride I cannot recall, fuelled by the usual idiocies to which men remain as childishly susceptible as ever: Country, Fatherland, Nation. I would say, God help them, but He went out with Humanity.

106

The Memory of Contentment

1817

Winter again: black trees, low cold sun. Smell of dead leaves, wood smoke. Breath blooming in the still air. Silence. Winters seemed longer, heavier, harder – or perhaps it was that winter thoughts had come to dominate my mind.

Careful as I was to form no close attachments, the time was approaching when I would have to begin planning the next life, and I was not sure I could summon the will. Another false death . . . how often can one man be lost at sea?

I dealt with my lawyers and managers by letter. Good old Bonnerby was long dead, but his son and, lately, his grandson have continued to serve me – or Them, as I call my successive selves. I would have to think of another name, construct another past. Even the thought of it exhausted me. Perhaps I could postpone the decision for another few years. I had houses in various parts of England and I moved between them, hiring staff as required. I dared have no permanent servants; in any case, I still missed Tunnie.

Over the last few years I had found myself increasingly unable to remain indoors; restlessness permeated my bones and I wandered the countryside for weeks at a time. I rarely needed food or sleep, but a man cannot, as it turns out, abide eternity. He has a beginning; he needs an end.

It was a frosty night. I was following deer paths through hilly woodland, not choosing my direction and with no idea of where I was. A small glow of light appeared through the trees. When I recognised Sally Bird's ancient dwelling by St Ælfhild's pool I thought I had stumbled upon a fragment of memory extruded from the past and dropped into my path. It was not so unusual. Memories had, lately, begun to seem more real than life. Had I thought I would forget things as they receded in time? Far from it. The more there was to remember, the more acutely I remembered it all.

Still believing that I was visiting a phantasm of my own past, I peered in at the window. There was the room I recalled from a hundred years ago: the shelves of jars and bottles, the dried herbs hanging from the ceiling, the warm flickering fire, Sally with her feet on the hearth. I was seventeen again, returned from the city soul-stained and heart-jaded.

She looked up and saw my face at the window. But this was not my Sally; the woman who came to the door had blue eyes and red hair and was surely no older than thirty.

'Come in,' she said, 'come in, stranger. Did someone send you? Do you need help?' And when I didn't answer, 'But you're frozen, come and sit by the fire. Thaw a bit, then you can tell me what you need. Sally Bird can help, whatever it is. Is it your wife with child? Or is it a sick child? The gripe? A fever? Never mind, you'll tell me as soon as your tongue melts. Here, drink this.'

I drank what she gave me, an elixir of berries and flowers, of earth and sun and distant summer. It tasted like the memory of contentment.

She watched me drink. 'So,' she said when I'd finished, speaking softly as though to a half-tamed animal, 'what ails?'

'The world, Sally, and my soul.'

'Oh, that.' She smiled, a smile like dark honey.

Somewhere in her was a spring of bright-flowing life, sweet and fresh. She led me to it and let me drink.

In the morning she made me an enormous bowl of porridge. 'A man can walk all day on a bowl of my porridge,' she said. I could probably have walked for a year on it.

As I ate, she talked. I learned that she'd been Sally Bird for three years, having taken over from her great-aunt, who must have been the daughter or granddaughter of my Sally.

'Tell me, Sally, I've been away for a long time. Are there still Damorys at Farundell?'

'Are there Damorys? Sometimes it seems there's nothing but Damorys. But you're a Damory yourself, surely you know that. You have the look about you. Handsome devils, the lot of you. Ah, you don't want to speak of it. Well, there's no shame in being a Damory by-blow, but it's not especially unusual. Let's see. The present Lord Damory's got two girls and one son by his wife, and a couple more in the village, and half a dozen, I hear, in London. But he's still young. His father now, the old Lord. When he died last year we tried to count them and gave up. No, no shortage of Damorys around here.'

I filled my flask at St Ælfhild's pool; Sally Bird waved from her door. The morning air was chill and damp. Mist lay over the surface of the lake and drifted across the meadows; a crow cawed as he chased a sparrowhawk across the wide white sky.

I waited among the trees above the house. Smoke rose from the chimneys; I caught a whiff of cooking odours. Several times I told myself to go away, but I lingered. Just one glimpse, I thought, as though with huge daring I planned a bite of forbidden fruit. I was afraid that I would be compelled to return again and again, but I need not have feared. When I saw them I knew: this was my last look. I had come to Farundell to say goodbye.

A man and a woman appeared at the door, followed by a boy of seven or eight. The child had a head of golden curls that it seemed I could feel beneath my hand. A carriage was brought round; they

climbed in and trotted down the drive. A wolfhound, held back by
a footman, slipped his lead and bounded after them, barking; the
carriage stopped, the door was opened, the dog jumped in and
they set off again.

107

The Body in the Chair

The world is round; I had run so far from Death that now I had
to meet him face to face. Having for so long thought myself
immortal, and lacking any clear sense of a natural destiny, I was
uncertain how to approach. Some notions are exceedingly hard to
shake off, and I could not help but frame my conjectures in the
language of my childhood: judgement and punishment or reward;
Heaven and Hell, or perhaps Purgatory. Even as I contemplated
these ideas I knew them to be absurd, yet I was unable to wash
them entirely out of my mind.

The technical details required careful attention; this body of
mine was not going to be easy to kill. Most deaths were ugly,
untidy and very unpleasant. I had an immense capacity to endure
pain, but that did not mean I liked it.

The easiest and least painful death is given by opium. A sufficiently generous dose of laudanum would send most people off on
clouds of lovely dreams; they would never know they were dying.
But opium no longer had any effect on me. The Elixir had, very
usefully, rendered me impervious to poisons – I had tested this,
cautiously. But it had also, very regrettably, made me completely
unsusceptible to intoxicating substances of any sort. I could not

get drunk; I could not even enjoy the mild pleasures of hashish or coffee. This alone made life not worth living.

I considered drowning. Having nearly drowned a number of times, I imagined that it would be relatively quick and painless. But I didn't think it would work; I feared my body would assert its will to live and, essentially undamaged, force me to survive.

I suspected that my body would survive anything other than really catastrophic injury. I wondered if beheading would do; it might well, but it would be tricky to arrange; also messy. I pondered how I might get myself convicted of some ghastly capital crime – attempting to kill the King, for instance – which could perhaps induce the State to do it for me. But I was unsure of the law. They might not cut off my head; they might draw and quarter me or something equally hideous and prolonged; they might hang me and I most certainly did not fancy hanging. In any case they would probably torture me first. Also I thought I'd find the presence of an audience – a jeering mob, for example – too distracting. This was to be the final act of my will, the culmination of my life; I wanted to be paying attention when it happened, not fending off rotten eggs.

No, it had to be private, elegant and absolute. I decided on burning: death and funeral in one, requiring neither assistance nor elaborate apparatus, leaving no mess, just a tidy mound of ashes. In India I had seen widows climb willingly on to their husbands' funeral pyres and perish in apparent serenity; if they could do it, surely I could.

For sentimental as well as practical reasons I chose the summer-house pyramid in the garden at Belwood as the site of my pyre. I'd left the property to each of my selves in turn, but had not visited the place for many years. The efficient Bonnerbys installed caretakers and saw to basic maintenance.

It was dark when I arrived. A candle burned in the window of the caretaker's room and an old man dozed in a chair – white hair, shabby black coat, spectacles awry on his nose – the Bonnerbys' caretakers all looked the same.

No need to disturb him. I went around the house to the garden and down the moonlit path to the pyramid. As my life had been an imitation of immortality, it seemed both fitting and, more importantly, amusing, to end it in an imitation of eternity. For all that Man had debased himself in innumerable ways, he was yet the only creature who could laugh about his own death. A small distinction, but precious to me.

I opened the french doors on all four sides and carried in armfuls of dry grass, leaves and fallen deadwood. I piled this in the centre of the floor and added tables and chairs. I'd brought a couple of bottles of whale oil and, on a whim, some frankincense and myrrh; these I distributed over the pile, soaking my clothes in the oil as well. Mine would be a bright and fragrant demise. Lighting a candle, I climbed to the top and perched on a chair.

I needed only the will to sit still; after all my wanderings, I thought I could do that. It was wonderful to know that I had taken my final step, that I had come at last to the place and the moment to which fate had, all along, been leading me: an amusingly circular bit of reasoning on which to end. I tossed down the candle.

The flames spread, slowly at first then very fast. The fire was so beautiful; I wanted to keep my eyes open for as long as possible. I'd planned to be thinking the most profound thoughts, but I forgot them all. Time seemed to stop, then unfold. I was watching, fascinated, as each licking filament of fire dissolved into a million spinning atoms of light when I glimpsed a figure in the doorway.

It was the caretaker; he must have heard me and come to investigate. I shouted at him to get out but he didn't move. Was he mad? Deaf? Extremely stupid? The flames were rising; he would soon be cut off. The doorway behind him was already outlined in fire. It was infuriating to have the peace of my final moments disrupted in this way, but intolerable that my act should harm another. Still the old fool stood there, grinning like an idiot. I flung myself through the wall of fire and pulled him out of the building.

He really was mad; he was doubled over with laughter. He straightened, wiping tears from his eyes, and pointed to the summer-house. The body in the chair was consumed in flame; it collapsed gently to one side and sank into the pyre.

I looked at it, I looked at myself, I looked at him, and looked again. I had seen him before; I had seen him many times. 'Are you Death?'

That set him off again and I had to wait until he was able to speak. 'Yes and no,' he said, guffawing as though it was the greatest joke.

'But I am dead, surely?'

Making an enormous effort at seriousness, he drew a deep breath like an orator preparing to declaim. 'Yes . . . and . . . no.'

Only God, I thought, could be so annoying. 'Are you God?'

'That is very sweet of you, my dear Lord Damory. I am not He . . .' a snort of repressed laughter, 'but we are as close as this.' He held up one finger.

'You're Mr Pym.'

He bowed. 'At your service.'

Epilogue

❧

Mind and Will

Precisely how I came to be stranded in this state is something I have not yet entirely understood, but there is no doubt that, as an experienced chemist, I should have known that the application of intense heat to a substance (my body) whose nature I did not fully comprehend was likely to have unexpected consequences.

I am not a ghost, which, as Mr Pym explained to me, is a mere fragment, a shadow, an aetheric automaton with no mind and no will. I no longer have a physical body, but mind and will I certainly still possess, and although I have had the opportunity to give considerable thought to their natures, they remain, in their way, as much of a mystery as Stone and Elixir.

And as for my own fate, that too is still unknown. Mr Pym tells me I have a role yet to play in the perfection of Man, but I never know when he's joking.

I'm here; I'm waiting, though for what I don't know.

Postscript. London, 1924

Everything has changed. I saw her today. In the back of a Bentley in Charing Cross Road. She looked straight at me with those grey-green eyes. I am certain that she saw me and recognised me; then the car sped away.

The greatest disadvantage of my incorporeal state is that I cannot hail a taxicab when I need one. But it doesn't matter. I have seen her. Rosalba is alive and I am . . . whatever I am. The story is not over.

Fate, though complete in itself, is the second in the
loosely linked *Time and Light* series of novels.
The first, *Farundell*, is also published by John Murray.

Notes

The opening scene in Mr B. Lytton's bookshop and the encounter with the mysterious Rosicrucian on Highgate Hill are my variation on a theme originated by Sir Edward Bulwer-Lytton in *Zanoni* (1842).

Fama Fraternitatis, or, A Discovery of the Rosicrucian Fraternity: the most laudable Order of the Rosy Cross is a 'real' book and Francis's précis of its contents is fairly, though not entirely, accurate. See http://www.levity.com/alchemy/fama.html.

Brother Renatus's Order's rule book is taken almost verbatim from the work of Samuel Richter, the early-eighteenth-century pastor and alchemist who wrote under the name of Sincerus Renatus. The notion of the 'Holy Guardian Angel' has been spliced in from *The Book of Abramelin* (Abraham of Worms, 15th c.).

Salih bin Nasrullah Ibn Sallum was a seventeenth-century Ottoman physician from Aleppo who – among other things – introduced Paracelsian medicine to the East. I trust he will not mind that I have made him immortal. Dr Moses Hamon (*c.*1490–1567) was physician to Suleiman I and sired a dynasty of Ottoman court physicians of the same name.

The descriptions of Constantinople, especially the arrival by ship, are taken in large part from Edmondo de Amicis's *Constantinople* of 1877.

The paintings of the Crucifixion and the Resurrection that Francis finds so compelling are part of the famous Isenheim Altarpiece. Now known to have been painted by Matthias Grünewald in 1515, it was for many years thought to have been the work of Dürer. I had always intended Francis to revisit Isenheim to see the Resurrection and Arlène. When I came across the story of the altarpiece's narrow escape during the destruction of the monastery in 1793 I had to include it. It's not known how, but the altarpiece was spirited away from a mob of looters and hidden in the nearby town of Colmar, where it is now on display in the museum. The Antonine monastery at Isenheim was burned to the ground.

For those wishing to time-travel to eighteenth-century France, I recommend the Cassini map, available online overlaid with Googlemaps. You can zoom in to an almost street-view level. It will guide you along every road, showing the post stages and the inns, the gallows and the ruined chapels, through woods and along streams, up and down every hill and valley. It will name every city, town, village and hamlet; indicate every vineyard, tile kiln, bishop's palace, cemetery, paper mill, church, cathedral, fortification and chateau. demo.geogarage.com/cassini/

Select Bibliography

Ackroyd, Peter, *London: The Biography*, Chatto & Windus, London, 2000

Edmondo de Amicis, *Constantinople*, Hesperus, London, 2005

Ball, Philip, *The Devil's Doctor*, Heinemann, London, 2006

Barbier, Patrick, *The World of the Castrati: The History of an Extraordinary Operatic Phenomenon*, Souvenir, London, 1998

Black, Jeremy, *The British Abroad: The Grand Tour in the Eighteenth Century*, Sutton, Stroud, 2003

Bon, Ottaviano, et al., *The Sultan's Seraglio: An Intimate Portrait of Life at the Ottoman Court*, Saqi, London,1996

Casanova, Giacomo, Chevalier de Seingalt, and Willard R. Trask (trans.), *History of My Life*, 12 vols, Johns Hopkins University Press, Baltimore and London, 1997

Churton, Tobias, *Invisibles: The True History of the Rosicrucians*, Lewis, Addlestone, 2009

Cruickshank, Dan, *The Secret History of Georgian London: How the Wages of Sin Shaped the Capital*, Random House, London, 2009

Denon, Vivant, *Travels in Upper and Lower Egypt*, 1803. free ebook.

Dobbs, B. J. T., *The Foundations of Newton's Alchemy: Or, The Hunting of the Greene Lyon*, Cambridge University Press, 1975

Dolan, Brian, *Ladies of the Grand Tour*, HarperCollins, London, 2001

George, M. Dorothy, *London Life in the Eighteenth Century*, Penguin, Harmondsworth, 1976

Girouard, M., *Life in the English Country House*, Penguin, Harmondsworth, 1980

Girouard, M., *Life in the French Country House*, Cassell, London, 2000

Hopton, Richard, *Pistols at Dawn: A History of Duelling*, Portrait, London, 2007

Hunter, Michael, *Boyle: Between God and Science*, Yale University Press, New Haven, CT, 2010

Kelly, Ian, *Casanova*, Hodder & Stoughton, London, 2008

Leroi, Armand Marie, *Mutants: On the Form, Varieties and Errors of the Human Body*, Harper Perennial, London, 2005

Mansel, Philip, *Constantinople: City of the World's Desire, 1453–1924*, John Murray, London, 1995

Mather, James, *Pashas: Traders and Travellers in the Islamic World*, Yale University Press, New Haven, CT, and London, 2009

McCalman, Iain, *The Last Alchemist: Count Cagliostro, Master of Magic in the Age of Reason*, Harper Collins, New York, 2003

McIntosh, Christopher, *The Rosicrucians*, Crucible, Wellingborough, 1987

McIntosh, Christopher, *The Rose Cross and the Age of Reason*, Brill, Leiden, 1992

McIntosh, Christopher, *Gardens of the Gods: Myth, Magic and Meaning*, I. B. Tauris, London, 2005

Midgely, G., *University Life in Eighteenth-Century Oxford*, Yale University Press, New Haven, CT, and London, 1996

Montagu, Lady Mary Wortley, *Letters*, various sources

Paracelsus, *The Hermetic and Alchemical Writings*, trans. A.E. Waite, 1894, republished 2007, Forgotten Books.

Pachter, Henry M., *Paracelsus: Magic Into Science*, Schuman, New York, 1951

Picard, Liza, *Dr Johnson's London: Life in London 1740–1770*, Weidenfeld & Nicolson, London, 2000

Powell, Neil, *Alchemy: The Ancient Science*, Aldus Books, London, 1976

Principe, Lawrence, *The Aspiring Adept: Robert Boyle and His Alchemical Quest*, Princeton University Press, Princeton, NJ, and Chichester, 1998

Rubenhold, Hallie, *The Covent Garden Ladies*, Tempus, Stroud, 2006

Peakman, Julie, *Lascivious Bodies: A Sexual History of the Eighteenth Century*, Atlantic Books, London, 2004

Somerset, Anne, *The Affair of the Poisons: Murder, Infanticide and Satanism at the Court of Louis XIV*, Phoenix, London, 2004

St John, James Augustus, *The Lives of Celebrated Travellers*, New York, 1844

Walpole, Horace, *Letters*, various sources

Webster, Charles, *From Paracelsus to Newton: Magic and the Making of Modern Science*, Cambridge University Press, 1982

White, Michael, *Isaac Newton, The Last Sorcerer*, Fourth Estate, London, 1997

Acknowledgements

Heartfelt thanks for continuing support, encouragement and advice to my agent, Judith Murray, to my editor, Kate Parkin, and to everyone at John Murray Publishers: Caro Westmore, Nikki Barrow et al. I am particularly grateful to Jane Birkett (copy-editor) and Nick de Somogyi (proofreader) who have saved me from untold embarrassments.

Thanks to Ronald Hutton for information about the English legal system in the eighteenth century.

I owe the greatest possible debt to the magnificent, delightful, erudite and irresistible Chevalier Seingalt, without whose constant, guiding presence the eighteenth century would have been far harder to imagine. Aside from a certain *je ne sais quoi* that I have come to think of as the essence of the times, his many fans may recognise the garters inscribed with erotic verses; the character of the Marquise du Bellay (his Marquise d'Urfé); the *ménage à trois* in the voyeur's *casino* in Venice, and other details.

The music of Robert de Visée, George Frideric Handel and Antonio Vivaldi has accompanied and inspired this work. I would particularly like to thank Hopkinson Smith (lutenist and theorbist), Andreas Scholl (countertenor) and Stefano Montanari (violinist) for their interpretative genius.